dear

LOCK&KEY

let yourself dream
let yourself wish

CAT PORTER

Cat Porter
xx

M000194929

Lock & Key

Copyright © 2014 by Cat Porter

Cover Designer

Najla Qamber

http://najlaqamberdesigns.com

Editor of 1st Edition

Chelsea Kuhel

www.madisonseidler.com

Editor of 2nd Edition

Jennifer Roberts-Hall

Interior Designer

Jovana Shirley, Unforeseen Editing, www.unforeseenediting.com

Skeleton Key Necklace

Blue Bayer Design NYC

http://www.etsy.com/shop/billyblue22

Without limiting the rights under copyright reserved above, no part of this publication may be reproduced, stored in or introduced into a retrieval system, or transmitted, in any form, or by any means (electronic, mechanical, photocopying, recording, or otherwise) without the prior written permission of the above author of this book.

This is a work of fiction. Names, characters, places, brands, media, and incidents are either the product of the author's imagination or are used fictitiously. The author acknowledges the trademarked status and trademark owners of various products referenced in this work of fiction, which have been used without permission. The publication/use of these trademarks is not authorized, associated with, or sponsored by the trademark owners.

ISBN-13: 978-0-9903085-0-8

CONTENTS

PROLOGUE

ONCE UPON A TIME I lost everything.

Then I ran away.

But I returned because I had to, and I stood on the edge and looked over.

Truth is a painful sword. It cuts deep and stings, but the pain evaporates, the blood dries, and in the place of such savagery is a gleaming absolution and an absolute purity.

It's blinding.

It hurts.

And it is utterly beautiful.

You can't escape it. Truth demanded a leap, I took it.

This is a story of my love for two men at two different moments of truth in my life. One man is gone forever; the other is very much alive.

Love not only stings when you lose it, when it's ripped away. When it first bites, it can sting just as deeply.

This is also a story about the love between my sister and me, and our redemption through two families—one bonded by blood, the other by brotherhood—that tore us apart yet bound us together forever.

Real life is messy and strange, and our ride through it left plenty of bruises, slashed hearts, a few lifeless bodies, and blood and smoke in its wake.

But it's our story, this rather mangled tale.

I SHOULD HAVE LEFT when I had polished off that first drink. That had been my initial plan, but the Doobie Brothers "Eyes of Silver" was playing on the jukebox, and that really deserved another drink for old time's sake. Not for the sake of the future, though. Isn't that why I'd stopped here in the first place? I was just over an hour outside of Rapid City, but I wanted to put off harsh reality a little while longer.

Just one more drink.

I gestured at the bartender with my empty glass. He winked at me.

My motel room across the highway was most certainly not a fabulous destination, and I just couldn't face another night watching bad reality TV or the usual sitcoms as I had done the night before at the motel in Montana. Tonight was different. No, I couldn't sit still tonight. The walls of the room seemed to stretch to hold me in. Dead Ringer's Roadhouse was a much, much better alternative.

It hadn't changed much in the sixteen years I'd been away. License plates from each one of the fifty states still covered the walls, but that original poster for a Doors concert in California was thankfully now secured in a thick brass frame. A dramatic spotlight glowed over it for all those who came regularly to pay their respects. I suppose the owners finally realized its worth. A vintage photograph, it too now solidly framed, of an old locomotive stuck in over twelve feet of snow during the infamous blizzard of 1949, took pride in its place on the opposite wall. Gentrification had arrived in this little corner of South Dakota. The same beer-soaked smell filled my nostrils, though.

Three pool tables stood on a raised section of the room where several older pot-bellied bikers played a game. The dart boards still dotted one wall as did the myriad of hunting trophies peering down at us from overhead—an eccentric variety of antlers, furry, glassy-eyed heads, and even a few stuffed fish, all mute, somber witnesses to the whirligig of flesh and alcohol below.

Hey up there, remember me?

I took in a deep breath and leaned back against the extremely long bar. In the center of the spacious Roadhouse was a sunken dance area, its long stretch of wooden floor polished and worn from years of use. Glass mason jars glowing with the light of votive candles spotlit each of the crowded tables surrounding the dance floor. I lowered myself back on my barstool and waited for my refill. The lights lowered a notch as the couple to my right laughed uproariously at a joke the waitress had told them.

I rubbed the back of my neck. I definitely needed to have a laugh and relax before I got into town tomorrow and faced the music. I was too wound up to sleep tonight. All my belongings, and there weren't many, were packed in my Toyota Land Cruiser. It's good to be mobile at a moment's notice, like I was when my sister called me a little over a week ago.

"Grace, I need you, honey."

She wouldn't have asked me to come home if it wasn't serious. I think both of us had been in denial over just how serious it was. I quit my job that day, packed my essentials, and came back to South Dakota.

Anything for Ruby. Anything.

But I wasn't going to think about all that right now. Right now, I was going to try to enjoy myself. Well, at least have a laugh or two. Or something. That's why coming to Dead Ringer's had seemed like such a good idea after I had checked in to the motel earlier. My home town was located almost two hours away on the other side of Rapid City, so there wasn't too much of a chance of anyone recognizing me here tonight.

After I had checked in at the motel, I'd taken a long hot shower, scrubbed the grime of the road off me, and eased the ache in my lower back from driving most of the day. I'd put on my black jeans and my favorite charcoal-gray T-shirt dotted with studs and tiny rhinestones along the wing design, shoved on my oldest pair of engineer boots, then set off for Dead Ringer's. My legs always felt solidly weighted into the ground with these treasured puppies on, which was always a good thing, especially now. They were definitely a nice change from the high-tops I had been wearing to stay comfortable as I drove.

I raised my chin and inspected my appearance in the huge, cracked antique mirror that hung behind the bar next to the Roadhouse's famous antique photograph of a nineteenth century gold prospector in the Black Hills. My grape lip-gloss had faded, of course, but my thick brown hair that I had highlighted off and on over the years had, as usual, achieved full volume all on its own. I had kept it bound in a ponytail all through my days of driving to keep it out of my face and off my neck. I combed my fingers through the layered waves that cascaded to my shoulders.

"There you go, hon." The bartender blocked my view, breaking my girlish reverie. He slid a whiskey neat towards me on a small white napkin.

I shot him a smile. "Thank you."

I drew deep on the amber liquid, and that delicious warmth flowed through me once more and settled in my blood. A Miranda Lambert song flared up, and suddenly a rumble echoed over the old wood floors as a good number of eager couples, both young and old, scrambled to the dance floor. Laughter and whoops swirled through the room. I took another swallow of my whiskey and savored its richness in my mouth.

This was good, comfortable. I tugged a strand of hair from one of my long silver earrings.

Was I really an upgraded version of the Grace Quillen who ran away from Meager, South Dakota sixteen years ago?

Ran away, absconded, escaped…

"Are you really drinking that without ice?" a deep male voice vibrated through me.

My eyes snapped up to my left, and I had to raise them up a bit higher to see the face behind that firm, almost purposeful tone. My fingers slid down my glass.

I drank in the large, almost black eyes lined with thick dark lashes that were pinned on me. His face was full of planes, angles and high cheekbones. He sported a long nose that must have been broken at some point, because it had an odd bump to it and a small scar on its side that travelled down his cheek. Those flaws may have blunted any overt handsomeness he might have been blessed with, yet they gave him an unforgiving, grim quality. My gaze settled on his full mouth. His smooth skin was a light bronze hue. He definitely had Native American blood in him.

He had to be over six feet tall with pronounced shoulders and a closely cropped head of dark hair peppered with just a bit of gray. There were faint traces of stubble on his face, and a small silver hoop hung from his right earlobe. His long arms and broad chest filled out his black hoodie that was zipped up most of the way. Faded and frayed blue jeans hung low and loose just below his waist and extended down a long pair of legs, which ended in heavily scuffed black leather boots. A worn-out road warrior.

He leaned against the bar, one feathery dark eyebrow quirked higher than the other at my glass of whiskey. "Never met a chick who liked it straight," he said.

I choked on the swirl of liquor at the back of my throat. He swallowed his drink, his solemn eyes on me as he waited for a response to his ridiculous remark. With my eyes locked on his, I put down my glass.

I smirked. "Well, well. Lucky you."

He shifted his weight and leaned in closer. "I meant the drink, not ..." I could swear his irises had silver threads in them at this angle. His full lips tightened. He didn't break into chuckles or a flirty pose. He really wanted an answer to his question.

"Yeah, I got it," I said with a slight smile. "Ice only dilutes the flavor. Why order a great whiskey if you're going to insult it with water or sugary soda?"

He studied me for a moment, perfectly still, then he nodded once and drank from his ice-filled glass, his dark eyes never leaving mine. "Very true. Insult—that's perfect."

I turned back to my drink. He moved in closer. "It's just that most women order everything with a diet, you know?"

"Women or was that 'chicks'?"

He let out a laugh. His face seemed almost boyish, then in an instant the relaxed look was gone and the somber returned.

"I hate soda," I said.

His dark, languid eyes riveted on me once more, and I swallowed hard. I could soak in those soothing pools of darkness.

"Guess you're not most women." His voice was warm, almost gravelly, and his eyes glinted at me as he drank. The chunks of ice in his glass clinked together, the sound filling the thick air between us.

"No, I'm not."

His teeth crunched on ice as he studied me. "I'll bet you don't like much diluted or watered down, huh?"

I tore my gaze away from those dark eyes of his and cleared my throat. "What are you drinking?"

"Vodka. Thought I'd change it up from beer tonight."

"Good idea," I murmured. "Change is always good."

"Keeps the blood flowing, right?"

I glanced up at him again. He was trying to make conversation with me. Being friendly to strangers is good for one's karma, isn't it? And I needed all the help I could get in the karma department. Why not indulge in conversation with the attractive Mr. Vodka On The Rocks?

"Ever tried it with a slice of lemon?" I asked.

A hint of amusement passed over his eyes, and I grinned. "The drink, I mean."

He shook his head and sighed. "No."

"You should."

My gaze swept over him once more. A tattoo crept across the base of his neck from his shoulder. Was it a feather? I tried not to stare at it too long. He looked to be around my age. There were lines around his eyes and mouth to match my own budding crow's feet. His face was a bit weathered. A wise, dry humor flashed from the crooked angle of his brief smile, which I liked. No, he wasn't some young'un hoping to score a cougar. My eyes rested on the bulky silver ring of a sculpted eagle's head he wore on the hand that was wrapped around his glass. I frowned.

He leaned over the bar and plucked a thick slice of lemon from the tray of condiments and dropped it into his glass. He swirled the vodka around the ice and the lemon and took a swig. His attractive lips puckered.

"It adds a little something without overwhelming it. I like it."

"I'm Grace, by the way."

His eyebrows lifted slightly. "Pretty name. Nice to meet you, Grace." He tipped his glass in my direction. "I'm Miller."

"Hi, Miller."

He signaled the bartender for another round for both of us.

"You don't have to do that." My hand darted out to his long arm. The wiry muscles under the plush softness of his hoodie tightened, and I snapped my hand back right away as if I had been burned.

"Why not?" His eyes scrunched together. He leaned in closer, his one elbow grazed mine on the bar top, his warm breath fanned my neck. "I usually don't do this sort of thing, but tonight, for a woman like you, I'm going to splurge."

"Oh, a woman like me?" I smirked into my empty glass. What did that mean? Mature? Older? "And why does a woman like me get the formal treatment?"

His eyes gleamed. "Because I admire your respect for that whiskey," he said in a smooth, honeyed voice that melted right over me.

I straightened my back as I absorbed his dark gaze. A buzz zipped through my veins. I knew I was already in trouble here, but this was ... fun. Isn't this why I came here tonight? To unwind, distract myself before the hell of tomorrow? What's a little flirting? It had been so long since I had actually felt attracted to a man.

Really attracted.

"I appreciate your appreciating it," I said. He grinned, and my mouth abruptly went dry.

The bartender slid our new drinks in front of us and took our empties away. My gaze shot up at Miller. His eyes were softer this time, like dark pools of full-flavored coffee. There was something calming to me about his gaze, like the calm that suddenly comes after a violent storm. Or was that before the storm?

He held up his glass and clinked it against mine. It might as well have been an alarm bell heralding our move into new territory. We had shifted gears, and we both knew it.

"To appreciation, then," he murmured.

His eyebrows bunched up for a second, and he let out a laugh at the banal sentiment. I liked that small, unfettered laugh of his. He immediately segued into serious once more, and we swallowed our liquor, our eyes fastened on each other.

Danger, Will Robinson.

My face heated, and I quickly diverted my gaze to scan the increasing number of patrons lining the bar. All I really wanted to do was look into those rich eyes again. I held my breath and tamped down the urge. Blake Shelton's "Ten Times Crazier" blared loudly through the Roadhouse.

Miller's glass slammed on the bar. "Come on, Grace. Let's dance." My head jerked back to him. He seized my hand and tugged me off my bar stool, his long calloused fingers pressing into my flesh.

"Dance?" My eyes widened, yet all the while I enjoyed the firm heat of his hand over mine. He led me through the crowd to the dance floor.

"I've got you, no worries," he whispered in my ear.

His arms slid around me and pulled me close to his solid frame. I tried to ignore the shiver that zipped across my skin, but it was useless. His very masculine scent of leather and musk intoxicated me immediately. My stomach fluttered as we moved easily to the music across the floor, his hand pressing against my back. He tucked me in closer, and our hips swayed against each other.

I blinked up at him. Miller was tall. I was five foot seven and considered myself average. But there was nothing average about me dancing with this gladiator. His large, hot hand at my lower back singed my skin through the thin cotton of my T-shirt. His face had softened, and his dark eyes seemed to shimmer over me. It was as if he were a different person from the somewhat brooding figure at the bar.

My long silver earrings prickled the suddenly sensitive skin of my neck as we danced to two more songs. Miller teased me about the two old cowboys at a table near the dance floor who had been allegedly ogling my ass, and we laughed over the melodramatic lyrics of the current song. My breathing began to return to normal.

Well, a more intense level of normal.

I liked being held in the long, lean arms of this man, a man who sent that glorious buzz humming through me. It had been years, hundreds of years, since I had been rendered nearly speechless by that rush.

I'm usually a sensible girl. Maybe I should have made some excuse and headed out the door, but I didn't. I liked the way he kept me close. I liked how his solid body moved against mine and led me through the music. His warm, heady fragrance ignited my insides as Kenny Chesney crooned softly about all the potential damage that could be done. It was nice to pretend I was just an ordinary woman dancing to "You and Tequila" with a sexy somebody at a bar off an interstate in South Dakota.

But I knew better.

I used to let go and have fun. Now, not so much. Sixteen years ago I had stopped harboring expectations for too much more than pleasantness in my life. I had learned the bitter lesson that low expectations were the best way to go.

Miller's hand slid up my back. He led us off the dance floor and back to the bar where our drinks waited for us. The place was crowded now and much noisier. We leaned against the bar and stood closer together than before out of necessity. His one hand slid over my left hip and secured me close to him in the pressing crowd.

"How did you like Ohio?" he asked.

I still chewed on the sensation of his hand gripping me. Crap, what did he just say?

"Excuse me?"

"Your Harley tee." Miller gestured to my back. "It's from Ohio. That where you're from?"

My lips curled into a slight smile. He didn't suspect I was a native. "I worked at the store in Dayton for a couple of years a while back."

I had been the general manager, actually, at that store and several others.

"No shit?" His eyes widened. "Careful, you're turning into my dream girl, babe. You know everything about bikes?" He took a drink.

Dream girl? Wouldn't that be swell? At the age of forty-two, I had enough baggage to charter my own cargo plane.

I laughed, and he gave me a quizzical look. "Not everything," I said, "but let's see." My eyes slid down his long legs slowly and obviously before resting on his boots. He grinned as he swallowed his vodka, enjoying the stroke of my deliberate attention. "I know your boots aren't the real deal." I took in another mouthful of whiskey.

He nodded. "Not this pair, but I've got several others at home came straight from the source."

I let out a laugh. "Going casual tonight then?"

"Hmm." He crunched on another ice cube, his gaze locked on mine. "Now I wish I had put them on, to suit the occasion."

"What occasion is that?"

"Meeting you, Grace."

The firm, crisp way he said my name made my insides tighten. His eyes remained on me as he polished off his vodka then licked the excess off his lips. I wondered what those full lips would feel like pressed against mine. The need to know suddenly overwhelmed me.

"So are you from around here, 'cause I know I haven't seen you before?" he asked.

"You'd remember me?"

"Absolutely." The edges of his lips curled into a slow grin that made my stomach dip.

"I'm from. . .around." I made a twirling gesture with my fingers. "Plenty of around."

"Like where?"

"Ohio, Wisconsin, Texas, Colorado, Washington State."

"That's plenty of around, Grace. You like to keep moving? Or maybe you need to?"

I turned to face the dance floor in order to escape his penetrating gaze. "Change keeps the blood flowing, didn't you say? It's good for the soul, too."

If I had any of my soul left anymore.

His eyes tightened. *Here come the goddamn twenty questions now.*

"You got any family?"

Bingo.

"A sister."

"Husband, kids?"

I smirked. "She does, yes."

"Not your sister, Grace. You."

"Me? No," I replied a bit too sharply. "No husband. No boyfriend either, if that's going to be your next question."

He lowered his head. "You off to somewhere new?"

I shrugged my shoulders at him.

"Not telling, huh?" He turned back around and settled his elbows on the bar. "Guess we all have our dark secrets," he muttered and polished off his vodka.

My ears pounded with the booming vibe of a Florida Georgia Line song. I cleared my throat. "I guess it's country music night tonight?"

"Almost every night," he said, an eyebrow lifting. "You in the mood for something else?"

I grinned. "A little Santana would be a good thing."

He grinned back at me. "Great band."

"One of the best."

Oh, I liked his grin. It was hard won, I suspected, yet worth it.

He gestured to my not quite empty glass. "You want another?"

"No thanks. I'm good."

"Mind if I try?"

"Go ahead." I pushed the glass towards him.

11

The sight of his generous lips clinging to my glass, and the movement of his long throat as he drank in my whiskey held me spellbound. I might as well have been witnessing some sort of supernatural phenomenon.

"Single malt?" he asked, his eyes on me. His lips puckered for a moment as he set it down.

"Yes. Only way to go."

On some sort of insane reflex, my fingers reached out to wipe a glistening amber drop that clung to the corner of his beautiful mouth. His hand caught mine and held it fast to the side of his face while his other hand wrapped around my neck and pulled me close.

"Only way," he breathed.

Any trace of oxygen was sucked right out of me as his warm lips touched mine and gently explored. Suddenly his tongue swept over my lower lip, and I tasted my beloved whiskey on his slickness. A groan choked in the back of my throat. The heat of his hand around my neck made my insides pulsate almost painfully.

I desperately wanted this kiss from him.

I opened my lips to welcome him in. The next moment our mouths assaulted each other, and our tongues devoured deeply. Somehow I didn't care that I was in a public bar where a herd of people pushed around us, music boomed, laughter and chatter droned in my ear.

All I thought or cared about was this demanding, hungry kiss.

My hands gripped his biceps, and his hard muscles flexed under the soft material of his hoodie. He pulled me into his chest, and his scent flooded my senses once more. This time I wanted to drink it in; let it entwine around me and hug me close. My nipples hardened against the thin satin of my bra.

Miller's teeth nipped my lower lip, and he hissed in air. . .or was that me?

I dug my fingers into his shoulders and crashed back down to earth. "I'm hot."

He kissed the edge of my jaw, while his finger traced my collarbone. "Yeah, you certainly are."

Waves of dizziness surged through me. "No, no, Miller, I mean, I'm hot, I can't brea . . ."

His eyes narrowed over me. His hand wrapped around my neck and his thumb stroked my cheek. "Let me get you some water." Miller turned to find the bartender and smirked. "I tend to have that effect on women."

"Oh, shut up!" I pinched his arm. He laughed, then his hand went to my waist and squeezed.

That particular heat flooded my female parts, those parts I thought I had put out of commission some time ago. Years of underwhelming responses to a variety of underwhelming men had dulled me. . .or so I thought. I was finally experiencing again what it feels like to be really turned on, wasn't I? My eyelids sank, and I lifted my heavy hair off my neck. There were different grades of turned on weren't there? Amused, aroused, pleasantly excited? Not this. This was more.

This was key jammed in the ignition and motor revving.

My lungs constricted as icy wetness slicked across my collarbone and down my chest. "What the . . .?" I gasped and let go of my hair. Miller smoothed ice cubes from his glass over my hot skin, letting one slip down my cleavage. "Oh, God," I moaned.

"That hit the spot?" He gently tugged on the wide V of my T-shirt to look for the errant cube. It had nestled between my breasts and was melting against my hot skin. I drew in a breath as his finger traced the satiny edge of my black bra and seared my flesh. He chuckled softly.

I let out a sigh. "Leave it, it feels great right there."

Miller took another cube from his glass and rubbed it around my neck then let it slide down my back. My pulse hurtled out of control.

"Holy crap!" I let out a laugh and arched my back as the ice cube slid down my heated skin and landed at my waist where my jeans gapped open. My lips parted as his long fingers found the cube, slid it in circles around my lower back then tucked it into the waistband of my panties where it melted down my rear.

I shook my head at him, pressed my lips together, and suppressed a laugh. Another cube followed down the base of my throat, slipped down my chest, and landed in my bra. Miller's cold, wet fingertips traced a line on the side of my neck.

"Feel better?" he asked. His lips brushed my forehead. He handed me a glass of water.

I nodded at him and drank. My inner buzzing continued recklessly like a car careening at top speed on a rainy highway.

He was good.

13

This was bad.

Miller's lips nuzzled the underside of my jaw, his fingers pressed in at my sides right at the swell of my breasts. A landslide of sensation careened through me, and only the word YES surged through my brain. My arms flew around his neck. He pulled me deep into his arms against his solid chest and the soft bulkiness of his hoodie. Our tongues tangled, my back arched into his embrace.

He tasted of cool freshness and golden warmth all at the same time. His hand slid up the side of my breast then quickly went down my back to the curve of my ass and squeezed. A shudder went through me.

"Grace," he whispered in my ear. "You got somewhere we can go? We can always go out back, I've got my truck with me tonight." His tongue licked at the shell of my ear.

Ah, the old quickie in the parking lot. No, I didn't want a slam-bam. I wanted more, a lot more. In fact, I had all night to indulge in this insanity. I tore my mouth away from his neck and stared at him.

"You're disappointing me, Miller. We're grown-ups, aren't we?"

"I don't feel like a grown-up right now, Grace. I don't think I can wait to even get you in my truck, you're driving me that insane," he breathed. He let out a small groan. "Jesus, you smell good. What the hell is that? Watermelon with roses?" His thumb stroked my nipple over my shirt, and my breath hitched in the back of my throat.

I was certainly pleased to hear my recent impulse buy of expensive perfume had been worth it. Both of his hands rubbed my ass and pulled me into his urgent hardness. The sudden intensity of the rush only made me ravenous for more. Geez, I was the one behaving like a teenager, or at least my hormones were.

Wait a second—that was actually refreshing news.

I released my hold on Miller in order to get a hold on myself. We were in a public bar, after all. I gulped down the rest of the cold water. Miller's large hands stroked up and down my back.

I didn't want to say no to this...to him. The need to touch him again overtook me with a sudden desperation. My hands slid around his waist and grazed over a thick leather and metal belt looped through his jeans. My fingers travelled up over the sleek, firm muscles of his torso. His breath caught, and heat rushed straight through me at the sound.

Yes, I wanted him badly.

But I didn't want to do this in a truck, a back alley or a parking lot for God's sake.

Just say it. Say it. Say it. Say it.

"I have a room at the motel across the way," I whispered in his ear. My fingers traced the line of his jaw. His arms squeezed me. I was breathless at the prospect of this sort of anonymous, midnight fling. I hadn't had a one-night stand in a very long time. Such nameless, faceless, raw experiences had lost their luster for me early on in my widowhood. They had left me feeling even more hollow than I'd already felt. I had begun to prefer friendly and affectionate casual dating instead. The going out, the laughs, the meals, the sleeping together were enjoyable, pleasant, nice. But I had nothing to give these men I had chosen, and so they had never lasted. And that was fine.

I shut my brain down, and my eyes riveted on Miller. Austerely attractive, brooding, tall, great lips, amazing tongue. . .

Once this was over that would be it, right? It would be done. I was just passing through anyhow. He obviously didn't live around here either or he'd be dragging me to his place, wouldn't he?

Oh crap, maybe he's married or he's got a girlfriend? Seriously, why wouldn't he be taken?

"I forgot about that motel," he said. "Perfect."

He planted a firm kiss on my mouth and ended it with a leisurely swipe of his delicious tongue. I pulled back from him, my hands against his chest.

"Wait a sec. . .how about you?"

Miller's gaze darkened, the silver threads all but disappeared, and his eyes burned straight through mine as he tilted my face towards his.

"How about me what?"

"You have a wife or a girlfriend?"

"No, I don't."

A flutter went off in my insides, and I bit my lip. This would be a candy bar, that's all this was. Chew, savor, and throw out the wrapper on your way out. End of story.

I grinned at Miller.

He slid two twenty-dollar bills out from his wallet and brandished them at the bartender, who hustled down to us. The bartender handed him his change. Miller left him a generous tip.

I managed to finally unlock the door to my room on the third try. Miller jerked the key from the lock, tossed it on the table, and slammed the door behind us. The room was engulfed in streaky darkness. He tore off his hoodie and whatever else he had on underneath, and I yanked off my shirt.

Our rapid, short breaths filled the room. His jeans along with his heavy belt hit the floor with a clang and thud. I fell back on the edge of the bed with an oomph to do away with my boots and socks as quickly as humanly possible.

He lunged at me, and his powerful hands undid my jeans and jerked them down my hips. I tumbled off the bed onto the floor, and we laughed. I felt the weight of him on me and reveled in it. My fingers raced across the lean muscles of his shoulders and back. I groaned in satisfaction as he unhooked my bra and freed my swollen breasts into his greedy hands.

Miller kneaded and licked them, and I gasped at the unexpected burning sensations rippling through me. He sucked hard on each nipple in turn, and I bucked against his hips, rubbing myself up and down on his erection like an animal in heat. I was an animal in heat; there was no help for it, though. If I stopped to think about it, I would stop myself. So I didn't think. I kept going.

His hand slid over my inner thigh and grazed the lace edge of my panties, and I let out a tiny gasp.

"I want you good and wet," Miller breathed in my ear as two of his fingers thrust past the damp fabric.

His knuckles swirled against my clit. I tugged my panties down my hips, but he took over, yanking them down my legs and flinging them to the side. Two of his fingers sank deep. I let out a low moan as they churned inside me. He groaned and muttered something under his heavy breaths. Bunched nerve endings detonated all over my body.

Shit, he knew what he was doing. What a relief.

He whispered over me. I raised my hips up and circled them in the rhythm that he worked me. "Yeah, Grace." The raw tone in his voice radiated its heat right through me. He moved down my body licking as he went. His tongue lashed across my clit, and I exploded right there and then.

"Yes!" I cried out, and Miller growled somewhere above me. Intense, almost unbearable waves of sensation rolled through my body.

As I floated in my own little stratosphere, the rustle and rip of a foil packet snapped me to my senses. I tore the questionable quilt off the mattress, scrambled up on the bed and squirmed on the cool sheets. I ached with the need to feel his smooth body rub against mine, filling me. All I wanted right this very moment was to consume and be consumed.

Miller sat between my legs and ran his ringed finger over my wet sex. He rubbed the cold bulky silver eagle in small circles over my clit, and my hips jerked.

"Miller—"

His eyes glittered over me in the muted light from the street signs outside. He brought the ring to his mouth and licked it. My hands wrapped around his powerful thighs to steady myself in a desperate attempt to prevent shattering into a thousand pieces.

He leaned over me, one hand planted in the mattress. "You ready for me, Grace?" he breathed. I tilted up my chin.

I was beyond ready.

He positioned himself and drove inside me. My body arched off the bed. My hands gripped his arms as I struggled to adjust to his thickness filling me, stretching me. I raised my hips to take him in further.

I wanted all of this, all of him, needed him like oxygen, like water.

"Shit, you feel good." Miller let out a groan and hooked one of my legs around his hip. He rocked deeper inside me, and my eyes flew open. My fingers rubbed into the base of his skull as we moved together and against each other quicker and harder. The glorious wave actually built inside me again.

"Grace—you got it?" he asked. "I'm not going to last much longer. You're making me fucking crazy."

How considerate of him to communicate.

17

I had learned how to be self-sufficient. There hadn't been much real communication with the men I had slept with over the years, just a lot of show on their part. I ground up into Miller and chased my peak. I tightened my inner muscles around him and circled my hips. His mouth hung open, his forehead furrowed with the strain. Then his gaze darted down my body. His hand dug into my hip, his teeth sank into my shoulder.

Miller stroked faster, over and over. The only thing left was to succumb to that rolling storm of sensation. It finally burst and crashed over me. My fingers dug into his back, and I released myself into that sweet, crazy haze. His grip on me tightened, his body suddenly stiffened. I held my breath as he jolted into me. He buried his face in my neck where he muffled a string of curses. Our bodies were veiled in a sheen of sweat. He raised his head, his eyes were fierce. His mouth crushed mine, and I hooked both my legs around his, my fingers raking through his short hair.

Miller's hand slid down my damp skin, stopping at my hip. "Babe, you are some kind of hungry," he said, his breathing shallow.

"Oh?" My nerve endings still vibrated with electricity. "You were pretty enthusiastic yourself."

"You fired me up." His fingers teased one of my nipples. "Has it been a while?"

Was I that obvious?

"Yes."

"How long is a while?" His voice was gentle.

"Does it matter?" I closed my eyes against the tingles his fingers created.

"Tell me." He pressed his pelvis against mine. I squirmed at the sweet pressure. My hands slid over his smooth contoured chest barely visible in the glow of light. Disappointment crept over me that I couldn't see that tattoo. "Grace?"

"A year. . . or so."

"Or so?" His eyes flashed through the shadows, his lips brushed mine.

"Hmm." My body shifted underneath his, but he didn't unpin his formidable weight from me.

"Why, babe? You're beautiful, you're. . ."

I put my fingers to his lips. "Needed a vacation from the bullshit, that's all." I didn't want to continue in this line of conversation. His lips sucked my fingertips into his mouth, and my defensiveness melted into a puddle at his feet.

"There is plenty of bullshit out there." He let out a sigh. "Plenty." His tongue traced a wet trail around my nipple as his fingers caressed my other breast.

"It's just not worth it most of the time," I whispered. My gaze was riveted on his mouth taking in my aching breast and sucking on it. My body tightened and released to him all in one wave.

"But you took a chance on me?" The edges of his lips curled against my delicate skin.

"Yeah." My fingers burrowed into his crop of very short hair.

"Was I worth it?" Miller rubbed my wet, aching nipple between his thumb and forefinger, then pinched it. I gasped, and my foot dug into his rear. "Did I make up for what you've been missing?"

I lightly kicked at the firm muscles of his sublime ass and smirked. "You made a dent."

His eyes narrowed over me as his thumb grazed my swollen lips. He didn't laugh, smirk back at me, or return with a clever comeback. He didn't take the bait. My ribbing, my jokes to distract and deflect from any kind of serious inquiry into me didn't seem to work with Mr. Miller, like it always had with other men. He remained still and studied my face, his warm fingers stretched out over my throat and around my neck, my heart thrumming at his touch. We studied each other in silence, our shallow breaths mingling.

"I'm honored," he whispered.

I believed him.

He pulled out of me slowly and leaned over me. His mouth hovered over mine for a second, his breath warm on my skin while my fingers lingered on the side of his face. His lips nuzzled mine gently, then he tilted his head the other way and kissed me again, very slowly. His mouth pulled away just a bit, then descended once more, even softer, relishing every part of my lips. His tongue finally found mine, but then he trapped my bottom lip in his teeth.

"Oh—"

"You good for another go?"

"Hmm." I rubbed the back of one of his long legs with my foot and savored the sensation of his body pressed against mine.

"That a yes or a no?" His warm mouth nuzzled my throat, his tongue flicked at my skin.

"Yes, yes," I said, and he only chuckled. The sound of his subdued laughter deep in his chest only turned me on more without a trace of shame.

"Let me get rid of this condom first." Miller pushed himself up off the bed. I sighed and stretched out. He licked my navel, and I laughed. He peeled the used rubber off himself and tossed it in the wastebasket between the bed and the table and quickly found another packet ripping it open. A very motivating sound in my current state.

"Let me do it," I said. I suddenly needed to touch his hardness, to feel it, to feel him. I sat up. Miller's face was partly visible in the shadows. He pressed the condom into my unsteady hand.

My fingers skimmed over his tense abs and wrapped around his cock. It was thick, warm, and slick with his release. My fingers stroked its hard length, and I bent over and licked around the smooth crown. I took his thickness in my mouth and sucked slowly from base to tip. Miller's fingers dug through my hair, and he raised his hips higher, hissing in air. My body jerked at the illicit sound.

"Babe. . . oh, shit. . . wait," he murmured. "I want to fuck you now, want to come inside you." His fingers found a nipple and squeezed, then released it just as quickly, a blaze of heat spiking through me. I slid the condom over his shaft and smoothed it firmly down his length.

His hand squeezed my shoulder, then he pushed me back against the mattress and my eyes lifted to his searing gaze. There was hunger in those dark orbs and a steely ruthlessness. No mercy. His mouth sank between my legs, and I let out a deep moan.

He took his sweet time.

"Miller!"

My back arched off the bed. He immediately flipped me onto my knees, raising my hips, and rubbed his hard length between my ass cheeks. His cock slid down, teasing my needy, grateful center. My breath snagged, my pulse jammed.

"Hold on, Grace."

My fingers curled into the tangle of sheets, and he drove inside me.

My eyes came unglued in the haze of a pale halo of light around the dark curtains of the single window in the room. I was pinned to the bed by an enormous weight, and the tingling in my limbs prickled. My insides were sore, and my skin smelled of sweat and musk. And sex.

Now it came back to me. Lots of sex.

I moved in small increments, and a still-asleep Miller finally rolled off me with a slight moan and settled on his back. I blinked at the sight of a large tattoo of a great eagle in profile. The eagle's wings were spread across Miller's shoulder and down his chest. I raised myself up on my elbow to get a better look. I never got to see it last night as we never turned on the lights. My fingers traced the outline of the majestic creature emblazoned across his tawny skin. One large wing pointed down, the other wing pointed up, and its end reached around the back of his neck. The image was rather elegant, dignified.

Miller's hand fluttered across his chest in response to my tickling touch. I bit my lower lip to suppress the giggle that rose in my throat. He let out a heavy sigh and twisted onto his stomach.

And then I saw it.

Ripples of pain tore through my gut.

It had to be an illusion. A cosmic joke.

But it wasn't.

My throat constricted. That ancient, wild thing inside me shifted and cut loose. That primitive beast that had taken me years to leash and constrain shimmered before me again in all its hideous glory.

No. No. NO.

Tattooed on Miller's back was the logo that had been forever burned into my brain, branded on my heart, and scorched onto my soul from a very young age. I struggled for air. My bleary eyes took in the familiar lines of the skull with one eye socket enlarged, and a great star glowing its fiendish light from its blackened hollow. The leering skull was framed by that indelible name.

21

My stomach caved in as if I had been punched, my mouth went dry, and icy darts shot down my spine.

"Holy shit," my voice broke. I clenched my jaw to stem the sour tide that rose in my throat.

"Get gone!"

My eyes widened as a voice from my past, from inside the deepest recesses of my soul, resounded in my brain and pummeled through my chest.

"Get gone now, sweetheart!"

I squeezed my eyes shut for a moment. "'Miller,' my ass," I whispered to myself.

We'd even had the goddamn Harley conversation, and he didn't mention he rode, or that he had a bike. He didn't even use it to get down my pants. Now that was impressive, Mr. Miller, or whatever your road name was. I sure was easy, wasn't I?

I gritted my teeth. Of course, this was all my fault. As if I hadn't known when I first laid eyes on him: Here was biker material, here was rough, rugged American man. This was the kind of man I hadn't let myself get close to in years. Was the attraction so overwhelming that I kicked all my logic out the door at the sight of him? Was I so much in denial about what made me tick? Obviously, the answer to those questions was a resounding yes.

My eyes fell on the eagle ring on his finger. I knew I'd seen that very same ring before on someone else in the good old days. My instinct had warned me last night, but I had brushed it off in the name of hot sex. Such an idiot. I had plummeted headlong into the very thing I had wanted above all else to avoid.

I had to get out of here. I had to get away from him. I eased up off the mattress and twisted my hair into a messy knot securing it with a band.

There had been a sign at the entrance of the bar that declared "No Colors." Any bikers who entered had to cover or remove their colors, the leather vests they always wore with their club patches, or not wear jackets that were marked with the same identifying patches. Dead Ringer's Roadhouse was a decades old landmark on this stretch of the highway. Plenty of riders passed through here, and the owner wanted to avoid any trouble.

Therefore Miller had himself covered up. But he was driving a cage—a vehicle, not a bike. He must have been making a delivery or a pickup somewhere under the radar. If you were in a cage you weren't supposed to wear your colors, mandatory gear on your bike.

Miller had probably stopped at the bar to take a leak and get a drink on his way home or on his way out. No, if he had time to spare to get laid he must have been on his way home to Meager. He had even pointed out his truck to me last night as we crossed through the parking lot on the way to the motel. I had actually smiled at the sight of his black GMC.

"Get gone now."

I stuffed my duffel bag with the makeup, face cleanser, body lotion, deodorant, and perfume that I had scattered on the small bathroom counter. I dashed to my jeans that lay twisted on the floor and yanked them up my legs, not even bothering to look for my missing panties. My bra poked out from under Miller's jeans, and I snatched it up and hooked it on. . .that I couldn't do without. I nabbed my socks and boots and shoved them on. My crumpled T-shirt reeked of last night's indulgences. I shoved it in my bag and plucked a fresh one, stretching it over my head and through my arms.

The heel of my boot stepped on something unusually thick, and my gaze darted down. A black leather vest with the club's logo on it and a variety of patches was stuffed inside his black hoodie.

I didn't know whether to laugh or cry.

Part of a silver and black patch glared at me. I could barely make out the words "Road Captain."

He had most definitely been under the radar last night. If he had only unzipped that hoodie in the bar, if I had seen even a hint of his colors, I would have run like hell on the spot. But no, I had to kiss him back, I had to suck on his beautiful tongue, I had to push my tits into his chest.

Stupid.

I bit down on my trembling lip as I slowly zipped my duffel bag closed. I nabbed my car keys, the room key, slipped on my old leather jacket, and swung my large studded suede handbag over my shoulder. My fingers gripped the doorframe as I turned to take one last look at Miller. The incognito biker's magnificent naked body lay face down on our snarled sheets. His sleek tattooed back rose with every deep and even breath of sleep. The hard angle of his lean jaw jutted forward on the smashed pillow, the lines of his intriguing face slack, his fingers curled around the edges of the pillowcase. The silver eagle ring glimmered in the soft pink glow of dawn sifting through the drapes.

That gorgeous hard ass my hands couldn't get enough of last night mocked me now. The sleek, powerful body that had held me, moved inside me, and gave me so much pleasure for hours was now only an ominous presence and left me numb. I slumped against the doorjamb, my eyelids sank.

"Get gone," I whispered.

I carefully turned the knob and pulled open the door, stepping out of the room into the cold cloudiness of a day that I had dreaded dawning for a long, long time.

Now it was here, and I had even more reasons to dread it.

TWO

"GRACE, YOU MADE IT!"

Alex, my sister's husband of five years, took a long drag on his cigarette and tossed it in a sand-filled canister at the entrance of Rapid City Regional Hospital. The collar of his gabardine overcoat was turned up against the early morning chill in the air. He pushed back from the wall and took me in his arms. His eyes narrowed over me.

"You look like shit, Gracie."

"Thanks, jerk." I scowled at him. "Smoking again?"

"It's insane. I know." He raked a hand through his mussed waves of dark blond hair. "I've been here most of the night." His weary brown eyes rested on me. "What's your excuse?"

"I didn't get any sleep last night, and I've been driving for over two hours straight since before six this morning. And without coffee, by the way." I put my arm through Alex's. "How is she?"

He shrugged. "The same. Not in any pain, thank God. It's the waiting that's the bitch right now. For this test and that one. They're putting off the next round of chemo until these new test results come in. They don't let Jake come too often. That's ticking her off, but he's only four. They have rules."

"He's staying with your aunt?" He nodded and led me into the lobby. "I can't wait to see him," I said. "So what's the story? Can I get tested today?"

"Sure, if you don't scare the doctor away first." Alex let out a laugh. I elbowed him in the chest. He threw his arm around my shoulders and pulled me into his side again. "You can tell me, Gracie. Did you go clubbing and hook up with some badass who kept you up all night?"

I crossed my arms. "Actually, I did indulge in the minibar at the motel last night, so I'll have to schedule the testing for tomorrow."

Alex smirked. "Minibar?"

I caught my reflection in a large mirrored memorial plaque behind Alex in the foyer. My strained eyes were slightly swollen and red with black smudges of mascara smeared under them. My face was pale, and my hair had frizzed out from the knotted band. Definitely spooky. I exhaled and let out a stiff laugh.

"Shut it, Alexander."

"Come on, party girl. Let's get some caffeine in your veins, put you in front of a mirror in the ladies' room, and I'll find the doctor. Then we'll see Ruby."

"Mrs. Quillen, your sister's small cell lung cancer is extremely difficult to treat in general. There was some initial responsiveness to the chemo and the radiation, but not enough," Dr. Braden said. "Some studies have shown that a bone marrow transplant may benefit the patient, but the percentages are rather low. It is a relatively new procedure and quite costly, I'm afraid."

I dug the heels of my boots into the floor as I rubbed my cold fingers together, my silver bracelets jangling against the desk of the nurse's station.

"I'll be here first thing in the morning to have my blood drawn. No matches on the national list yet?" I asked, but I knew the answer.

"No, unfortunately. You should ask anyone you know to get tested. We might get lucky that way. Every moment counts."

My sister's life was coming down to test tubes filled with blood and soggy swabs in plastic baggies. Seventeen of them so far, but still no hope in sight. I suppose I shouldn't say *no* hope. Being pessimistic wouldn't help her, or Alex, or their son Jake. And being pessimistic wasn't Ruby's way. It never had been.

Out of the two of us, Ruby was the beautiful one. We had the same hazel eyes, but Ruby had a thick mane of honey-blonde hair like our mother's. My hair was a light brown color like Dad's. She was taller than me by two inches with long legs and a slim, but curvy body. I was curvy, too, but I had to work at the slim part. She was two years older than me and my best friend, always had been.

Ruby had a big, loud personality that I envied and adored. I'd loved dancing in the glow of her brash aura. Our differences had never been a source of divide between us. In fact, we'd cherished them. As we grew up, we'd found how well my quiet clicked with her loud. We'd needed each other. We were the opposite sides of the same coin, Mom used to say. Even she had liked that about us.

Our little brother Jason was nine when he'd gotten run over by a car while out riding his bike on our street after school. He died in the ambulance on the way to the hospital with my mother holding onto his broken arms. Jason was her baby, and he was the apple of Dad's eye. His death had devastated all of us. Ruby and I had tried to ignore Jason's empty chair at the dinner table each night. Dad had stopped showing up for dinner, and Mom had stopped cooking altogether. In fact, Dad had never really pulled himself out of his pit of shock, grief, and anger.

Mom had taken the stiff upper lip route to new heights, but her drinking had given her away. Our parents would only exchange information and do their own thing, bumping into each other in the house on occasion. Ruby had dealt with the delightful harmony at home by getting loud and wild, while I had done the opposite. I hadn't wanted to be in my parents' faces or make any waves. I'd kept quiet in the background and concentrated on school.

Ruby had been the one that got us into trouble over and over again. Half the time it was fun but a lot of the time, especially as we got older, it was freaking scary. She had plenty of brazen bravery, but oftentimes crap luck. Her brain was sharp as a razor's edge, and she'd been able to put a spin on at least 80% of the trouble we'd get into and find a loophole out.

We had a pact from our girlhood: *"Love you no matter what, so just suck it up."*

By the time she'd gotten into high school, Ruby's evenings out often had ended with Mom catching her sneaking back in through my bedroom window. I would clutch onto Ruby, but my mom would drag her out of my arms and into the kitchen. The slaps would crack over Ruby's smirking face. Once, twice, three times. *"Punishment doesn't work with you! Grounding you sure don't work! What's it gonna take, you good-for-nothing tramp? I'm not gonna let you take your sister with you on your little joyride to hell!"* My mother's shrill, shrieking desperation would fill the house every time. I would cover my ears and slump on the floor between my bed and the nightstand when it would get really bad.

Ruby's great big appetite for tasting all that life had to offer eventually had gotten her into drugs. I had tried to dabble right alongside her, but it had made me anxious, and I'd never enjoyed it like she did. That's when I'd lost her to the rave parties and a variety of eager boy-men in their fancy trucks. Then followed the menacing outcasts on their loud bikes who seemed to have endless supplies of pot, mushrooms, cocaine, and an assortment of pills.

I'd gone back to getting ready for college. That would be my escape from Meager. But I'd always been there to pick up her pieces when she'd needed me to, because Ruby and I only had each other. Forever and no matter what. So we sucked it up.

PAST

The first time I met members of the One-Eyed Jacks was because of Ruby.

We were in high school then, at a keg party out on a ranch in the hills outside of Meager. A lot of people had shown up and the beer had finished early. Ruby and her friends had mouthed off about it, of course. Loudly. Tim Squiers, a football player whose advances she had rejected earlier, had come after her during all the commotion she had instigated.

I was on the other end of the property with my girlfriends, trying to keep clear of the impending chaos. The yelling intensified, and Ruby's name was being tossed around. My friend Tania and I went running. Panic and horror were words too weak to describe what jolted through me at the sight of Ruby kicking and screaming, being dragged off by Tim with one of his pals holding onto her legs, their buddies cheering them on.

A few bikers had shown up to sell some weed. I knew in my gut they were my only hope of saving my sister from those bastards. I took off.

"Grace, come back here, don't you dare!" Tania yelled after me.

But I did dare. I had to save Ruby.

I ran like hell.

Three leather-clad bikers were perched on a group of large boulders around a fire drinking from whiskey bottles, fumes of pot and tobacco clouding over them.

"Hey, excuse me guys, can you help me?" They stared at me. I rattled on like a windup toy. "Those jerks have my sister! He's slapping her around, and all his friends are laughing. They're gonna take turns with her. You've got to help me. Please!"

"Is that what all that ruckus is about?" A young attractive biker with hair just touching his shoulders jumped down in front of me, a cigarette dangling from his mouth. He wore a leather jacket over his colors, so I couldn't see his patches. Big brown eyes frowned at me. "They got your sister?" he asked.

"Motherfucking football assholes!" hissed another, taller one. He hopped down from his perch. His long dark hair was in a braid down his back. He rubbed his hands together and let out a cackling laugh. "Time to kick some school-boy ass. We got this, little girl." His fingers tweaked my chin. The name "Jump" was patched on his leather vest.

I stumbled after them, and with a roar they pounced on Tim and his friends, beating them to a pulp until they bled all over their varsity letter jackets and begged for mercy. It had been quite a tornado-like display. There was no hesitation on their end. The bikers knew how to give a punch as well as take a punch, even dead in the face. They seemed utterly unfazed by any pain. Fighting was obviously not simply a hobby or a sport to them. It was serious business.

The brown-eyed one delivered a shuddering Ruby straight into my arms. "There you go, little sister," he said, his voice low, his eyes glued to mine.

"Oh my God, thank you. Thank you so much, thank you." I held on to a shaky Ruby.

One of his brothers stood next to him and wiped the blood off his face with his sleeve. He had vivid green eyes and very long dark hair. He let out a ringing laugh. The name "Boner" was on his leather jacket.

"Hey, it was a good time," Boner said winking at me.

"Glad we could help," the brown-eyed one said. "You keep out of trouble, you hear? And get her to do the same." He jerked his chin in my sister's direction.

"Yeah, I know. Thanks again."

His steady gaze remained on me. "I bet you don't get into much trouble though, do you?"

I swallowed hard. "No, not really."

Big Brown Eyes tilted his head at me and grinned. A shiver snaked through my insides. That was new for me. The thrill of the unknown, of temptation, of something wicked perhaps. A thrill, not fear. I let that sensation dissipate in the air between us.

"Too bad." He jerked his chin up at me. "See you." Big Brown Eyes and his brothers left us and got on their Harleys. They revved up their bikes and thundered off one by one.

My father went over to the One-Eyed Jack's clubhouse first thing the next morning. He shook each and every one of the members' hands, looked them in the eye and expressed his sincere gratitude for their standing up for his girls. He told them that he had struck a deal with Tim's father. Dad wouldn't press charges against Tim and his pals, if they didn't press charges against the club members who beat up the boys. Outlaw justice had been served, and that was good enough for Dad.

The men appreciated his show of respect and gratitude. All of this left me speechless. Ruby only laughed, even though it hurt her broken rib. It was probably the nicest thing Dad ever did for us. Then he went back to tuning us out.

Our father was a long-distance trucker who was gone most of the time. Out on a job the week after my eighteenth birthday, he just didn't come home. The divorce papers had arrived in the mailbox soon after. Our mother had decided to celebrate her newfound liberty from "the pig," as she'd fondly called him, by going on a three-day bender at the nearest Native American casino with her girlfriends. She'd returned home more bitter than ever.

She'd calmed down somewhat over time, but the rancor remained. Two years later, she got killed driving drunk on the interstate. She had lost control of the car, drifted into oncoming traffic, and crashed into a truck. It was a startling sight, and one that Ruby and I had insisted on seeing, much to the policemen's horror. We'd needed to see it in order to believe it.

Ruby had tucked my hand in hers as we'd stood on the edge of that streak-marred asphalt. Silent tears had rolled down my cheeks, my chest bursting. A sudden primal need for my mommy, the mommy I hadn't had in years, ripped through me.

Ruby had squeezed my cold fingers. "That's it then, little sister. It's just you and me now," she'd whispered in a choked voice. I'd hiccupped in air and glanced up at her. Her eyes were glued to the crumpled mass of twisted metal, her face stony. My watery vision had blurred at the scuffed and worn tips of my only pair of leather cowboy boots. She'd silently led me back to her car, and we took off.

I was twenty at the time and Ruby twenty-two. Ruby had moved back in to the house with me after having deserted boyfriend number who-knows-what. Thankfully, our house had no mortgage as it had been our father's parents' house. With basic expenses covered by our procession of odd jobs, we'd gotten by.

Ruby's immediate life plan, of course, had been to have lots of parties. And we did. I would often get stuck with the nightmarish cleanup while Ruby would take off with her friends or some new guy and disappear for days. Eventually she'd come back, usually more strung out than the last time.

This had gone on for a couple of years. In the meantime, I'd stuck to my life plan and after saving a bit of money, I finally registered at Western Dakota Tech in Rapid City to study business management. I also worked nights at Pete's Tavern, a local bar in town that Ruby had frequented since she was fifteen. Naturally, she'd gotten me the job.

One look at me, and Pete had known I was more dependable than my sister. At first I'd cleaned up in the kitchen, and within two weeks graduated to wiping down tables and clearing empties. Finally, Pete had put me out on the floor one night when one of his regular waitresses hadn't shown. I'd gotten to serve drinks and rake in real tips.

Life was good; life rolled on. I enjoyed my extremely busy routine. Ruby, however, became utterly unpredictable. She would be gone for longer stretches at a time. When she would be back, it would be with a crew of people, mostly bikers and their women who would park their phenomenal, shiny, massive Harleys in the driveway and crash all over our house.

Many of them I knew from Pete's. However, I took to locking my bedroom door. Too often I would find a trio of them screwing wildly on my bed, another couple on my floor. On those occasions I would take off and spend the night at Tania's house to try to get some sleep. Luckily, my quilt fit into the washing machine.

Then stuff around the house had started disappearing. I had ignored it at first, couldn't believe it, but it got harder and harder not to believe it. It had started with dad's tools in the garage, the stereo, the small television in my parents' room, my mother's gold cross, and then my grandmother's pearl bracelet. That had infuriated me. That was all we had of grandma, other than the house. Ruby wouldn't listen. She'd see the look on my face and either laugh, give me a hug, or start a conversation about nothing at all. Or if she was in one of her deeply sullen moods, she'd act like she couldn't see me. That broke my heart.

Early one morning I had found used syringes in the bathtub as I was getting in the shower, and it had knocked the air right out of me. Suddenly Ruby dabbing makeup on the inside of her left arm the other day made sense to me. The small plastic baggies I kept finding stuck in the sofa and the garbage, and the coffee grinder that seemed to be a new, permanent fixture on the coffee table had also made horrible sense.

The numbness I would feel when my mother would have her drunken tirades seeped through me once again. When I'd pulled up alongside the curb after work one morning a few hours before dawn, Ruby was getting on the back of Jump's bike. She only shot me a quick grin, and they'd roared off into the dark. That was the last I would see of her for over three weeks.

NOW

"She's having another round of tests again. Could be a while." Alex frowned. "Have a seat here, Grace, and we'll wait."

I slumped down on the hard plastic chair in the brightly lit hallway in front of Ruby's hospital room and dumped my bag in between my legs, parking my near-empty cup of coffee on a small table piled with dog-eared magazines. My head fell back against the wall, my eyelids sank, and memories flooded my brain again.

PAST

His hand burned into my wrist. "You're the little sister, right?"

I let go of the glass I had just set down on the table in front of the One-Eyed Jacks biker. Pearl Jam pounded over Pete's sound system, and I had to bend down close to the attractive guy who sported a hint of a goatee and caramel-colored hair, which just grazed his shoulders.

"Excuse me?"

"You're Grace, right?" he asked in a hypnotic, gravelly voice.

I wrenched my hand away from his, propped my tray up on my hip, and scowled at him. "Who wants to know?"

He grinned at me; a wicked, sexy grin that sent flutters through my belly. He leaned back in his chair and rubbed his hand along his handsome scruffy face. Big brown eyes smiled up at me, and the angles of his jaw seemed to widen as his lips curled at the edges.

Holy crap. It was Brown Eyes from that keg party drama years ago.

I hadn't seen him much since that night. A few times here at the bar, but never at the house with Jump and his buddies. A Sergeant at Arms patch was sewn on his leather vest along with a number of other colorful patches marking his warrior victories and wild sex-capades, no doubt. Pete had once explained the patch thing to me. He had said they were like medals of the life, their colors and symbols only translatable by other brothers.

"Oooh, an officer?" I asked. "Are you a gentleman, too?"

I liked sassing. It was my defense mechanism when I was scared, but it also charmed people because I had a feminine, sweet face, so they never expected it from me. Ruby's face wasn't as delicate, and she was all attitude, all the time. People always expected a smart mouth from her. At least that's what Mom had always said.

His brown eyes flashed at me, and he grinned. His friends cackled and snorted. At his side, Boner, the green-eyed one with the long hair, muttered, "Watch it, little sister."

Brown Eyes only jerked his chin at another one of his compadres who was in the chair behind me. The blond guy jumped up right away. With his foot, Brown Eyes yanked the chair up against the back of my legs.

"Sit." His voice rumbled through my chest.

"I've got work to do." My voice quaked, but I kept up the scowl anyway.

"Sit down." He rubbed his hand over his abs, his suede brown eyes never leaving mine. One of his eyebrows arched high on his forehead, and my breath snagged in my chest. I guess people always did what he told them.

I sat down, my back straight, my knees glued together. Brown Eyes leaned forward, his elbows on his thighs. His eyes were the color of dark syrup, their golden flecks glinting at me.

"I'm Dig."

"And you seem to know who I am."

"I need to talk to you about your sister."

"Okay." My shoulders tensed.

"Not surprised, huh?"

I shook my head, my lips pressed together. "Is she all right? I haven't seen her or heard from her in over three weeks at least. Do you know where she is?"

"Your sister created problems for us, and these problems gotta get gone."

My pulse thudded in my neck, and my mouth went dry. "Okay."

"She's been hanging with my boys."

"Yeah, I know. I've seen lots of you at my house." My eyes darted down the table at the other men who had already finished with the pitcher of beer and were waiting for me to bring them their shots.

"Ruby works for the club from time to time," Dig said, tilting his head at me. "At the Tingle."

I blinked up at him.

It all made sense now. The Tingle was the strip club just outside of Meager that the club owned. Ruby slept in pretty much all day every day, but was up and out all night every night. That had to be where all her cash had been coming from lately. She had been leaving me plenty of money the past few months for the bills and my weekly run to the supermarket, even extra for clothes shopping.

"Great." I glanced around the bar. I hoped Pete wasn't aware I was yakking with a customer while I should be taking orders. The place was filling up fast, and I needed to end this quickly with Dig.

"Listen up, little sister." His fingers went to my chin and brought me face to face with him once again. "She got involved in a deal that went south. Smart bitch, but a little too eager. She got herself arrested today with one of my brothers."

My stomach buckled. "Where is she? Can I go see her? Was she with Jump?"

"Yeah. Calm down, Peanut." Two of his fingers curled around a strand of my hair and twisted it into a coil. "I need you to do something for me."

"Me?" I let out a squeak.

My life flashed before my eyes. Dig was probably going to tell me he was dragging me back to their clubhouse to turn me into a club slave or house mouse or skank or whatever the hell they called it, to pay for Ruby's wrongs.

My jaw slackened. The room spun.

In one quick and efficient maneuver, Dig plucked the tray from my white-knuckled grip, pulled me into his lap and dropped the tray onto the now-empty chair. His hard chest was a solid, impenetrable wall against the side of my body. His tobacco scented breath filled my nostrils.

One of his hands stroked my back while the other, on which he wore a variety of heavy silver rings, most notably a large gleaming skull, clasped my thigh. His firm grip coursed right through my jeans like an electrical current. I shuddered despite my earlier determination to play it cool, especially when his nose stroked the line of my jaw and up my cheek.

"Little sister," Dig's low husky voice dripped over me like melted chocolate. "What I need from you is to talk to Ruby. I need her to understand a few things so she can say the right thing to the cops. She's actually in a perfect position to help us resolve a few

35

important issues. And if she does this for the club, we'll help her, and we'll look out for you."

"What do you mean—help?" My heart pounded outside my chest.

"We always help our own." His hand squeezed my thigh tighter.

"Your own?" The back of my throat stung. "Is Ruby yours?"

Dig shook his head. "Not mine. She's done a couple good deeds for us here and there. The club is prepared to help her out now in her time of trouble with lawyer's fees, and whatever else comes up, like maybe rehab once she's out. We'd also look out for you, Peanut."

I bit my bottom lip. "Why do I need you to look out for me?"

"You're going to be on your own in that house, going to school, working here." Dig seemed to know a lot about me. His hand continued its conquest of my flesh. "There are people who know your sister, and they aren't the nicest kind of people. They aren't happy with her or with us right now. We've got a slim window of opportunity to make this right, and I want to take it. The club needs to do this in order to keep the peace, but that will only happen if Ruby does this thing for the club. Otherwise, we're going to have a serious mess on our hands, and you'll both be flapping in the wind. It won't be pretty for any of us."

"Oh." I squirmed in his lap.

Oops. Not a good idea.

His erection jutted against my rear, and my back went rigid. Dig only tightened his grip on my leg to steady me. His other hand slid up my back to my neck and pulled my face in closer to his.

Holy crap. This is what Ruby meant by "alpha male maneuvers."

His full lips were only a breath apart from mine. His spicy cologne and tobacco-laced manly aroma hinted at a foreign, exotic world. "You get me, little sister?" he whispered.

"Yeah."

"Yeah what, Peanut?"

I swallowed hard. "I get you. Just, um, tell me what you want me to tell her to do or whatever you just said."

His ringed hand stroked up my thigh, his thumb grazing my crotch. I glanced down. One of his silver rings was made of a .44 caliber chamber.

"You still got that pissant boyfriend?" His voice was rough and gravelly again.

I shook my head. How the hell did he know about Trey Owens? The whole thing had been a whole lot of nothing that had lasted maybe three weeks. Trey frequently dropped by Pete's with his friends and insisted on freebies, or he'd come to my house unannounced to watch ball games with bagged popcorn and cheap beer. He'd try to get down my jeans and up my shirt during the commercials. My disinterest irritated him. His irritation annoyed me. The big attraction was over real quick.

Dig's warm fingertips skimmed my back under my tight Pete's T-shirt and lingered at my bra strap. His light touch suddenly transformed into a massage that radiated waves of heat through me.

"How about we meet for breakfast tomorrow at that diner in Pine Needle, and I'll lay it all out for you. Say around ten? Sound good?" His lips brushed my ear, and I nodded, mesmerized by what his hot hand was doing to my flesh. His hardness poked at my rear. I could barely breathe at this point.

After all, I was a virgin.

My sister had repeatedly tried to get me to "lose it," as she called it, but I had no interest in "losing it," "giving it up" or "getting rid of it." I wanted my first time to be a memorable, special moment. Not some sort of sloppiness in the back of a car or a truck, or a quickie on the sofa during commercials for Monday Night Football.

I didn't want to regret it after, nor did I want to laugh about it years later like Ruby did. I wanted to be thrilled and gratified by the memory. My sister had smirked at what she considered to be my oddball corniness, but she admired my resolve and romanticism, nevertheless. I didn't have to be in love, I argued. I just wanted there to be something big and real between me and the guy when it happened. And he had to be a good guy who I was really attracted to and who really wanted me, too, not just any good looking dick on legs.

Like now, perched on Dig's lap, trapped in his arms, his lips and hands scorching my skin. This was breathlessly big and thrillingly real, wasn't it?

"You want to let my star waitress get back to work, Dig? I got a business to run," Pete's grizzly voice sliced between us.

Dig's hands dropped from my body and relaxed at his sides. "Later, Peanut." He grinned and winked at me. My pulse skipped a beat, and I scooted off his lap and grabbed my tray.

In a few months I would become Dig's old lady.

THREE

NOW

"GRACE, WAKE UP."

My eyes adjusted to the harsh, bright lighting of the hospital hallway.

"Ruby's back in her room," said Alex. "She's waiting for you."

I popped out of the hard chair, and my hand immediately went to my stiff neck and aching shoulders. An elderly man swished a large mop across the floor, and the heavy smell of pine cleaner pierced my nostrils. I let out a cough as my hands rubbed down the legs of my jeans. I slid my handbag over my shoulder and followed Alex into my sister's room.

"Grace!" Ruby exclaimed, her arms outstretched. Her beautiful silky blonde hair had long since fallen out and now her head was wrapped in a teal blue scarf. Her skin was pale, very unlike her usual golden hue. She looked thinner, yet bloated at the same time. I ran to her open arms, and we rocked each other back and forth.

She laughed. "Shit, you look just a little better than me, what the hell?"

"I've been driving for long stretches to get here. I couldn't get any sleep last night at this crappy motel, so I just decided to get back in the car and come straight here."

Ruby's tired eyes slid to Alex, then back to me.

"I may have had a whiskey from the minibar. Or two." I shrugged at her as I sat at the edge of her bed.

Ruby let out a small laugh. "Oh, that's why you're having your blood taken tomorrow?"

"Yep. They need a clean sample."

She squeezed my hand. "Thanks, honey. It means a lot to me."

I frowned at Alex. "Did she just say thank you?" I turned my frown on Ruby. "I'm your sister, I'm your best shot. It's a no-brainer."

Ruby nodded stiffly as her eyes welled with tears. My stomach clenched. Ruby never was the crier. I had always been the Miss Sensitive at our house.

"Rube?" I crushed her to my chest once more.

"Honey, it's okay." Alex rubbed her arm.

"It's so good to see you. It's been such a long time," Ruby mumbled.

"Meeting me the past three Christmases in Denver, Dallas and Seattle doesn't count?"

"I mean seeing you here in South Dakota," she said. "Sorry. It's just frustrating. I finally go and get my shit together and now this. For the first time in my life there's nothing I can do about it. You know me. I don't do helpless. I like plans of attack."

"You mean no plans and lots of attack," I said.

Alex chuckled. "You got that right." He leaned over and planted a kiss on Ruby's cheek.

"Whatever." She made a face at us. "All I can do now is sit back and wait for test results and listen to the doctors drone on about their data. It makes me cranky. Deal with it, you two." Ruby wiped at her eyes.

"So that's what we do. We deal." I stiffened against the catch in my voice. "Don't fret about me. I'm here to stay. I brought my stuff with me in my car."

"Really?"

"Really. Of course I'm staying."

"You'd do that for me, Gracie? Stay here?" Ruby asked. "I know it's gotta be rough for you to be back for the first time since. . ."

"I'm fine. Anyway, this is Rapid City, not Meager."

Ruby let out a whoop, and her arms flew around my neck.

"I'll leave you two. I've got to get to work." Alex bent over Ruby and kissed her slowly, his hand stroking her face. "Love you, Rube."

"Love you too, baby," she murmured.

The door clicked shut behind him. I shuffled through my bag to look for the packet of gum I had bought the day before at a truck stop.

Ruby let out a heavy sigh. "Amazing isn't it?"

"What's that?"

"You'd think it would have been HIV that would be the end of me, what with all the crazy shit I've pulled. But nope, it was Momma's revenge that sank its teeth into me instead."

My eyes shot up at her. "What are you talking about?"

"The cancer, Grace. Mom's DNA sucks. Aunt Jessie died of ovarian, Aunt Lucy had stomach or something nasty like that, and Mommy Dearest had pancreatic cancer."

"What?"

"You didn't need to know back then. You had enough to deal with. That's probably what made her extra crazy the last couple of years—her looming death sentence." Ruby's head dropped back onto the pillow, and she let out a sigh. "Whatever."

I tossed my bag to the end of her bed and leaned over her, my hands planted in the mattress at her sides. "Listen to me, Ruby. You are going to beat this thing. Stop it in its tracks. All of us are in this together: you, me, Alex, and Jakey."

Ruby let out a sob. I winced at the raw sound. "That's what I think of all the time, Gracie." Her voice was small, raspy. "I can't leave my baby behind. He's everything. I love being his mommy." Her weary eyes filled with water again. I took her hand in mine and squeezed it hard. "Getting pregnant was a total surprise, a complete gift. God can't take that away from me now. He just can't."

A knife ripped through my chest, tearing through my heart.

Ruby struggled to sit up. "I'm sorry, so sorry, sweetie. I don't mean ... you know I didn't ..."

"I know, honey." The tears finally spilled from my eyes. I had been holding onto them since I'd left Seattle. Ruby wiped at my wet face with her cold fingers.

"I want to live this life I managed to patch together," Ruby said through a watery smile. "It's a good one, Gracie. Alex and I have been really happy. I never knew what that was before. I didn't know I could have that. You did, though. You had that."

"I always wanted that for you." My voice hitched in the back of my throat. "You deserve it. And you're going to keep it. You got to hold on with everything you've got. Everything. Every damned thing."

Ruby nodded and bit her lip. I buried my face in her neck. Her fingers smoothed down my hair, and she planted a kiss on the top of my head.

My beautiful sister had always braided and unbraided the strands of her life however she damn well pleased, and now she was suffering the random cruelty of fate in an utterly different way. When years ago the club had asked her to take the fall for them, to plead guilty to selling drugs and go to prison, I had verged on the hysterical, but she had eerily taken it in stride.

Ruby had only nodded silently at me when I had told her what Dig wanted and about the club's pledge to look out for us. She had only stared at me as I stammered it out over the prison visitor's telephone, my shaky hand glued to the glass between us. This lung cancer was different, though. You couldn't cut deals with cancer. This was utterly out of our control.

This was hell.

"We're going to lick this thing, Rube. We are," I said. "I'm home now. It's my turn to help you."

I swallowed back the sourness that rose in my throat and peeked up at Ruby. Her tired gaze had drifted outside the window.

"Hey hon', welcome to the party."

There was a party tonight at the One-Eyed Jacks clubhouse? Perfect.

"You sure you're at the right place?" The cute, blond, twenty-something recruit asked me.

Of course, if I were twenty years younger and wearing next to nothing, he wouldn't have asked me that question. I grinned at the two prospects at the gate of the property, an old go-kart factory from the sixties with its own small raceway at a still-desolate corner on the north edge of Meager. Bikes of all shapes and sizes were lined up like ominous shiny metal soldiers in the lot. Two pickup trucks stood sentry at the other end.

"I need to see Jump."

The blond recruit with a hint of a mustache squinted his eyes at me. "Really?" He leaned over the gate towards me and grinned. "And who are you, sweetheart?"

"Tell him Little Sister is here to see him."

His features froze. "What?"

"You heard me."

He stared at me, and his partner's eyes went wide as he got out his cell phone and pushed a button. "Kicker? Yeah, um, got a lady out front here to see the prez. Says she's Little Sister." He pushed a thick mass of dark hair away from his face revealing a scar down his forehead. He looked me over top to toe. "Yeah, got ya." He shoved his phone back in his jeans. "I'll take you in."

The blond recruit unlocked the gate and held it open for me as I walked through. The other one jerked his chin at his brother. "Dawes, I'll be back." Dawes nodded at us.

"My name's Tricky, nice to meet you."

"Nice to meet you, too."

"Kicker, our VP, is waiting for you." He gestured towards the main entrance.

We moved through the vast courtyard past the line of bikes. I recognized Miller's black GMC truck in the lot. I sucked in air as we approached the main building. At the double metal door, a goateed, black-haired man, muscular arms folded across his wide chest with a VP's patch on his colors, wearing pointy cowboy boots waited for us.

"Hey, I'm Kicker." He shook my hand. "This should be good."

I only smirked.

He turned on his heel, and I followed him through the double doors. My eyes blinked at the familiar smells as we strode through the main hallway. . .metal, faded alcohol and stale tobacco that had once been the fragrance of happiness and contentment to me. Loud noises and cheers came from the distance. My black leather boots made a distinct clomping sound on the bare concrete, the same concrete I had once strode over in what felt like a past life.

I used to belong here.

Did I still?

My damp hands smoothed down my short, slim denim skirt as I sucked in my tummy and adjusted my favorite black leather belt with the intricate silver embroidery. I gave a final tug at my black blouse that draped down my front and pushed back my hair over my ears past my dangling earrings. Dig's silver skull ring sat on the index finger of my right hand. I traced over my short gold and silver necklaces, a tiny cross and a peace sign Ruby had given me a million years ago.

My hand smoothed down the one long silver chain I wore and settled on the medallion hanging from it. I fingered the skull engraved in the silver with a single diamond chip in one eye socket, like the One-Eyed Jacks logo. Dig had given it to me as a wedding present. My thumb traced over our names that were engraved on the back. Whatever tonight turned out to be, Dig was here with me and I would get done what needed to get done. For Ruby. I may have lost absolutely everything once upon a time, but I would do my damnedest to make sure that didn't happen to my sister.

Even if it meant coming back here.

We made the next turn in the photograph-lined hall. Sucking sounds, muffled moans and heavy breathing filled the space. I turned my head down the shadowy hall to the right that led to the bedrooms. I could barely make out a red-headed woman spilling out of a tiny white bikini top on her knees as she sucked off a tall man facing away from us wearing a knit cap. His hands were fisted in her hair as her head bobbed over his dick.

Kicker turned to me and shrugged, and I rolled my eyes grinning. He stopped and leaned back into the hallway. "Yo, Lock!"

Mr. Blow Job jerked his head towards us in the shadows.

"Wrap it up, dude. You're gonna want to be inside for this one."

Lock flicked his fingers at us and pumped his hips into the girl's greedy mouth. *How efficient.*

I had ceased to find these sorts of things embarrassing a very long time ago. It was part of the shameless freedom of club life. Maybe it was awkward and crude, but I didn't find it shocking or as very dramatic as I had when I'd first walked into this clubhouse twenty years ago. That was the day I had left the courthouse choking on tears because my sister had just been sentenced to a year and a half in jail for a crime she was not responsible for.

FOUR

PAST

THE JUDGE'S GAVEL CRACKED AGAINST WOOD, and my body shuddered.

Mom used to say: "*You play, you pay.*" Ruby Hastings now had to pay.

I knew Ruby must have had a hand in the drug deal she was being accused of, but Jump certainly had engineered it and was the main player in the equation. Not to mention the two members of the Demon Seeds, the rival gang, with whom she also hung out.

Ruby had been sleeping with Jump, but she wasn't his old lady. In truth, she was a club bitch who was going to take the fall. She didn't merit their loyalty or support. However, as Dig had mentioned, Ruby had come through for them time and time again on odd jobs and little missions. I never knew what exactly. "Club business," she would mutter and wave me off. "Don't ask me that shit," Dig had said over that breakfast he'd treated me to. Was it drug deals? Did the club pimp her out undercover when she worked at Tingle to rival gangs or drug dealers? My imagination swam with the lurid possibilities.

All of Ruby's badassness and diligence had earned her a certain measure of respect, though. If her going to jail was somehow going to "resolve major issues" for them, and she had been loyal to the club in the past, I was confident they wouldn't let us "flap in the wind" as Dig had pointed out. Somehow that didn't comfort me much, though. That only meant I was in trouble, too. Ruby most certainly was aware of this, so she agreed to go down for all of us.

I was used to fending for myself, but Ruby had always been around, flitting about like a moth to a bright light in the darkness, sometimes out of sight but always fluttering back. I never felt alone; she would always return eventually.

This was different.

Ruby rose from her chair, and the officers immediately clicked handcuffs on her wrists. She turned slightly, her hard eyes finding mine, and I knew what she was thinking. I could hear her voice burning through my heart.

"Love you no matter what, so just suck it up."

But now those words took on a whole new meaning. My sister was taking on a heavy burden, a responsibility for herself, for me, for the club. The force of it positively flared from her stony gaze. Her body stiffened, and she slowly turned away from me as the officers pulled her out of the courtroom. The club lawyer tucked his papers and folders into his briefcase and clicked it shut.

Acid rose in the back of my throat.

I drove home in my dad's old Chevy Jimmy. I should've felt grateful he had left it behind, but I didn't. What was left? Just me and everyone's castoffs. The sobs broke from my chest and wouldn't stop. I could barely see the road ahead of me. I barreled through the front door of our house, collapsed on my bed, and heaved for air and salvation.

But I knew there was none to be had.

I twisted onto my back and listened to the sudden silence in the house. Silence all through my room, Ruby's bedroom, the bathroom with dated fixtures and dull tile. Silence down the narrow hallway treaded with worn green carpeting, its walls dotted with small framed squares of Grandma's embroidery of strawberries. Silence in the living room stuffed with two bulky couches in that tired blue and green striped pattern. Silence in our parents' bedroom, which had been empty for a long while, because on a jag Ruby had sold the furniture and donated their clothes just as she had emptied the basement of years of clutter except for the washer and dryer.

There was sheer silence for once in the house, save for the ticking of that ugly oversized clock in the shape of a sunflower with huge petals that had hung in the kitchen since day one. My grandparents had first nailed that cheesy clock on the kitchen wall over the small wooden table. Yellowed with age, that clock had ticked away the years of spotty contentment and shrouded misery in this house all through my childhood.

Now that ticking seemed to presage all the emptiness that lay ahead for me and for Ruby.

Screw that.

I got up from my bed as I wiped my wet face on my forearm, marched to the kitchen, flung open a cupboard, and snatched one of Dad's favorite beer glasses. Why the hell had my mother kept them anyway? What the hell kind of crazy ass house was this? Laughter stung in my throat.

I hurled the glass at the clock.

The clock face smashed into a shower of bits and pieces that flew all over the kitchen. I shook myself, and pieces of glass fell like treacherous snowflakes from my hair and clothes. I grabbed the rest of those beer glasses and threw them at each and every petal of the now ruined sunflower clock. Glass showered through the room.

Then I started on my mother's wine glasses that she'd gotten from a gas station on a special offer. She had been so proud of them. *"They're nice, aren't they?"* she had mused aloud to herself over and over when she had first arranged them in the cabinet.

Everything was "nice" in here wasn't it? "Nice," if you didn't ask too many questions. "Nice," if you didn't look too hard. "Nice," if you didn't expect anything much.

I hated anything "nice."

I aimed each glass at a different deer on the faded brown hunting-themed wallpaper in the kitchen. My aim improved with each throw.

A half empty bottle of tequila flirted with me from the top of the fridge. I jumped over the sea of sharp remnants on the kitchen floor and snickered at the harsh chomping noises my boots made. I reached up, grabbed the bottle, and took a long swig. The liquor burned down my throat, and I coughed, wiping the side of my mouth with the back of my hand. I nabbed the keys to the Jimmy and left the house.

Who the hell did Jump and Dig think they were anyhow? Kings of the freaking county, no doubt. Where were they when the judge passed down her sentence on Ruby? Having a beer and getting their dicks blown at their precious clubhouse most likely.

Hell no.

I jostled my way through the throng of people in the courtyard of the clubhouse. A raucous party was in full swing. *What a surprise.* Members of the Demon Seeds, the rival club involved in Ruby and Jump's drug deal gone south, were here partying with the One-Eyed Jacks. The boys had kissed and made up, so this must be a celebration-at-Ruby's-expense party. Did my invitation get lost in the mail?

A fire blazed in the center of the yard, and the aroma of charred meat filled the air in a haze of smoke. I tromped through the yard, the bottle of tequila still in my hand. I had a good buzz on. Enough to let go of any inhibitions, but enough to still retain my self-respect.

Boner bounded in front of me, his green eyes glassy. "Little Sister, whazzup?" A cigarette hung from his fingers, and his one arm was hooked around an overly made-up and very drunk blonde with an unsettling amount of teased hair.

"Where is he?"

"Who?"

"Dig. Where is he?"

"Oh, he's partying...somewhere. Not sure." Blondie only cackled. "Sure is nice to see you, babe, but I don't think you wanna be here." Boner took a long drag on his cigarette, and his eyes widened. "Why don't you go on back home, huh?"

Home. My insides blazed with fire.

"Where is he?"

The blonde giggled and leaned towards me wobbling on her heels. "He's at the shed."

"Aw shit," muttered Boner. He popped the cigarette out of his mouth and rubbed his forehead. "Don't go back there, Little Sister. Don't."

"Yeah, yeah." I brushed him off and charged in the direction of the shed.

A big circle of men and a few women stood in front of the large steel shed which housed the bike repair shop of the Club. An in-the-wild-jungle-like vibe hung in the air, a tangible, raw menace that made my mouth go dry.

Shit, maybe I should have listened to Boner and not come out here.

Everyone's eyes were glued to some sort of extravaganza playing out before them. Several fires roared from rusty steel drums, which cast a golden-reddish glow over everyone's faces. Undisguised carnal intensity was etched on their features and it hit me like a furnace blast. Was it a fight? Some sort of death match?

I squeezed through the gaps between several men who didn't even register my presence because their attention was riveted by the show. My pulse skidded to a halt.

Four naked women were on the ground getting banged, giving head, and getting it up the ass by a number of men in a number of combinations. The sound of slapping skin, moaning, and grunting filled the hot air. Plenty more men waited in line to have their turn while they smoked weed and drank from bottles. They spurred their buddies on with a colorful array of language and howls of laughter. Others were getting it on with their own women as they watched.

The vivid spectacle burned through my eyeballs and positively knocked the tequila buzz right out of me. A wave of nausea rushed up my throat. I pushed back through the men, but got stuck.

"Oh, yeah, look what I found!" a voice growled in my ear. "A sweet piece of cherry pie."

Two massive hands ran up my rear over my skirt and around my waist, travelled north and settled on my breasts. My body was jerked back into a rock hard wall of muscle and stench.

"Ain't it my lucky night? Got me a pretty piece."

"Hey, that's Ruby's little sister," said a passing female voice. I looked up. It was one of the biker chicks always at our house. My mouth fell open, but her name suddenly escaped me. She disappeared into the crowd.

The beast's hand fisted in my hair, and he yanked my head back. "No shit."

"Let go of me!" I scratched at his arms, and shoved against him. Big mistake. One of his hands grabbed at my crotch and drove my ass between his legs. The air got sucked out of me, pain flaring through my chest.

"Aw, this is gonna be good. I won the fucking jackpot tonight," he growled in my ear.

I raised the tequila bottle over his head, but it was plucked from my hand.

"Let her go, Vig!"

Dig. *Thank you, God.*

I struggled in Vig's grip, but it was useless. Laughter ripped from his chest. "Don't be an asshole man, just having fun. Now fuck off."

I turned my face, and a coarse patch on the sleeve of his leather jacket grated against my cheek. The smell of his sour sweat and the booze on his breath erupted a tide of nausea in my belly once more.

49

"She's that cunt's little sister, ain't she?" Vig's voice seethed. He squeezed my breasts and my crotch all at once, and I let out a loud gasp.

"I said let her go," said Dig. "You don't want to do this, man."

"You're not being a good host, Diggy. You don't share the house pussy with your guests?"

I struggled for air in Vig's tight grasp. My eyes darted up and found Dig's. The lines of his face were hard, a muscle in his jaw pulsed. He handed off my tequila bottle to a grim-faced Boner. "She ain't house pussy. Now let her go."

"Why should I? She's here ain't she? Why do you give a shit? You've had your dick up in plenty of bitches for days. What the fuck you playing at?" Vig twisted me in his arms once more. "I just saw some cunt sucking your dick."

Oh, too much information.

My stomach flipped over as images of Dig getting hot and nasty with lots of different women flitted through my thoughts in a frenzy. But I was in the lethal clutches of a Demon Seed who didn't like my sister, for crap's sake, and there wasn't time to indulge in jealous fantasies.

Jealous? Of Dig and other women?

Revolted, maybe. Jealous no way.

Dig and I had actually spent some time together over the past months while waiting for Ruby's trial to come up. He had been as good as his word about looking out for me. He and Boner and a few of their brothers regularly came to Pete's and drank while they played pool. I knew he was there to check up on me as he had never come in so frequently before. Dig would show up every time, the others rotated.

I hated it at first. Then I began to like it.

The guys wouldn't let the other waitress, Mandy, take their drink orders. Her eyes had shot daggers at me, and she'd mouthed "bitch" across the bar at me the first time that happened. It got to the point where Pete had made sure that my section always included the Club's ever-reserved set of tables.

At first Dig would nod at me, or give me the badass chin jerk, which frankly made my knees wobble almost every time. Throughout the evening, we would exchange sassy comments. He'd flash me his wicked grin, and I'd roll my eyes and shake my head at him. My insides had melted at each and every exchange, but I'd worked hard to ignore that phenomenon, which only increased in regularity. I was Little Sister, after all, not biker ~~girlfriend~~ bitch material. He was just being sweet and flirty, wasn't he?

One night Trey had shown up at Pete's with his pals. He'd grabbed my arm and yanked at me to sit in his lap, and the shots lined up on my tray had gone flying. Dig and Boner were on him in a flash. Boner had pulled me out of Trey's grasp as Dig had wrenched Trey out of his chair and popped him in the face. Blood had gushed over his shirt and hands. Most everyone in the bar had clapped as Trey and his pals had stumbled out of Pete's.

Dig had turned to me, his eyes grim. He had run his bloody knuckles down my cheek, leaving behind a smear of blood. He didn't say a word, only rubbed off the blood, planted a kiss on my forehead, then he'd returned to his table and sat back down with his brothers as if nothing had happened. Trey never came around Pete's again.

Inevitably, all sorts of women would hover over the bikers' table, sitting in their laps or at least trying to, and they'd eventually leave together. Even Mandy would leave with them once in a while. But no matter how his evening ended, Dig would always find me in the crowd and flick his hand at me in goodbye.

At home very late at night or in the wee hours of the morning, I would sometimes hear the roar of pipes down the street or the rev of a bike's engine that was springing back to life. I would smile into my pillow in my bedroom in my empty house.

One afternoon I had bumped into Boner at the supermarket. He'd taken my arm in his and said he was going to help me shop. He'd yapped on and on about crazy shit that made me laugh, but it had gotten to the point where I couldn't keep track of what I was looking for on the shelves. Then he'd surfed through the aisles on my shopping cart and narrowly missed several elderly ladies. We must have been in there for almost two hours.

I'd invited him home for dinner, and he'd called Dig. I'd cooked them chicken cutlets with homemade mac and cheese and a huge spinach salad. Dig had brought the beer. Later, Boner had given me a quick hug and kiss on the cheek good night, but Dig had only stared at me, his jaw set.

"Dig? What is it?" I'd asked.

"Hmm? Nothing, baby." His hand had reached out, and his knuckles had stroked my cheek as my breath had snagged. He'd never called me "baby" before. I was always "Peanut" or "Little Sister."

"Lock up, okay?" he'd said softly.

"Yeah, okay." He'd turned and strode down the front walkway. I'd closed the door, bolted it, and peeked through the curtains to watch them get on their bikes. Boner had waved at me. Dig had busied himself with his bike. Suddenly their engines exploded, and they'd zoomed away into the night.

But now those happy thoughts couldn't keep me from gagging when Vig's tongue slicked over my neck. Dig's eyes blazed.

I had to do something to flip the balance. I didn't want to be responsible for some kind of battle or war between two bike clubs already in a tenuous truce. Pete's voice infiltrated my brain: *"Always be respectful and polite with these guys, and they'll show you the same. Don't ever sass them, or you're asking for it."*

Somehow, I didn't think respectful and polite was going to save my ass right now or defuse the situation. By now our little standoff had attracted a crowd of onlookers.

My hands pushed against Vig's chest. "Hey, excuse me, but I'm Dig's woman! We got into a major blowout last week, and I took off, so of course he's been banging everything in sight! He does it to get back at me, like all the other times we've broken up. He's a man-whore and I'm a mouthy bitch, but I'm back now and I'd like to fuck my man tonight, show him what he's been missing, if that's all right with you?" I gulped in air and grimaced at Vig.

He looked at me as if I was an alien who had just landed on Earth.

Laughter and snickers rose around us. Vig cursed under his breath and pulled on me again. My head twisted towards Dig. His eyes glittered over me, his chin high.

"You heard her, man," Dig said, his voice cold and hard as iron. "Get your hands off my property and there won't be any trouble."

Holy crap, he called me his "property" in front of everybody. That was quite a social step up from a mere "bitch" in biker-speak.

"You wait one more second and there's gonna be a shitstorm, motherfucker," said Wreck. My eyes shifted in the direction of his voice. Wreck was the One-Eyed Jack's Road Captain and one of Dig and Boner's closest friends at the club. He was a real 1%'er who had been a club member since his teens.

"Vig!"

A rough voice cut through the crowd and a stocky, burly man who had to be in his early fifties glared fireballs at our little clusterfuck. My eyes went to the patches on his worn-out colors. Cowboy, the Demon Seed president.

Not good.

Vig cursed under his breath, and shoved me hard into Dig with a grunt. I immediately flung my arms around Dig's torso and planted juicy kisses on his pecs over his tight gray T-shirt.

"I'm sorry, baby. It's all my fault," I stage whispered for effect.

Dig's arm slammed me against his body, his hand sliding down my back. I took the opportunity to throw my arms around his neck, hop up and hook my legs around his waist. His hand landed over my ass under my short cotton skirt and rubbed my curvy flesh over the thin fabric of my pink panties that I was sure were now plainly visible to our audience.

After my harsh imprisonment by Vig's foul body, I sank into Dig and reveled in the sensation of his hands on my flesh and his masculine spicy scent. His touch and smell became my elixir of life in that moment of sheer relief. My fingers raked through Dig's soft caramel hair, and I nuzzled his neck and face, doing my best impression of a property chick who was horny for her man. I loudly murmured sweet skanky nothings in his ear. His hold on me tightened.

"What the fuck?" Cowboy said. My stomach rolled. I shut my mouth and pressed my fingers into Dig's back.

"We're good, bro," Vig said, his voice controlled, even. "It's all good."

"Oh, yeah?" Cowboy's bloodshot eyes narrowed and shifted between Vig and us.

"Yeah," Dig said flatly. "We're good." Macho chin jerks followed all around, and Vig turned and pushed through the crowd, the bulk of Cowboy at his side.

My grip on Dig's back relaxed.

"Can I get down now?" I whispered in his ear. His hand continued to burn right through my panties, plus my crotch sat right on the side of his waist at an angle making it hard for me to breathe, let alone think coherent thoughts.

He exhaled on a hiss. "You're not going anywhere."

"Huh?" I jerked my head back to face him.

"They know who you are now, you little idiot!" His eyes flashed at me. "Ruby's a fuck-up to them. Don't think they wouldn't take the opportunity to take it out on you." He slid me down his body and held me as I found my footing. Dig grabbed a fistful of my hair and tugged my head back. His face leaned into mine. "What the fuck are you doing here anyway?"

Shit. He was mad at me.

I pushed at his chest, but his free hand gripped my bicep yanking me closer to his body. My eyes stung. He stared at me. "Peanut, what is it? What the hell's wrong?" he asked, his voice softer.

My lungs squeezed together. "Ruby. . .Ruby got sentenced today. And I couldn't hug her goodbye, I couldn't do anything. All I could do was get in my car and go back to that house. That h-h-house. She's in a cell with God knows who, and. . .and. . .you're all partying 'cause she's going down for you. This is a victory party, isn't it?" I rubbed at the edge of my eyes and sniffed. "So yeah, I thought I'd come here and join in on the celebration just to top off my day. Got any champagne on tap?"

Dig's eyes tightened. "You knew the score, Little Sister."

"I knew, but it's something else to actually live it, Dig!"

"Shut it, Grace. Now, you're gonna be really living it. You show up here tonight on your own and get into it with Vig of all people, and then even their prez catches wind of our little scene." He dragged a hand through his hair and exhaled. "Thank fuck Boner and Wreck found me and we got to you in time."

"Well, thank fuck your blow job finished up when it did!"

His eyes flared, and he tugged me closer. I winced at the pain. "You better forget the attitude and the tears and get your sweet ass in gear, Little Sister. You just put a whole new concept in motion, and now you got to play it."

I scowled at him. "What concept?"

"Babe." He shook his head at me. "The concept you planted in Vig's pea brain about you being my woman. It was smart and well-played, but now you got to follow through on it. Actually, it's a damn good idea. It'll make you totally hands-off. For a while at least."

I was lost. "What?"

"Look, it's Friday. The Seeds are here until Monday, which means you got to stay with me so we can play happy couple until they clear out."

I rocked back on my boots. "Excuse me?"

He grabbed the sides of my face and crushed our mouths together. Electricity coursed through my body, and I lost my mind along with my breath.

"Would it be that difficult, Peanut?" he murmured against my lips.

Hell no, it most certainly wouldn't be hard to pretend I wanted his hands on my body and his mouth on me. I only shook my head at Dig, knowing I would give myself away if I even attempted speech. My heavy gaze fell to his lips. I really liked the way they felt on mine. Demanding, rough, giving.

I was in trouble.

"I didn't think so. So play along, baby. You've been around us long enough to know the drill."

My eyes shot wide open. "Wh-what do you want me to do? Drop to my knees and suck you off right here, right now so they can see?"

"Jesus, Grace!" He frowned at me. "Relax. Just go with it. And I mean it, go with whatever I throw at you, no pulling back, no hesitation."

His stern face suddenly relaxed and his tongue licked around my ear then slid down the side of my neck, erasing any memory of Vig on my skin. I let out a small cry. Dig's hand cupped my breast and pressed into my flesh. My eyes flew open once more.

"Can't you pretend you want to fuck me, Peanut? That you can't get enough of me?" My breathing came to a complete standstill, and the blood rushed through my veins like a tidal wave. "Can't you pretend you're hungry for me, baby?" he whispered hoarsely.

My insides clamped together, and my fingers gripped his taut biceps in a death lock. "I'll try."

"No, Sister. You fucking do it. We put on a believable show, even make my brothers believe it. You got that? There'll be no room for anyone to make a move on you as revenge against Ruby or the Club's decision for her to take the fall."

"You mean the Demon Seeds aren't happy with the outcome?" My voice quaked.

55

"I can't get into it with you but yeah, a few of them have been grumbling, especially Vig, so we need to nip any potential hazards in the bud. You being one of them."

"I've never been called a potential hazard before. In fact, just the opposite."

"Think of it as a new adventure in your formerly quiet life." A smile curled the edges of his mouth and he stroked my lips with his thumb. Sparks flew over my skin under his heated gaze and his feather-light touch. "Great lips, by the way," he murmured.

I rolled my eyes at him. "Glad you like them."

"I do. Which is a very, very good thing, huh?"

"I guess."

He smirked. "So did you come here tonight to punch me out?"

"Something like that."

He took me in his arms and filled his hands with my ass. "Now you got all weekend to take that aggression out on me in other ways. You just showed us you got it in you. Am I right?"

I nodded.

"That was really sexy, by the way," he said into my hair. I blushed from head to toe and punched him in the chest. Dig chuckled. "You ready?"

"Sure." I let out a sigh.

He smacked my ass.

"Hey!"

His jaw set in a rigid line. "I need enthusiasm, babe."

I glared at him. Challenges always did appeal to me. I slid my hands over his ass, pulled his pelvis into mine and stroked his bottom lip with my tongue, then slid it in his mouth where it lazily tangled with his tongue. Then I retreated and sucked on his lower lip nipping it with my teeth.

"I can work with that." Dig's hands skimmed the sides of my body. "Remember, stick with me, never let go. Don't be chatty, just smile, and don't show interest in our conversations. Just show them we're together and that you can't wait to fuck me. Okay?"

"Okay, I get it. I'm your arm candy."

His lips pressed into a firm line. "No, baby. You're my pussy candy. That's how they're all gonna be thinking of you, so get it straight."

My face heated. Geez, what was I thinking? This was hardly going to be lighthearted fun at the senior prom.

Dig took my hand in his. "Let's get something to drink."

We clung to each other for the rest of the long evening. I was determined to play it cool and hard but horny, of course. This would be just some meaningless show, a performance I had to put on. Dig was an officer of his club, and he had to show his respect and hospitality to his guests, and I had a role to play.

We made our way around the entire compound so he could hang out with the Demon Seeds. He didn't introduce me to most of them, and they didn't pay me much mind other than a quick flick of their eyes.

Tonight I was just his piece or his pussy or property or whatever, so we worked it to make the appropriate statement. He constantly kissed me in a raw, possessive way, making my mind and all my girly parts unravel in a tailspin. He didn't stop me when I ran my hands through his hair or over his chest. I slipped them often in his rear pockets and groped his ass as we walked or stood hip to hip while he conversed with other bikers as I pretended not to pay any attention.

So far so good. I handled it all pretty well. Didn't I?

All of this "acting" certainly wasn't much of a hardship or a labor for me. Dig was a very good-looking man. His thick locks of golden brown hair were always in his expressive eyes, whose amber tones seemed to deepen and change along with his many moods. His tight rear and powerful legs filled out his jeans incredibly well, and his chest was very well defined. This I knew because I had really enjoyed smashing my face into it earlier when I'd broken free of Vig.

As the hours wore on, my admiration for his physical assets skyrocketed into a full-on attraction. Images of Dig at that high school keg party years ago skipped through my beer-addled brain. He had certainly filled out since then. More muscles, more hard edges. More authority.

Over the course of the night any conviction I had in this being purely a charade or a show crashed around me. My skin became hypersensitive to his every touch, and my body began to crave his fierce attention. My rational self continually reminded me that this was all an act, not to confuse it with anything real. But the intense burn never let up, not for a moment.

Dig backed me up against a wall by the main bonfire and leaned into me. "Hanging in there, Peanut?"

"Yeah," I breathed. My heavy gaze fell on his twitching lips.

Dig's fingers unfastened the tie on my Indian print blouse, making my cleavage visible. His head dipped down, and his lips laid a trail from my neck to the top of my breasts. A shudder went through me, and my knees wobbled.

Crap, I hoped he couldn't tell how fast my heart was beating. My innocent status was probably glaringly obvious. I was certain it was a big laugh for a guy like him.

"Grab on to me, Grace," he whispered into my neck. "Kiss me. Make it good."

Once given responsibility, I leap into action. Or had I been waiting for permission?

I took his face in my hands and swept my tongue between his lips. His one hand kneaded my breast over my thin peasant blouse, and his other was planted against the wall at my head. My hands slid down the dip of the taut muscles of his lower back to his beautiful rear and pulled him into my body.

"That's it, baby," he murmured against my skin.

His hand left my breast and went up my skirt, slid under my panties, over my ass, and pulled me in between his legs where his hardness jammed up against me, right where I needed it most. I gasped. My body surged into his as heat swelled in my center. Being with him tonight was like having a hallucinogenic drug constantly pumped into my veins.

Absolutely crazy.

Throughout the night Dig's eyes would catch mine as if he were checking in with me, and they were serious, never mocking or scornful. I found it assuring and much too compelling. I would smile at him, determined to prove myself. All night he either had a hold on my hand or an arm around my neck, or one at my waist or on my ass. Whenever we sat I would be in his lap, his hand clamped over my bare thigh. Like right now.

Why the hell did I wear a skirt today?

We had moved to lounging on a sofa that had been brought outside. Dig was in the middle of an otherwise perfectly normal conversation with two Demon Seeds about a winter bike run in Florida, but all the while his fingers were under my skirt, circling my mound over my now rather damp panties. He asked his pals about campsites and motels while I rapidly turned into jelly and silently whimpered into his neck, tremors of pleasure and need swirling through me.

This sure wasn't high school where holding your girl's hand or throwing an arm over her shoulder denoted your claim.

Never having had a steady boyfriend before, just a number of dates and several necking sessions, this evening's relentless exhibition of possession startled me. Boner got me another beer (thank heavens) and grinned as he raised his bottle at us. Wreck gave me a wink and a lopsided smile, then went back to the redhead on his lap. Jump came over and talked with Dig for a bit, softly pinching my cheek when he left us.

Demon Seed old ladies socialized with the One-Eyed Jack's old ladies, the upper echelon of the tribal women. An unexpected smile from a One-Eyed old lady eased the tension in my chest, but for the most part they ignored me. Of course, I got lots of curious stares and a number of hard, icy glares from the "party pussy" throughout the evening. Dig's blow job babe from earlier was probably one of them. I was positive among them were many past Dig hookups and plenty future hopefuls whose ambitions I had thwarted. They looked like they could chew me up and spit me out in one go. I gulped down more beer.

Most of the women at the party were considered hanger-on females in the social ranks of this little kingdom. They sauntered about as they made their rounds in the hope of some "aaaaaction!" as my sister would say. Who knows how many Dig had already hooked up with since he'd become a member of the One-Eyed Jacks? A countless array, I'm sure. I shoved that brutal thought out of my blurred mind.

One weekend, and you are done. This will be over very soon.

Not soon enough.

I lifted my eyebrows at the outfits most of the women wore. Frankly, I was dazzled by the show: strappy leather bondage type tops, see-through sparkly tank tops, string bikinis, ripped skin-tight jeans or tiny shorts that barely covered their asses, thigh-high boots, platform high heels, and second skin mini-skirts or mini-dresses that could barely be defined as skirts or dresses, in my opinion. They wanted attention, and they were getting it.

A lot of them had big hair or very long, shiny tresses. A few of them showed off their bare breasts (both fake and real, yet all impressive), and all of them had crazy manicures and glossy, pouty mouths. I chewed on my bare lips. I was the schoolgirl who had stumbled in on the naughty masquerade party.

Hours passed in a haze of alcohol and loud laughter. Dig suddenly pulled on my hand and dragged me over to the edge of the property where there was a row of parked cars.

I suppose all of his club obligations were taken care of? *Yippee.*

Shadowy figures moved about us in the dark. Groans, muffled shouting, grunts, slaps and assorted cries filled the air. My eyes widened at the surreal and freakish aural entertainment. I recognized his black Camaro up ahead.

Oh shit.

Charade over.

"Dig?" My voice wavered in the dark.

He pulled me up onto the hood of his car and into his arms, his warm breath fanning my face. His thumb brushed over my lips. My tongue darted out, and I tasted his salty skin. Suddenly all the pent up sexual tension of the evening exploded between us, and we lunged at one another, groping, biting, sucking on each other's flesh.

His tongue traced my breasts over the thin fabric of my cotton bra. My back arched and my nipples hardened painfully. I almost wished I had worn some sexy, tiny bikini number like the other women I had seen. Fortunately, the bra I was wearing tonight was one of Easy Access Ruby's front closure numbers. Dig snapped the button open and released my breasts. He squeezed them together and took them in his mouth. A sob escaped my throat, and my eyes fluttered closed. I was never more grateful for a hand-me-down piece of clothing in my life.

The sounds of the Jeep next to us being jostled, flesh slapping against flesh and heavy grunting, made us stop for just a bit. We listened to the woman's shouty moans and a curse-filled running commentary by the two men about how they liked it and what they wanted her to do. This was another twisted form of stimulation. Who needed clear visuals? That certainly would have been overkill.

"Oh, God." I exhaled and pressed my half-naked body into Dig's.

He chuckled. "Getting turned on by the show, baby?"

"It's sort of. . .inspiring." I reached for his mouth again.

Dig let out a throaty laugh against my lips and his hand burned on my bare thigh under my skirt. His thumb hooked into the thin elastic band of my panties, and my heart pounded furiously against my ribs. I flexed my hips, and his fingers sank over my throbbing wetness. My entire body shuddered, my mouth breaking away from his for a moment. He only drew me closer and kissed me harder. I clung to him as his fingers worked me then slid inside me. Sparks flew over my skin.

I suddenly didn't care that we were out in the open yard in some sort of crazy orgy-esque environment. I didn't care that we were laying half-naked on top of his car. All I wanted was for my newfound pounding hunger to be satisfied by Dig.

"That's it, Grace." Dig groaned into my mouth, and that sound only made me crazier. "Let it go, baby," he whispered as his thumb stroked my clit.

My entire body snapped and shuddered with force. I came hard for the first time in my life. I had touched myself before, but it was nothing compared to this. This was ... I didn't know what this was, but it was fantastic. He caressed my aching breasts with his rough hands as my orgasm hurtled through me. His tongue tortured my burning nipples.

"You've got great tits." He swallowed another. "Beautiful."

Oh hell, I was on my way to coming again. Was that even possible? I needed to ask Ruby.

My legs hooked over Dig's and my pelvis rocked against his body. I was desperate for friction, desperate for more of him. Beer bottles broke against the cement of the courtyard. A Red Hot Chili Peppers song blared over the speakers, and the beat pulsed right through my ragged nerve endings.

"Oh, Dig."

He unzipped his pants.

That unzipped my brain.

"Wait!" My hands shot out to his shoulders. His dazed, hooded eyes fell on mine. "I've never done this before."

"What, baby?" he mumbled through short breaths. "Done what?"

"Sex. I've never had sex before."

His body went solid. Shit, he was going to push me off the side of his car now and kick me to the curb. After he exploded, of course.

"Never?"

"Never."

"Peanut. . .Jesus," he breathed. His eyes softened over me in the half-light, and his hand caressed my belly. My bare legs rubbed against his soft denim clad ones to stem the tide of the throbbing deep inside me.

"I want to, though. I want to with you, Dig." I exhaled the words bravely out into the universe, and silence fell between us. A lock of his hair fell over his smoky eyes, and I bravely slid my fingers through the wavy strands. His chest heaved for air against mine.

Whoops and cheers exploded in the distance by the bonfire. The noisy threesome next to us had finished up, and their laughter echoed over us. The red tips of their lit cigarettes flared in the dark as they left one by one. My stomach rolled as I waited for Dig to say something, anything. He took in a breath, planting his hands on the hood of his car. Shit. He must think I lied to him, and that I'm just some silly tease.

"I want you too, baby," he said finally, his voice a husky whisper in the darkness. "But not like this. Not for your first time. No." Dig's thumbs softly stroked the sides of my breasts.

"Oh, but . . ."

"Shh." He suckled my breasts again. "You're all worked up for me now aren't you?" My breath caught at the illicit tone in his voice. "I'm gonna take care of that," he whispered. He laid a trail of kisses down my torso, my belly and then he flipped up my skirt. A devilish grin split his face in the half light as he tugged my panties down my legs and over my boots then shoved them in his pocket. The cool air tickled my pulsating, wet sex. He pushed my knees open wide and his gaze darted down between my legs. I was exposed.

I felt dirty, wild.

And I felt free.

A muscle across his bare chest flexed as he pulled my knees up. His hands slid under my rear. I licked my dry lips. "Dig, what are you doing?" My thighs tensed under the tight grip of his fingers. That wicked grin lit up his face once again.

"I'm going to suck on you 'til you scream, Grace."

The party continued on around us, and I did scream Dig's name. Several times. All for the good of the club, of course. Oh, the raunchy things he whispered against my skin, full of hot promises, daring me to new heights.

When we finally came up for air, things had quieted down. There was still partying going on, but without its previous intensity. Others were sleeping it off all over the courtyard, and probably more were sprawled all over the building.

I got my bra and blouse back on, but Dig refused to give me my panties back. "Not until the weekend's up, Peanut. So far, so good. You see it through, you get them back."

Oh, I'd see this through all right. Dig had lit a fire in me I didn't know existed and yet always yearned for. He pulled tightly on his belt, his eyes on me. Every nerve ending in my body vibrated under that fierce gaze. He kissed me hard then linked my fingers in his, and we returned to the party.

He checked in with his president, and a while later led me inside the building. We passed Vig, who was snorting blow with two women in the dimly lit hallway. He glared at me, and I quickly averted my gaze. Dig's hand tightened over mine. We turned right down another hallway, and he unlocked a door and led me into what I assumed was his room. He locked the door behind us. A small night light in the bathroom illuminated the room with an eerie blue glow.

He yanked his T-shirt over his head and threw it to a corner littered with clothing, then unbuckled his belt and unfastened his jeans. "Gonna shower." Dig brushed past me and went into the small bathroom.

That was something else I'd never done before. I had heard Ruby in the shower at home with a man plenty of times, her moans and laughter audible through the heavy cascade of water.

Here it was. Dig and I wouldn't be fumbling with each other in the dark after too many brews. Being face to face and naked together under the unforgiving light of his bathroom would make this entire surreal situation real, wouldn't it?

The water ran. My pulse raced through me despite my fatigue as I shoved off my boots and peeled off my clothes. I pulled back the shower curtain and took in the dramatic sight of the large, sinister One-Eyed Jacks skull tattoo on Dig's contoured back. Long, curving lines of muscle were slick with water and shampoo suds, and a beautifully detailed snake was tattooed around his waist. I entered the small stall and drew the plastic curtain.

He handed me the shower gel over his shoulder, and I emptied some of the creamy liquid into my hands. My fingers worked the lather into his firm muscles and my hands ran down his smooth lower back and hips, then over his high ass. I kissed the indent of his spine and leaned into his body as I slid a soapy hand around his waist over that snake and down his sleek abs to where his hard shaft waited at full attention for me.

Dig leaned back against my body and exhaled. He put his hand over my shaky one and showed me how to touch him. I stroked him until his cock pulsed in my grasp. Dig groaned and planted one hand against the shower wall, the other went behind him and wrapped around my middle, holding me tight against him.

The warm water sprayed over us. He came in my hand, then tilted his head and stared at me. I stared right back. He turned around and kissed me. This moment was mine, and I tucked it in my brain and in every cell of my being to keep it with me for when this weekend was over.

I stood there immobile as Dig slathered my breasts with the soapy gel. He slid his fingers between my legs and I choked back a cry as they worked their magic again. My body jerked in his arms against the cold bathroom tile. Dig's hands cupped my breasts and he kissed the side of my face as I came back down to earth. He released me and began to shampoo my hair. I looked up at his beautiful face in a complete haze of sensation.

We dried each other off and collapsed onto his bed tangled in each other's arms and legs, and quickly fell asleep. The following morning when I woke up, I took the opportunity to admire his powerful body while he slept. His streaky dark golden hair had fallen over his face and I swept it back, gently kissing the angles of his jaw.

My tongue designed wet circles over his chest as my hand slid over his hip and down a muscular thigh. My fingers grazed his cock. He was rock hard. *Morning wood*, I believe Tania had called it. I smiled and took his stiff length in my hand.

"Grace?" Dig stretched out on the bed, rolling onto his back.

I crouched between his legs and gently licked around the tip of his hard shaft.

"Baby," he murmured, propping himself up on his elbows, his mussed dark golden hair in his eyes.

"Show me how, Dig," I whispered. "I want to make it good for you."

His bleary eyes ignited with heat, and he let out a groan. "Fuck me."

NOW

Here I was again.

The roar of voices mixed with laughter and the reverberating music assaulted me and Kicker at the large archway marking the entrance to the main room of the clubhouse. I tried not to give too much thought to the idea that I would probably see Miller One Night Action. I couldn't think of that now or what it might be like to see him again because I'd go nuts. And I couldn't afford to go nuts.

I was on a mission.

I took in a deep breath as I stepped through the archway. The main room was where everyone hung out, and the offices, the meeting room, the kitchen, and the bathrooms and the hallways leading to the men's rooms all led off this large center room. The bar looked the same except fresh posters of hot women in bikinis on motorcycles had replaced the ones I remembered. The same blue and red neon clock—advertising a now defunct beer brewery—still faithfully ticked away the correct time on the wall, albeit with only part of its neon still glowing.

I moved towards the bar. The same dusty shelves filled with a combination of empty and full liquor bottles lined the wall overhead. My fingers pressed into the ancient cherry red vinyl topped stools. What tales they could tell. Now scuffed and scratched, those high stools remained like steadfast silent witnesses to raucous, wild exuberance, risky determination, and so much bitter grief.

The Scorpions blared over the greatly improved sound system. The pool table still held pride of place at one end of the room where a group of four men played a game. Three unmatched shabby sofas were filled with couples necking and laughing, as well as an older biker with a young woman in a ponytail who giggled on his lap while he fondled her and whispered in her ear. That had to be Willy with that straggly gray beard. Dear, sweet Willy always had a thing for the young ones.

Three younger men were in deep conversation under a cloud of fragrant smoke on one sofa, practically oblivious to the two young women who gyrated to the music on the big round coffee table in front of them. Another young woman dashed around serving drinks.

"Who's this, bro?" a familiar scratchy voice came from behind me. My eyes slid closed against the dip of my stomach. I turned around and faced my husband's best friend who stood behind the bar. My gaze locked on his sparkling green eyes.

"A whiskey, neat. Please."

Boner's eyebrows bunched, and his mouth hung open.

"I'm gonna go get the prez," Kicker said from somewhere behind me. "He was in a meeting."

"Holy shit." Boner shook his head. "Holy shit!"

"Do me a favor, Boner. Pour me the drink first, yell after."

Boner snatched a glass and plonked a whiskey bottle in front of me. His arms shook with tension. He lifted the bottle and started to pour, his maniacal eyes glued to mine. The whiskey topped out over the glass, and the amber liquid flowed over the bar. "Fuck!" he waved his hands over his head, still holding onto the bottle. "Fuck!"

"What the hell's wrong with you, man?" Willy charged our way, his long, gray beard swaying. Willy was one of the oldest members of the club and had first nominated Dig to be VP before it all went to shit. I grinned at Boner as I leaned over the bar and sucked in the whiskey until the glass was no longer overly full. The harsh warmth soothed my aching throat.

"It's Little Sister, you assholes! Little Sister!" Boner's voice boomed.

The room quieted down a few degrees, and a sharp female voice trilled, "Who the fuck is she? Somebody's sister?"

Boner's big green eyes burned right through my heart. He shook his head at me, let out a great big whoop, and bounded over the bar top. He took me in his arms and lifted me up, squeezing the air out of me. My eyes filled with water. "Oh, honey," I murmured in his neck, holding him close as he swung me around and around.

"Put her down, man!" shouted Willy.

Boner planted a juicy kiss on my mouth then released me from his death grip. I hugged him once more as a tear slipped down my hot skin. He wiped away the salty streak, cursing under his breath.

Boner and Dig had been best friends long before they had joined the club. They had come up to South Dakota from Colorado on a pilgrimage to Sturgis and had stayed on, eventually hooking up with members of the One-Eyed Jacks. They had become prospects together and patched in together.

Willy folded me in his arms and hugged me. His hands cupped my face as he smiled. "Oh, my baby girl, my sweet baby girl, it really is you. Fucking A!" His voice drifted, his eyes crinkled.

This was belonging. I had forgotten how it felt.

It felt damned good.

The music stopped. "Hey, come on! What's going on?" shouted several women.

A door slammed open, and the hot air in the room became a living thing, intense, expectant, vibrant.

"Where is she?" a voice I recognized thundered through the room.

"Our girl's right here where she belongs!" Willy said.

The women on the table stopped chattering and turned, and the men stood up from the sofas and chairs. Jump smiled at me from the open door of the president's office. He was just as handsome as ever; his hair, still in a long smooth braid falling right down his broad back, was now threaded with gray. His face had creased with time, his belly was fuller, but his large brown eyes still burst with drive and spark.

Jump and Dig had been officers together. They had shared a secret language that had made making tough decisions and directing the club under their prez a streamlined operation most of the time. Jump's colors now bore the president's patch.

"Get over here, Sister."

I charged across the room and lunged at him. Jump lifted me up in his thick arms with a great big shout and squeezed me tight. He put me down and planted a kiss on my forehead. "Where've you been?" He turned his head slightly. "Alicia, baby, where are you? Get the hell out here, woman!"

Alicia, Jump's old lady, tall and thin, straight long blonde hair down her chest, expressive kohl-lined blue eyes, just as I remembered her, strutted towards me slowly. Alicia had been a close friend from the start and my mentor at the club, not only in all things womanly—clothes and makeup, men and sex—but also in all things biker—riding and old lady etiquette.

"Grace?" her voice rang out in the room. "Oh, Grace." She wrapped me in her arms and hugged me tightly on a deep sigh.

"Who the hell is she?" a thin-voiced woman asked from somewhere behind me.

Alicia's face tightened, her eyes narrowed. She spun us around to face that voice. It belonged to the redhead in the white bikini top I had seen giving the blow job to the guy in the hallway earlier.

"This here is one of the classiest old ladies this Club has ever seen, you two-bit twat," Alicia said in her still sexy, raspy voice, which was another trace of home to me. She put a hand on her hip, her eyes glinting. "And if you don't shut your face and show her some respect, you're gonna get kicked out of here on your ass!"

My breath caught in my chest, but not over my old friend's fiercely proud and loving words. Redheaded Two-Bit Twat had her curvy body draped around Miller, who sported a slouchy black knit cap. He stared at me, his posture rigid, his jaw slack.

Oh shit.

His eyes squeezed shut.

Miller and the redhead were the blow job couple I'd seen in the hallway.

MILLER

IT'D BEEN EXACTLY SEVENTEEN DAYS since I last saw Grace at that motel.

Now she stood four yards away from me, right here at the clubhouse. Her beautiful greenish brown eyes locked on mine, and a phantom fist punched me in the chest lodging itself there. Everything suspended in mid-air.

Excitement spilled over the room like a rushing river. She seemed a little anxious by the tension in her shoulders, but happy. She was home, after all. The club had been her home just as it had been mine, the place where both of us had done a lot of important growing up. It was also the home she had once shared with her husband.

There was that, too.

When I had first seen Grace at Dead Ringer's that night, I couldn't take my eyes off her.

She'd been drinking straight whiskey. Not just drinking it actually, but savoring it. Enjoying it. Really enjoying it. It had made an impression on me. She had obviously chosen something she really, really wanted and was enjoying the fuck out of it her way. I liked that she didn't seem uncomfortable or embarrassed at being on her own at a bar. She didn't seem like she was out fishing for a hookup or any male attention. The woman wanted to enjoy her drink.

I'd stopped at the Roadhouse on my way home from a drop to hit the bathroom, splash some water on my face, and have a quick drink before the last stretch of road home. It was late, it had been a long two days on the road, and I'd needed a break before I went back to the same old, same old. Seeing as I was on my own, I'd decided to enjoy my five minutes of peace. I hadn't had a vodka in a long time. Beer, bourbon and tequila were always on the menu at the club. I was over it.

Like I was over a hell of a lot of things. I just wasn't sure what to do about it.

She was beautiful. Not in a conventional—wow, she's gorgeous—kind of way. Grace's beauty was in her quiet, her simple. It sprung at me when she grinned, and it seeped through me when she looked a bit sad or faraway, which was pretty often.

When I'd first spoken to her, she'd turned quickly to face me, one sexy eyebrow lifted. Her big hazel eyes had been tight with suspicion, yet had quickly thawed into amusement. And what a color those eyes were. They seemed to shift from greenish-brown to a grayish-green color over the course of the night. She'd gotten a kick out of our debate about liquor and change, laced with plenty of innuendo. I'd gotten her to smile a couple of times, and she'd caught herself and bit that sexy lower lip of hers.

I'd introduced myself using my real name. I didn't want to hear my club road name come off this woman's lips. I'd wanted something different from her, and I'd gotten it. Every time she'd say 'Miller' in that warm tone, heat jabbed me in the gut.

I figured Grace had to be around my age. There were a few creases at the edges of those beautiful eyes, yet her skin was creamy, fresh with a few freckles over her cheeks, the kind that had probably come up in her younger years then stayed. When she laughed, she lit up, she let go. That was beautiful. Yes, she was beautiful—my kind of beautiful. Then she would go back to holding on tight to something inside her; something she refused to share.

I could have kicked myself when she turned away from me and leaned back against the bar to check out the crowd as some sort of signal for me to change the subject. A sudden need to touch her had engulfed me. I'd wanted my hands to skim over that smooth skin under that tight Harley tee and discover every secret curve. We'd stood very close at the bar. What the hell was that magic scent. . .her perfume? Her shampoo? I couldn't put my finger on it, and it had driven me crazy. It was something not too sweet, but mellow, like early summer. Hell, I wasn't big on dancing, but I had to do something to get closer to her.

Once I had her in my arms and we moved together to the music, she finally relaxed. My cock wasn't the only thing that stood at attention; it was as if my blood had kicked up through every goddamn vein in my body. That night I hadn't been shopping for a hookup, hadn't even crossed my mind.

It was easy for me to get laid back home. Whenever the need struck, a selection was always available. But the same expectant, willing eyes batted up at me over and over again. There were different faces often enough, but they all wanted the same things from me—a way in, a notch up, an attachment.

But Grace was different.

No, that night I'd stopped at Dead Ringer's because I'd just wanted to enjoy a drink, listen to some music, lose myself in the buzz of the crowd, then get back in the truck and get home. But there she was in her sparkly T-shirt, tight jeans, sexy silver jewelry, and harsh leather boots that on this kind of woman made my mouth water.

Her body was all tight curves; a body she obviously took care of without going overboard. Even whatever makeup she'd had on was real; I could see her, a pretty her, not a pumped-up version. I'd wanted to sink my fingers into her long, thick hair. There was nothing about her that was there to put on a show or jack my cock and jerk my chain. It was all ... *Grace*.

And I wanted to know that woman. I wanted a piece of that no excuses-been there-done that-no drama honesty. She didn't feel the need to let it all hang out and dangle it in your face. She could take it or leave it. I liked that. I liked her.

A lot.

I'd seen something else in her eyes. Something I recognized because I lugged the same shit inside my soul. Suspicion, sadness, bitterness? All of it initially had flashed up at me, but then she'd tucked it away and got back to her drink. Still, she seemed familiar, but I hadn't wanted to waste any time trying to figure it out just then.

Maybe I should have.

I'd kissed her. My insides had exploded when she'd opened her mouth and given it up to me. Then she'd given it back to me. That had been it. I couldn't keep my hands off her, and I couldn't help myself with the ice cubes. Had it been high school of me? I didn't give a shit. It had got me touching her curvy ass, her sexy tits, and my tongue had gotten to glide over her hot skin. I can still feel how her pulse had jumped at the side of her neck.

I'd gotten so desperate for her that I suggested the back of the bar or my truck. Stupid. Her eyes had flashed at me. What an idiot. My mouth had started to ramble non-stop. I prayed for mercy. Then she invited me back to her room at that motel on the other side of the parking lot.

My hands shook like an eager kid's when I'd taken out my wallet to pay the bartender. That was a brand new feeling for me, but I'd pushed that aside. Neither of us could get the motel room door unlocked fast enough. Once I slammed the door closed behind us, we both ripped our clothes off, and I finally got my mouth and hands all over her. And it was sensational.

Then I got inside her, and I was ... gone.

I had looked Grace in the eyes and watched her come. She had sparked a curiosity in me and, more importantly, a particular desire that I thought had faded a long, long time ago.

The desire to feel.

Her eyes had been wide open with everything I gave her as if it were new, different. The mere fact that she'd been so eager for me drove me insane, made my heart race, and my dick pound. I hadn't wanted to stop. She'd been eager, but not rabid or showing off like some women around the club get when they're desperate to have you and want to show you how good it can be with them if you keep tapping their ass. No, that wasn't Grace.

She'd enjoyed it, and I had a feeling she hadn't let go like that in a long time. And I was right. She'd been relaxed, happy to be in that crap motel room with me, touching me, kissing me, letting me do all sorts of shit to her while she clung to me and moaned out my name over and over again. Somehow her genuineness loosened that slab of cement inside my chest.

The next morning when I'd woken up alone, I'd gotten pissed that she had cut out on me without a word. Not just because it had been the first time that had happened to me or I'd wanted another go, but because I actually liked her.

Imagine that?

I'd kicked the wrinkled sheet off me and rubbed my eyes. I hadn't even found out what her last name was, where she was headed, what the hell she was doing in South Dakota, for fuck's sake. All I had were her black panties that had gotten gnarled up in my jeans on the floor.

LOCK&KEY

Did I have to throw the memory of us in the pile with all my other hookups? I didn't want to. It stung, and it pissed me off that it stung. Grace didn't belong there with all those nameless, faceless, forgotten women, and she certainly didn't fit there. I wasn't sure where she fit, but I knew for certain not there.

The feel of her soft skin still burned all over me.

I'd inhaled the scent of our sex on the sheets mixed with faint traces of her memorable perfume. I'd lain still taking it all in on that creaky motel bed as the sun showed the first signs of morning. I'd checked my watch. Shit. She could have crossed into Wyoming for all I knew. I had gotten dressed, shoved her panties in my pocket, and left.

A couple of hours later when I'd dragged my ass back to the clubhouse to check in with Jump, I'd passed the photo wall in the main room and my eyes instinctively went to the shot of Dig and his wife.

I'd stopped dead in my tracks.

Those eyes.

That smile.

It's her.

Grace was Little Sister. She was Dig's old lady from a lifetime ago.

In the past sixteen years, Sister had literally not been heard from again. Not even from Alicia who had been her close friend. I figured she had come back to town to see her sister who I'd heard lived nearby in Rapid. That had given me a spark of hope.

Now that spark had just exploded into fireworks right here in the middle of a full clubhouse.

"So what's so great about her? I don't get it," Heather muttered, twisting a lock of her brassy red hair between her fingers.

Goddammit.

Grace had seen me getting blown by Heather earlier when she'd passed us in the hallway with Kicker. The blood backed up in my veins.

I peeled Heather off of me and moved forward. The bitch squealed from somewhere behind me.

"Lock, what the fuck?"

I didn't bother looking back at her, but judging from her shriek, I was sure steam was coming out of her ears.

73

Men jostled past me to greet Grace. The brothers she had never met—Bear, Peck, Dready shook her hand. The men she obviously knew from the old days like Clip, Willy, and Boner stayed close to her.

She was here. My dream come true.

Heather's long fingernails dug into my arm. "Hey, what the hell's wrong with you?" Her eyes flared at me.

What a fucking disaster.

Heather hadn't let up for months. I'd dipped in several times, but she had been way too clingy and too loud for my tastes. Tonight I had been jonesing for something I would probably never have again, something I hadn't realized at the time was so profound. Tonight, I'd taken that frustration and self-loathing out on Heather.

I had let her hang on me, and she'd pulled out all the stops as usual to get me to take her to my room and fuck her. I finally shut her up by shoving myself into her mouth in the hallway. But there was no relief in it nor any end to my torture. In fact, it had only pissed me off and frustrated me even more.

Same ol', same ol'.

Until I'd noticed a woman hit up Boner at the bar with a cryptic smile like she had always belonged there, and it all began to make sense.

Little Sister.

Grace.

That beautiful name. A small breath, my secret prayer.

Jump flung an arm around my shoulders and pulled me forward. "Lock, this is Little Sister. I don't think you two ever got a chance to meet. Ain't that crazy, considering?"

Yeah, way fucking crazy.

My chest constricted. Couldn't I just throw her over my shoulder and get us the hell out of here? I took her small hand in mine and squeezed it. Her eyes dug into mine, her lips parted.

Shocked, huh? You don't know the half of it.

I swallowed hard as her cold, soft hand settled in my large one. It was a hand whose touch my body knew too well, and a swell of heat tightened my insides. That primeval pull zapped through the two of us, that electricity in our touch still there.

"Nice to meet you," tumbled out of her mouth.

"Pleasure," I breathed. Her eyes darted to Jump's then back to mine.

"Lock is Wreck's little brother, can you believe that?" Jump asked. His other hand clapped down on Grace's shoulder.

Her eyes went round. "You're Wreck Tallin's little brother? The soldier?"

"Yeah." A muscle clenched along my jaw. "I'm Miller."

She made a noise in her throat and turned over our joined hands. Her eyes found Wreck's eagle ring on my finger. "Miller. Of course." She bit her lip, her face flushed.

She knew who I was. It must all be coming back to her. The boy she used to pass in the hallway in high school and smile at sometimes. Her good friend Wreck's little brother of whom she heard so many stories. The endless photos that Wreck had no doubt showed her of a soldier in uniform sitting on a tank, on patrol tightly holding his automatic weapon, handing out chocolate to refugee children.

"Wreck was so proud of you." Her hand squeezed mine. "He would tell me stories—"

"My brother loved to tell a good story. He'd mentioned you and Dig to me in his letters a lot."

Wreck had been twelve years older than me, and a veteran. He had been a mentor to Dig in his early years at the club. While I had been serving my last tour of duty, Wreck's throat had been slit during a fight at a bar while the boys were on a run in Texas. His sudden, unexpected death had shattered the club, and just two months later Dig had been murdered.

"That's his ring isn't it?" she asked.

"Yeah, it is." My fingers tightened their grip on hers, the heat unbearable. Both of us stared at the ring, stared at our hands clasped together.

I'd noticed at Dead Ringer's how she'd done a double-take when she had seen my ring. In bed I had stroked her with it. I don't know what the hell had come over me, but she was lying there having just come hard, purring with the satisfaction I'd given her. Her gorgeous body was all lush and relaxed. Totally irresistible. I'd wanted to ignite her all over again.

Jump's voice brought me back to reality. "We saved the ring for Lock before we buried Wreck."

My hand was on fire, my cock stirring in my jeans. I finally loosened my grip on her hand and let go, but I didn't want to. Her gaze darted up at me.

Jump released me and slung his arm around his old lady. "We came to see you in the hospital plenty of times, Sister, but you were out of it for a long while. Then when you finally came to, you were either hysterical when you saw us or just plain dead in the eyes. Wasn't good."

Well, don't we have plenty in common?

I remember that feeling well when half my unit had been blown to bits in a mine field. It had later been cemented in the pit of my chest when I was told Wreck had been killed, and I was thousands of miles away, in another world, on a covert mission I couldn't get out of.

"It was a smart thing to do though, leaving," said Alicia. "Ruby said it was better for you to start over somewhere new. Clean slate. She was right, wasn't she?"

Grace nodded slightly.

Clean slate, my ass. No such thing. *Oh, Grace.*

"What you went through was brutal, honey. No denying it," Alicia said. "I always hoped we'd see you again, and here you are. Look at you. You look great, so pretty."

Grace blushed and let out a small laugh, her features brightening for a moment as if she were a shy young girl hearing a compliment for the very first time.

Something pinched in my chest. Something new.

"And you're still a hot mama!" Grace said in a throaty voice that sent a ripple of heat right through me. She took Alicia in her arms, and they clung to each other. A sob escaped Grace's lips, her body convulsed.

"Suzi, get her a whiskey!" I shouted as I grabbed her one arm.

Alicia pushed Grace down into an armchair. Boner came running with a glass full of whiskey. She gulped the liquor and swiped away the wetness brimming in those beautiful eyes. Jump and Alicia sat on the end of the sofa next to her.

"Where you been, hon'?" Jump asked, a hand squeezing her shoulder. "You come back to stay?"

"I've been moving around," Grace replied. "I could never sit still in one place long enough. I never felt I could settle down."

I squeezed my eyes shut. All that evasiveness and wariness she had offered up to me at the bar suddenly made sense, as did her crazy nomad existence over the past years.

"I came back a couple of weeks ago because Ruby's sick. She needs me, and I need your help."

"I heard she's been in the hospital," said Jump. "You need help with the medical bills?"

"No, nothing like that. She's got good insurance. It's cancer. She needs a bone marrow transplant. I thought maybe you all could come get tested, put out the word, as well. We don't have a match yet." She brought the glass to her lips once more and drank. "I don't even match. Found out today. Do you believe that? I was supposed to match. I'm her goddamn sister."

"Honey, I'm so sorry," Alicia murmured, her hand went to Grace's knee.

Grace cleared her throat and straightened her back. "Jump, I was also hoping you could help me find my dad. If he's still alive, he's the only relative left. It's worth a shot."

"Lock's good at investigative shit," Jump said. "You just give me whatever you got on him, and we'll get on it. Right, brother?"

"Absolutely," I said.

She took another gulp of her drink "Thanks," she whispered.

My pulse skidded at the sound of that throaty whisper. The same whisper that had taken my breath away seventeen nights ago with "*Oh, God, yes. Don't stop. Miller, you feel so good. What are you doing to me?*" My hand slid down my chest.

"Ruby gave her son Dig's real name, didn't she?" Alicia asked.

Grace gave Alicia a small smile.

"That's sweet," Alicia said.

"Sure is." Boner eased down on the arm of Grace's chair and ran a hand over her hair.

Grace took another drink, resting an arm on Boner's leg. Her eyes darted up at Alicia. "She did it for me, you know."

Alicia squeezed Grace's hand. "Yeah, I know."

Holy shit, that's right. Grace and Alicia had been pregnant at the same time sixteen years ago, but Grace had lost her baby in the attack.

Boner rubbed her shoulders. "Dig saved Ruby's hide more than once, helped her get on her feet after all was said and done. And he sure made her little sister real happy." His voice was unusually gentle, his eyes soft. He leaned over her and planted a kiss on her forehead.

Shit, here was infamous club history I had always heard about, playing out before me. Volatile, crazy-ass Boner's sudden transformation into a soft-spoken, caring big brother with Grace was nothing short of amazing.

Grace parked her empty glass on the table. "There's something else I need to know."

"Shoot," said Jump.

Her eyes cut to his. "Where did you bury my husband?"

GRACE
PAST

MY AND DIG'S LITTLE CHARADE, that wasn't much of a charade, was now over.

The entire weekend Dig and I had been inseparable, but we didn't do "the deed." We had done everything but in his bed every night and every morning, and by the time Sunday rolled around I was desperate for him. He was desperate for it too, but had kept himself in check. His self-control amazed me. Dig was a hundred times the man that someone like Trey Owens was or could ever hope to be.

I figured it was because he didn't want me to get attached to him if he deflowered me. Bikers didn't do attachments, did they? They were all about freedom, their bike, the open road, and a good time on their own terms. Several of the older members of the club had old ladies and kids, but a twenty-seven year old sexy man like Dig? He certainly wasn't boyfriend or relationship material. He could have anyone he wanted whenever he wanted, and I was sure they lined up for him regularly. I had no delusions about that.

Yep, I knew that once my lunatic weekend in One-Eyed Jacks Land was over, I would get right back on the bus to Reality.

The party ran through late Monday morning when the last of the Demon Seeds roared out of the gates. Soon after, Dig brought me to my house on his bike.

This was the big goodbye.

I held my breath as he popped the kickstand. I leaned on his shoulders and swung off his Harley.

What should I say? 'Thanks for the good time?' *God, no. Um ...*

Dig dismounted and followed me to the front door.

Oh. Very polite.

I shoved the key in the lock and turned the knob. "Get your bikini," he said. "We're going to the Hippie Hole for a swim."

My eyes popped open. He invited me!

It was a pretty warm day for mid-September in South Dakota. When we had left the clubhouse earlier, all the men were setting off for their favorite swimming hole in Big Falls with plenty of beer, weed, and food to unwind after the long weekend. Dig hadn't said a word about it, and I hadn't asked.

"Oh, okay." On the inside, I jumped up and down for joy.

We entered my house and passed the kitchen to get to my room.

"Peanut, what the fuck?"

I turned around. He stood in the center of the glass-strewn floor of the kitchen, his eyebrows knit together.

"Oh." I shrugged and let out a sigh. "I had a spaz before I came looking for you at the club Friday night."

His lips twitched as he stared at me. He shifted his weight, his heavy boots crunching on shards of glass and plastic underfoot. Emotion flickered across his features, and he took in a breath.

The sudden silence in the room pressed in on me. "What?" I swallowed past the lump in my throat. "What is it?"

"Come here," he said, his voice gruff.

I didn't hesitate. Under his burning gaze I scooted over to him, my boots chomping over the debris. He lifted me up in his embrace, hooking my legs around his waist. I wrapped my arms around his neck, and his mouth took mine in a gentle kiss. His hands pressed into my ass under my skirt.

"This shit's over for you, baby. You're with me now. You got that?"

My heart pounded in my chest. I only nodded at him, my fingers rubbing the back of his neck

"Ruby will be fine in jail, we've got her protected. I don't want you worrying about her. She'll be out in no time, you'll see. I'll take you to visit her whenever you want." He studied my reaction. "Either you stay with me, or we can stay here. What do you say?"

Together with Dig. We were together.

You're with me now.

My legs tightened around him, and I bit my lower lip. Dig's head tilted at me. "What is it?"

"I'm with you, now?"

"Yeah, baby." His lips brushed my mouth.

"Does that make me a club bitch?"

He laughed. "Hell, no. It makes you mine. This sweet ass is only mine." His fingers dug into my bare skin and my insides seized.

"Oh." My fingers played with the worn collar of his faded club T-shirt.

He pinched my rear, and my eyes shot up to his. He scowled at me. "Come on, spill it."

"I was just wondering. Does that mean you'll still be, um, partying like before?"

I just couldn't come out and say it in plain English. What if he laughed at me and said something like: *"Of course, Peanut, I'm a tough biker dude. Gotta have me lots of different women. Deal with it."* I knew I'd be crushed. All this was already too good to be true. My heart stopped as I waited for his reply.

"What did you call me at the party—a man-whore?"

I dragged my fingers through his hair. "You are."

His eyes softened over my face, and he grinned. "If I got it good under my own roof, I won't look for it elsewhere."

I smirked at him. "Well, now. That's quite a deal then." He chuckled. My fingers traced the side of his stubbly face. "You won't get bored?"

"You don't bore me," he said, his voice just above a whisper.

"Hmm."

"Hmm?" He grinned at me. "As long as you're not too much of a bitch, we'll be cool."

"Women are not always bitches, you know."

"Peanut, I don't think there's any bitch in you at all," he murmured against my lips. "You're nothing but sweet." His tongue drove into my mouth. His eyes remained on me as he lifted my body higher in his hold.

"There's more to me than sweet."

"Believe me, I've noticed. I'm looking forward to figuring it all out."

I soared to the top of the world right there and then in that haunted house. He put me down on my feet and my boots crushed the glass once more. It was the most beautiful sound I'd ever heard.

"I want to see your room."

"You do?"

"I want a bikini fashion show, then you're gonna strip for me."
His hand went under my skirt and rubbed the bare flesh of my rear.
He shoved me into his erection.

"What about the Hippie Hole?" I asked, short of breath.

He grinned down at me. "We'll get there, baby. Now move
that sweet ass of mine." He swatted my rear.

As requested, I modeled my one and only bikini for him and
made a dramatic display of it, then I began to take it off. Slowly. I
had no idea what I was doing, but it didn't matter. Dig loved it,
both of us laughing the entire time. He took his very hard dick out
from his jeans and stroked himself while he lay back on my pink
and yellow daisy quilt admiring my moves.

He crooked his finger at me. "Get over here, babe. My boy
needs you." That wicked grin of his made my insides curl. I crawled
up on the bed, and we fooled around. I thought we would have
sex, but we didn't.

"Louder, baby," he said against my wet skin. "Nobody's home.
It's just you and me in here."

His fingers and mouth kept working me, and I gave it to him
louder. I was breathless from the orgasms and all the laughing. It
was deliciously illicit to behave so brazenly in broad daylight in my
parents' house, in my pastel bedroom with the white eyelet curtains
drifting in the breeze.

This was my house now, and for the very first time I could
actually let it all hang out whenever and however I wanted to.

And I wanted to. I wanted to with Dig.

"One day soon I'm going to fuck you in every room in this
goddamn house," he said as he shoved his boots on.

"Promise?"

He planted a kiss on my forehead as he took his colors from
my hands. "Hell, yeah."

I bit the inside of my cheek at the sudden harshness in his
voice, the frown shadowing his face. Dig knew what it was like to
grow up in a haunted house.

"Let's get moving." He put his leather jacket on.

We got on his bike and zoomed toward Big Falls. Holding
onto Dig as his bike forged through the wind at heart-stopping
speed made my pulse jump in my throat and a new kind of energy
pump through my veins. My legs squeezed around the machine of

wonder that roared over the asphalt, my arms clinging to Dig's strong body.

This is where I want to be.

It was a fact, a truth that seared through me.

When we got to the Hippie Hole I stumbled off the bike in a daze, a smile plastered on my face. His eyes slid to mine as he unpacked the blankets. He reached in his saddlebag and handed me the burgers we had bought on the road. Dig took the helmet from my hands and planted a wet kiss on my lips.

"That your first long ride on a bike?"

I nodded.

"You liked that, huh?"

I could barely manage a grin.

"Yeah, you liked that a lot." Dig shook his head and laughed, his golden brown hair falling in his eyes. "Let's go, goofball." He planted a kiss on my lips again. "Got a bit of a hike ahead of us." I linked my fingers in a belt loop on his jeans, and he led me to the swimming hole.

Boner's blonde skinny-dipped and splashed water at several other women, all of them hangers-on from the weekend party. Alicia, Jump's new woman, was sunbathing in her tiny white bikini on a large pink towel. We had met at the clubhouse over the weekend, and she had been somewhat friendly.

I wasn't sure where I fit in with the women in terms of the tribal hierarchy, but I didn't care about defining or analyzing anything at the moment. I was with Dig, and that was good, it felt right. That was enough for me. More than enough.

Dig and I swam, we made out in the water. We ate too much junk food and drank way too many beers. Later in the afternoon we got high on their homegrown pot as Willy played a few tunes on his guitar. His voice wasn't half bad either. We crashed on our blankets, me tucked into Dig's side. The cool breeze blew over our bare skin and lulled us to sleep.

"Peanut!" Dig whispered in my ear and shook my arm.

I cracked an eye open. The sky was a dusky pink; it would be twilight soon. "Is something wrong?"

"Baby, get up. Got to show you something," he whispered. I looked around at our group sprawled out on the green hill. Everyone else was still asleep. "Come on, get up," he insisted.

I exhaled and clambered up on my knees. Dig gathered up our two blankets that had been layered on the hard ground, took my hand in his and led me up the path leading to the bikes. We took a steep left down another trail.

"Dig? Where are we going?"

Sleep still claimed my muscles and joints. I really didn't want to go for a hike right now. We walked on for a few more minutes until we came to a small clearing where there was a grove of trees and long, hanging branches. I had to duck my head. It was as if we were in our own private room of green. He quickly laid out the blankets and pulled me down on my knees.

"What's all this?" I asked.

He put his hands on my thighs. "I wanted your first time to be something sweet like you are, baby. You deserve this, not my room at the clubhouse, not your shit box of a house."

He kissed me as he untied the ties on either side of my bikini bottom. The fabric fell in his hand, and I raised myself up an inch so he could yank it away. My insides seized at the rush of air and fabric against my delicate flesh. He tugged on the tie around my neck, and I undid the one around my back. My top dropped, releasing my breasts. His hungry gaze swept over my naked body, and my face enflamed. There in the soft twilight, I felt suddenly shy in front of Dig, even though he had gotten to know every inch of my body over the past three days.

My heart hammered in my chest. "Is that why we haven't . . .?"

"I didn't want it to be with the Demon Seeds around and all that craziness at the club. I wanted time with you. Thank fuck they finally left." He pushed the hair out of his face and licked his lips. A deep fluttering pressure surged within me. He had planned this.

"Dig"

I wrapped my arms around his neck and kissed him deeply, the way we both liked it, and he moaned in my mouth. He drew back and removed his faded cut-off jeans. He folded my shuddering body in his arms, and we held each other in silence. His hot hands kneaded my rear and stroked my back.

"I've never had it special, Grace. Never interested me to tell you the truth. But I feel something for you, been feeling it a while now, just didn't want to deal with it with your sister's thing going on. Then you showed up at the party, and I couldn't ignore it anymore." His teeth grazed his bottom lip. "I don't like complications, but it's not so complicated between us. Is it, baby?"

I shook my head, utterly mesmerized by every word that fell out of his fantastic mouth. I reached up and kissed him again.

"I want to make you mine, Grace. Want to come inside you," Dig breathed against my lips. "I don't know what this is, but you're all I can think about. I've got to have you."

My heart swelled and exploded. "I want you inside me, too. Make me yours, Dig," I whispered.

He pushed me down onto the scratchy blanket and reached out to the side and grabbed something. My gaze darted down to his hand. Blue, purple, yellow, and white wildflowers were bunched in his fist. He tore the petals off the stems, held his hands high over my body, and scattered them over my feet, up my legs.

The flower petals and buds fell like magic fairy dust in the fading light which filtered through the trees. My skin tingled with every gentle touch of the tiny petals on my blazing skin. He continued up my body and scattered them between my legs, along my tummy, around each breast, up to my throat, then over my mouth and eyes, my hair. I took the small petals in my mouth and laughed.

"You like that?" he asked.

"I love it. Don't you stop."

He chuckled. His fingers traced the petals around my breasts, and he planted kisses in between them.

"You're my wildflower, baby. You're all these gentle, simple colors, but you're a survivor too, like me. Strong enough to grow on these rocks."

I reached up for him and crashed my mouth into his. Tears slid down my hot cheeks. He moved away for a moment to fit himself with a condom then leaned over me once more. His fingers trailed down my thigh. His mouth dipped between my legs, and he kissed and licked at my trembling flesh. Flower petals fell from my skin with every jerk of my body's joyful submission. I closed my eyes, tilted my head back, and filled my lungs with fresh air. My fingers slid through his thick locks, and I whimpered his name over and over again.

Dig lifted himself up and slid inside me slowly. Every nerve ending in my body and my brain quivered and expanded, and I angled my hips towards his.

I'm his special, and he's mine.

"Oh shit," he groaned in my neck as he rocked in deeper, filling me.

I winced at a sudden twinge of pain. My breath caught in my throat, and I froze. Our eyes locked together.

He kissed my jaw and whispered, "It's okay, baby. Relax for me. It'll pass in a sec."

I closed my eyes and struggled with the burning sting. My body stiffened, and I took in a deep breath.

"Grace, look at me. Open up for me, baby," he murmured. His fingers went between us and slid over my clit. My insides flooded with heat, and my eyes found his again.

There was nothing more I wanted in this world than to open up for Dig. I wanted him inside my body and inside my soul, like I wanted to be in his. I knew that my most secret wish had come true. I released my pent-up breath, unclenched my muscles, and opened my entire self to him. His fingers slid away and he settled deeper, slowly moving inside me. Our bodies crushed the scattered petals between us.

He let out a deep groan. "My wildflower," he breathed in my ear. We clung to each other.

I will never forget that moment in my entire life.

It was beautiful.

It was real and big and true.

And that was us.

Every year when the first warm days of spring would blessedly roll around once more, we'd pack up the saddlebags on Dig's chopper and take off for a day long ride, always ending up at the Hippie Hole before we went home. Sometimes we would do it alone, but sometimes it was with a bunch of the guys and their women, and we'd make it an overnight. And always, when the partying would settle down, Dig and I would trot off to our tree and have lots of sex and then a snooze. After the sun would set, we'd head back to the party and celebrate the stars sparkling over us in the big night sky with more sex and plenty of tequila and weed.

It was at the Hippie Hole where, years later, we celebrated our wedding anniversary with an overnight, after finally having decided on making a baby, and we had made love for the better part of the afternoon in our little green hideaway. And it was there that two months later I had told him I was finally pregnant.

He had gone nuts.

Dig had grabbed me, his kiss landing hard on my cheek when I'd turned to face Alicia who had shouted at us, waving a disposable Kodak camera. I'd squealed and nabbed the beer he had been drinking out of his hands before he got a chance to toss it in the air and probably hurt someone. I'd held onto him and couldn't stop laughing. His infectious wild energy surged through me as Alicia had snapped a photo of us with Wreck.

Three months later it would all be ripped to bloody shreds.

I don't think I could ever go back to that swimming hole again. Not ever.

Let it be for other young lovers with a different, sweeter fate than ours.

NOW

My eyes froze on the small, almost inconsequential framed photo hanging on the wall of the clubhouse main room among the myriad trophy shots of the men sporting a variety of firearms or posing on their bikes.

My breath constricted in my lungs as my gaze passed over my own young and beaming face laughing at the camera, a beer bottle in my hand. Dig had crushed the side of my body to his front with the taut muscles of his bare arm tightly clasped around my middle. He was kissing my cheek, his face in profile. Wreck was on the other side of him, his mouth open in a great big howl, his one arm raised high gripping his beer bottle, the other clapped on Dig's shoulder.

A shadow fell over the glass. Warm breath heated my shoulder.

"You can't know how many times I've looked at that picture over the years and wanted to know who that woman is, who she *really* is." Miller's deep voice filled my ear, my eyes shut tight. "That gorgeous, deliriously happy woman in that sexy black bikini making her man feel on top of the world, both of them so full of life." His finger tapped the photo. "That is pure, unadulterated joy."

"Please, stop . . ."

"I've been fascinated with her since I got back from the army sixteen years ago, and I walked back into this clubhouse and saw this picture. Knowing that my brother Wreck loved you like a little sister, knowing Dig and the kind of man he was, and then to see him like this, took my fucking breath away. Still does."

"Miller, don't."

"And then over two weeks ago, I came in here after being out of town on a run, after being with you, and saw this photo again, and I practically doubled over. It clicked why I was immediately drawn to you, why I thought I knew you somehow when I first spotted you at the bar. Christ, I had my dream on my hands, and in my mouth, and I never fucking realized."

"I'm not a dream," I whispered.

"No, you are absolutely not a dream. You're Grace Quillen. The woman who almost bled to death on a country road, yet found the strength and presence of mind to take her husband's gun to protect herself, her man, and his bike. You're so real it's killing me right now to stand two inches away from you, smell your goddamn perfume, and want to do nothing but touch you, kiss that unbelievable mouth of yours, drag you to my bed, and bury myself inside you again."

"Please, stop."

"I didn't grow up dreaming or wishing for things, Grace. Then I saw this woman in this motherfucking picture, and I let myself dream, let myself wish." He exhaled.

We stood in silence facing the photo.

"Why did you leave the motel like that?" he asked, his voice now quiet.

I shrugged. "I had to get on the road early."

"You took off way before early, Grace. Tell me."

I needed to end this conversation immediately.

"What's the matter? Your big manly pride hit a new low just because a woman left you first without begging you for another session or a goodbye kiss?" Miller only glared at me. "What difference does it make that I took off first? Was it bad etiquette on my part as a female? Wait—were we going steady, and I didn't realize?"

He leaned in closer to me, and I could smell him, clearly see the silver in his dark eyes. All my senses swept me back to being against his hot, smooth skin in that motel bed.

"I liked it Grace. You and me. I liked it a lot."

"It was just sex."

"No, it wasn't. And it sure as hell isn't anymore."

"What is that supposed to mean?"

"It means now I get your loneliness and confusion. Now I get—"

Something in my brain snapped. "Well, there's one thing I'm not confused about—seeing you in the hallway getting your dick blown by that redhead. You don't waste any time, do you, *Lock*?"

"For shit's sake." He grimaced. His hands flew up to the sides of his head, and then they fell away.

I took in a breath. "Listen, that morning I woke up and saw your tattoo and your colors, and I . . ."

He cursed under his breath, his lips drawing into a firm line. "I get it, Grace, I do. But I can't pretend I don't know you. I can't pretend that what happened between us didn't happen. I don't want to."

My hands gripped my waist. "Why not?" I asked. "You've had years of experience at that sort of thing around here, haven't you?"

His eyes flashed at me. "You are not those women."

My gaze darted around the room. His sexy redhead shot daggers at us from her seat at the bar. My eyes cut back to his. "I can't do this right now—whatever *this* is. I've got a sister who's dying, a brother-in-law and nephew who are hanging over the edge."

"Yes, you do, and that's harsh."

"It is. And I've left everything behind to be here for them."

He tilted his head at me. "What was there to leave behind, Grace? You've been doing that on a regular basis for years now, haven't you?"

The breath burned in the back of my throat. "It took everything I had to walk in here tonight and keep it together after all these years."

"I'm sure it did."

"Lock, I'm not Little Sister," I whispered, my finger tapping on the dusty glass over the small photo. "I'm not that woman anymore."

"Bullshit."

"I'm not. Little Sister vaporized on the asphalt in Meager sixteen years ago. Vaporized."

SEVEN

"HERE HE IS, SISTER." Jump squeezed my elbow. My chest tightened as my gaze rested on the stone marker. The breeze tugged on my hair.

All the men of the One-Eyed Jacks had ridden in formation to Rock Hills Cemetery, a patch of burial ground dating back to pioneer days. They had parked their bikes one by one then stood with me. Jump and Alicia had led me here to Dig's grave.

The vast sky with its puffs of popcorn clouds took my breath away. Here was one of the many beautiful, natural phenomena of the Great Plains. We were tiny specks on this patch of stone-enclosed green.

The club's skull logo was engraved in the stone just above the words "Jake 'Dig' Quillen", Loyal brother & Beloved Husband." I closed my eyes for a moment and savored the rush of cool air that wafted over us.

I'm here, baby. Finally here.

That's what had tortured me for years, on top of all the rest of the horror, that I'd never had a chance to formally say goodbye to my husband. I'd never touched his cold cheek or planted a kiss on his stiff chest before they sealed the lid of his coffin. Nor had I been a part of his big biker funeral send-off. I never got to see all his brothers gather who would have ridden to Meager from hundreds and hundreds of miles away to pay their respects to a loyal member of their brotherhood. Nor had I heard a preacher or someone say a few kind words in his honor in order to send his soul to a better place and ease mine just a little.

All these years I had never truly felt in my bones that he was at peace and, therefore, neither was I.

Instead, at the time of his funeral, my doctors had me on a twenty-four hour suicide watch after my desperate attempt the night before. My head had only shook back and forth against the flat pillow, and an endless river of tears had spilled down my bruised and swollen face. My wired brain could only replay over and over again those horrible, shrieking final moments. My insides were empty, my soul had been ripped to shreds, yet Dig's hoarse, rough voice had still echoed through me, pleading with me.

"Get gone, baby. Go, sweetheart."

I stepped forward, crouched, and laid my bouquet of wildflowers on the blades of green grass. My trembling fingers pressed in on the cold unforgiving stone, brushing over the engraved letters of his name. Tears slid down my face. Here in this tiny patch of cold hard ground directly beneath me were the remains of my husband.

His remains.

What did that mean? The life force had been removed, driven off, vanquished. Now there remained only a mass of particles, remnants, residue.

A stinging pressure caved my chest in. The door I had left ajar all these years was finally closing. Dig being dead and gone was no longer an idea that I could distract myself from or keep at arm's length with new places to live, new jobs, new faces, new bed partners. It was stone cold real, and it settled deep in a corner of my heart right where it needed to be.

"Rest, baby," I whispered.

My fingers scrunched the cool sharp blades of grass as I rose, and I steadied myself with a hand on his tombstone. I slid my sunglasses back down over my aching eyes as someone took hold of my arm and slipped it through his. I tilted my face to the side, and Boner gave me a watery smile. My fingers gripped the sleeve of his worn leather jacket.

"Ever since your results came back negative, that spark of hope drained from her eyes. It's not there anymore. I hate this," Alex said, slinging his arm around my shoulder as we walked through the parking lot of the hospital so he could have a smoke. "She's trying to keep up her happy face for Jake, that's one thing, but she's doing it for us now. It's killing me to see her like this."

I held onto his hand that hung at my shoulder and wrapped my other arm around his waist. High in the clear midday sky, the sun glared over the sea of metal cars in the visitor's lot. "We can't think like that, Alex. Jakey can't see you like this, either."

"Why do you think I'm dumping it on you?" He took a deep drag on his cigarette.

I bumped his hip with mine, and we both let out brittle laughs. "Good, dump away."

He exhaled. "I'm so glad you're here, Grace."

"Me too." My vision got misty, and I cleared my throat to fight it. "How about I pick Jakey up from pre-school and take him out for dinner and ice cream, so you can have more time with Ruby or go home and enjoy the silence for a couple of hours. Sound good?"

"Sounds great." He gave me a weary smile and planted a kiss on my forehead.

The roar of pipes blasted in my ears. My head jerked around. Lock straddled a Harley Fat Bob a few yards from us. He removed his helmet, the line of his jaw harsh, his full lips twisted. His broad shoulders were pronounced under the worn patched leather jacket, his long lean legs fitted with dark blue jeans were taut against the massive bike. Today he sported black Harley boots with chain detail.

The sight of him far surpassed caffeine first thing in the morning.

Alex's arm tensed around me. "I'm assuming you know this guy?"

I clenched my jaw as I took in all that was Lock. Dizzying sensations swirled through me at the memory of those powerful legs tangled up in mine, pinning me down.

Grace, back to Earth.

His fingers raked through his cropped black hair, and the small hoop earring on one ear swung lightly. His mirrored sunglasses obscured his dark eyes, but his stiff, unhappy vibe was palpable. I ground the heel of my one boot into the asphalt.

"They must all know you, huh? Even after all these years?" Alex said in my ear. "Their prodigal old lady has returned and all that?"

"Shut up, Alex," I said through gritted teeth. Lock lifted himself up off his hog in a powerful yet graceful move that took my breath away. He leveled his gaze at me, his lips pressed into a firm line. My mouth suddenly went dry.

"He doesn't look too happy. I think you better go talk to him. I'll go." Alex released me and turned to move. My hand pressed into his middle.

"Oh no, let me introduce you." I hooked my hand in his arm and dragged him toward Lock.

"Not necessary," Alex said. "I could really do without this right now, Grace."

"Lock." I nodded at him. His features remained tight.

Lock leaned back against his bike, a lone muscle pulsing in his jaw. "Don't waste any time do you, Sister?"

Alex's eyes widened. I only smiled. "Lock, this is Alex. Alex is my sister's husband. I think I mentioned him to you another time." Lock's lips parted, and his face relaxed. He raised his sunglasses over his head. "Alex this is Lock."

"Good to meet you." Lock thrust his hand out to Alex.

"Same here," Alex said, shaking his hand.

Lock's shoulders loosened. "Sorry to hear about your wife and all that your family's going through right now. I can't imagine how difficult this must be."

My mouth fell open. He was not only polite, but empathetic and articulate.

I was really in trouble.

"Thank you." Alex released his hand. "It is difficult, but we're thrilled that Grace is here with us now."

"I'll bet," said Lock. "We're glad she's back too."

Alex shot me a wide-eyed look. He dropped what was left of his cigarette to the ground and squashed it with the toe of his polished shoe. "I'm going to head up to Ruby now." He gave my shoulder a squeeze. "Call me when you get Jake, okay? Nice to meet you, Lock." He lifted his chin at us as he left the parking lot.

"Nice guy," Lock said.

"Very. My sister is a lucky woman."

"Alicia said I'd find you here. I have some information on your dad, and I came to see if you wanted to grab a cup of coffee."

"You do? Already?"

"Wasn't too hard, Grace."

"The club still has women working at the DMV?"

He smirked. "No. Somehow I managed this on my own."

"So he's still alive and kicking?"

"He is."

"Where?"

"In Montana, just over the border from North Dakota."

"Montana?"

Lock nodded.

"Montana?" My brain fired burning particles off in the direction of what I hoped was Montana.

"Grace—" Lock's hand gripped my bicep.

My eyes blinked up at him. "Tell me."

"Why don't we go get that cup of coffee and talk about it?"

"Montana."

"C'mon, let's go."

I suddenly snapped out of my huff and landed in a new one. "Where are we going?"

"Grace—coffee." He flicked his sunglasses over his eyes once again and mounted his Harley. The Fat Bob roared to life underneath him. "Get on."

"What?"

He held out his helmet to me. "Get on the bike. Let's go." Lock hit the accelerator, a muscle in his jaw pulsed. My mouth watered before the combined greatness that was the Fat Bob and Lock straddling it.

"Grace, get on the goddamn bike!"

I snapped the helmet from his hand, fit it over my head, and got on his bike. We took off, and my body lurched forward. Lock zipped through the back exit of the hospital parking lot and into traffic.

"Hey, where are you going? There was a Starbucks down the block!"

"You need to get out of the hospital routine for a bit," Lock said over his shoulder as he guided the bike onto Route 44. "Takin' you to Meager to a great coffee place. Town's changed, picked up. Think you'll like seeing it." My insides hardened.

The Harley tore out of Rapid City, my heart in my throat. It had been a long while since I had been on a bike with someone who really knew what they were doing. Lock was no Sunday rider. He was an organic part of his machine. My hands eased over his waist. No use being shy about this. It certainly wasn't my first time on a bike, not to mention that Lock and I had already done the deed, hadn't we?

Even so, my palms prickled against the smooth leather of his jacket.

"Erica Drake?"

"That's right." Erica laughed. "Oh my gosh, Grace! It's good to see you again."

Erica's revamped cafe in a revamped Meager was remarkable on all counts.

The adrenaline rush of the forty-five minute ride here on the back of Lock's bike and the surprise of the sophisticated new Meager Grand Cafe were a delightful reprieve from my tense early morning at the hospital. The walls of the renovated cafe turned coffee house were painted in cool hues of robin's egg blue and gray with dark wood trim framing the interior. Small cushioned chocolate brown and gray sofas and apricot upholstered arm chairs dotted the room. Large framed black and white photos of the magnificent granite spires, tunnels, and bridges of the Black Hills punctuated the walls.

Warm streams of sunlight poured through an oversized picture window that offered an ample view of Clay Street, Meager's winding main drag. From here, you could lie back and people watch all day. A single fresh red flower in a tiny vase on each table added a stroke of bold color. This was modern country elegance, not a jot of backwoods hokeyness in sight. I loved it.

"My aunt and uncle had the cafe that used to be here, remember?" Erica asked.

"Of course I do. Drake's Cafe. You used to waitress on the weekends and in the summers."

"That's right." Erica let out a small laugh. "They sold it to me about five years ago, and I made a few changes."

"Just a few? It looks great. And this—" I held up my hazelnut latte, "— smells fantastic, and the muffins and cookies look irresistible."

My eyes swept over the glass case chock full of a delectable variety of baked goods coated in powdery sugar, white glaze, chocolate, and jam. Small sandwiches burst between squares of crusty bread and beckoned from their trays.

My stomach growled. "I think I need one of those huge cookies right now."

Erica grinned. "I'd recommend the chocolate chip with pistachios and dried cranberries or the lemon ginger spice. We bake everything here ourselves." She bent over the display case, and her eyes suddenly widened at something behind me.

I followed her gaze. It was Lock. He stared at us as he stood at the opposite counter, slowly stirring his Super Grande Brazilian Roast. My heart skipped a beat. Yes, he was an impressive specimen. Even in a relaxed pose there was something primal about him. Either he was ready to pounce or shield you. I wasn't sure which.

"Grace? Which cookie would you like?"

"Oh, um, I can never say no to chocolate."

A slight smile creased Erica's mouth as she reached into the case with a slip of wax paper to grab one of her jumbo gourmet cookies for me. "Here you go. On the house."

"Thank you, Erica."

"Come back another time, and we'll catch up, okay? How's Ruby doing?"

"She's ... okay."

"Give her my best."

"I certainly will. Thanks." I stuffed several dollar bills in the hand-painted tip jar by the cash register.

"Thanks, honey. You have a good afternoon now," Erica said.

Lock had moved to a small sofa at a table by the bay window. I put my handbag down on an armchair and sat next to him. Our eyes trailed the light traffic on Clay Street and the pedestrians who strolled by enjoying a day out in our tiny town.

I was pleased to see the large red sign for Pepper's Boot Shop still hung outside the family owned store of wonders that sold all manner of boots to farmers and ranchers and trendy young folk. Mom had taken us there and bought us our first pair of real leather cowboy boots when Ruby was a freshman in high school. *"Good quality is worth the price,"* she had declared as we tried them on and pranced up and down the narrow aisles of the store. *"Can't keep wearing those cheap imitations, they're bad for your feet. Nope. My daughters are going to look good and feel damn good about it."* The three of us had

97

squealed with laughter and gone out for lunch afterwards, brandishing our shopping bags. That was a good day. A very good day.

The tiny fifties-era post office still clung to its corner on the winding end of the road. Marla's Eatery, which once only catered to the retirees who went for an early morning breakfast and then headed back for lunch, still stood alongside the venerable Pete's Tavern next door. In between were a few new shops I had never seen before—an organic produce co-op, a vintage clothing store, and a boutique called "Lenore's Lace" with purple gothic style lettering on a dramatic black banner, which flapped in the breeze.

Steve's Auto Repair had survived, as had Kellerman's Hardware and Grocery with its classic red brick facade. The aging firehouse endured on its own in the distance. There was now another gas station in town, all shiny and modern, but how could it possibly compete with the grand old Prairie Pumper still holding court on the corner of Clay and Anderson?

I settled into the couch next to Lock and sipped on my latte. An elderly couple from the next table glanced over at us then went back to chatting quietly. A young couple in their early twenties with matching dyed black hair murmured over their laptops at the small table on Lock's side.

"You okay? Was it a bad idea coming out here?"

"No. Actually, it was very thoughtful of you. Thank you. I don't think I would have come out here on my own otherwise. It's good to see the old town refreshed and revived. This place is terrific." My gaze wandered to the stone fireplace in the far corner of the room, perfect for the many colder months of the year.

"I thought you'd like it."

I sipped my coffee. "Erica and I were pals in high school."

"She's good people."

"I remember you too back then, actually."

"Oh, yeah?" Lock sank back into the sofa and rubbed a hand down his jeans over a long, muscular thigh. "What do you remember about the high school me, Grace?" He took a sip of his coffee.

"You would slink around the hallways, hiding your eyes behind your long hair. Mostly I remember your book covers."

"My book covers?" He made a face and took another long gulp of coffee. "Yeah, well, I could never stop doodling. Still can't."

I placed my cup on the table in front of us. "Oh no, no, no. What regular kids did was doodle on their brown paper book covers or write the lyrics to their favorite songs like I did. I still remember etching "Born to Run" on my Chemistry cover. You, however, created mini murals on yours full of wild imagery, a real opus of colors."

A smile curled his lips. "You saw one up close? You were a year ahead of me. We didn't have any classes together, didn't run with the same crowd."

I let out a laugh. "Yeah, you spent most of your free time on the smoking patio, can't say I did. No, I think the first time I noticed them was at an assembly. We were both late getting to the auditorium, and you and I ended up standing in the back next to each other. Your book cover caught my eye. It was a comet hurtling through the sky with space aliens and flying horses with wings. Something like that." I grinned at him. "It was definitely some sort of cataclysm in the galaxy."

Lock rubbed his hand over his face and continued to look out the window. His lips twitched.

"What is it?" I asked.

"I like the words you use."

"Oh."

"Opus, cataclysm—that about sums it up," he said. "For shit's sake, how can you remember something like that?"

"Like what?"

"A minor detail from over twenty years ago—a freaking book cover that belonged to a kid you didn't know, never even talked to in high school?"

"It wasn't minor to me. Anyway, I liked high school, Lock. I still remember a few things from back then. That book cover was so unique and unusual. It. . .dazzled me. I always looked out for your book covers after that. You were a little spooky back then, though. So yes, I remember."

He chuckled. "Spooky?"

"Not spooky as in scary or weird. Spooky as in something deep and big was going on behind those bleak eyes and long black hair." His dark gaze held mine, and I sank back into the sofa. "Then you started playing football, and you grew out of spooky real fast." He threw back his head and laughed as I grinned. "You filled out, got taller."

His features relaxed, his mouth turned into a sensuous smile that made me sit up. "You noticed that, did you?"

I rolled my eyes. "Me and all the rest of the girls, Lock. It was hard not to."

He made a face. "That's what eating three square meals a day does for a growing boy."

"Things were bad on the reservation before Wreck brought you to Meager?"

"We didn't have much on the res. Wasn't much to have, but there were good people there. The last two years there with my dad were tough though, let's just put it that way."

I was sure Lock was putting it mildly. His eyes had gotten hard once more. Time to change the subject.

I knocked my knee against his thigh. "I like your Fat Bob, by the way."

"You do?"

I nodded from behind my coffee cup.

"I've got an Ultra Classic Electra Glide at home," he said.

"Holy shit, really? A CVO?" My eyes widened. I knew my Harleys, not only from my years with Dig at the club, but all the years I had worked at the Harley Davidson stores around the country. The Electra Glide was a pricey custom Harley with premium features. It was a beautiful touring bike, sleek and powerful.

"I decided to spend some money on myself for a change a few years ago and sprang for a brand new bike. Then I bought the Electra Glide for longer trips. What the hell have I been saving for all this time, you know? I've been riding my own choppers for a while, and I've got quite a collection, what with Wreck's old bikes."

"Good for you."

"I'll consider giving you a ride, if you keep being nice to me."

Oh goody. Flirty Lock was back.

I let out a laugh. "Can I be your fender, baby?"

A shadow swept over his features for a moment. "You're no fender, Grace," he said, his voice low.

I squirmed in my seat. Yes, at my age I certainly was beyond being the chick on the back of a member's bike, there just for the ride and the good time. I was never that girl anyway.

"Yep, those days are long gone." I broke off a piece of cookie, then sunk back in the sofa and concentrated on the buttery chocolate melting on my tongue.

He leaned into me. "What I meant was that you were never a fender from what I've heard. You were straight up fine girl to classy old lady, doing good things for the town, the community, the club. Still are classy." My eyes snapped up to meet his penetrating gaze. It was almost painful, as if he were looking for something inside me.

Do you see it, Lock? What is it?

That animal-like arousal he inspired in me stirred again, that needy ache stretching between us.

Lock's gaze returned to the window, his hand wiping across his chest. "When's the last time you saw him, Grace?"

"Who? My dad?"

"Yeah, Raymond Hastings of Montana."

"A couple days after my eighteenth birthday. Ray took off on a rig heading for Oregon and never came back."

"Very nice."

"Yeah, it was something else. A wife, two kids. Guess he figured he was leaving us his fancy mansion in Meager and his rusty car, so he didn't have too many regrets. When he didn't come home, we thought maybe he had gotten into an accident. We checked with everyone we knew, the police, even the trucking company, but there was no accident. Two weeks later he sent divorce papers to my mother and that was that."

"Very slick."

I took a small sip of my flavorful coffee. "Did he get married again? Have more kids? Tell me. I'm a big girl, I can take it."

"No, he never remarried. He lived with a couple different women off and on, but he's been on his own for several years now. He owned a couple of rigs and did pretty well for himself in the oil boom up north."

I put my latte down on the table with an audible clunk. "Really?"

"What is it?" Lock put a hand on my knee. An unfamiliar warmth slid through me at his touch, at the low, gentle tone in his voice.

"It's just that the man I knew, the man I remember, was always so disinterested in everything around him. My parents didn't even fight much because he would just walk away, take off. End of discussion. She would rage on by herself, throw stuff around the house. I never thought he had much imagination or desire for anything outside his little box of a life. He was usually quiet, distant, which only got worse after my little brother got killed. Ray pretty much checked out after that."

"You had a brother?" His hand pressed into my thigh.

"Jason was nine when he got run over on his bicycle by a drunk driver. It was awful. My parents never recovered from it."

"How old were you?"

"I was thirteen, and Ruby was fifteen. Everyone just went their own separate ways mentally and emotionally after that. Five years later Ray was gone." My palm rubbed over my cheek. "Now you're telling me that he actually created something big for himself, something that must have brought him a lot of satisfaction and self-respect. He couldn't do that with us? I suppose he had to get away from us to be a better, productive person."

"Maybe it was just your mom he needed to get away from," he said. "Marriage isn't for everybody, you know."

I held his gaze. "Is that how you feel about marriage?"

His eyes tightened. "I've never met anyone I wanted to make that sort of commitment to."

"Really?"

"Tried living with a woman once. It fell apart pretty quickly. That was it for me." We averted our gazes back to watching people cross the street, to cars and pickup trucks cruising past.

"I was never under the illusion that my parents had a romantic love story going on. They got married young when Mom got pregnant with Ruby."

Lock took my hand in his as he let out a heavy breath. My gaze darted to our joined hands that now rested on his thigh, and a peculiar tickle rose from my palm, travelled up my arm, and swirled in my chest. I liked how his tanned fingers were woven with my much paler ones. Holding hands with someone was such a simple thing, but it didn't feel so simple right now.

For some reason, it didn't feel awkward or uncomfortable sitting here with him, watching the world go by and recounting our past horrors; It was a relief. I eased back into the sofa, my hand still in his.

"I'm going to take you to Montana," he said.

"What?"

"We'll go together."

"What are you talking about? You don't have to do that. Just give me the address, and I'll go."

His hand released mine and squeezed my thigh. "You shouldn't have to do this alone."

"That's right, I shouldn't." I fought the tears that filled my eyes. "Ruby should be with me to ream his ass. But alas . . ." I didn't want to cry over my dad and my sister, and I certainly didn't want to cry in public, in my own hometown, and with Lock.

"Come here." He pulled me into his chest and stroked my back.

The ache in the hollow of my chest faded, and I couldn't help but ease into the solid warmth of his body. This felt too good, being soothed by this man who could be demanding and yet gentle with me. His lips brushed my forehead, and his clean masculine aroma filled my nostrils stirring my nerve endings. His scent reminded me of Earl Grey tea with an edge of rough thrown in.

Oh hell, I should push him away. Sit up, suck it up, drink my coffee, and put my game face on. But I didn't want to. It felt too good here in Lock's arms. His steady heartbeat drummed under my ear, and I focused on that.

"Lock . . ."

"Shh." His face leaned into my hair.

"You don't have to take me. I can handle this on my own. It's just my father."

"Not a good idea." His voice rumbled in his chest, and his fingers slid under my hair and stroked the back of my neck.

I blinked up at him. "Is something wrong?"

"You can't go alone. In fact, you shouldn't go at all. But we get that this is huge and you need to take care of this shit in person."

"We? You mean the club?"

"Yeah."

"But this has nothing to do with the club. I have nothing to do with the club. What does it matter?" I pushed against his chest and sat up.

"Baby, you're one of the most famous club old ladies that ever was in all of South Dakota. You've been MIA for sixteen years after your old man, a club officer, got mowed down. Not to mention you were the only witness to the shooter."

"I also shot him dead, Lock."

"Exactly. The cops couldn't do much with your statement. You were never able to give a very thorough one, which was good for the club, of course."

"A hysterical depression didn't allow me to be too communicative."

"That's right. Don't you see? You're back now. You're here. It won't be long before the cops come knocking on your door to revive the case if they're in the mood. Your sister was really smart to get you as far away from here and the club as possible. But now that you're back it might call up the ghosts wanting to make sure you don't remember anything from that night that you might possibly tell the police about."

"I really don't remember much from that night. He was wearing a ski cap, his weapon pointed right at us. That's all, that's all I remember. I knew better than to get the police involved in club business, anyhow."

My breath quickened as he took me in his arms, his free hand rubbing the side of my thigh. I leaned into him.

"I'll bet you did," he murmured in my hair. "Don't forget, your shooter was related to a Demon Seed, Grace."

"Vig's nephew."

His tight gaze was focused out the picture window, his hand pressing into my back. "And you killed him. There's bound to be blowback."

Yes, indeed.

"I've spent the past sixteen years licking my wounds in a self-imposed exile pretending everything would be fine. My killing my old man's killer didn't heal me, though, and time didn't heal me either. It only dulled the pain."

Lock tucked me closer into his warm body. "I know the feeling." He leaned back into the sofa, taking me with him. My hand went to his on my knee, and my fingertips slid over the eagle ring.

I let out a sigh. "I loved your brother, you know. Wreck was good to me. He was at the shed shop every day working hard and teaching the younger guys about their bikes. He even took time with me, telling me stories about the old days, about what being out on the open road was really like, what it meant to him."

"Yeah. Those were good stories. Building bikes, the crazy shit they got up to on runs, living by his own rules."

"That was everything to him. Wreck was the real deal, genuine 1%."

"And that's how he died," Lock said.

Wreck's sudden and violent death in Texas had haunted Dig, put him on more of an edge than he'd already been on. It had changed something for him those last two months, made him think differently and make different decisions about a lot of things.

My fingers trailed down to the cluster of knotted leather cords at Lock's wrist. "Wreck took me under his wing like the older brother I never had. I have to say, his kindness helped me get settled in the life."

Lock's brows pulled down as he watched my fingers twist the thin leather cords, teasing his skin. "I'd looked forward to being part of the club with him, you know. I wanted to prospect under him, ride with him like a brother. But I took on another tour of duty, stayed away too long, and it was too late. I'll always regret that."

"Lock . . ."

"It's all right though. The club was his only family, and it became mine too. I've had that thanks to Wreck."

I smiled. "As messed up as it sounds, if Ruby hadn't gotten involved with the club and gotten into trouble, I never would have gotten involved with Dig. We knew each other before, but it was after Ruby got arrested that we got close. When she got sent off to jail, the club became my family."

"And they always will be, Grace. You know that, don't you?"

I sighed. "Yes, I know."

His gaze drifted out the window once more.

"Is it enough for you?" I asked.

His head snapped back at me, and he frowned. "I'm not so sure anymore. I'm not questioning the brotherhood, just my role in the club. Things have been feeling routine for a long time now. Hitting forty last year made me start wondering."

"It's okay to want more out of life, you know," I murmured.

"It's one thing being grateful for what you have, it's quite another being satisfied. I know that only too well." He studied me, his one hand squeezed my leg. "Wreck told me how he'd found you beaten up and locked in the cellar of your father's house on the reservation."

"My dad had broken my nose, but by the time Wreck found me it had already been a couple of days. I've got a nice souvenir of my brief time with Daddy." His fingers flicked over the bump on the bridge of his nose.

I was sure the scars he carried on the inside ran deeper than the one on his face.

"Our mother hooked up with some real shitheads over the years, one right after the other. My father was just one in a long line of many."

His fingers slid over mine at his wrist. "Wreck found me, got me out of that fucking cellar, and took me home with him. He didn't even know me, but that didn't matter to him. We were brothers." I leaned my head against his shoulder and uncurled my hand to his fingers gently tracing my palm. Soothing. Erotic. The air nipped from my lungs.

"I was a pain in the ass half the time, but he dealt with it. He missed out on a lot of club runs because of me, but he didn't mind, never complained. He was Road Captain at the time too, so that must have been rough on him and a pain in the ass for the club. They gave him a pass on it, though, because I was his family." I smiled against his shoulder.

"For a long time Wreck spent more time fixing bikes and cars to keep the money coming in, than hanging with the boys. Once I turned sixteen he started going out again, riding to rallies, partying. That simple shit made him so happy, especially riding with his brothers. I was glad when he got back to it full-time. I didn't want to be the reason he stopped being a full-fledged Jack."

"You were loved," I whispered. My words hung between us.

His eyes slid closed, his lips tightened.

My fingers entwined with his. "He'd showed me a picture of you on your first bike, the one you had rebuilt together."

"He did?" His eyebrows lifted. "The Indian Chief was a classic, Grace. A thing of beauty."

"You looked so happy sitting on that bike, Lock."

"Not spooky?" His fingers squeezed mine.

I laughed softly. "Not spooky at all."

"It was one of the best moments of my life," he said, his voice husky.

"You know, back then a lot of the guys had gotten caught up in the drugs, the partying, or the business of making money any way they could," I said. "Not Wreck. He liked partying and all the rest of it as much as anyone, but his soul was in his bikes, the road. Most of all, in you."

His fingertips grazed the stack of silver rings on my middle finger. "I'm glad you got to know my brother like that." His eyes pierced mine. "Makes me feel good that back then a good girl liked you appreciated the kind of man he was. He deserved that, someone like you giving him that love and respect." His heavy gaze fell to my mouth, and my insides launched into orbit.

I shifted on the sofa and took a sip of my latte. "Why did you go into the army, Lock? Why not just become a member of the club right off?"

He sighed, his hand remaining over mine. "Wreck wanted me to have more life experience before I made the commitment. He took that really serious, and I respected it, understood it. I was itching to get out on my own anyhow and push my limits. I ended up doing two tours of duty in Bosnia."

"I remember Dig calling you to tell you."

"Yeah. Wasn't good." He exhaled.

"Dig told me the three of you would go out riding and shooting," I said, a half-smile on my lips.

"Your old man gave me my first gun. He taught me how to take good aim. Dig always had my back and got me out of a few nasty scrapes as a screwed up teenager before I signed up for the Army. I owed him big time. He was a fearless son of a bitch, and I learned a lot from him." Lock's jaw tightened.

I imagined my husband taking a young Lock under his wing and teaching him his way around a bike and a weapon. It was pretty nuts the way our lives were connected in a crazy zig-zag through the same people and places. We shared so much of the same past, and yet we had only just met.

Lock made a noise in the back of his throat. His shoulders had gone rigid. Had talking about Wreck and Dig with me made him uncomfortable?

"Grace, listen, that part of Montana is Demon Seed territory. You can't just go waltzing over there on your own. Not you. You going into their territory after having been gone so long will put you on their radar. They might get ticked that you went in without a heads-up and see it as a sign of disrespect on our part, or a threat."

"But I'm a citizen. I've been one for ages now."

"To them you will always be our property, Grace. You know that. You're branded as Dig's old lady. Can't change that fact." Lock focused his attention on his coffee mug once more, a muscle pulsed in his jaw.

"No," I murmured. "I can't change that."

"Don't you think they'll be wondering if you've been laying low on purpose all this time plotting your personal revenge and this is you making your first move with or without our backing?"

"I don't want to put the club at any risk. I'll back off, be out of everyone's hair. No problem."

His head snapped to me. "Don't think like that, Grace. You're not in anyone's hair. This is your home. You have every right to be here. And to be honest, it's a good shot in the heart for the club to see you and think about those times again."

My skin heated under the intensity of his glare. I turned away, my gaze falling on a teenage couple kissing hard outside on the street. The girl was leaning into her boyfriend, standing on her tiptoes, her fingers buried in his shaggy hair. A corner of my heart squeezed. If only things could stay that simple and fresh forever.

"Jump sent out a friendly request to the Demon Seeds for me to take you in to see your father," he said, his voice lower.

"Why you?"

"Why not me? I want to keep you safe."

My heart ricocheted against my rib cage. "Okay. Are they gonna let you ride with your colors or do we go in a cage?"

His hands clamped onto my legs and swung them over his as he swept me into his lap. My breath hitched as his warm hands braced the sides of my face, his full lips touching mine. He tasted of coffee and spearmint. His burning, dark silver gaze wound a hot coil straight through me.

"Want you on my bike," he said against my mouth, his voice husky. "If you're up for the trip."

"Electra Glide?"

A black eyebrow quirked. "Oh, yeah."

I grinned. "Definitely the bike then."

The edges of his lips tipped up, and he took my mouth in a gentle kiss that became urgent very quickly. His tongue devoured everything in its path, and I happily let it have its way. A groan escaped my throat as he shifted me in his arms, and I slid deeper against his chest, a place in which I was beginning to find I liked to be. Very much. My hands tucked inside his leather jacket, pressed around his lean torso and dug into his back, my swollen breasts were crushed against his chest. I reveled in his taste, in his solid heat taking me in.

"They put something in the coffee today?" a thin voice scratched above us. "Why don't you tell me what it is, so I can get me some too?"

Lock's body stilled under mine. "Motherfuck," he said against my lips.

I turned my head to the side of Lock's. A bright mane of red hair and two piercing green eyes hovered over us. It was Lock's blow job bikini babe from the other night at the club.

A brittle smirk twisted Red's face. "I didn't figure you for vanilla in a plain old Today's Special."

Oh no. She did not just say that.

My hands slid around Lock's shoulders. I straightened my back, crossed one leg over the other on his lap, and tilted my head at her. My eyes narrowed, taking her in. Her face tightened under my stare. She was an irritated hornet ready to sting, but I was no little girl intimidated by her showy stance.

Hold on—was she Lock's new girlfriend? *Perhaps I should rethink my attitude.*

"It's none of your goddamn business, Heather," Lock said. "Cut the shit. Get lost." His one hand moved over my thigh and cradled my hip.

Nope, not his girlfriend. *Reload the attitude.*

Heather hitched a hand on her waist over her skintight leggings. Her pastel blue open-neck sweatshirt emblazoned with a huge Pink logo slipped off a curvy shoulder and revealed bare skin. Her coral fingernails decorated with glittery designs curled around her cardboard coffee cup so tightly that I expected the steamy contents to explode at any moment. Her artificially tanned skin flushed and her mauve-colored lips bloomed into a pout.

Here it comes.

"Fuck you, Lock! Don't come looking for me next time you get yourself a raging hard-on!"

Heads snapped our way, gasps erupted about the room. Erica's eyes widened at the counter, and the light buzz of chatter in the coffee house was suspended while Heather held center stage at the Meager Grand Cafe. She waited for our reaction. Lock and I continued to hold onto each other, staring blankly at her.

Heather's eyes sizzled. "Asshole!" She turned on a dime, her long, bright red hair swishing against her back, her high-heeled booties clacking mercilessly on the polished wood floor. She pulled on the door, shot us a final death glare, and stormed out.

Lock's gaze darted over me. "You okay?"

"Yeah. Don't you need to go after your girlfriend?"

Just confirming.

"She's not my girlfriend." His lips began to move again, but I quickly pressed my fingers against his mouth.

"I don't need an explanation. And you don't owe me one. I know what *that* was, and I know what *this* is. No worries." I clambered off his lap.

His grip on me tightened, and he pulled me back over his legs. "Whoa. Stop right there."

"Excuse me?"

His brows snapped together. "Number one: Heather's just a club bitch making a play where there is no play to make and, most importantly, she had no right to even make it."

Poor Heather. She had obviously forgotten that vital line item in the Biker Babe Handbook: To fuck a biker is a privilege. If you are chosen, consider yourself lucky. Never question, never say no, and never ever make your own demands.

"She and I have hooked up a few times," Lock said. "Same as she's hooked up with a lot of the guys. This, I'm sure, is not news to you. And although I do appreciate that, with all your club life experience, you get that without my having to explain it to death and without you getting yourself into a snit about it, I still find it necessary to make a reference to it."

Un-fucking-believable. Alpha arrogance coupled with articulate, gentlemanly concern.

Hold on, I liked it.

I bit down on my lip, shoving back my amusement. He was certainly fired up. Was that good or bad?

"Number two: You made a play of your own back there."

My face prickled with heat. "What?"

"It was priceless. You didn't get pissy or bitchy. Didn't say a fucking word. No, what you did was smooth and subtle. Don't think I didn't notice, and don't think I didn't find it hot." His hooded gaze fell to my mouth. "Extremely hot."

I shot him a glare.

He ignored my glare. "Number three—"

I made a face.

"You and me are happening. It's not an illusion, and there's nothing confusing about it. It just is."

"It just is?" I said. "What the—"

"Yeah, Grace. You and me. It's happening."

"Lock, there is no 'you and me.' You and me barely know each other. We have a few things in common, like dead biker relatives and a sexual episode, but that's about it."

He leaned into me, his features dark. "A sexual episode? Are you kidding me? We can't keep our hands off each other, woman."

I made a scoffing sound and jerked off his lap, but he tugged me right back on once more. I shot him another glare. The corded veins in his neck seemed to pound at me.

"Grace!" His voice was low, his tone slightly threatening.

"Keep it down, would you? We've made enough of a scene in here as it is. Even Erica's watching."

"I don't give a shit who's watching. Admit it." The silver in his eyes glinted at me. His face was now only inches from mine. The air was sucked out of me. "Say it," he said. "You know it's true."

I let out a heavy sigh.

"Grace?"

"Okay! Yes, I'm attracted to you."

"How nice. And?"

Demanding, bossy, son of a . . .

"Babe, " he practically growled. His thighs tightened into absolute rocks under mine.

"And I liked sleeping with you."

"You *liked sleeping with me*?" His eyes flared. "We fu—"

My fingers flew to his mouth. "For God's sake!"

He snorted air from his nose like a wild horse and latched onto my hand at his mouth, pulling it away. "Grace!"

I leaned into him. "I liked *fucking* you a hell of a lot," I whispered. "How's that? Is that better?"

He lifted an eyebrow. "Oh, much better. Extremely accurate, in fact."

"Good. But a good fucking doesn't constitute a 'you and me' of any kind."

Lock's dark eyes simmered. "Are you shitting me?"

I groaned, and my head sank in my hands. The couple at the next table stared at us. "It was amazing," he said. "We clicked, it was a whole other level of—"

"So we have chemistry."

"It was more than chemistry. There was something honest about it, something real."

"Come on, that night all we shared was booze and desperation."

He shook his head, his jaw stiffening. "We didn't drink that much, and I wasn't desperate. I wasn't even looking, and you weren't either. Don't make excuses, Grace, and don't you bring it down. Don't."

"You're right. I'm sorry. But we don't even know each other. So we're attracted to each other, we indulged—"

His fingers pressed into my flesh. "We indulged, all right. Imagine if we get to know each other better?"

Yes, imagine.

His dark eyes bored through mine demanding a reply.

"I can't do this, Lock. I told you, I'm here for Ruby."

"When was the last time you did do it?"

I glowered at him.

He leaned in close to my face. "That's what I thought."

I shook my head at him. My gaze fell to my oversized stainless steel watch that hung loosely on my wrist. "Dammit!"

"What is it?"

"I need to pick up my nephew from school and take him out for an early dinner. Could you take me back to the hospital so I can get my car?"

"Let's go." He lifted me out of his lap, then took my hand in his and led me towards the door. He stopped to tuck several bills in the tip jar.

"Thanks, guys." Erica waved at us.

Lock lifted his chin at Erica, and I waved as he tugged me out the door.

The cool air wrapped around us. "Crap!" I groaned.

"Now what?"

"I have no idea where to take him. I don't know Rapid like I used to."

Lock shook his head and laughed. He swung his arm around my neck as we made our way towards his Harley. "I'll take you out."

"You don't have to do that." I took the helmet from his hands.

"I want to, Grace." He took the helmet out of my grip and fit it on my head. "And I'd really like to meet Jake. Anyway, you'll get better service if you got me with you."

"I'll just bet," I muttered as we climbed on the back of the bike.

EIGHT

"LOCK IS A FUNNY NAME, huh, Aunt Gracie?"

"It's a nickname, Jakey. Just like your Uncle Jake's nickname was Dig, right?"

"Yep." He nodded his head. "So my nickname's Dig, too?"

"No, honey. You've got to earn your nickname. It's unique, and it sticks."

"What's oo-nique mean?"

"Unique means original or one of a kind. Like you are to Mommy and Daddy and me. There's only one Jakey for us."

He grinned up at me. "Why 'Dig'? Is there a reason?"

"You know, he never told me. It was some sort of big secret." I wiggled my eyebrows at him. His eyes went round, and he burst into giggles.

I couldn't tell my nephew the real meaning of Dig's nickname. Digging a hole in the Hills deeper than any of the other recruits to hide a few dead bodies wasn't the sort of thing you shared with a little boy.

"What about Lock?" Jake asked.

"I don't know that, either. I just met him though, so I didn't think it would be polite to ask."

"Oh," he said, pursing his tiny lips.

"I know his real name is Miller. You want me to find out about his road name, honey?" Hang on, maybe that wasn't such a good idea. Maybe I wouldn't want to know.

Jake's face lit up, his clear hazel eyes beaming up at me. "Ask him, Aunt Grace. Please! It's gotta be some super tough reason to go with that super tough bike."

Oh brother. The fascination begins early.

"You liked his bike, huh?" I grinned down at him. Jake nodded as he kicked his feet against his mattress.

"Me too." I laughed and dropped down next to him on his red race car bed. I drew his Spiderman comforter over us and kissed the top of his fluffy blond hair. "You know, Lock had a brother who was good friends with me and your Uncle Dig. His nickname was Wreck, and he used to fix cars and bikes. He was a really good rider and driver, the best. He never once got into an accident on the road."

"Why did they call him Wreck then?"

"It's called irony, sweetie. It's sort of like a joke. He used to fix up everyone else's car and bike wrecks, never one of his own."

Jake frowned at me.

"I'll explain it better tomorrow. Too tired now." I yawned. "Can I sleep with you tonight, Jakey? Your bed is just too cozy, and my tummy is so full I don't think I can get up again."

"Yay!" he shouted. Jake put his hand in mine under the warm, thick bed cover and his little fingers tickled my palm.

"That was a mighty good buffalo burger, wasn't it? I've missed those."

"But Aunt Grace, you had yours with cooked onions and blue cheese. That's gross!"

"Only cheddar and bacon allowed?"

"That's right. That's the perfect burger. Lock knew that too."

"Yeah, he's really smart, just like you. Fine, next time cheddar, bacon and barbecue sauce only."

"Can we go for ice cream again tomorrow?" He grinned up at me.

"You're a little ice cream freak, you know that?"

His eyes lit up. "I know."

"Did you brush your teeth?"

"Hmm."

I tilted my head at him narrowing my eyes.

"I did, Aunt Grace!"

I leaned over Jake and sniffed loudly over his cute mouth and neck. He giggled, and his small warm hands rubbed my face.

"You did brush. Good for you!" I laid a sloppy kiss on his cheek. "How about we go for ice cream after we see Mommy tomorrow?"

Jake's eyes clouded. "When's Mommy coming home?"

"I'm not sure, honey. The doctor is going to let us know. I don't like not knowing either."

I rubbed circles over his chest, and his tiny mouth stretched open as he yawned. I drew his warm little Batman pajama-clad body next to mine, planted a kiss on his soft cheek, and stroked his back.

The Mickey Mouse night-light glowed next to us, casting shadows against the wall from the race car mobile hanging from the ceiling and the large Tramp stuffed animal on his miniature desk. I had bought him that toy at the Disney store in Dallas a couple of years ago along with the *Lady and the Tramp* DVD, and it was still his favorite movie. Tramp stood at attention over us, his large soft brown eyes full of reassuring doggy love. He was our trustworthy bodyguard against the Boogeyman of the long night that lay before us. God knew what would find us in the morning.

"Love you, Aunt Gracie," Jake breathed and rolled over. My eyes rested on the large framed photo of Jake, Ruby, and me that Alex had snapped in front of a huge pile of nachos at a restaurant in Denver two years ago. Our excited faces hummed at me in the delicate light.

"I love you too, Jakey," I whispered.

"What do you mean you're looking for Ray? I don't want to have anything to do with that shithead, Grace." Ruby's face tightened as she attempted to sit up in her bed.

I had to tell her. Lock and I were set to leave first thing tomorrow morning.

"We need to explore all our options, Ruby. Like it or not, he is our biological father. There is a possibility he is a match, and I'm going to find out. I'm not leaving this stone unturned. No way."

"Isn't he too old for this sort of thing?"

"He's just at the cut off point, but it's still worth the try."

Ruby pressed her lips together. She shook her head, and her eyes narrowed. "How did you find him? Oh, let me guess!" She raised her hands in the air. "You asked the club for help?"

"Yes, I did. Jump was all over it. Their Road Captain, Lock, found Ray right away."

"Lock?"

"Yes."

"The biker my son currently worships thanks to you?"

"Lock took us out for dinner last night."

"And ice cream."

"And ice cream."

"Cozy."

I crossed my arms. Her wan eyes settled on me. "He's Wreck's half- brother," I said. "The one he saved from the abusive father on the reservation? The soldier?"

Ruby's face relaxed. "Oh, yeah. I vaguely remember him lurking around the club. He was just a kid then. Wasn't he in your class or something?"

"He was a year younger. His real name is Miller."

"Right. Quiet, rebellious type, but way too young for me. At least back then." She smirked. "Now, hey . . ."

I grinned at her. "Back then, you liked your men mature and sophisticated."

Ruby barked out a laugh. "If I had the energy I'd throw this pillow at you."

"Consider it thrown."

Ruby sighed, her eyes resting on me. "You going on your own?"

She was just like our freaking mother. "No, mom." I made a face at her. "Lock is taking me."

"Oh?"

"The club doesn't want me going out there on my own. You should be pleased."

"I'm tickled pink. Some things never change."

"Apparently not."

She waved a hand in the air. "I hate that it's my fault that you have to do any of this—Club protection, asshole parent."

My gaze darted down to where my fingers twisted an errant thread on the thin bedspread. "I'm kind of curious to see Ray actually."

"Oh Jesus, you must be joking." Ruby frowned at me. "Don't be. Please don't do this."

"He's been living practically next door all this time. And yet not one word. Mom died, nothing."

"He's a coward, Grace. That's why," said Ruby. "I don't care how unhappy he was, he could've handled it very differently. Instead, he stepped on all of us, every single one of us, and never looked back. I stopped wondering about him a long, long time ago. I cut that shit off so I could breathe, but I guess you never did."

"Even when me and Dig. . .that made the six o'clock news, didn't it? He could have come then. Why didn't he?"

Ruby took a gulp of air from her oxygen mask, then put it down. "He did."

My pulse pounded in my ears. "What?"

"You were still in your post-surgical coma when he showed up at the hospital."

"Ruby?"

"He stayed for a couple of hours. Talked with the doctor and took off again." Ruby sank back on the bed.

My eyes flared at her. "Why didn't you tell me?"

"Gracie, you had so much going on, and you were not dealing with any of it very well. You wanted me to tell you that the sweet daddy who abandoned us popped by for a visit while we were trying to keep you sane, alive, and in one piece?" She took more air in from the mask.

"What did he say?"

"I took one look at him and told him to get lost. I pushed him, threw a fit, and Jump and Boner had to pull me off him. Security showed up, and he left. A nurse told me he came back much later that night, stayed until morning in your room."

My mouth went dry and my lungs squeezed together. I rubbed the sides of my head with my hands. "Oh, God."

"What? Does that absolve him of everything now? Grace, you always want to believe the best in people. That's a gift you have, but don't waste that on him. Maybe it's a good thing Lock will be with you. I'm sure that man can spot bullshit a mile off. That'll keep it real for you."

I rolled my eyes at her. "What would you prefer I do? Ah! How about we sneak into Ray's house in the dead of night, have Lock incapacitate him in his sleep, I retrieve his bone marrow and we take off? Sound better?"

"And how are you going to "retrieve his bone marrow" smarty pants?"

I shrugged. "I'll look it up on the internet."

Ruby's head sunk back on the pillow, and she laughed, her body shaking. I snapped the oxygen mask back over her face.

"I'm guessing you like what you see?"

The chrome, silvery brown and black custom paint job on Lock's new Harley gleamed in the soft light of early morning in the club yard. The machine seemed to be moving even as it stood perfectly still. I licked my bottom lip as Lock leaned in over my shoulder, his warm breath tickling the side of my face.

"What's not to like about a CVO Electra Glide?" I asked.

"It's great for long trips. The older I get, the more comfort my body demands. This definitely qualifies. Have you ridden on one before?"

"Once in Texas, but just for a short test run."

"You must have ridden plenty of new bikes working those stores."

"I did. But you know better than I do, it's not the bike that makes the rider. I dated a few weekend warriors over the years. They would spend amazing amounts of money all the time on bikes and gear, but so what. It was never the same. They handled the bikes differently. I felt it," I murmured.

Lock aimed a smug grin at me and went back to packing my rain gear in his saddlebags. That buzz ripped right through me at the sight of him all decked out in his aviator mirrored sunglasses, his leathers, the hoodie over his head. I averted my gaze.

"Nice rain gear," he said.

"Thanks. The skies change here so quickly. Better prepared than wet."

"Absolutely."

"And these." I handed him two frozen water bottles. His lips twitched.

"I told you, you're no ordinary fender, baby." His voice wrapped around the words lazily. "Organized." I grinned back at him. No matter how cool the weather may be, out on the asphalt, under the burning engine of the bike for a long stretch of time, the two of us in leathers and under helmets, things would get hot very quickly. Ice melting into cold drinkable water would be an asset.

"By the way," Lock said. "I was thinking we could stay in North Dakota and get on 16 and shoot through the Teddy Roosevelt and the Grassland instead of staying on I-94 through Montana. 94 is quicker, but it's a highway, there'll be traffic, and 16 is open range, a much better ride."

"Definitely, 16."

"It'll take longer."

"I know. Doesn't matter. 16."

A slight smile curled the edge of his lips. "Good." My pulse spiked at the warm lick of pleasure in his voice.

Jump and Alicia strode over to us. "Ready to head out?" asked Jump.

"Yeah," Lock said. Jump put his hand on Lock's shoulder and pulled him away for a private chat.

"Any problems?" I asked Alicia.

"Demon Seed crap, what else. Those assholes are still on our backs after all these years. The boys like their club the way it is. Those mothers want us to patch in."

My eyes flew open. "Become Demon Seeds? Is that some kind of joke?"

"They've become a big regional organization now. The One-Eyed Jacks have kept things small, the chapter in North Dakota, the chapter in Colorado. Just like you remember, but that's it."

"So they want their grubby fingers in our humble pie, huh?"

"Something like that. Anyway, Jump cleared everything for you and Lock, so things should be friendly out there." I only nodded. Alicia's hand reached out and patted my upper arm. "Lock's a good guy. You can trust him."

My gaze darted down to my black leather boots. "He seems. . .nice."

"Nice?" Alicia barked out a laugh. "You know better than that, hon!" I blinked up at her. We both broke out into laughter.

"By the way, how did he get his road name?"

Alicia let out a sigh and flipped her impossibly straight blond hair behind her shoulders. "You remember, he was on some kind of special assignment when Wreck died, and he couldn't make it home for the funeral?" Well, when he finally did get back from soldiering just after your thing, and with both Dig and Wreck gone, we kept waiting for him to explode, let loose. Never did. He kept to himself at Wreck's cabin. From a kid he was always kind of quiet and introverted, but after all that, he took it to a whole new level."

Alicia shook her head slightly. "He took on lots of scary shit for the club one right after the other, got into plenty of fights at parties and bars. The usual crap, but throughout all of it, he was so contained, even in a fight and definitely after. He'd walk away, bloody, bruised, get on his bike and take off like some Terminator robot. Days later, he'd be back for more."

"Kept it locked down," I murmured.

Alicia nodded. "Many a woman has tried to get under that exterior of steel, but none have succeeded."

"Oh, yeah?"

"He's been through plenty of women, but only a few steady ones over the years. None of them ever lasted." Alicia quirked an eyebrow. "But hey, if you're looking for a simple good time, why the fuck not? Go for it. I would."

I tugged at my waistband. "I was just wondering about him, that's all. He strikes me as a bit unusual."

"He's a good guy underneath. But where women are concerned, if he's not interested, he'll let you know, and you need to believe him. That's the way he keeps it. Some girls think they can win him over or rescue him. I see it all the time."

"All the time, huh?"

"Oh yeah, and it never works. It always ends badly for them. Actually, there was one the other night after you left the party. The twat pitched a fit." She rolled her eyes.

My face heated, and I averted my gaze.

"Anyway, just keep that in mind. You know how that shit goes." She got her car keys out of her handbag. "I've got to get back home, get Wes to school."

Alicia and Jump's son. They have a son.

Something twisted deep in my chest. "What grade is he in now?"

"He's a sophomore in high school this year," she said, her eyes beaming. "You wouldn't believe the shit I put up with."

High school.

She pulled me into her arms and gave me a hug. "Take care, Sister. Good luck with everything."

"Thanks for being here so early to see me off."

"Of course, babe. When you get back we should have a girls' night out, huh? Love you."

Alicia sauntered over to Jump in her skinny jeans and high-heeled boots and gave him a kiss. She gave me a final wave as she climbed into her navy blue Jeep Grand Cherokee.

"Good luck with everything, Sister." Jump gave me a quick hug. "Lock will take care of shit for you."

"Thanks for everything, Jump."

"Sure thing, sweetness."

"Later," Lock muttered, a scowl on his face. A bandana was now knotted around the neck of his tight charcoal gray henley. Over his hoodie he wore the club's thick leather riding jacket. Long, lean, dark.

I held my breath as he moved closer to me. He handed me a pair of ear plugs. "Once we hit the highway, you might need them for the wind noise."

I smirked and opened the palm of my hand to reveal my own pair.

He shook his head. "Shit, I'm an idiot." His fingers brushed the side of my face.

Oh crap, there it was again—dark, dangerous, *and gentle*.

He zipped up his jacket. "Let's roll."

I secured a bandana around my forehead to catch the perspiration that would surely come under the helmet and fit the lid Lock had given me over my head. With one hand on his shoulder, I mounted the bike.

Montana, here we come.

The trip would take almost five hours. I peered over Lock's left shoulder and took in the road being eaten up by the massive Harley. I smiled at the memory of Alicia's lecture to me on my first long bike run with Dig: *"Don't shift your weight unnecessarily on the bike. Your old man has got enough to concentrate on commanding that machine at high speed once he gets on the highway."*

Being on these roads once again after so many years away made my chest constrict at the sight of the raw, bleak landscape. A Sunday rider I'd once dated in Texas had remarked to me that the Dakotas were *"a whole lot of nothing that lasted forever."* I dumped his ass after that.

The ancient hills and rock formations dotted the now sun-filled horizon before us on the road. The wide gold and green bands of wheat and alfalfa fields side by side made me smile after all this time away. Aging grain silos stood sentinel while towering sleek wind mills churned in the company of the occasional shiny cell phone tower.

The farmland eventually gave way to rolling expanses of dry yellow brush dotted with pockets of green trees and wild grasses. A flutter went off in my chest as I took in the wide-open space that stretched out into infinity. No, it wasn't dull to me. There was profound beauty in this raw, quiet majesty.

Had I ever truly appreciated that beauty years ago?

The fresh cold air ripped around us. There was nothing like tearing through it on the back of this formidable Harley with Lock.

Once we got on 85 the wind kicked up along with our speed. I stayed close against Lock's body and held on tight. Not a chore. I sat as still as humanly possible to decrease my resistance for him, not letting the hard wind get between me and the bike or me and him. My lips curled into a smile against my helmet.

We stopped less than three hours later just over the North Dakota border to get a bite to eat and hit the bathrooms. I got off the bike, removed the helmet, and bent over to stretch out my lower back. The moment I stood up again, Lock's hand grasped the side of my face and his lips crushed mine sending me spinning.

"What was that for?" I shoved at his chest. My tongue swiped at my aching lips.

"I think you know, Grace."

I think he liked having me on the back of his bike.

It had been a very long while since I'd ridden such a long distance. Lock made it a smooth experience. He was attuned to his machine, fully concentrating on the road, relaxed but attentive. Wreck had taught his brother well, and Lock had achieved that harmony, that oneness with machine, road, and air that I always believed was rooted in a deep, compelling passion for riding, a need in your very soul. That vital feeling of wholeness and freedom had swept through me as we rode. That rush still swirled inside me right now. Of course, the effect had only intensified with that kiss and Lock's heated glare.

"I'm going to hit the ladies' room." I shoved the helmet into his hands and charged through the parking lot on shaky legs.

Within the next hour we circled the Teddy Roosevelt National Park with its dramatic Badlands terrain of jagged stone valleys and deep gorges. My heart stuttered at the vast, forbidding wilderness to the east of us. As we pushed further north on the winding trail of US 16, a sudden lightness filled me as we sped through the prettier sweeping prairies and boundless lush grasses of the Little Missouri Grasslands Park.

Once we crossed the North Dakota-Montana border towards Sidney, monstrous traffic reared its ugly head. Rigs and semis of all shapes and varieties, most of them ginormous, ruled the roads. The number of passenger cars had quadrupled over the years, effectively clogging these small country routes. Oil boom, indeed. "Man camps" and RV parks had sprouted up everywhere as temporary housing for the army of oil workers. Unfortunately, there was no sign that housing, restaurants, or retail stores had caught up with the obvious demand.

Once we entered Sidney, Lock's GPS directed us to Ray's house, which was in a very trim and tidy neighborhood. I hadn't wanted to stop and make myself glossy and presentable. I just wanted to get there, see him, say whatever I had to say, and be done with it. Oh, yeah, and convince him to get tested.

My tangle of nerves, insecurities and emotions about my father were already a ball of hot mess rumbling inside me. If I had to take a moment to change my clothes and look in the mirror to put on makeup and brush out my hair, a riot would surely set off in my already overtaxed stomach and pounding head. Then I would probably only want to bite Ray's head off or burst into tears rather than be civil and calm.

Time to get this done.

We got off the bike. I swept my hair back into a tight ponytail and swiped on some cocoa flavored lip balm, the comforting fragrance easing my frazzled nerves just a bit. Lock studied me, his arms crossed at his chest. I took in a deep breath as we made our way up the pebbled walk to the front door.

"You okay?" His hand cupped my elbow.

"Not really, but it doesn't make a difference now."

His dark gaze focussed on me. "Grace . . ."

I stopped. "Thank you for doing this. For bringing me. I ... I ..."

"Hey, take a minute." He wrapped an arm around my shoulders and pulled me in to his chest. The aroma of leather, sweat, metal, and gasoline filled my lungs, and my muscles instantly relaxed. "You sure you want to do this now? We can come back later tonight or even tomorrow morning?" His deep voice vibrated through his chest and into mine. His fingers pulled through the thick strands of my ponytail and rested on my neck.

"I need to do it now."

"All right." He released me from his embrace. "I'll be right out here, okay?"

I shook my head. "I'd like you to come inside with me. Could you do that?"

Lock's eyes softened over me. "Of course." He brushed his lips against my forehead.

My eyes took in the glossy red door with the brass knocker, and my finger pressed in on the button with "Hastings" neatly printed over it.

The door swung open.

My own hazel eyes stared back at me from behind a pair of wire-framed glasses. Ray was still trim, tall, but a mustache now covered his top lip. His chestnut hair was now streaked with silver.

Time stood still for a nanosecond. Then it rushed right back through me along with my heartbeat.

"Grace?"

"YOU'RE STILL WITH THE CLUB?" Ray's eyes flicked over Lock. Twice.

"No, I just got back to South Dakota actually."

I placed my glass of water on a coaster next to Lock's empty bottle of beer on the large wood coffee table where several hunting and fishing magazines were arranged in a neat stack. Ray's house was impressive. No faded curtains or worn rugs here like the ones he had left behind in Meager. No outdated, old fashioned furniture either. Everything in Ray's living room seemed organized, neat, clean, new.

My eyes scoured the room to search for clues about the father I no longer knew. The three of us were perched on matching navy blue twill sofas. A white entertainment unit filled the center wall, framing a large flat screen television. A number of home theatre gadgets and an extensive collection of DVDs lined the shelves. Beige wall-to-wall carpeting flooded the room with a lifeless spartan veneer. Dull navy blue drapes lined the windows, sealing out the sun and the neighbors. A tall chrome-stemmed lamp with a stiff white shade stood in the corner. Not one framed photo or personal object was visible. We might as well have been sitting in a sample room at a furniture store.

I cleared my throat and shifted forward on the edge of the sofa. "Actually, I haven't been home for sixteen years now."

"I'm sorry about what happened to you and your husband," Ray said.

"Thank you. Ruby told me you had come to the hospital."

"I had to see for myself if you were okay."

I held his tense gaze for a moment. "I wish you had stayed. At least until I had come to."

"Ruby made it clear that I wasn't welcome. Of course, she had every right to feel that way." His lips tightened into a thin line.

I took another gulp of water. "Look, I didn't come here to go over old history." I shot him a look. "I'd like to, believe me, but I've got bigger fish to fry right now. I came here because I need your help."

"My help?" His eyes crinkled. "What do you need?" His features instantly tightened as he sat up straighter. The shithead probably thought I'd come for his money.

"Ruby's married now. She has a little boy, Jake." I handed him the small creased photo of the three of them I had ready in my jacket pocket. He studied the photograph. "Alex is an engineer with a big oil corporation and Ruby's a drug dependency counselor. Jake's headed for kindergarten next year."

My throat tightened. I curled my toes in my boots, grinding them into the floor as I took in a shallow breath. "Ruby has lung cancer." His hazel eyes snapped up at me. "She's had chemo, but she needs a bone marrow transplant to have a chance. It's a long shot. A long, long shot, but we need to try. We haven't found a match yet. I'm not even a match. I should have been, though. Siblings are supposed to be the best match."

The side of Lock's formidable thigh pressed into mine, and I was grateful for it. I swallowed hard. "You're the only blood relative I know of, so I had to come find you."

My father's body went rigid. His tense gaze darted back to the photograph in his hand. "Ruby?" he said, his voice small.

"I'd like you to get tested. I have the name of a doctor here where we can have it done. It's a blood test, and maybe a swab inside your mouth. Then we see if you're a match."

Ray's jaw slackened, his eyes held mine.

"That's it. That's why I came." I gulped down more water. "The photo's for you."

The silence simmered in the room.

"Ray?" Lock said, his hand settling on my knee. The tight pressure of his fingers on me stemmed the panic that spawned inside me.

"Can you do this for Ruby?" I asked, my voice thick. "She's a mom now, Ray. She needs you. Your grandson needs you. Please? This is all we've got left." Ray's glassy eyes fell on mine. He nodded his head stiffly.

Lock and I followed Ray in his golden brown Buick Enclave to the doctor's office that Dr. Braden had contacted for me and set up an appointment. As Ray filled out his paperwork, I leaned against the wall of the crowded reception area, my hand enclosed in Lock's large, warm one.

"I really hate doctors' offices, hospitals, all of it."

"This will all be over in a few, Grace," he murmured in my hair, squeezing my hand.

The nurse motioned for my father to follow her inside.

"This is just the beginning, Lock. Just the freaking beginning."

"Grace, you've got to eat. Eat something, come on."

I poked at my grilled rib eye and mashed potato with my fork.

"You want something else, maybe?"

I shook my head at my dish.

"Swear to God, Grace, I'm going to come over there and feed you myself."

"Geez, okay!"

"Eat, baby." He leaned over the table on his forearms. "The night is young, and we have to celebrate."

"Celebrate? Celebrate what?"

"You getting your dad tested. No tap dancing, no blowups, no drama. Clean and neat. Done." He tipped his frosty mug of beer at me and drank.

"That's what you like, huh? Clean and neat, no drama?" I cut into my juicy steak and chewed on the tender, buttery meat.

"I like to get the job done with minimal fuss, if that's what you're asking." He pushed his empty dish to the side and studied me.

"Can't argue with that." I dipped another piece of grilled meat into the pool of steak sauce on my dish and put it in my mouth. I swirled my fork through the creamy mashed potato.

Lock's legs tangled with mine under the table. I blinked up at him, my mouth full of food.

"You're feeling the sting now, aren't you?" he asked. "Seeing Ray and not getting anything out of him except a soggy Q-tip and a vial of his blood?"

I swallowed my food. How did he know what I was feeling before I had even the opportunity to digest it, sort it, put a name to it?

Lock pushed out of his side of the table and slid next to me in our booth. "You did good today, Grace. You were amazing—in control, keeping it focused. You got the job done for your sister," he murmured in my ear.

"But now we're back to waiting again." I put a small forkful of mashed potato in my mouth. "All this waiting and hoping. Ruby and Alex were pleased when I talked to them before, but we all know we're just at the next level of waiting, with another process to endure, then another."

"That's usually the way."

"It stinks!" I blurted.

"Yeah, it does." His warm hand wrapped around my neck, and the banging in the pit of my tummy eased. "But that's the way of it. Of most things, not just medical shit. But what you accomplished today was huge. Huge."

His eyes loomed over me like a balm soothing my jagged nerves. I drank in their languid potion, but forced myself to return my attention to the mound of buttery mashed potatoes on my plate.

"Eat," he ordered.

I made a face at him and finished eating. I arranged my fork and knife on my dish, wiped my mouth with my napkin, and settled back against the firm upholstery next to Lock. His warm, leathery scent filled me with heat and crazy thoughts.

"Can we drink now?" I asked. Lock let out a deep laugh. He took my hand, and we got up from our table and moved to the bar.

Lock's thumb rubbed over the rim of his nearly finished glass of single malt whiskey. I averted my gaze and drained my glass, shoving aside thoughts regarding this evening's hotel accommodations. For our second round, we chose a local microbrewery beer.

"God, I love lime!"

"You love lime?" he asked.

"It's delicately sour. But there's a hint of sweet all over it pulling you back in. It's a fresh and clean kind of sweet. Lemon can be truly sour. Lemon is definitely yellow, but lime's unique green is all about the fresh—fresh air, fresh water, but with this terrific twist."

Lock only grinned at me and shook his head.

He's very cute when he's all smiley and relaxed. I squeezed my legs together and pushed up against the bar. "What is it?" I asked.

"Nothing."

I let out a laugh and shoved his shoulder. "Come on, say it."

"What?"

"Come on!"

He leaned in closer to me. "I agree with your assessment of lime."

"My assessment?"

"Yeah."

"Oh, okay."

"You don't get it."

"What don't I get?"

His fingers tipped up my chin, and his warm lips touched mine feather light. "That's how I see you, baby—fresh with a hint of sweet. Possibilities." His voice had gone low, rich, deep.

Uh oh.

I swatted his arm laughing. "Cut it out."

Lock pulled me into his arms. "That's what I got for you, sweetheart. Don't tell me to cut it out."

My heart beat raced as his sinewy strength pressed into me. I wriggled in his arms. "What are you talking about?"

He tightened his hold on me. "How I feel about you," he murmured, his ebony eyes widening over me.

"You've known me for two seconds, Lock." I turned my face and gulped down more cold beer.

"I know what I need to know, and what I know is all good." He took my beer from me and set it down on the bar. His other hand rubbed my bare waist sending sparks shooting over my skin.

How the hell did his hand get under my shirt without my noticing?

"Actually no, not just good. The best." His lips nuzzled the side of my jaw, and a shiver snaked through me. I tried to pull away from him, but it was impossible. "Babe, stop." Goosebumps shivered down my arms at the way his husky voice wrapped around the endearment. "I want you, Grace. Bad. I got you on my bike . . ."

My body stiffened. "I knew this was a mistake. That's not what this is, and you know that. You're just playing bodyguard for the club."

His fierce eyes lashed me. "I'm not *playing* anything for any-body."

"Lock—"

"Already had a taste of you. I want more," he breathed. "Tell me you don't."

His lips touched mine, and my pulse went haywire. His tongue coaxed my lips open, swept through my mouth, and took what it wanted of me. Lock made a growling noise at the back of his throat and bit my lower lip.

Screw good intentions and self-preservation.

I pressed myself into his hard chest, and this time my tongue took over the little dance inside our mouths.

"You got company, man," the bartender's voice stopped us. Lock's hand dug into my waist. My eyes darted in the direction of the bartender's sober gaze.

A Demon Seed stood on the other side of Lock. "Peg" and "VP" were patched on his colors, and a sneer was etched on his face.

"Welcome to the neighborhood."

"AM I INTERRUPTING?" One side of Peg's mouth tipped up in a smirk.

Lock raised his chin, his eyes hard.

Peg's gaze flickered over me. "This here's Little Sister?"

"Grace Quillen." I gave him a nod. Lock's grip on my waist tightened.

Peg pulled his face back and gave me a brittle smile. "Right." His hard gaze shifted to Lock. "Take care of your business?"

"Yeah, we're done. Just having a drink before we head out," Lock replied.

Peg nodded and knocked back the bourbon the bartender had set down in front of him. "Little Sister, would you mind if me and Lock had a few words? Won't be long."

My gaze darted to Lock. A muscle in his jaw pulsed, and his eyes narrowed at Peg.

"Sure, of course." Lock's arm remained tight around me. "I'm going to hit the ladies' room," I said in his ear. My hand squeezed his as I unlatched it from my waist.

"Five minutes."

A chill stole over my skin at the tension in Lock's voice. I grabbed my leather jacket and strode through the dimly lit bar. Once in the bathroom, I took care of my business, washed my hands, and smoothed back my hair with my fingers. I slipped on my jacket, swung open the door of the bathroom, and four hands dug into me in the shadowy hallway, shoving me in the opposite direction from the bar.

My body jerked in their grasp. I shrieked. "What the hell?" A sweaty hand covered my mouth.

"Shut it, bitch. We're goin' for a little ride," a scratchy voice said in my ear.

I bit the hand at my mouth, and it flew off. "Get the fuck off me!" I shoved against their iron hold. "I'm not going anywhere with you."

"Cover her fucking mouth, asshole!" another voice ordered.

I could barely see in the darkness, but I kicked my leg out towards the hulking shape in front of me. A sharp howl burst over me.

"You bitch!"

They dragged me kicking and thrashing further down the hall, out a door, and into the cool air. They packed me onto the back of a waiting bike. The bold red words "Demon Seeds" on the back of the rider's leather jacket seared my vision.

"Hang onto me or you'll fucking fall off, and we wouldn't want that now would we?" he snapped at me over his shoulder. The pipes roared to life, and we twisted out of the parking lot, one other bike on our tail. My heart ripped out of my chest.

This shit was actually happening. It didn't really surprise me, though.

I shuddered in the icy wind. My hair whipped around my face, lashing at my eyes and skin. We finally pulled off the road and headed onto a long rocky driveway full of weeds. An old rusted warehouse loomed in the distance. He cut the engine.

"Get off."

I swung off the bike. There were a number of Demon Seeds standing outside the warehouse staring at us, their bikes parked out front. It would be pointless to make a run for it.

"Take her," the voice muttered as he lit a cigarette for himself. He had "Dime" and "Sergeant at Arms" patched on his jacket. I should be impressed. They sent their official tough guy for me.

Two Seeds came forward and grabbed my arms, dragging me to the entrance of the warehouse. Dime opened the metal door, and we entered the cavernous interior, our boots shuffling over the cement. They let go of me, shoving me forward.

"Little Sister," came a rough voice. A figure stepped forward from the shadows.

Vig, the Demon Seed of my Christmas past, grinned at me. His bulky features had bulked some more over the years and his wavy brown hair was now mostly gray and held back in a messy ponytail. He sported glasses and a full beard now, but those bushy eyebrows and bulging eyes hadn't changed, nor had the beefy hands and arms. The only difference was that this time stitched on his colors was a president's patch.

"It's been a long time, pretty."

"Why are you doing this?"

Vig chuckled. "I wanted to see you, Little Sister, one on one."

"It's Mrs. Quillen. I've been a citizen since my old man got killed."

"I don't give a fuck what you call yourself. You're the One-Eyed Jack's Little Sister."

I sucked in air. "If you wanted to talk to me, why didn't you just come to the bar? Why all the drama?"

"I wanted to see you alone, look up close into those sexy eyes." He stretched out the last two words, and my skin crawled. "Can you blame me?"

"Great, you're looking at them. Can I get back to my beer now?"

He only laughed.

"Vig, I was under the impression that you had approved of my quick visit."

He gnawed on his bottom lip. "Why did you come, Sister? Answer wisely or this ain't going to go very well between us."

I shifted my weight. "I came to see my father. He lives in Sidney. Haven't seen him in over twenty years."

"Why?"

"Why what?" My eyes widened at him.

"Answer me, dammit!"

"Vig. . .you want my family saga now?" I sighed. "He took off when I was a teenager and I haven't seen the man since. I just found out where he lives."

"What's his name? Where does he live?"

"He's just my dad."

Vig took a few steps towards me. "I hate repeating myself."

"Ray Hastings on Blackmore Terrace."

"I want to make sure you and me are on the same page. You get what I'm saying?" His face was in mine. His thick fingers stroked my jaw, and my lungs constricted sharply. Vig was a bear of a man. Being mauled by him would not be pleasant. I wouldn't put anything past him when he wanted to make a point.

"Yeah, I get it," I said.

"Good. I don't want no trouble, you know. Your boys have had a tear up their ass for years since your old man hit the pavement. They couldn't get their shit together for a long time there, striking out left and right."

"Understandable, wouldn't you say?" I clenched my jaw. "Especially since Dig's killer was your nephew?"

He shrugged. "Things have been quiet a while now, but you should never underestimate a sleeping tiger. I gotta be ready for anything."

"You don't have to worry about me, Vig. You know that. You know me. I just came to see my dad. But don't you think this will piss off the One-Eyed Jacks and make things a little awkward?"

He tucked a cigarette between his lips. His eyes creased as he bent his head into his lighter and flicked it on.

"Unless, of course, you want things awkward and temperamental, right?" I asked.

Vig raised his head, exhaling a wave of smoke. His smug gaze settled on me as he held out his pack of Marlboros.

"Want one?"

I shook my head.

He took another deep drag on his cigarette. "Look, you showin' up after all this time makes me wonder. Especially after our agreement."

"Understood."

"So I'll ask you one more time. What are your intentions?" His eyes squinted at me through the haze of smoke. "Is that clear enough for you, Grace Quillen?"

"I came back home because my sister got sick. She's got lung cancer. I'm not sure if she's going to get better. I had to come, Vig."

"That's too bad. She was something else, crazy ass bitch." Vig barked out a laugh. "Nerves of steel, that one."

"My coming back has nothing to do with the club. I've had nothing to do with the club since I left."

His eyebrows shot up. "So why are you here with Lock?"

"That's just Jump being protective, looking out for me. That's all that is. Like you said, I'm their Little Sister."

He let out a rough chuckle. His fingers looped in my belt and pulled my hip into his gut. "They keeping you on a tight leash, just like Dig?"

"He was my old man, Vig."

Wreck's voice whispered in my soul: *"Expect anything and everything ahead of you on the road. Anything can happen at any time and most likely will."*

I remained utterly still, pliable, but stiff. My eyes had to be as dull as my heart thudding in my chest right now. His hand slid up my torso.

"Jake's a real cute boy. You gonna be taking care of him now that Ruby's sick?"

An icy shiver stole down my spine.

"That got your attention now, didn't it?" He took another drag on his cigarette.

"That's the only reason I'm back," I said, my voice suddenly small, but steady. "The only reason."

He dropped his butt on the floor and smashed it with his boot. "You're a good sister, aren't you? And I think I've shown my respect for that and for your deep losses all these years, haven't I?"

"Yeah, Vig, you've been a real stand up guy. But that came with a steep price, didn't it?"

He tilted his head at me. "All these years I've been watching you, listening. You been working hard, been a good girl, laying low. Ruby and her man coming to you on the holidays every year. Real sweet. But her boy, Jake. Oh, he's something, huh? Almost five years old, ain't he? Just loves that strawberry ice cream."

I remained perfectly still, but my stomach pitched, and it wasn't from the sour odor of his skin.

A cell phone rang, and he reached into his pocket. "Yeah?" His eyes bulged, his lips twisted into a sneer. "Relax, motherfucker. I just wanted to have a private chat with her, for old time's sake."

Lock.

"Don't worry, she's right here and in one piece. I know, man. . . .she's your club property. I'd like to convince her to come over to the red side, but I'd need more time to break her in the way I like 'em." Vig winked at me.

I shook my head at him.

He shoved the phone against my ear. "Say hello to your boy."

"Grace?" Lock's voice was tight, forceful.

"I'm okay."

Vig snapped his phone back. "If you shoot my boys I'm gonna have your brown ass, then I'm gonna play with your woman. And that you ain't gonna like." Vig's eyes screwed up tight while he listened to whatever curse-filled threats Lock dished out. "Cool it, she's leaving now." He tapped the screen on his phone and stuffed it back in his pocket.

"That crazy as shit half-breed motherfucker managed to get my three men down and is holding a gun on them until he gets you back. Never fails to impress me," he said, his thumb swiping at the corner of his mouth.

I glared at him, letting out a heavy exhale. He leaned in closer to me. "You're not gonna pitch a girly hissy fit with him and Jump about our time together are you? I think you know better than that. Bad idea you starting something."

I snickered. Yes, blame the woman for 'starting something.' Men like Vig never ceased to amaze me. His stubby fingers gripped my chin, and he leaned in and planted a kiss on my lips. My throat burned.

There was always a kiss to seal the deal, wasn't there?

"Nothing changes, pretty."

I only gritted my teeth and nodded.

His hand slid down to my hip and squeezed. "You give little Jake my best."

I held his stony gaze as he jerked his head at the two bikers behind me. They grabbed my upper arms once more, turned me around, and the second we got outside I gulped in the chilly evening air. Dime was on his bike waiting for me. They shoved me on the back, and he gunned the engine. I leaned into the curve as we tore out of the gravel road.

The engine vibrated through me as if I were made of hollow tin. I tilted my head up at the dark sky streaked with ghostly clouds, the cold wind beating at my skin. I knew that all my dread about returning home for a long list of reasons was utterly insignificant now in the face of Vig threatening my nephew.

Would we ever be free of this shit?

I have to make us free.

The bike suddenly took a turn off the main road. We were at the bar parking lot again. Lock stood over three men on the ground, their hands bound behind their backs, their faces swollen. Blood ran down one side of Peg's face, his lip broken. Lock had his gun on them, his jaw cemented closed. The bike slowed down, and he charged over to us, his eyes hard as stone. He trained his gun on Dime. The engine cut, and Lock pulled me off the bike and into his body, his free hand fisting in my hair, his gun remaining on Dime.

"Relax man, they just talked," said Dime.

"Fuck you! Grace, you all right? Did he touch you?"

"I'm fine." The words came out tight.

A shadow passed over Lock's eyes as they swept over me in the dimly lit parking lot. He pressed me back into his chest.

"Cut us loose, fucker!" yelled Peg from behind us.

"We're gonna follow your asses over the border and then call it a night," Dime said. Lock motioned at him with his gun, and he hopped off his bike and sprinted over to his brothers.

"Grace," Lock breathed into my neck, his hands digging into me. I took in the earthy aroma of his skin and clung to it, filled my lungs with it.

"I'm okay. Let's just go!" His hands smoothed over my shoulders, arms, over my rear, my legs, up around my hips and around my torso. "Lock?"

"They might have put a bug on you or a tracking device, fuck if I know. Did that fucker touch you? Did any of them touch you?" I bit the inside of my cheek, and my eyes strained under his hard gaze. My hands moved over everywhere Vig's hands had touched me. Nothing. Lock let out a snarl as he stood up before me. "Let's move."

He took my hand in his and tugged me over his bike. I shoved the helmet over my head and leaned into his broad, leather-covered back, my arms around him. I forced my wobbly thighs to tighten around the Harley as the engine roared to life. Within minutes the Demon Seed bikes came up next to us and behind us for the fifteen-minute ride to the North Dakota border at Fairview. I pinned my eyes on the road over Lock's shoulder.

The large green sign declaring our entrance into North Dakota loomed ahead. My chest tightened. Lock's hand gripped mine at his waist. The Demon Seeds, eerie figures against the multiple fingers of lightning cracking the black sky, made a u-turn and headed back to Montana.

We rode on in the darkness, drops of rain thudding on my helmet. Lock's body tensed under my hands. Luckily, there was an underpass up ahead, and we turned and parked under it. I dismounted, my body wavering, and he clasped my arm.

"I want to get us to a hotel in Watford City for the night. Let's get our rain gear on and head over. I don't want to stay anywhere near here. Too easy for them to find us." My weary eyes shot up at him. "They might come back and play," he continued. "I'm not taking any chances."

Lock turned and unlocked the compartment on the bike where he stashed our rain gear. He was all efficiency, planning, all for me. I couldn't breathe anymore, everything felt tight, constricted. I unsnapped the top button of my leather jacket, and the cool air whistled against the burning skin of my throat and chest.

My gaze was transfixed on the jagged lightning bolts cracking through the immense, thick, billowing swirls of cloud. A tremendous supercell filled the vast dark sky like an ominous alien spaceship, a convection of rotating clouds. I had forgotten what it was to witness this thrilling, forbidding display over the Great Plains.

"Grace?"

How could I have forgotten this?

Lock's hands gripped the sides of my face. His eyes smoldered in the half-light. My need for him detonated right through me and took away every thought, every rationale, every excuse, every shred of modesty. I opened my mouth to speak. To say what? I was numb, still that hollow tin creature, but now about to splinter.

Lock pulled me into his chest, his lips burning against my cold, damp forehead. He pushed me against the hard concrete wall, and I inhaled his leathery gasoline scent as if it offered salvation. His body pressed against mine, and I let out a groan. The pounding rain shimmered on the concrete. The lights from the passing cars on the highway illuminated the harsh angles of his face in flashes.

"Baby." His hands wrapped around my neck, his lips moving against mine, the tenderness in his voice shattering.

I surged up on my toes and kissed him. His one hand shoved underneath my jacket, searing my bare skin. A truck roared over us on the highway, the concrete pylons vibrated and thundered. Lock's arms tightened around me.

"Grace," tumbled from his lips. It sounded like he was pleading, asking for mercy.

So was I.

ELEVEN

"LOCK, IT'S NOT YOUR FAULT."

He pushed open the door to our room in the upscale hotel in Watford City he had checked us into. He still wouldn't look at me. His face set in stone, Lock threw our bags on the floor and switched on the light. My eyes strained in the brightness. A massive wood headboard towered over a king-sized bed, which beckoned to me immediately. Huge cornflower blue and oatmeal colored pillows lined the coppery brown bedspread. A flatscreen television propped on a dresser faced opposite, and a small kitchen was at the end of the room. I let out a heavy exhale. This was an unexpected and most welcome oasis of luxury.

He peeled my wet rain gear off me. "Take a shower, Grace."

I nodded and headed for the bathroom where I stripped off the rest of my clothes, got into the large shower stall, sliding the glass door shut. I stood motionless and stared at the rows of beige tile as if they would direct me what to do next. My hand reached out and turned the large chrome handle of the faucet. The jumbo shower head above me released a thousand prickles of hot, steamy water over my weary body, the stinging heat melting the tension in my aching joints. I smoothed the small rectangle of soap over my skin and with a face towel rubbed every inch of myself. I rubbed hard and swallowed down the sour bile rising in my throat.

Vig didn't like me being back home again and being with the club. He knew all about Jake. I hadn't seen Vig in all these sixteen years. And in all that time there hadn't been any bumps on that crazy road that I had agreed to travel. Should I be grateful?

I squirted shampoo into my hands and worked it through my scalp and all through my mass of wet, thick hair.

Did I say grateful?

Years of lying low, moving on, rolling on. I had done everything Vig had asked me to do. Time and time again. Now it was time for it stop. It had to stop. Sixteen years ago I couldn't protect my unborn baby, but now I could protect my nephew.

I said grateful, didn't I?

Laughter erupted in my throat and made its way out of my mouth. I buckled under the water raining down on me. My laughter drained into deep choking sobs as my head thudded against the glass shower stall door.

"Grace?"

The shower door gave way, and Lock's arms came around my middle. He held me close, his eyes taking me in, and I only wanted to drown in them. He gently drew my head back onto his chest, his soaked henley and jeans now sticking to my naked body.

"It's okay, babe. It's over."

If only.

My body shook, and he held me securely. His other hand smoothed my hair back. I buried my face in the sopping wet fabric of his shirt, the water cascading over both of us.

"I'm here," he said. "I'm right here. I got you." I sank into his chest. His one hand slid down my back to my rear and rubbed my bare flesh, settling on my lower back. "Baby, this is all my fault."

"No, don't say that. Not true," I said into his wet shirt.

This is all me. This is a mess that only I can clean up.

I don't know how long we stood there under the shower together. Eventually Lock reached over and shut off the water. With a large towel he mopped my face and rubbed my hair. I stood still as he dried my body, then pinned the towel around me. He ripped off his wet clothes and took a quick shower himself. I waited for him mutely as he dried himself off. He took my hand and led me out of the bathroom.

He tossed the decorative pillows on the floor, peeled back the bedspread, stripped both of us of our damp towels, and we got into the bed together naked. We lay there in silence, Lock's cool, smooth body wrapped around mine. I sank into him and quickly drifted off to sleep.

A commercial for a pizza chain droned in my ears. My lips brushed against a firm wall of warmth. My eyes unglued.

"Sorry, did the TV wake you?" Lock's rough voice asked.

"What time is it?"

"Just after midnight."

"Did you get any sleep?" I asked.

"No."

My eyes drifted to the TV screen. Pepperoni and extra cheese. "Are you hungry?" I asked.

"I could eat. There's a fridge freezer thing in here with all kinds of food."

"I'll check it out."

Frankly, I was more than happy to get myself un-naked and out of the bed. I got up and donned one of Lock's huge T-shirts from his duffle that lay open by my side of the bed. I tossed him a pair of his boxer briefs, and he grinned at me. I unzipped my bag that was still by the door and grabbed a pair of panties to put on.

The fridge was indeed full of treats. I microwaved a frozen pizza and set a large towel on the bed as a tablecloth. We ate and drank beer while we watched the news on TV, then cleaned up.

Lock settled against the headboard, and I sat down next to him, but he pulled me into his embrace, wedging my body between his legs. I leaned back against his broad chest. A survival documentary began on the Discovery Channel, but he clicked off the TV, tossing the remote to the side.

"I was supposed to protect you from this shit. I should've seen it coming," he said, his voice gravelly. "We're together, we don't separate."

I put a hand on his thigh and squeezed. "I think this conversation needs booze." I got out of the bed and went to the minibar, returning with a selection of tiny bottles.

Lock released a heavy sigh. "They got balls to make a move like that. Jump is gonna flip."

"It's Vig. We go back. You know, Dig and I started up when he saved my foolish ass from Vig at a club party I shouldn't have even been at. They had words. It wasn't good. It just made an already tense relationship between them worse. And that crap lasted over the years, tainting every confrontation they ever had."

"He was involved with Ruby's set up, wasn't he?"

"Yes, and how that went down had pissed him off to begin with. The Seeds lost out on some big drug deal, but Ruby saved everyone's ass by going to jail. He didn't care so much. Me being her sister, made the whole situation more sour. Lock, please, this is all Vig. It's not on you."

"If anything had happened to you . . ."

"It didn't. He just wanted to mess with us, as usual."

I crawled over the bed and leaned forward to reach Lock's packet of cigarettes that had tumbled to the edge of the mattress.

"Grace, what's this tattoo?"

"Hmm?" I leaned my head over my shoulder. My black panty had ridden up my rear, and his fingers traced over the ink on my bare cheek.

"It's my wildflower."

"The blue flax?"

My eyes went round. "You recognize it?"

"Impressed?"

"Yeah," I said softly. "I am."

"My grandmother and her friends knew all the wildflowers that grew around the reservation. They'd drag me on hikes early in the morning to collect a whole variety of plants and herbs." His finger tickled over my flesh. "I like it," he murmured.

"Wildflower was one of Dig's nicknames for me."

His hand swept over my hip, and he pulled me back in against his chest. I handed him the pack of smokes. He took one out and lit it with his chrome Zippo, then dropped the lighter back on the nightstand next to his gun. He inhaled deeply, his finger tracing over the scar on my right thigh. My eyes went to the nightstand where the stainless steel finish of his Colt 1911 glinted at me under the lamplight.

Lock exhaled a stream of smoke and put his cigarette between my lips. I took a drag as his mouth nuzzled my shoulder. He shifted and tapped the ash into a glass filled with water on the table. We sat in silence for a while.

My fingers drew a circular pattern on his knee. "That moment on their bike, heading into the unknown. . .I don't think I've felt that kind of fear since the attack. Wreck and Dig had prepped me for moments like that."

He put his cigarette to my lips once more, and I inhaled. I leaned my head against his chest and exhaled the smoke. "I actually felt relieved once I saw Vig." I let out a slight laugh.

Lock's hand tightened on my arm. "I can handle fear."

I glanced up at him. "You must be old friends with that feeling, right? The army, the club..."

"It's the helplessness I can't deal with. That's not an option for me. When I realized they had you, and I didn't know where you were, what they were doing to you." He exhaled a thick plume of smoke and dropped his cigarette into the glass. The butt hissed in the water. "I should've seen that coming."

My head sank against his shoulder. "Helplessness is the worst. Seeing Dig crushed under his bike. All that twisted metal and there was nothing I could do."

Lock's hand wrapped around my throat. "Don't. Not now. You keep that. I can't hear it now."

I tilted my head up and pressed my lips against the side of his face. "Okay." We held each other's gaze, and heat stabbed my insides.

"Kiss me, Grace," he whispered.

I kissed him gently relishing the ashy taste of his mouth, his full lips. My fingers dug through his closely cropped black hair.

I grinned. "I liked your long hair in high school."

"Yeah?" His eyes glittered over mine. "It was down to my shoulders, like a good res Indian."

"Don't talk like that." I turned in his arms and kissed the corner of his mouth, then the side of his nose over his scar. "It's part of who you are." He said nothing, only brushed away strands of my hair from my face and shoulders. "It's true," I said, kissing him again.

He bit my lip, and I gasped, crushing my mouth into his. I pulled myself up and straddled him, and he tore the T-shirt off me and threw it to the side. Lips and tongues explored and sucked on skin, curves, flesh. I was under his spell.

"I want to see that one day," I said in between short breaths. His large hands kneaded my breasts, his thumbs stroking my nipples.

"See what?" His hips flexed against mine. The friction he created between us ignited my insides.

"You with long, black hair. You. . .connected again."

Lock cursed under his breath and took a nipple in his mouth like a hungry man, sucking on my breast. I cried out at the stinging rush of pleasure, my back arching. His cock stiffened against my thigh, and I reached down and stroked him over his briefs. He let out a heavy breath, his hips jerking up. My entire being ached with need for his body, for him.

"Babe," he breathed. "You want this? Don't do this if . . ."

"I want this. I want you."

He stripped off his boxer briefs, and I sat up and tore off my panties. He held my hips and kept me on my knees facing him. Two of his fingers hooked inside me gently coaxing me to life while his thumb swirled over my clit. His tongue eagerly teased one of my nipples. I grabbed onto his shoulders and licked my lips, moaning softly. He slid his wet fingers out of me, and my entire body wobbled and shuddered.

"Take me in, baby," he breathed.

I settled over him, tucking him into my entrance, taking his thick cock in slowly, that exquisite shiver shimmering through me. A sob escaped my lips.

His eyelids sank, and he hissed in air. "Oh, fuck. . .Grace . . ." His head rolled back against the headboard.

He filled me tightly, perfectly. Waves of sensation flooded my entire being. "Lock, you feel so good."

Suddenly his hands clamped down on my hips and halted my movements. "Shit. Hang on," he said, his voice strained. My hands dug into the taut muscles between his shoulders and neck. "Grace, I want you to know I'm clean, I got tested the other day, and I haven't been with anybody since you walked into the clubhouse. I've got condoms in my bag."

My hands smoothed over the sides of his face. "We don't need a condom."

His eyes searched mine. "You on the pill?"

I shook my head. "I can't have kids. They had to cut me up after I lost the baby. They took most of it."

He let out an exhale, his hands digging into my flesh, his ebony eyes spilling with tenderness.

"Shh." I brushed his mouth with my lips, and my fingers smoothed over the eagle's wing that rose up his shoulder and neck. I raised myself up once more and lowered myself slowly, taking him in again. I rocked my hips over him needing him as deep as possible, a cry escaping me. A mess of quivering sensations rioted through me as my body adjusted to his demanding thickness, his hot hands searing down the skin of my back, curving around my rear, keeping me close. He watched me, his lips parted, the two of us moving together, needing each other.

"You're beautiful, you know that?" I murmured. "So beau—"

His mouth slammed over mine, and I lost myself in him, spiraling, whirling. All that mattered was the rasp of his tongue against mine, his hard, fantastic length filling me without barriers, him driving inside me. I clutched the top of the headboard and moved over him faster, meeting his every thrust.

"Grace." Lock's voice was rough. His fingers bit into my flesh.

I groaned. "So good. Oh, God—" I embraced him and slid his earring between my lips sucking on his flesh, sinking my face into the heat of his neck.

A growl escaped his throat. "That's what I want," he said against my skin. "Want you to feel good."

There he was, giving himself to me. This man was always giving to me, always considering me.

My lips brushed across his temple. "I do," I breathed. "You do this to me. You make me feel good." A storm of urgency overwhelmed me. My throbbing pulse soared, wound its way around us, pressing us together.

His fingers fisted in my hair tugging my head back. The silver in his dark eyes burned through mine.

"You're doing me in," he rasped.

His teeth nipped at my throat as his hand went between us, his fingers flicking over my clit. I flew hard plummeting through the air. My hands slid over the rippling muscles of his shoulders, my limbs utterly weightless.

Holy crap, what the hell was this?

Such a sharp, hard response had become rare for me. I had spent sixteen years mostly fumbling and taking care of my own business even when I was with men, many of whom only put effort into their own performance, assuming I enjoyed their presentation. Lock, however, was focused on what we were doing together. He wanted me there with him, and I definitely wanted to be there too.

I didn't want this to end. I was greedy for Lock. Very greedy.

My arms pressed around him. I wanted to give him what he needed. "Don't stop. You take whatever you want, however you want it."

Lock yanked me down underneath him, pulled my legs up high, and ground into me. A groan roared deep in his chest. His jaw slackened as he hammered into my hungry body.

"Grace . . ."

TWELE

"YOU OKAY? You haven't said much since you got back."

I shrugged my shoulders. "I'm fine."

"Fine?" Ruby's eyes narrowed. "How I hate that word."

I continued to stare out the window crossing my arms across my chest. "I'm going to need the key."

"What key?"

"The key, Ruby."

"Oh. Okay. Right. Anything wrong?"

"Nope."

Ruby pulled the oxygen mask off her face. "What happened in Montana, Grace? Other than the happy father-daughter reunion?"

"Nothing."

"You slept with Lock, didn't you?"

I didn't answer.

She grinned at me. "Was it good?"

"Rube—"

"I don't need details. That's not what I mean, stupid. I mean, was it good for you?" She drew a deep breath from the oxygen mask. "I know there hasn't been anyone in your life for a while. Which is all your fault, of course, but that's another discussion. Now you're thrown together with a badass hottie from the One-Eyed Jacks." She reached out and squeezed my hand. "I just hope he blew your panties off—that's what I meant before—because you deserve to have your panties blown off."

I smirked. "I deserve the proverbial 'good time' from a 'hottie'?"

"You deserve way more than that. You deserve the whole enchilada, but that, too, is another conversation." Ruby rolled her head to the side and took in a gulp of air. "So first things first."

"Like what?"

"Tell me." Ruby let out a wheezing sound.

I told her everything from the very beginning. Except for the Demon Seeds abduction. She didn't need to hear about that.

"So what's the problem?" Ruby's eyes narrowed over me. Her arm went over her forehead as she settled back onto her pillows.

"There's no problem."

"Grace, how did the two of you leave it?"

That was just it. Lock and I didn't really leave it anyway at all.

At the hotel the morning after, Lock had woken up first. Already showered and dressed, he'd brushed my lips with a quick kiss and headed out the door to check us out and pay the bill for the room. While he'd been gone I'd taken a shower and gotten dressed. I'd put our wet clothing from the night before into plastic bags and packed up my small duffel bag.

A grin had curled the edges of my lips as I swiped my lashes with mascara. My girly parts were sore, and I actually liked it. He'd woken me up in the middle of the night with his mouth between my legs, his tongue exploring secret hollows, whispering precious, raw intimacies against my skin. We'd gone a couple more delicious rounds, one very energetic and creative, the other slow and sweet. The intense ache Lock had left behind each time burned through me still; satisfaction laced with fervent craving.

The door had opened, and his large frame had filled the entrance. He'd put a protein bar on the dresser in front of me along with a tall insulated cardboard cup filled with freshly brewed coffee. He'd taken a swallow from his and glanced at the bags.

"You ready?"

My gaze had darted up at him, and he'd quickly averted his eyes. His voice was clipped, his mouth downturned. I'd tightened the cover of the tube of mascara and shoved it in my bag.

"We'll make a stop for an early lunch before we cross into South Dakota," he'd said. "That okay?"

"Sure."

Suddenly, he'd been in a rush. He'd scooped up our bags from the floor and had held the door open for me. I'd tucked the protein bar in my jacket pocket and picked up the helmets and my coffee cup.

"Lock?"

"We should get moving." He'd pulled the door shut behind us, and my heart had thudded in my chest at the sound of the slam.

Great. Welcome to Lock Down City.

Over two hours later we'd stopped at a burger joint in Bowman. Lock had wolfed down two huge burgers. A half-eaten grilled chicken sandwich had stared up at me from my dish. He'd been very quiet the entire meal. In fact, he'd barely looked me in the eye. When he'd spoken, it was in a flat voice, his responses terse and short. I'd flagged the waitress and ordered a hot tea to settle my rioting stomach.

Had he regretted last night?

Is it something else? Maybe it's something I've said, and now, after he's chewed on it, he's reconsidered being with me?

I'd wiped a smear of mustard from my thumb with my napkin and glanced up at him. He'd seemed overly intent on his food. I'd wanted to make conversation, say something, anything.

"You grew up on the Pine Ridge Reservation, right? That's where Wreck had tracked you down?" I'd asked from behind my steaming mug of tea.

His eyes had scrunched at me. "Yeah." His tone had been almost suspicious.

"I wasn't sure if it was Rosebud or Pine Ridge."

His dark eyes had darted up at me from his dish. "Pine Ridge. My dad is Lakota Sioux."

"What's your last name?"

"Why?"

"I don't know it, and I think Native American names are interesting. They tell a story."

"Miller Flies As Eagles."

"Really?"

"Really. My dad didn't use it when he was rodeoing though. Too exotic for him, wanted to fit in better. He used his mother's maiden name, LeBeau."

"Does your eagle tattoo have to do with him?"

"Hell, no." Lock had shaken his head, wiping his mouth with the paper napkin, then tossing it on the table. "My father took me from my mother because I was a boy. My mother didn't have much interest in me anyway, and she didn't have much money either. She already had Wreck, and he was twelve years old when I was born. She wasn't thrilled about the whole diaper and bottles thing all over again. Cindy was a rodeo groupie, and a baby would've cramped her style, so she let him take me. Guess she should have invested in better contraception, huh?"

I'd bitten my lip and stared at him as he'd chomped on a french fry.

"My father was barely around the res, though. Always on the circuit. And when he was home he was miserable, didn't know

151

what to do with himself, let alone with me. His mother, my grandmother Kim, is the one who took care of me. You'll like this, Grace. Her name was Kimimela. . .Butterfly."

My legs had stiffened under the table. That was one of the most beautiful things I'd ever heard. "Butterfly Flies As Eagles?"

He'd taken a swig of coffee. "Yeah. That was my Gran. Gentle and beautiful as a butterfly, but fierce and proud as an eagle. She taught me more about being a Lakota man than my father ever did. When she died, it all went to shit. The tat's for her." His eyes had flared at me. "And it's for Wreck, too. He was real proud of being a vet, very patriotic, had lots of flags and—"

"—and had eagles all over his house and the shed." I'd smiled at the memory. "You painted a lot of them before you went into the army, didn't you?"

He'd blinked up at me. "Yeah, I did."

"It's a gift, what you have, to draw like that, paint that way. It's very special."

He'd snorted. "Special? Grace, I've been passed around most of my life, gotten bits and pieces here and there. The only special I've ever known came from my Gran and Wreck."

"What happened to your parents?"

"Dad stayed on the res after his big career came to a finish, had a few odd jobs here and there, but mostly devoted himself to alcohol. I haven't seen him or heard from him. Wreck had found out that our mother had landed some rodeo organizer and ended up in Oklahoma with a few more kids and a nice house. Everyone blond and blue-eyed. Don't think I would have fit in with that American dream, do you?"

"You never . . .?"

His eyes had tightened. "What for?"

"She's never tried contacting you?"

He'd only shook his head at me and went back to the last of his fries.

I'd squirmed in the hard wood chair. "The eagle is a very special symbol isn't it? He's considered the spiritual link between heaven and earth, the carrier of prayers? A connection with the Great Spirit, a symbol of higher truth, honor, and bravery, right?"

Lock's opaque eyes had slid back to mine. "Very good, Mrs. Quillen." He'd wiped his hands on his napkin then crushed it in his fist.

"I paid attention in school, Mr. Flies As Eagles. It's a little unusual though, your eagle. Is there a reason his wings are spread out like that, one pointing up and the other down?"

His eyes had glinted at me, as he'd taken in air through his nostrils. His one hand had pushed against the table as he'd pressed back into his chair.

Is he bracing? Maybe he's never shared this before? Maybe I should shut up already?

"One wing points up for my Gran because she taught me how to fly. The other wing points to the ground for Wreck because he gave me a second chance at life after all my dad's shit. Wreck's the one who taught me to let go and ride free over the earth."

I'd wanted to lunge at Lock across the table over our greasy, crumb-filled dishes, wrap him in my arms and kiss the base of his throat where the tip of the eagle's wing pointed up to the sky. Suddenly, I was desperate to taste his skin on my tongue and hold him tight.

But I didn't moved, didn't breathe. His large espresso eyes had held mine and the world fell away. A delicate stillness had shimmered between us through the clatter of dishes, the ding of the cash register, and the raised voices and laughter from the recesses of the kitchen.

Our waitress had appeared out of nowhere and smacked the bill on the table. I flinched. "There you go. Have a good one!" She charged past.

Lock had torn his eyes from mine, his hand covering the bill, crumpling it. He'd taken out his chained wallet and threw several singles on the table for a tip, and, without a word, strode towards the cashier. My heart shrunk. I'd swallowed down the lukewarm tea to drown my disappointment.

The ride home straight down Route 85 had been uneventful and smooth. I'd concentrated on the rhythmic, vibrating chant of the engine and the flat grassy prairie that had rushed by us. My breath had caught at the sight of wheat fields billowing in the wind looking more like waves on a golden ocean.

Over two hours later we'd entered Meager and arrived at the club. Lock had parked his Harley in front of the shed where Boner had been crouched on the side of a chopper. He'd dropped his wrench on the ground, wiped his hands on a dirty rag as he smiled at me.

"Hey, baby. Everything go all right with Big Daddy?" Boner had taken the helmet from my hands.

"It was okay. We talked. He got tested. We just have to wait and see now."

Lock had busied himself over his bike. He'd marched to my car, put my small duffel bag on the ground, muttering "Later, Grace" at me and had strode off towards the clubhouse lighting a cigarette.

"What's up his ass?" asked Boner.

I'd pressed my lips together and shrugged my shoulders. "It's been a long day. He's tired."

"Yeah right, having you on the back of my bike for two days would be real tiring," Boner had said. "For fuck's sake!"

I'd forced a grin across my lips. "You ought to know, Boner. You babysat me plenty of times." I'd brushed my lips against his stubbly cheek, and he'd wrapped an arm around me and squeezed tight.

"Love you, Sister."

"Me too, hon. Big time." I'd planted a quick kiss on his lips and let go of him. "Gotta get to Ruby. Fill her in."

"All right. I'm gonna swing by the hospital for a visit, but you keep in touch, yeah? Or I'm going to come find you, and it'll be ugly." He'd swatted my ass, and I'd scowled at him over my shoulder. He'd blown me a kiss, and I'd blown one back.

I'd gotten in my Land Cruiser and started her up, my P!nk CD blaring over the speakers. Thank God for P!nk. I'd swerved out of the lot, taking off.

My mind had been tranquilized from the long ride, but my muscles still ached, and my Lock hangover showed no signs of wearing off anytime soon, on my body or in my brain.

"You like him, don't you?" Ruby's voice broke through my replay of this morning's events. I only gave her a blank look. I really didn't want to dissect this right now. "You want to see him again?" Ruby's eyes lit up. "Get back in his bed?"

I sighed. "Yeah, Rube, I like him."

"Why is that so hard to admit?"

I shook my head. "Things got emotional between us somewhere along the line. I don't know exactly."

"Emotional?"

"What I mean is we seemed to know how to reach out to each other. We understood each other. I felt . . ." My one hand gestured in the air.

"You felt something you haven't felt since Dig?"

My forehead knit together. "That sort of intensity, yeah. There was something raw there all knotted up with . . ."

"His big, beautiful dick?"

"Ruby!"

"Or . . ." Ruby's eyes flew open. "His pecs?"

"Oh, for Pete's sake. Will you stop talking like a teenager?"

"It's annoying isn't it?" She grinned at me and sucked in oxygen from her mask. "Come on, tell me about his pecs."

I threw myself on the edge of her bed, and we both laughed.

"He does have a perfect chest," I said. "Not overly bulky. It's lean, defined, and just. . .perfect." I curled up next to her, and we both shook with laughter.

I had missed this with Ruby. We always gabbed on the phone regularly, but there was nothing like being together, like this. Only I would have preferred her not being attached to an oxygen tank in a hospital bed.

"So where's the problem?" Ruby asked.

"From the beginning I've been the one keeping him at a distance. The last thing I need now is to get involved with a member of the One-Eyed Jacks." I rolled on my back and rubbed at my eyes. "But this trip opened up something in the both of us, and just as I started feeling comfortable with him and with these feelings, he pulled back. He couldn't look me in the eye this morning except for the strained conversation over lunch. Then when we got to the club, he barely said goodbye. He just walked off. It was cold."

"He got that nickname for a reason," Ruby said.

I chewed on my lip. "Maybe the real me just doesn't add up for him."

"You want to translate that for me? Before I smack you upside the head?"

"Ruby, he told me himself. He's been fantasizing about 'Little Sister' for years. He heard stories about me from Wreck, from the guys. He's seen the photos of me and Dig on the walls of the clubhouse. I'm this idea in his head and, no matter what, maybe I'll always be someone else's old lady to him."

"Dig is dead and buried, Grace."

"I know that. But now that Lock's had me, maybe I just don't live up to the ideal or the fantasy he's had in his head. In the harsh light of day, maybe he realized he's just not that into me, as they say. Could be as simple as that, you know." I let out a heavy sigh. "Come on, Rube, a guy like that is better off screwing the hot young things that are always chasing after him around the club anyway. How about that?"

Ruby stared at me from behind her oxygen mask. She tugged it off her face. "Once again, honey, you are overthinking things. If he wasn't interested, he wouldn't have insisted on taking you to Montana, and he certainly wouldn't have been panting for seconds after his first taste. And from what you've described, he was pretty damned enthusiastic about you between the sheets."

"Exactly. Between the sheets, yes."

"Okay, so he's just another asshole biker. Big surprise."

My stomach tightened. "No, I don't think so, he's . . ."

Ruby smirked at me. "And there we have it."

"Bitch."

"Oh yeah. You like him. A lot," Ruby said. "And by the way, what he said to you at the clubhouse, that was frigging poetic."

I shook my head at her. "He was just freaked out that night. He got carried away when he said all that. That's it."

"I had my dream on my hands and in my mouth, and I never fucking realized."

I gnawed at the inside of my cheek. That heat flared through me again, but this time the soreness only stung.

"Now he's stepping back," I murmured.

"What about what he said to you at Erica's? Insisting that you two were happening?"

I made a face, shrugging my shoulders.

"Stop it, Grace!"

"What? Don't actions speak louder than words?"

"Did you ever think maybe he's putting the brakes on in the harsh light of day not because he's feeling too little, but because he's feeling too much? Maybe what he feels for you is really intense, and that's new for him."

"Maybe."

"That's always a lot for a guy to deal with. And for a guy like Miller, who has nothing except his bikes and the club, who has always kept things tight in order to survive, it's probably a hell of a lot. It means change and letting go. And then letting someone else *in*. That's a big deal for anyone. It happens to be a big deal for you too."

I bit the edge of my thumb. Ruby slapped my hand from my mouth.

"No witty, clever comeback?" she asked.

"Nope."

"You want more with him Grace, you should explore it."

"That's just it, though," I said sweeping my hair from my face. "I don't think I'm capable of more. So his pulling back is just as well."

"Oh please. Have you tried? Since Dig, really tried, ever?"

"You know the answer to that."

"Yes, I do," said Ruby. "The answer is a big fat no. So here's a better question: Did you ever want to *this* badly?" She held my gaze. I didn't answer. Ruby leaned her head on mine. "It's okay to like him, you know. It's a good thing, Grace."

I blinked up at her. "Is it? I haven't done the real relationship thing at all since Dig. I just can't. And from what Alicia told me, he's barely done it himself."

"Okay. Humor me here. For the sake of this conversation, forget the cringeworthy words "relationship" and "commitment.""

I rolled my eyes at her.

"Grace, listen." Ruby took hold of my hand and squeezed. "Do you want to live something rich and whole with one other man? Do you want to give to him and accept what he has to give you and create something new together? Something special, exciting and safe, just for the two of you? Wouldn't you like to do that with Lock? From what you said, you two obviously have the chemistry for it."

"We certainly have chemistry."

"It's not hard when it's the right person, honey." Ruby rubbed my fingers and grinned. "In fact, it's a delight."

"You think I don't remember what it can be like?"

"Do you? Don't you want it again? You can. But you have to choose it, Grace. Have the goddamn balls to say yes to it. We make our own choices in this life. And by the way, the choices our parents made have nothing to do with us. You understand that, right?"

I turned my face away from her and swallowed.

She nudged my arm. "It's never too late. You know, it wasn't easy with Alex, but it was so right. We managed, and it was worth it." She seized my hand. Her breath hitched in her throat and her eyes filled with water.

"Ruby what is it?"

"Don't let this sink Alex," she whispered.

"Stop. Don't talk like that."

"I'm being a realist." Her chest struggled for air.

"I'll kick his ass."

She grinned weakly. "I made him promise to kick yours too."

"Of course you did."

She cleared her throat. "Think about it, Grace. Actually, no, don't think too hard about it. Just dive in. It's been too long. You're a sensible forty-something now. Although, shit, you've always been this sensible, just not so fucking uptight." Ruby let out a hoarse laugh.

"I'm not uptight."

"For God's sake, you used to be this hot biker chick. My sweet little sister, the scary biker's old lady. And I ended up marrying the clean, upstanding white collar citizen with two college degrees. Who would have thought? Oh, you definitely had Mom rolling in her grave for years!"

I snatched the small tissue box from her side table and flung it at her. She tossed it back at me, the both of us laughing.

"Grace, you want real, you got to get real. And don't tell me you don't want real. You've always been about the real. It took me a long while to catch up with you."

"Aw, after everything I've put up with from you. I'm really touched." I tucked the box of tissues at her side.

She grinned at me. "It's good to see you so hot and bothered about a man. Finally! There's only so much mediocre fucking a woman should tolerate in her lifetime." Her eyes held mine. "Hang on to Lock, Grace. Try."

Years of mediocrity and making do ended that night for me at Dead Ringer's when I'd looked up from my whiskey and set eyes on a dark-eyed, enigmatic man.

"I'm *not* hot and bothered," I said.

"You sure as shit are!"

"Shut up."

Ruby rolled her eyes at me. "Enough about you, bitch. What are you cooking for dinner for my husband and son?"

"Black bean soup, your highness."

Ruby snorted. "Oh, Grace, they're gonna love that."

"You bet your bony ass they will."

She threw the tissue box at me again.

THIRTEEN

"LOCKDOWN?"

"Just for you, Little Sister." Jump stuck the toothpick back between his teeth.

"What do you mean just for me?"

"You're on Demon Seed radar, woman. Got to keep you safe after that shit Vig pulled. I ain't taking any chances. You're staying here at the club where we can keep an eye on you 24/7."

My mother was right. History does repeat itself.

"For how long? A couple of days, a week?"

"We gotta see how this is gonna play out."

"I can't do that, Jump!"

"Club voted on it this morning, Sister. Unanimous. You're in, starting right now."

Shit, they'd had an emergency meeting on my account?

"Jump, I got Ruby in the hospital in Rapid."

"I know that."

"And Jake." My voice got sharper along with my pulse. "Alex is going on a business trip for four days, and I've got Jake. I can't—"

Jump's brow twisted. "Bring him with you!"

"Are you joking?"

"Grace!" Alicia said.

I slumped in the easy chair in Jump's office. Ruby was going to love this. Not to mention Alex.

"Jump, it means a lot to me that the club has my back. But the thought of my nephew being in any danger. . ."

"That's the fucking point!" Jump leaned over his desk, his massive hands planted in piles of papers, bills and bike magazines. His long braid of gray-black hair slipped over his shoulder.

"This is to keep both of you safe, Sister," Alicia said, touching my arm. "Look, we've been planning that bone marrow donor drive in Meager, right?"

I exhaled. "Yeah, that's the other thing."

"You're all set up already, right?" Jump asked. "You've got all the women helping. They can take care of the final legwork in town and at the hospital for you. Alicia's got it. Right, baby?"

"Of course I do. I told you, we do a lot of fundraisers ever since you started the first one years ago. We've got this, Sister."

"You got phone, fax, and internet access here," Jump said. "The women will keep an eye on the kid whenever you need, there are even a few kids around Jake's age. Alicia's already got a room set up for you." Jump frowned at me again. "Look, Sister, you told me yourself Ruby's old man is always working and getting home late. Now you're telling me he's going out of town. You wanna be in that house in Rapid, where you don't know anybody, with the boy, on your own?"

He had a point.

"Okay."

But I didn't like it.

I would be stuck at the clubhouse for many days and nights within spitting distance of Lock. Going out of my mind distance. A Lock whom I hadn't seen or heard from in the day and a half since we'd been back from Montana. It was over, for whatever reason. But this lockdown would be rubbing salt in that wound. For me, at least.

I dragged a hand across my forehead.

"Now what?" Jump asked.

I crossed my arms and shook my head. "Nothing."

"You bitches never cease to amaze me."

I rolled my eyes at him.

Alicia laughed and wrapped an arm around her old man's shoulders. "And that's the way you like it, baby."

Jump raised his chin. "I'll have Dawes drive you to Ruby's house. You get packed, get the kid, and we're good. Now get moving."

"It'll be great, sweetie. You'll see." Alicia smiled at me. "We'll have fun."

"This is so cool, Aunt Grace!" Jake let out another whoop and jumped on the queen size bed in the club guest room as if it were a trampoline.

Jake's miniature jeans, sweatpants, sweatshirts, undies, socks, and pajamas were all stacked next to my shirts, jeans, socks, bras, and panties. I folded the last of his tiny T-shirts, sandwiched them in the drawer, and slammed it closed. The over-painted pine dresser shuddered.

This was real. I was living back at the club.

At least I had Jake to keep me occupied and the Bone Marrow Drive to keep me busy. Super busy. I would make sure of it.

Surprisingly, Ruby and Alex didn't have a problem with our staying at the club, especially with Alex going out of town.

"What are you not telling me?" Ruby had asked.

"It's just a precaution. My being back in town has made a few people uncomfortable."

"Like who?"

"Vig, who is now president of the Demon Seeds, by the way."

"Goddammit! Did he try something?"

"No. We ran into each other in Montana that's all."

"Why didn't you say anything? What the hell is going on, Grace?"

"It was no big deal, Rube. But Jump doesn't want to take any chances."

My sister's eyes had narrowed over me. She'd reached up and pulled me down in a hug. There had been no lecture, no sweeping analysis of events. Just a hug. "I'm sorry this shit is still hanging over you after all this time," she'd murmured.

"I've got it."

"That's what I'm afraid of." She'd released me and opened her small cosmetic bag on her table. She'd handed me a tiny red cardboard envelope. Ruby had studied me as I'd snapped it open and laid eyes on the safety deposit box key for the first time. The little brass key that I would use to clear our pasts and our future. Not to mention my rather screwed-up present.

I wouldn't let any hell from my past touch Jake. Ever.

I'd snapped the envelope closed and tucked it in the zipper compartment of my handbag.

"You okay?" Ruby had asked.

I'd flashed her a grin. "Never better."

Her eyes had held mine as she'd sipped water from her styrofoam cup. "Can't wait to hear about your stay at the club. I want to hear all the dirty details, my dear. All of them. Because there will be much dirtiness going on. Just, please, not in front of my son."

Jake, of course, was thrilled to be staying at Biker Central.

He launched off the bed and onto the floor. "You think Lock is here?"

"I didn't see him when we got here. Maybe he finished work and went home."

"Doesn't he live here, too?"

"I'm sure he has a room here, but he must have his own place somewhere else, everybody does."

"I'm going to go find him!"

"Hold on, sweetie!"

Jake flew out of the room. I pulled the door closed behind me and followed him out into the courtyard where a group of kids were on the slide and swing set.

"Hey, Sister!" Mary Lynn, Kicker's old lady, waved at me. Mary Lynn, a tall brunette, had six year old Melinda and four year old Carrie trying to climb the monkey bars.

I smiled. "Hey, Mary Lynn, how are you?"

"Jake just ran into the shed." She let out a laugh as she lifted Carrie onto a swing. "Boys and their toys!"

"Exactly. We'll be out in a minute."

"Hey there, Grace," said Suzi, Bear's old lady. A little toddler boy held onto her hand.

"Hey, Suze. This is Luke?"

"Sure is." She let out a giggle.

I crouched before the strawberry blond, blue-eyed boy. He gurgled at me and tapped my nose with his finger. I grabbed it and kissed it. His eyes widened at me, and he gurgled again.

"Hi, Luke. Aren't you a cutie pie?" My gaze darted up to Suzi. "He's gorgeous, Suzi. He obviously took after you in the looks department."

Suzi was a curvy, tall blonde with a girl-next-door pretty face, which, unfortunately, she often masked with too much makeup. Bear was not the most attractive specimen in the club. He had a huge muscular body and dark features that seemed frozen in a permanent snarl. They made quite a striking couple.

"He does have his daddy's stubborn streak, though. What can you do?" Suzi laughed.

Luke's chubby hand popped up and tugged on my hair. "Oh no!" I exclaimed dramatically. The boy mirrored my clownish expression as I untangled his fingers from my hair. "I'll catch you guys in a bit."

If I survive this, that is. I made my way towards the shed.

The rusted metal sign "Wreck's Repair" still hung over the large doorway of the shed. I stepped in and was assaulted by dozens of hanging American flags and eagle mementos. Wreck's cherished collection of street signs, vintage oilcans, and gasoline company signs, military posters, old photos, paintings of Lock's covered every inch of wall space. All of them emblazoned with eagle imagery.

"That's it, you see that cable? All we have to do is connect it. . .hold on, right there. That's it, little man. You got it. Way to go, Jake."

Lock's deep masculine tone blended with Jake's innocent laughter and simmered in my chest. His large figure huddled over Jake's small one, their hands nestled in the bowels of a Harley FLH Electraglide that was raised up on a platform. Lock's head was covered in a blue bandana, his long back and wide shoulders arched against the bike. My mouth dried immediately at the sight.

I cleared my throat. "How's it going?"

Jake twisted his adorable head towards me. "Aunt Grace, I helped Lock fix a busted cable on this bike! Come here! Look!" His eyes were round as saucers, his mouth motored on about pliers and chains.

Lock stood up straight and turned towards me. Warmth flared over my skin.

His dark eyes swept over me quickly. "Hey."

"Hi." My stomach filled with a thousand butterflies batting their goddamn wings. I shifted my weight and returned my attention to the Harley.

"You settled in?" he asked.

"Yes, thanks."

"Jake, show your Aunt Grace the new cable."

Jake's eyes became serious, and he reached out for my hand. I gave it to him, and he tugged me over to the bike. "Here it is, Aunt Gracie. You see it?"

"I see it, honey. Look at that! You did that?"

Jake beamed up at me, his cheeks pink. I moved a few steps to the left out of Lock's way.

"You going to help me this week, Jake?" Lock asked. "I could use an assistant around here. The other guys don't know what they're doing half the time. I sure could use your help."

"Really? Yes! Can I, Aunt Grace, huh?" Jake's face nearly burst at its seams.

"Sure. Sounds good to me." I turned to Lock and mouthed silently, "Are you sure?"

He nodded at me then turned to Jake again. "Why don't you grab the broom from the corner down there and give our workspace a once over so it'll be ready for us tomorrow?"

"Right!" Jake literally bounced up off the balls of his feet and dashed off towards the back of the shed. He grabbed onto the giant commercial broom and pushed, stumbling with it across the floor.

I let out a small laugh. "Geez. That used to be my job."

"What?" Lock asked.

"I used to come in here late afternoons if I didn't have school or wasn't working and bring Wreck a beer. We'd talk while I swept up. Later, I graduated to keeping his books organized."

"I got a fridge in here now. You want a beer?"

"Water would be great if you've got it." He went to the corner where there was a small refrigerator by the desk. He pulled out two small bottles of water and walked back over to me. Our fingers brushed against each other over the cold, wet plastic.

"How's your sister doing?"

"Stable. Which is good."

"Any news about your dad's test?"

"Not yet, but should be any day now. Hopefully." He cracked open his bottle and chugged on the water. I watched and held my breath. "Thanks for letting Jake hang out with you here. He likes you."

He looked down at his legs and brushed dust from his faded khaki cargo pants. "I like him too. He listens, really wants to learn. And he's able to focus on a task. That can't be too typical for a boy his age."

"He's a smart one." I cracked open my bottle and gulped at the cold water.

Lock turned away and directed Jake in his sweeping internship. I busied myself taking in his appearance. He wore a faded navy blue hooded sweatshirt. His cargo pants hung very nicely over his lean hips and his massive work boots were covered in dust. He leaned over the pile of dirt and bits Jake had collected and showed him how to gather it up and dump it in the trash. During his demonstration, I took the opportunity to enjoy the view of his sculpted rear and long, powerful legs.

Oh, brother. This was only my second hour of life in club lockdown. I needed to get it together and calm down. Now.

I chugged down my water.

"Hey, Aunt Grace, did you see the painting Lock does?" Jake took my hand and dragged me towards a chopper on a pedestal. "Look at that. Isn't that cool?" Jake's voice swelled. "Lock painted a bike!"

My jaw slackened as I took in a ferocious green-eyed black panther soaring through orange red flames over the gas tank. The entire bike was detailed to match.

"That's incredible."

"You like it?" Lock's dark gaze settled on me.

"It's beautiful."

"Got to finish it with a few more layers of gloss."

I grinned up at him. His dark eyes widened and immediately shifted down to the rag in his hands.

"Jake, put the broom and this rag in the back closet, okay, buddy? You organize it any way you want," he said.

"On it!" Jake darted off towards the rear of the shed, his arms full of broom, rags, pail, in search of the fabled utility closet.

I turned back to Lock's black panther.

"What is it?" he asked.

My hand brushed over the smooth leather seat of the bike. "It's. . .magical."

He scoffed. "It's just something I do for some of the guys once in a while. No big deal."

"It is a big deal. I hope you're getting paid big bucks for this sort of custom detailing. That's quality work. You should be doing this sort of work full-time, Lock."

"Nah, it's a side thing." The edges of his long, full lips curled into a slight smile. I suddenly remembered the taste of those lips on mine, and my insides twinged. His smile faded, and the silver threads in his eyes seemed to harden.

"How's it going, Jake?" he called out, his eyes never leaving mine.

"Good!" Jake shouted from the back.

I could slice the tension between us with a bread knife. Why was he pulling back? Why was he so cool and indifferent? My brain came up with half a dozen fitting adjectives for Lock's behavior and attitude towards me, but no plausible explanations.

"Why are you doing this?" The words tumbled out of my mouth in a rush of air before I lost my nerve to utter them. Or hear the answer.

"It's better this way."

"Oh." I nodded, pretending I understood.

To hell with that.

"I don't understand. Why is it better? For you? You seemed to want this before. You were the one trying to convince me. Did someone say something? Jump? Alicia?"

"No, no one knows shit." He wrenched the cap closed on his empty water bottle. The bottle top cracked.

"Then what is it?"

"It's better to cut it off now rather than later. I just. . .I can't."

My heart crawled up my throat. "You can't?"

He frowned and smashed the empty plastic bottle in his hands. "You were right, Grace. Too much shit going on for you now, too much shit happened in the past, and all of it right here. It's bad timing." He tossed the crushed bottle at the recycling bin across the room, and it landed perfectly.

Yep, just not into me.

My real life tarnish had dulled his shiny fantasy. I was much too complicated.

I crossed my arms and looked around the shed as if the piles of tools, bike parts, and Wreck's plethora of Americana artifacts could possibly provide me with explanations for my stupidity. I bit down hard on my inner cheek. My initial instincts had not been wrong.

Why did I ever listen to him? Why did I believe all his little declarations? How stupid of me to have read more into a purely physical act (or five or six, whatever) and mistaken it for something else, like sharing, caring, or some sort of compelling voodoo. Was I that lonely? That pathetic?

Back to my Candy Bar Theorem.

"Jakey, let's go." My sharp voice echoed through the shed. Lock slammed tools into a metal drawer.

The intercom buzzed. "Yo, Lock. Little Sister in there with you?" Kicker's voice boomed over the speaker.

Lock went to the wall unit and pushed a button. "Yeah. She's here with Jake." His hand rubbed the back of his neck.

"Deputy Sheriff just showed up. Wants to talk to her. He's out front."

"Motherfucker," Lock muttered. His eyes flashed over Jake then shot up at me. He put his hands on his hips. "Um, sorry, Jake."

"Mommy now says 'Motherfudgemycake' instead of that word," Jake said. "You should try it too, Lock."

Lock let out a laugh as his fingers tousled Jake's blond hair. "Maybe I will, little buddy."

Jake's bright gaze darted up at me. I gave him a wink and a slight smile.

"The cops want to talk to me?" I asked.

Lock frowned. "Deputy Sheriff came himself to see you."

I crouched down in front of my nephew and squeezed his arms. "Jakey, why don't you go out front with Mrs. Davis and her kids and try out that slide and the monkey bars? I've got to go talk to someone for a few minutes. Is that okay, honey?"

Jake nodded at me. "Okay."

I planted a kiss on his cheek, and Jake zoomed out of the shed. I followed him, Lock on my heels. A police cruiser was parked out in the lot. Kicker and the two prospects, Dawes and Tricky, stood with the Deputy Sheriff. My eyes adjusted in the glare of the sun on the figure waiting for me. My muscles stiffened.

Deputy Sheriff Owens? Shit, it was Trey Owens.

"Can I help you?" I asked him.

Trey's blue eyes were a shade duller than I remembered. He wore the uniform well, but that lazy, cocky attitude was still mighty evident in the tilt of his head and the way his hands were hitched on his hips.

Trey grinned. "How are you doing, Grace?"

"Good, thanks, Trey."

"You two know each other?" asked Lock, his voice brittle.

Trey smirked at Lock. "We go way back." His eyes slid back to mine. "Don't we, Grace?"

I crossed my arms and let out a sigh. Lock hardened into a wall of muscle at my side and cursed under his breath. Trey's eyes picked over Kicker, Dawes, Tricky, and Lock.

"You wanted to talk to me, Deputy Sheriff?"

"Still shacked up with these lowlifes, huh?"

I moved two steps forward, right into his face. "Get to the point."

His eyes lit up. "Wanted to let you know that we might need you to make a statement about your husband's murder. There are still some holes in the case. Now that you're back and able to put two sentences together."

"Douchebag," hissed Lock.

Trey's eyes tightened. "Watch it."

"That's not very good to hear," I said. "A sixteen year old murder still unresolved? Doesn't say much for your department. And as a victim of that extremely violent crime, I think I'll have to voice my concern to the appropriate authorities. I took care of the perp for you, but you still couldn't figure the rest out for yourselves?"

Dawes cackled with laughter. "Oh damn, that's a good one." Tricky punched his arm.

Trey's tight eyes scanned the men. "The outlaw criminal element in our little town is pretty damn slippery. That's what that says, Grace."

"Mrs. Quillen."

"Mrs. Quillen." Trey's lips twitched. "Anyway, I didn't say the murder was unresolved. I said there were still holes in the case. There's a difference." He tilted his head at me. "We need to talk about one of those holes."

"Oh?"

"Maybe you'd like to discuss it in private?"

I took in a deep breath and walked with him. "What's this about?" I asked once we were out of earshot of everyone else. My eyes darted to Lock. He glared at us, his jaw clenched.

"This is about stolen gold," Trey said.

I blinked up at Trey's amused face. "I don't understand."

He rested his hands on his hips once more. "I'll bet you don't, Grace. But I'm sure your husband would know what I was talking about, but he can't do any explaining, now can he?"

"For God's sake, Trey."

"You must remember the old man who had panned gold in the Black Hills and was robbed and brutally hacked to death in his motel room just outside of Deadwood? There wasn't a lot of gold, a small amount of raw grains and flakes, but it was worth a few back then. It's worth a hell of a lot more now, of course." He planted his hands back on his hips. "The old man's suspected killer was a known drug addict and two-bit hustler. We'd had him on our radar for a while. Of course, you must know that his uncle was a Demon Seed, Vig, their current president. Well, our hustler disappeared the day after the old man was murdered and the gold disappeared as well. Word was our hustler's disappearance was drug-related. And we all know your husband was definitely drug-related."

"And? That automatically means that Dig had something to do with his disappearance?"

"I don't believe in coincidences, Grace. Dig had been seen in the vicinity of that guy's last known whereabouts, another motel further east. And then within the week your husband gets gunned down by the hustler's little brother who you ended up shooting."

"In self-defense."

"Yes, in self-defense," he agreed. "The only logical explanation for him to kill Dig would be as revenge for his brother's death. I'm thinking Dig killed that hustler, and I'm also thinking maybe Dig took something they considered theirs, and that made the brother real angry? Had to be worth a lot to a scumbag like him to come gunning for Dig Quillen though, don't you think?"

I stared at him, perfectly still.

"And the brothers' blood connection to a Demon Seed who are known rivals of the One-Eyed Jacks, makes it all the more interesting a package, in my opinion." Trey leaned in to me. "By the way, you think Dig took that gold after he killed the hustler? Where's that gold now, I wonder? It just vanished into thin air."

I pulled on the silver chains around my neck. "As you can see, Deputy Sheriff, I'm partial to silver."

Trey chuckled and shook his head. "Go ahead, Grace. You play it this way. In fact, you play it any way you damn well like. But know this, word's out that you probably know something about it."

My scalp prickled. "Word's out? What does that mean?"

He took a step closer to me. "I got me little birdies in lots of pies. So if I were you, I'd watch my step. You play games with these fuckwads, you just might get yourself splattered on the road, same as your man. Then again, you always liked playing games, didn't you?"

"You done?" Lock stood at my side, his eyes burning fiery lasers through Trey.

Trey's thin lips tipped up as he opened the door to his cruiser and got behind the wheel. "Keep in mind what I said, Mrs. Quillen." From his open window he glanced up at me one last time, then started his engine, shifted into gear, and left the property.

Lock moved in front of me. "What the hell was all that about?" His hands were jammed in his front pockets, his eyes hard.

"I dated him for about 2.2 seconds a couple of years out of high school, and he was a jerk then. Amazing how some people never change. Dig got in his face a few times. When Trey became a cop later on, the animosity stuck. Then the speeding tickets and the warnings came flying. Most of it crap. How long has he been Deputy Sheriff?" Lock studied me, ignoring my question.

"Two, three years now," Kicker said, now at Lock's side.

"So what was all that chit chat about?" Lock's eyes flashed. "Did he come here to ask you out on a date?"

"Oh, for God's sake!"

A muscle along Lock's jaw pulsed. "What's he after, Grace?"

"Like you said, now that I'm back he wants to poke around Dig's murder case. They're missing key details."

Lock's eyes narrowed. "Why do I think there's more to this than you're saying?"

"I guess that's your problem." I turned and stomped off in the direction of the playground.

"Uh oh," Dawes said behind me.

"Shut the fuck up," Lock muttered.

FOURTEEN

"HE'S VERY HANDSOME."

Alicia smiled at me as we lounged on one of the sofas in the clubhouse. "Who, sweetheart?"

"Your son," I said. "Wes is going to be a real heartbreaker."

Wes racked up the balls on the pool table. He ran one hand through his long wavy brown hair, his other wrapped around a pool cue. His indigo blue eyes sized up the placement of the balls, then he leaned over the table to take his shot, a self-satisfied look etched on his face. James Dean had nothing on him.

After all the excitement in the shed, rambling around the playground with the other children, a hearty dinner of spaghetti and meatballs I'd made for everyone followed by lots of brownies that Alicia had brought over, Jake had finally collapsed around ten o'clock. Rather late for his usual schedule, but this week at the club would be anything but usual. At least I was certain he wouldn't wake up again in the middle of the night and maybe get scared being in a strange room. It was now midnight, and the grown-ups were hanging out.

"My boy is already a heartbreaker!" Alicia let out a laugh and threw her arm around me. I grinned at her, but as I watched Wes take his next shot I bit down on my lip to keep it from wobbling. My eyes stung. I tore my attention away from Alicia and Jump's gorgeous teenage son before I lost it.

If my son or daughter had lived would he or she be shooting pool with Wes right now? Would my daughter have a crush on him? Would my son be his best bud? Would my son have popped me a sweet smile just like Wes was giving his mom right now from across the room after he took that great shot? My eyes squeezed shut.

Dammit, I thought I'd gotten past this.

You will never be past this.

Especially when the possibility from an alternate universe was staring me straight in the face here in this goddamn haunted house. I swallowed hard. My eyes caught Lock's intense gaze. He tilted his head at me, his eyebrows pulled down. He'd noticed. That was sweet, but that's all that was—a kind inquiry into my well-being.

I wished we could talk. I wished I could sit with him, my hand in his, his heartbeat under my ear taking away the strain in my chest.

The front door burst open down the long, winding hall and boisterous laughter and booming voices got louder as they approached. Five men in One-Eyed Jacks colors from the North Dakota chapter along with three women strutted into the room.

"All right!" Alicia let out a loud whistle and clapped her hands together. "It's Butler!"

I shot up from the sofa, a rush of adrenaline coursing through me.

"Little Sister?" came Butler's gruff voice and hearty laugh. "Woo! Look at you, baby!" Blond, blue-eyed Butler charged towards me and swept me up in his arms. He sported more earrings in his left ear than I remembered and a couple in one eyebrow. His blond hair was still full, but instead of it hanging over his shoulders, it now stood in stiff tufts on his head. The stubble over his weathered face gave his striking good looks a rougher edge, and his body had not gone soft with time. He took my face between his hands and planted a brief kiss on my face, then a longer one on my mouth.

"Oh my God," I stuttered. "It's so good to see you!"

"Hell, sweetheart." Butler planted another kiss on my forehead then pulled me out of his arms. "You're still one hell of a walking hard-on!" He burst out into gales of laughter, as did I and the rest of the club.

Everyone except Lock.

"I've been in Colorado for a couple of weeks. Heard you were back, and I had to come see you on my way home." Butler's hands squeezed my waist. "You look great, babe. You doing all right?" The lines along the edges of his eyes scrunched up with his broad smile.

Butler and Dig had been close friends and together would organize all the winter runs in Southern California, Florida or Texas for the three One-Eyed Jacks chapters. Butler's old lady Caitlyn and I would, on special occasions, join them and ride along with Wreck in a van packed with the tools and all the bike parts necessary for such a long trip. Otherwise we were stuck home alone waiting for our men to get back, calling each other constantly to see who'd heard from whose old man for any news, good, bad, or dubious.

"What a terrific surprise!" I wrapped my arms around his massive torso as my gaze rested on the president's patch on his leather jacket. Butler ran his fingers through my hair and brushed his mouth across the top of my head. This felt good, seeing Butler again, being reminded of a time when everything rolled along easily. Or at least seemed to.

Today a fierce jumble of emotions had slapped me upside the heart valves one after the other.

What more?

The music blared louder, bottles popped opened, laughter hooted and bubbled over.

It all sounded good to me.

"Jake's room is all the way at the end, you can't hear much back there," Alicia said.

In the clubhouse kitchen we loaded food into bowls and platters to bring outside to the party. "I'm not worried. He had a big day, and he's a heavy sleeper. He's definitely out for the night."

"Must be good to see Butler again huh?" Alicia's eyes gleamed.

"It is. Where's Caitlyn though? Those two were inseparable."

Alicia froze. "Sweetie . . ."

"What? What is it?"

"Caitlyn was in a bike accident about three years ago."

An icy shiver raced down the back of my neck. "What happened?"

"They were on their own in the middle of the Black Hills coming back here from a day at the Reservoir. A car bumped into them. It was nothing major, but Caitlyn's foot got pushed into the primary chain. Butler didn't have a primary cover on his Panhead."

"No."

A primary chain rotated at 1500 rpm. Caitlyn's foot might as well have been mashed into a high speed meat grinder.

175

"Her foot was gone before the bike even went down," Alicia said. "She bled to death before an ambulance could get to them. They weren't even speeding. Just the two of them out for a nice afternoon ride. The idiot driver of that car took his eyes off the road for just a moment, but that's all it takes."

Outrageous, gorgeous, over the top Caitlyn. . .gone. My hands clamped onto the bowls of cheese puffs and the chili flavored corn chips.

"It was horrible. Butler was a fucking mess," Alicia said. "He blamed himself for it. Even went nomad for a year. It changed him. He's better now, but different."

Butler had even left the club for a year and went out on his own? Guilt and pain are certainly powerful little demons.

"I think I get it."

"I'm sure you do." Alicia's eyes settled on me, and she let out a sigh. "Come on, let's get this stuff out there."

We headed outside, and I plonked the bowls of snack junk on the big table. An arm wrapped around my middle and squeezed, and I held my breath.

Butler let out a growl against my cheek. "It's so good to see you again, so fucking good." I smiled at the emotion in his voice and the warmth of his large body against mine.

"I feel the same way." I turned in his arms to face him. "Alicia just told me about Caitlyn." My arms went around his waist. "I'm so sorry, Butler. So sorry. I. . ." His lips stiffened into a firm line. "Are you doing better?"

"Sure." He shrugged his shoulders. "It doesn't sting the way it used to, but it's like nothing's stable anymore, like the earth is tilted a different way now, and I just don't get it. Then it passes, but it's still there. I can feel it underneath everything." He raised a pierced eyebrow at me. "Am I right?"

"Yes, you are."

He squeezed my shoulder. "We both took off, huh?"

I met his steady gaze. "I couldn't face everybody or this place without Dig here. Then I kept wondering why the hell did I survive? Why did I get to live and Dig and the baby had to die? Maybe if I hadn't insisted on going out for a ride that afternoon, maybe—"

"Ain't no maybes, Sister. That's a losing game we keep playing with ourselves, 'cause it just doesn't change the facts, does it?" His hand wrapped around my neck. "When I came down to see you in the hospital, you didn't recognize me. That killed me. I wanted to be there for you, but I didn't know what to do. I freaked."

"I don't remember too much. I remember voices, pieces of conversations, but I was too far gone."

"Yeah, you were," Butler said. "I just thank God Caitlyn had insisted on giving Ruby a break that night and stayed with you in your room. Ruby had been exhausted that night. If Caitlyn hadn't been there—" He inhaled sharply through his nose.

I pressed my lips together and gave him a watery smile.

"I'm glad you made it through. Feels good to hear you laugh, see you smile." Butler's hand cupped my face. "Tears are over, beautiful." His warm lips touched mine.

"That's right." I straightened up and pushed at his massive chest. "Go get me a beer, big man."

"Coming right up." He winked at me and headed for the bar.

"Ain't life grand, Sister?" Boner came up behind me and slung an arm around my shoulders. I gave him a kiss on the cheek.

He released me and trailed after a blonde who strutted by us. "Yo, sweetness, where you going?"

I let out a laugh, and then my breath caught in my throat.

Lock sat on the sofa with one of the girls who had come in with Butler. She had gorgeous long, silky raven hair, big brown eyes, dangling turquoise earrings, and large breasts stuffed into an orange tube top. A mini skirt barely hid what was between her thighs, and cowboy boots were at the end of her long, toned legs. She slid onto his lap with a deep giggle and traced the edge of his eagle wing tattoo with a long wine-colored fingernail.

A red rage flared inside me. *That's my tat, bitch.*

She plucked a cigarette from the pack in his shirt pocket, and a slight grin broke over his face. He pulled out his lighter from his pocket and flicked it on. The girl leaned in and touched his wrist as he lit her cigarette. My jaw clenched. I always hated it when Dig would light another woman's cigarette. There seemed to be an instant of sensual intimacy in that quiet exchange that always bit at me.

It bit me now. Hard.

Another one of Butler's girls, a blonde with pink highlights, perched herself on the arm of the sofa on the other side of Lock and raked her fingers through his cropped hair, laughing at what they were saying.

I had no right to be jealous, but my body was having its own violent reaction to the Lock spectacle before me. He wasn't mine. He was not my boyfriend, not my lover, not my man, not my anything. He had made that clear in the shed. We happened, it's over. End of story.

Wasn't that what I had wanted all along?

"Beer, my dear," Butler tucked a beer into my hand. My fingers gripped the icy bottle. I wasn't sure if I wanted to drink its contents or send it flying across the room.

Butler clanked his beer bottle against mine and threw an arm over my shoulder. "To living, Sister. Living large." He took a long pull from his beer, and I did the same. Butler held me closer to his body and kissed the side of my face. I swallowed more of the icy brew.

To hell with it, I couldn't help it. *I have to look.*

My gaze slid back to Lock. His black eyes glinted at me. Even across the great room their dark heat seeped right through my veins as two very willing young women filled his hands. My pulse pounded in my ears.

Why did he have such power over me?

Butler leaned in and whispered something in my ear; I didn't even know what he'd said. I couldn't listen. I was listening to Lock's eyes, translating his glares, and he extracted from mine.

I chewed on my lower lip. *Why are you doing this?*

Lock's eyes narrowed. *Why are his hands and mouth all over you all the fucking time?*

My eyes remained bolted to Lock's magnetic glower. The blonde leaned down, her breasts rubbing against his shoulder. Grinning, she whispered in his ear and lazily stroked his chest.

Heat blasted my face. *Is that the way you want it?*

Lock didn't move a muscle. Suddenly, he grabbed the blonde's arm and pulled her down into the sofa next to him, and she barked out a laugh. A brick settled in the pit of my stomach and crushed everything inside me. Lock had pushed me away and shut us down. And now here he was getting busy right in front of me, yet he had the nerve to be ticked that I was hanging out with Butler?

This was Butler, not some skanky hook-up, but an old friend. Lock had two club sluts panting over him, touching him everywhere I had caressed and kissed him, everywhere I still wanted to touch him. Pretty soon all this would lead somewhere as it usually did—the hallway, his room. Maybe with both women.

Wasn't he the popular one? Oh, what did it matter? He's probably fucked them before anyway.

I gritted my teeth until my gums ached. He obviously wanted to make a statement this evening, and he was doing a grand job of it. Why was this so damn hard? I was usually so good at letting go and moving on.

I needed to get over it. I needed to have some fun with my old friends tonight.

More people had shown up and the party had moved outside to the yard. The prospects grilled burgers and hot dogs. A keg had been tapped, and a bonfire burned, the flames and heat licking out at us. Alicia had somehow managed to whip up huge heaping bowls of macaroni salad. Suzi and I, and a couple of the other female hanger-ons, stacked piles of paper plates and filled cups with rolled up napkins and plastic utensils.

Several of the men had started a fight for betting. Cheering and heckling filled the air. I found Butler in the crowd. My brow snapped together at the sight of a shirtless Lock fighting with one of Butler's brothers.

"He's good, I haven't seen him fight in a while," Butler said.

"Oh?" Did I sound uninterested enough? I hoped so.

Lock's bare upper body glistened with sweat. His long sinewy arms were taut and close to his body. He suddenly snapped one arm out, then the other, and punched his opposition repeatedly. His opponent shuffled back howling. Lock's leg shot out and cracked against the guy's jaw. Blood gushed down the poor guy's teeth and across his mouth. Lock's hooded eyes were those of a predator bearing down on his prey. He took a few hops back and waited for the other guy to come to his senses.

Butler hung his arm around my shoulders and took a drag off a joint. "He coulda been a contender, to quote one of my favorite examples of American cinema." I laughed. He had always been obsessed with Marlon Brando. We'd been through his DVD collection many, many times with Dig and Caitlyn.

"Lock was that good?" I asked.

"Oh, yeah. But he was never interested in taking it anywhere when he got out of the army. Wanted to stay put."

Stay put?

I'd once remarked to Lock how he wasn't connected. How wrong I was. He certainly was connected to everything Wreck had given him: Meager, the club, the repair shop. He was connected to all these things and to his brothers. All of it was home to him, and home was obviously vital to Lock. Unlike me. I had cut myself off from everything and everyone I knew and once held dear.

I was the disconnected one, wasn't I?

"He's made the shop a success, right?" I asked.

"Oh yeah. He's organized and very determined. Hell, it's good for the club to have a couple of honest businesses going."

I rolled my eyes. "Just a couple." I bumped my hip against his, and a wide grin split his face.

"Yeah, just a few to deflect attention from the real moneymakers," he said against my ear. He offered me his joint, but I shook my head at it.

Lock knocked his opponent down again. Loud cheering and shouting broke through the night air. The fight was called. Lock offered his hand to his fallen opponent and helped him up on his feet. The black haired woman in the orange halter top gave Lock a small towel and a bottle of water. He lifted his chin at her and wiped at his face and neck.

Butler and I turned to walk away, but Heather caught my eye. She stared at the black haired woman and Lock who were now laughing together. Heather's cheeks were flushed, her face pinched. I almost felt sorry for her. She muttered something under her breath as she watched them. Another girl pulled her away. Lock, the conquering gladiator. I dug the heel of my boots into the asphalt.

Butler and I ate together with a group of his brothers and Dee, an old lady from his chapter whom I knew with her old man, Judge. I chewed my food with intent, but could barely taste the smoky hot dog or the creamy macaroni salad. When we were done, Dee and I cleaned up our table, then she came with me to check in on Jake who luckily was sleeping soundly.

We went back out to the party and danced to some old time rock and roll, then Butler grabbed me, and we ended up at the makeshift bar to get some real booze. I was definitely ready for something stronger.

"What are you in the mood for tonight, babe?" Butler's lips brushed my ear. He stood behind me, his arms wrapped around my waist.

"Hmm." I grinned up at him. "Tequila."

"You got it." His one hand let go of me, and he motioned to Dawes behind the bar. Just then a couple stormed past and bumped into us. I got knocked out of Butler's loose embrace, but he immediately grabbed me, pulled me back into his arms, and kissed me. My insides tightened at the sensation of his mouth against mine.

"What'll it be?" asked Dawes.

I tore my mouth away from Butler's. "Two shots of tequila!" I shouted out.

"Make it four, man!" Butler smirked. Both his hands angled my head closer to his, and we kissed again, his tongue gently sweeping through my mouth. He tasted of tangy barbecue sauce and beer laced with acrid tobacco.

I punched his chest and let out a laugh. "I forgot you had that tongue piercing."

His blue gaze intensified. "Now you finally get to try it out, beautiful." I shot him a look, and he crushed his lips onto mine once more. The ball of his piercing rasped all over my tongue. "Always had a thing for you, baby," he whispered.

My fingers curled into his thick cotton shirt. To hold on? To push him away? What the hell was I doing? I didn't have a clue. And at this very moment, I wasn't sure I cared.

"Always had a thing for you."

I knew that.

The rub was I did too. . .once upon a time.

Before he had hooked up with Caitlyn, Butler used to pay me lots of attention. So much attention that Dig had caught on and didn't like it much. Then one night things had changed. I'd caught Butler watching me and Dig having sex in the woods where we had camped for the night on a weekend run to a campground outside of Mount Rushmore.

Butler had stood against a tree not far from us. A tourist he'd picked up was on her knees giving him head, but he'd been watching me ride my old man. Our eyes had locked in the full moonlight. It was chilling and erotic, and I'd known it was wrong, but I'd been unable to look away. Dig had whispered something

181

hot and nasty in my ear just as he slammed his hips into mine, and I'd groaned loudly. Butler had fucked the girl's face harder while his gaze had remained pinned on me. Dig had bit the side of my breast suddenly, and that had sent me over. At the same moment, Butler's neck had stiffened as he'd blown his load into the girl's mouth, his hips thrusting.

We had come together long distance.

Guilt and shame had flooded my insides when Dig finished a moment later and pulled me down for a kiss. I had sunk my face into his neck trying to blot out the image of Butler coming. That's as far as it ever got between me and Butler, and it was far enough.

Before that night he'd regularly tossed flirtatious barbs and suggestive looks my way that I'd only laughed off and taken in stride. But after that night in the woods, I made it a point to steer clear of him.

Tonight, though, there were no reasons against us, none at all. And Butler felt good. His desire intensified in wave after wave as his mouth possessed mine, his warm hands pressing deeper into my flesh.

It would be so easy to lose myself in it.

"Yo, Butler. Drinks!" Dawes shouted out.

"What's with the ice?" Butler asked.

My eyes shot to the bar. Four small glasses of tequila were accompanied by an extra large plastic cup filled to the top with ice cubes and a slice of lemon.

"Hell if I know," Dawes said. "Lock said you'd need it."

My blood froze. My head snapped up, and like a heat-seeking tracking system, I hunted for Lock.

There he is.

His black eyes smoldered at me, his jaw set. He now wore a denim shirt with the sleeves cut off at the shoulders. The bunched muscles of his arms and chest rippled in the harsh light from the big overheads. He inclined his head at me, and my pulse raced.

"What the fuck?" Butler let out a throaty laugh. "We don't want to cool down, we want to heat things up!" He snatched up a shot and drank. He handed me one, and I knocked it back. The liquor burned all the way down my throat. Butler's hand slid down to my ass and squeezed as he tossed back his second shot and handed me my second.

Kicker came up to Butler and whispered something in his ear and Butler nodded, his hand dropping from my side. He took out his cell phone and showed Kicker a map on his phone as they both rattled on about a schedule.

My eyes darted back over to Lock. The black-haired wench swayed to the music at his side. She handed him a shot glass then stood up on her tip toes and pressed against him. Her tongue swirled in a tight circle over the side of his neck. Lock looked up and met my gaze once more. He raised his glass in my direction and drank.

My head exploded, and I downed my second shot of tequila.

What the hell was his problem? He got what he wanted, didn't he?

"I need to go check on my nephew," I whispered in Butler's ear. He nodded and returned his attention to Kicker. I charged through the throng of people and darted into the clubhouse before I lost it. Imagine, I need to go inside to get a breath of fresh air?

I hustled through the dimly lit main hallway and made the turn for the bedrooms. My head pounded, and I stopped and pressed my hand against the wall to steady myself for a moment. The reverb from some heavy metal song marched up my arm. I sucked in a deep breath.

"What's the matter, Little Sister? You had enough or want some more?" Lock's deep voice taunted me. I spun around, and there he was filling the hallway. Dark emotion pounded off him charging the space between us.

My chest contracted. "What did you say?"

"There I was thinking that you needed time to deal with your past before you moved on to something new, but I was wrong." His brows snapped together, and his small hoop earring swung. "You're too busy climbing all over your past."

"Who the hell do you think you are?"

"I know who and what I am. Do you?" His black eyes flared at me. "Is Butler another one of your former flames? As if the fucking deputy wasn't enough."

"What's it to you?"

"Answer me."

"I've never hooked up with Butler, if that's what you're implying. I was a faithful old lady."

He smirked. "So now's your big chance then, huh?"

"Well, there's an idea."

Lock's hands wrapped tightly around my neck, crushing me into his body. His tequila-laced lips brushed mine, and I gasped for air. His tongue lashed through my mouth. Feverish sensations exploded inside me.

Hell no.

I pushed back against his chest struggling to pull away from him.

"You can't have it both ways, Lock. You've got a problem with me and an old friend spending time together after so many years, but you've got skanks climbing all over you, kissing you, touching you. What's it going to be?"

His jaw tightened. "They're just the same old tits and holes, Grace. They're nothing, they don't take any effort. I'm old enough to know the difference."

"Really?"

A hand slid up my side resting on the swell of my breast as his thumb stroked my pebbled nipple. I shuddered but fought my body's ridiculously instant, heat-filled reaction.

"Just can't keep away from you, no matter how hard I try," he muttered against my lips, his humid breath mingling with mine. My nerves jumped and caught fire at the raw timbre of his voice.

"Then don't," I breathed, my fingers curling tightly in his shirt. I opened my mouth to him, and his tongue claimed mine, lavishing and punishing as it scored through my mouth. The kiss was hostile, hungry. His insistent fingers undid my jeans, pushing them past my hips. I gasped as his cold fingers slid against the warm skin of my tummy, sinking in the pulsating wetness between my legs.

"Aw, fuck," he groaned, sinking against me.

A rush erupting in my veins, my body twisting with need. I wanted more of him, wanted him to pound into me with his own burning desperation, obliterating us both.

"You gonna let him in here?" his voice simmered. I stilled, my eyes flying open. Two of his fingers squeezed around my clit and the sensation burst through me like a flame, but my heart shrank.

Why did it have to be like this? A stolen moment with me pinned up against the wall. Right here where he had gotten blown by Heather and who knows how many others.

My hips jerked against his hand, and I snapped my legs together. "Screw you!"

He slammed me back against the wall and bit my lip. I fought for breath as he yanked my jeans down further, his one hand sweeping inside my panties down my ass, the other down my front. The smooth coldness of his eagle ring grazed me right on target, and my knees buckled as his fingers seared my sensitive, swollen flesh. No matter the outrage surging through me, my body submitted to his ruthless strokes.

"Oh God, don't."

"You gonna give it away to Butler tonight, baby?"

The knot of tight pleasure built and towered over me. My head pressed back into the wall, and I strained for whatever oxygen remained in the hallway. Pain, pleasure, and heartache riveted me to that hard wall, riveted me to him. He let out a brutal snarl, and my flesh vibrated with the raw, primitive need exploding between us.

"Lock!" I struggled, but was I fighting him or begging him for more?

"Want me to fuck you now?" The cruelty in his voice, vengeful and bitter, incinerated a hole in my chest while my body throbbed for the release I knew only he could give me.

He slid his wet finger out of my pussy and traced my lips with it, while his other hand dug into my ass. A cry escaped my throat, and his eyes flared. "This is what I do to you," he whispered roughly. "Remember that." My heart stopped. Was that triumph in the gleam of his eyes?

Suddenly, he thrust two fingers inside me, and I gasped. He pressed his forehead to mine, our short, choppy breaths mingling, his lips just degrees out of my reach, but he wouldn't give them to me.

I wanted to escape, I wanted to wrap my arms around him.

I was denied both.

His thumb pressed on my clit, his fingers hooked exactly where they should, and my enflamed body finally shattered. I squeezed my eyes shut and saw stars. My fists opened in a pathetic attempt to grip the wall for dear life.

Holy shit, he had serviced me in the goddamn hallway. He had turned the tables very nicely.

My teeth pierced my lower lip imprisoning the moan in my throat. I wouldn't give him the satisfaction. Lock drew in a long, shaky breath and released me. He stood back and tugged at my panties, then yanked my jeans up around my hips, jerked up the zipper and fastened the top button. His hot breath fanned my skin, but an icy chill swept over me.

He was done.

"That should take the edge off for now, yeah?" he rasped.

I froze.

How did we turn so ugly?

Who the fuck does he think he is?

My hand shot out and palmed the full throttle erection in his jeans. He grunted, grabbing my wrist.

"And how about your edge, huh? You going to blow your load inside one of those skanks now? Or maybe both of them, big man?"

"Should I save it all up for you, baby?"

Tears stung the backs of my eyes. I released him, and my head sank back. He planted his hands on the wall on either side of my face and leaned into me, his dark impenetrable eyes glinting in the shadows.

"I know I can't compete with your past, and you've got to do whatever it is you need to do. I get it. I get that whatever you're feeling being back here is big. I get all this shit, babe, believe me." He swallowed hard. "You want Butler? You feeling it for him? You should go for it."

I pushed against him, but it was no use. He was a wall of iron barring my escape, but also a fortress whose walls I couldn't scale.

His nose slid slowly against my jaw. The tangy aroma of his sweat and faded spice made my head spin, and I shuddered. He inhaled against my neck, his lips dragging across my sensitive skin.

"But at least I'll know when he fucks you tonight, I got in there first, and you'll be thinking of me."

I slapped his face hard. My hand burned, my arm shook.

Lock only nodded and pushed back from the wall, his lips pulled in a firm line. He walked away from me, his heavy footfalls echoing in the dark.

FIFTEEN

I STUMBLED TO MY ROOM and was relieved to find Jake still in a deep sleep. I scrubbed my hands and face, brushed my teeth, reapplied my makeup, dark and smoky around the eyes this time. I ripped off my jeans, tore off my damp panties, cleaned up, and put on a fresh pair before pulling up my jeans again. I charged back out to the party.

"Hey, beautiful, there you are."

I grinned at Butler. He handed me his beer, and I finished the rest of it in one swallow.

"I wanted to take you out for a ride tonight, but with you on lockdown it ain't gonna happen." His lips brushed mine as my fingers curled into his leather jacket. Someone whistled behind us and Butler laughed, hooking his arm around my neck. I leaned into his solid body.

Butler lit a joint and handed it to me, and I took a long drag. He winked at me, a wink full of heat and wicked promise. I let the smoke burn in my lungs, turned my head to the side on the exhale, and my gaze found Lock.

He sat on one of the wooden picnic tables. That black-haired beauty danced to the music in between his open legs and had pulled down her halter top to expose her large, firm breasts. He laughed at something she said, drained his beer bottle, and tossed it into the nearby garbage can with barely a look.

"Hey, Butler. Who's that woman with Lock? Didn't she come with you?"

"Who?" Butler turned, and a smile curled his lips. "Yeah, that's Iris. She's been hanging with us for almost a year now."

Lock leaned forward, grabbed her hips, and pulled her into his body. With her arms wrapped around his neck, she gyrated to the music against him, her long hair swinging across her bare back.

"That's quite a show."

Butler chuckled. "That's nothing for Iris, baby. Nothing. She's just getting started." I clenched my jaw and reached for the joint in Butler's fingers once again and took another drag.

What had Lock said? *It's better this way.* Sure is. No mess, no muck, no worries.

No connection.

The night carried on. Butler and I laughed at Boner's crazy jokes and Dawes's shy come-ons to the girls. Clip got busy not with one, but with two women. Dee, Alicia, and I gabbed about exercise DVDs over more tequila shots. The three of us eventually ended up standing on a table holding onto each other, singing vintage Grateful Dead tunes that blared over the speakers and laughed and laughed. It felt good not to have a care in the world.

Or at least pretend I didn't.

Butler whooped and whistled loudly. "Get down here, Joan Jett!" Warm hands wrapped around my waist. He swept me off the table, and I let out a loud yelp. My girlfriends cheered and clapped.

His lips nuzzled my neck. "Fuck me, you're something else."

I only laughed, and his blue eyes shined back at me. Butler kissed me as he gently put me back on my feet. He took my hand and led me into the clubhouse.

We peeked in on Jake who slept soundly, then he took me down the opposite hallway to his guest room. He locked the door, and in a tequila, beer and weed-induced haze laced with plenty of anti-Lock bitterness, I got naked with Butler in the dark.

"Fuck, look at you. Get on my face now, I want up in that pussy at long fucking last," he said, his voice rough.

"Gee, who could resist that invitation?"

He roared with laughter. I did as requested.

All I wanted was to be swept away into something far, far away. His hands groped my ass as his pierced tongue danced through me.

"Always wanted you, baby."

"I know."

"You wanted me too, smart-ass." He let out a growl and smacked my rear. Harsh bites of sensation burst through me like fiery needles. I fell back onto the mattress against his body.

Butler reached over to the nightstand and ripped a condom packet between his teeth. He smoothed the rubber over his cock.

My heart thudded in my chest. I was really going to do this.

Just like Lock was going to have Iris and maybe even the pink-blondie. Both of them begging him for it, begging for his mouth, begging for his . . .

Butler's cool hand slid up the inside of my thigh, pulling me closer. "Come here." He rolled on top of me and kissed me. Waves of dizziness filled my head. He raised himself up and pushed inside me letting out a groan.

"Damn, you're killing me."

"I bet you say that to all the girls," I said through gritted teeth.

I battled with memories of Lock's fingers exploring me, his tongue teasing my skin, his hand curling around my smaller one. The memory of his steely gaze in the hallway smoldered in my chest like dry ice.

That huge cup of ice with the lemon.

Iris's half-naked body grinding into his.

"You'll be thinking of me."

Son of a bitch.

Butler let out a laugh, and his hands went to my hips, gripping them tightly. "I've always been an asshole, baby, but that's one of things you liked about me."

That was true.

Twenty years ago, I had found his Nordic good looks, sweet charm, and volatile edge to be a fascinating package. Back then I had a faraway girly crush on this blond, blue-eyed devil, but it was like having a crush on your brother-in-law—totally off limits, simply not done. Or like having a crush on a celebrity—impossible to come true, but fun to fantasize about. Butler had been my bad boy fantasy crush like the one I had on Axl Rose back in the day. That was the thrill and the extent of it for me, the fantasy.

Until that night in the woods. That spooked me out of the crush and made me realize that this was not a harmless fantasy.

I loved Dig, and my husband and I were dedicated to keeping each other happy. (Not to mention how fooling around with another brother is a totally evil thing to do to the brotherhood, and I was not that woman.) We'd been thrilled when Butler and Caitlyn had gotten close and she wore his property patch, and then he had put a ring on her finger. They had been genuinely happy together. Eventually things had settled down, and the four of us had made for great company and good times.

But now, here I was, getting my taste of Butler.

Careful what you wish for.

Butler pulled my legs higher against his hips. "We've got all night to make up for years of wondering about it."

Club slut.

That would be me.

My head pounded, and I deserved it. I deserved a baseball bat to the brain, in fact. And to the pelvis. Are chastity belts still available? I should get one, lock it on myself, and throw away the damned key.

My lifelong good girl status had just been officially flushed down the toilet. At my age, too. My sudden lack of impulse control since I had crossed the border into South Dakota astounded me. What the hell was in the water?

I clambered off the bed and scrounged around for my clothes. I got dressed in the half dark; the light in the bathroom had been left on. I leaned over Butler's immobile body on the bed. My hand found his wrist, and I angled it to get a look at the dial of the large sports watch he wore.

"Thank God," I muttered. It was 5:44 in the morning. I let go of Butler's wrist, and his arm plopped on the mattress. I went into the bathroom. My eyes widened.

Three lines of white powder lay on the small bathroom counter by his keys, and an open plastic zippy bag full of what I assumed was a stash of coke. A hell of a lot of coke.

No wonder he had the exuberance of a bull last night even after all the booze and weed. No wonder he couldn't keep it up and finish what he'd started. He'd tried valiantly, but then he had dozed off, much to my relief.

I took care of my business and washed my hands carefully in order not to get any water on his pricey stash. Then I got the hell out of the room.

At this hour most everyone should have been passed out. I crossed through the main lounge to get to my and Jake's room. The couches were littered with sleeping bodies, and a half-naked couple was in a tangle on one of the pool tables. Snores rose from another corner of the room. I watched where I stepped as bottles, cups, and smashed cigarette butts were strewn everywhere.

"Little Sister."

I froze. Oh, hell no—who was that? I turned my head in the direction of the voice. Jump leaned against the door of his office and motioned for me to come in, his face grim. I tiptoed over a smattering of crushed potato chips and a puddle of yeasty beer on the floor and entered his dimly lit inner sanctum, and he closed the door behind me.

"Is something wrong?" I asked. "Did something happen?"

"You tell me."

"What?"

"Did you fuck him?"

"Excuse me?"

"Butler—did you fuck Butler?"

"Jump—what . . .?"

The lines around his eyes creased. "Answer the goddamn question!"

"Yes."

"Good," he said.

"What?"

"We got a problem."

"Jump, it's just after five in the morning, my head is killing me, and I'm having a hard time putting two and two together here after a very, very long night."

"I got a problem with Butler, and I need your help, seeing how you just made our lives a hell of a lot easier." He sat on the edge of his desk. "Have a seat."

I dropped my boots to the floor and slumped in the dung-colored vinyl armchair in front of his desk. My eyes grazed over the photos of past presidents of the One-Eyed Jacks. Each face more dour than the next, a few of them cocky and defiant. All of them dead and gone, some by natural causes, most of them by the hand of another or at the mercy of a road machine.

"You need my help?"

"I need you to get close to that fucker."

"Are we talking about Butler?" My fingers rubbed at my sore eyes.

"Yeah, Sister, keep up. He's been getting sloppy the past couple of years. Getting into scrapes with local law instead of keeping them happy. He's been dipping into the profits for himself and reaching out to gangs he shouldn't be. He's more erratic than he's ever been, and that's saying something. He's strung out half the time, and it ain't only the green he's dipping into."

I leaned closer to Jump. "Well, he's got quite a snowy mountain stash in his room right now."

A harsh grin split Jump's face in two. "After years of this shit, I'm surprised he can still get it up. Hell, I'm surprised he's got a nose left."

I exhaled and crossed my arms and legs. "I think he's working with Vig," Jump continued. "Vig's been wanting us to patch in for a while. He wants our territory badly for his expanding drug empire and whatever the fuck else he's into these days. He wants our contacts out west for himself. He's hooked up with big, national clubs to compete with the crime organizations that have moved in up north. Drugs, whores, and guns are big business up there."

I'd been aware for some time how the FBI, the ATF, even Canadian authorities were all over the Bakken now dealing with the higher crime rates. With the influx of tens of thousands of workers camped all over the shale oil reserve region that bridged North Dakota, Montana and Canada, Vig had his work cut out for him.

"Vig wants us in to swallow us up," Jump said. "But we ain't interested in being a part of his racket, his way. We got our own thing going, it's low on the radar, and it does well. I ain't got no mega-watt aspirations with the big outlaw clubs. We're good with our own network that we've built up over the years. I don't need to extend our reach that way. Shit's good now. Got it the way Dig and I always saw it—lean, independent."

"Okay," I murmured, my weary gaze meeting his.

"Butler always wanted to take it bigger, higher. Plus he's a hothead. Hotter than Dig."

"Yeah, he is."

"This shit's causing rifts among the brothers. I can't have it. Butler's making shit deals left and right to keep the money coming in up there. He's driving our train into a collision course on purpose so we'll have to accept the Demon Seeds' terms. I ain't having it. Not on my watch. No fucking way. What happened with you in Montana stirred the pot again. My boys are jumpy enough as it is."

"I don't need to know all this."

"This you need to know."

I frowned. "Why? I'm not even part of this club anymore."

"You will always be a part of this club, woman!" he growled. My blurry eyes focused on his tense lips under the full mustache. Jump took a deep breath and ran his fingers through his beard. Once. Twice. Three times. His large brown eyes tightened. "Sister, I need you. The club needs you."

I stretched my legs. "I'm not getting this. You lost me."

"Butler's been a mess since Caitlyn died. Anyway, he always wanted to tap your ass."

"Can we get to the why you need me part already?"

"I need you to stick to Butler. I need information on him, from inside his clubhouse. He's up to something with the Demon Seeds, and I need to know exactly what it is before it explodes in our faces."

My head snapped up, my tired eyes trained on Jump.

"He wants you, you want him, it's the perfect opportunity. You slept with him now, it's done. Keep going with it."

I sat up in my chair, my back rigid. "Wait, stop—hold on. What the hell are you talking about? I have no intention of continuing anything with Butler. It was a one night thing. Believe me, one night was enough. It was a mistake. I don't even—"

"You two got history."

"Ancient history. That you love to keep bringing up."

Jump tilted his head at me as he moved behind his desk and sank back into his large swivel chair. "Sparks were flying between you two last night, obviously." His ringed fingers drummed on his desk.

"You can have sparks with plenty of people. I'm not interested in Butler."

"Get interested."

"Jump—"

"Make it last until we get what we need."

"And what the hell do you need?"

"We need to know what his long range plan is."

"You want me to spy on him?"

"Shouldn't take long. He's getting sloppy with all the blow he's doin'." Jump's lips curled into a small grin. "Come on, Sister. You know Butler. He'll be good to you. You just get on the back of his bike, baby, and enjoy the ride."

"Don't you try to twist this into some romantic bullshit. I know how this crap goes down."

Jump slammed his hand onto his desk. "This is for Dig, Sister. For this fucking club."

"You want me to whore myself for the club? Even better, for my dead husband?"

Jump pressed his lips together. "It's a good plan. You'll have protection. I'll have Lock on you."

My lungs contracted. Oh, that just made it all better.

"I'm not asking you to marry him and live up there," Jump said, his fingers drumming on the desk. "I'm just saying . . ."

My eyes sank closed. "I know what you're saying."

"Sister . . ."

"Don't!"

"If he invites you to come up and hang with him, you go. You don't stay long, you got Ruby and her boy now," Jump said, his voice lower. "A few days here, a couple days there, no big deal. You get him talking, you listen, you watch. I'm not asking you to take him out, babe. That's my job if it comes to that."

"What a relief."

"What's it gonna be?" Jump's voice was noticeably sharper.

"Were you waiting up for me now?"

"Saw the two of you all over each other last night, and I was hoping you'd end up in his bed. I knew you'd be checking in on your nephew, so I've been waiting for you. The boy's fine, by the way. Alicia's with him." He exhaled heavily. "Just make Butler believe you'd like more and wait for that invite up north."

My brain clicked along and all the train cars finally got into a row and connected one by one. I rubbed my hands across my face.

Jump poured bourbon into a glass from an almost empty bottle. His eyebrows knit together. "What the fuck is it now?"

"When did Lock tell you?"

"Tell me what?"

"About Vig in Montana," I said. "When we got back here or on the phone before we got home?"

Jump shrugged. "He called me in the morning before you left the hotel in Watford City."

My shoulders slumped. "Is that when you both came up with this terrific plan?"

"Why? What does it matter? I'm not gonna tell you about my business with my brother." He gulped his drink.

"Screw that. Either I'm in this or I'm not. Which is it?"

"Oh, you're in this all right." His eyes flared at me, a stern finger pointing at me. "Made an impression on me that Vig pulled you out like that in Montana. Why would he do that?"

"He's fucking nuts, unpredictable. That's news to you?"

Jump leaned back in his chair leveling his stony gaze at me. "Maybe you got something he's after?"

I tucked my legs under the chair. "Me? What the hell would I have? Dig didn't share club business with me."

Jump swiveled his chair slowly, still holding my gaze. The metal creaking of his chair filled the sudden silence between us. "There's nothing you need to tell me? Nothing I should know?"

My fingernails dug into the tattered vinyl arms of my chair. "There is nothing you need to know, Jump."

He drank from his glass scratching the side of his bearded face. "We all got to do shit we don't like for this club at some point. I'm not asking you to do something you haven't already done though, am I?" He smirked at me and raised his glass of liquor. "You just fucked him, so what the hell? Obviously you ain't got ties to any man, so enjoy getting laid while you're at it." He snorted and drained his glass.

I swallowed hard, my legs stiff, my arms shaking slightly as I clasped the edges of my seat. He deposited his empty glass on the desk with a heavy thud, and I flinched.

"You don't call me or text me from there. You need to talk, you call Alicia and talk woman shit only, and I'll have her check in with you. We'll come up with a few code phrases if things get hot for you or you need a meet. Lock will always be nearby, and he'll be able to get to you quick. We do this clean and smart."

I shook my head letting out a dry laugh. "Clean and smart?"

"This is our chance, Sister. You want Vig or Butler or anybody to destroy what Dig and Wreck and the rest of us put our blood and sweat into for so long? You want to see those fuckers rip apart the club that took care of you and your sister like family?"

"Don't you talk to me about Ruby or my old man!" My voice shook.

His brows slammed down. "You ain't no whore, Sister. You're working an angle for your boys. For your club. Just like the rest of us do every goddamn day. We all got to do what we gotta do."

I glared at him.

He sighed heavily and poured himself the last of the bourbon. "Look at it this way. . .Butler's been hurting for a while, same as you. You two might be the best thing for each other right now."

A chill slithered down my spine. "I hate you, Jump."

"Don't give a flying fuck right now, baby. But I do give a fuck about all of us surviving this shit. And now you're a player." His stony eyes settled on mine as he leaned back in his chair and swiveled to the side once again.

"You in?" His ringed fingers curled into a fist slowly knocking out a beat on the surface of the desk. His One-Eyed Jacks skull ring leered at me, demanding the answer Jump wanted to hear. Once a symbol to me of support, loyalty, and allegiance, now that ring seemed more like a threat, a menace, a burden.

I recognized the challenge in Jump's determined eyes, in the way he leaned back in his chair. There was an arrogant swipe in his laugh when he made the remark about me getting laid, and a harshness in the way his jaw set as he waited for my answer now, taunting me, daring me to prove him wrong. He didn't believe me about knowing or having something Vig was after. The way he'd never believed in my innocence regarding my involvement with Butler all those years ago. Jump had blamed me for Butler's exile and silently resented me ever after for getting in between the brothers.

The walls of the suddenly stifling room pressed in on me. Jump had nudged me into the path for which he knew I had a weakness. He was right; he didn't have to do much work, I had a hand in this myself. Like a pawn on his chessboard, I had slid this way and that in the shadows of the knights and kings.

But I still had my own move to make on that very same game board. I just had to figure out when to make it.

I did agree with Jump. If Butler was working with Vig, the One-Eyed Jacks definitely needed to know what they were planning to preserve their club. And by helping them, maybe I could resolve my crap with Vig, barter with him somehow, and, most importantly, ensure Jake's safety.

I clenched my jaw to fight the tremor in my chin. My throat tightened. "I'm in."

"Good." Jump drained his glass.

I got on my feet, pulled open the office door, and trudged back across the lounge to Butler's room.

Motherfudgemycake.

My head swam.

Lock had known the morning after at the hotel in Watford City that Jump wanted me in play for Butler. Jump didn't know about us; no one did. Wouldn't that explain Lock's sudden freeze, his pulling away and letting those other women crawl all over him at the party? Was it all a show to drive me away and get me mad?

And I bought it.

And landed in Butler's bed.

Lock hadn't seemed too happy about it, judging from that brief, yet oh so intense episode in the hallway. He still wanted me, like I wanted him. Despite Jump's master plan, despite all the bad timing in the world, despite Lock's historic inability to feel or form attachments, he wanted me. That was cold comfort, though.

Would he still want me after this was done?

More importantly, would I be able to look at myself in the mirror after today?

Focus on protecting Jake. Only on Jake.

I closed the door behind me, took in a deep breath, peeled off my clothes, and got back into bed with Butler. His arm snaked around my waist pulling me in close to his warm body. His face sank on my chest.

"Caitlyn," he mumbled.

My breath hitched. I ran my fingers through his thick tufts of hair then down his damp face. "Shh."

Maybe with my little part in this nasty masquerade I could actually help Butler get untangled from his own mess. Maybe I could soften the inevitable blow between him and his brothers.

Maybe.

I would certainly try.

SIXTEEN

MILLER

"SHIT, LOCK, THAT WAS FAST!" Iris let out a peal of laughter twisting back onto my bed.

I snapped the condom off my cock and flung it aside. Iris crawled over the mattress to me on all fours. "How about you tie me up, like last time, huh?" She grinned, licking her top lip. "I liked it a lot. Got me real hot."

I stood at the edge of my bed and shoved my pathetic dick back in my pants. Two eager hands reached out towards my hips. I smacked them away and pushed her back. "Get the fuck out."

Iris let out a huff then scrambled up on her knees, spreading her legs wide and squeezing her tits together. "Come on, baby. Anything you want. You want my ass?"

I belted back up, wincing. "I want you to get the hell out."

"What's gotten into you?"

"Leave, for fuck's sake!"

"Fuck you! I don't need this shit." Iris whipped herself off the bed, shoved her skirt up her body and nabbed her top. She stormed out the door, slamming it behind her. I stared at my bed. My skin tightened, my throat burned. I ripped the sheets off the mattress and threw them across the room.

How the hell did I get here?

The club got us here. I got us here.

My lungs constricted. I threw myself on the edge of the bed, and my head sank into my hands.

It all started in Montana. Started and ended.

When the Demon Seeds had taken Grace, I'd lost it. I had failed her.

How had I not seen that coming? Probably because my cock was otherwise engaged and had hot-wired my brain into dysfunction.

When she finally came back I couldn't stop touching her. Once we got to the underpass and later at the hotel, the emotion bled out from her. She needed me, and she let me take care of her. She had been all brave woman, and then it had sunk in and gashed her. But she didn't need saving, she needed me to feel alive again, feel intact. Or maybe just to feel.

Later that night she tried to make me feel better about her hellish afternoon. She comforted me, soothed me like a warm bath with her quiet sincerity. I didn't know what to do with that. I hadn't had that in such a long time, if ever. Then she gave me her body, and I gave her mine.

And I fucking loved it.

For the first time in a very, very long time I felt I was a part of something bigger than me, beyond the usual, the everyday. It was intense, and it felt right. It didn't break me or sap my soul. Being with Grace built me up, gave me more; a more I wasn't familiar with. And the big news was I didn't want to fight it, didn't want to push it away.

I'd woken up early the next morning and had turned her out of my arms so she lay on her tummy. I traced over the wildflower on her sweet ass with my fingers.

Here was the girl I had noticed in high school always giggling in the hallway with her girlfriends. Here was the girl my brother loved as if she were his own little sister. Here was Dig's woman now in my bed. That abundant life they had shared and the loss of it were branded on her skin forever. That tattoo was Grace's patch as was that ugly scar on her leg.

My fingers travelled down her thigh and dwelled on the scar the bullet hole had left behind. Her shouldering so much pain and loss on her own humbled me. It drove her still, that horror, that immense void, and probably always would. I knew about that shit.

I lugged around enough of my own personal rot—my father's bullshit, losing my gran, the blood and body parts-filled battles I had managed to survive, along with the sickening torture and mindless destruction I had witnessed. Keeping it all tight had become my state of being.

I knew no one could come along and just change it for you. There was no magic wand. There were no keys to that lock—not great fucking, not a few kind words, nor the promise of a warm smile or a tight hug. Those can take the sting away, but to think anything more of them is stupid.

At least that's what I'd always believed.

But now I wanted more of the fucking, more of the kind words, the warm smiles, the hugs.

I wanted them from Grace.

I wanted to rack them up, collect them, and keep them safe. I wanted to plunge into them and wrap myself up in them.

Wrap myself up in her.

That morning at the hotel in Watford City I had called Jump after I'd paid the bill in cash at the front desk. Grace was still sleeping in our room. I'd stood in that sun-filled lobby which reeked of lemon cleaner and listened to Jump muttering over the phone.

"Something's going on between those two," he'd said.

"Vig and Sister? Like what?"

"Fuck if I know what she's been doing all these years. Why would Vig pull her in for a private one-on-one, especially after giving us the all-clear?"

I'd had to agree with him there.

"I don't think he wanted private time with her for a trip down memory lane," he'd continued. "She must have something they're after or she knows something. Maybe he'd wanted to put the fear of God in her. Only one way to find out what's going on. Fuck. Our Vig problem has just taken on a new dimension."

"Hang on, man, this is Sister we're talking about."

"Lock, she was Dig's old lady. Don't ever forget that. Those two were very tight 'til the end. Don't tell me a little bit of him didn't rub off on her. No telling what's really going on." Jump had grunted. "You get her back here, and we'll keep her on ice. Butler's been in Colorado the past two weeks, and I'm damn sure that on his way home, he'll stop here to see her and tap her ass. And I'm going to keep tabs on both of 'em."

My nerve endings had caught fire. "Back it up, what the fuck are you talking about—Butler and Sister?"

"How the hell do you think he ended up in the north when he started out down here with us?" Jump had laughed. "That's how the North Dakota chapter got really shaking, man. He was always breathing heavy over her. Fuck knows what really happened between those two. Dig nipped that shit in the bud, reamed his ass. Butler took off and headed up north full of piss and steam. But business had to move along, and a couple years later he and Dig finally managed to play nice again about the time Butler hooked up with his old lady."

I'd known where this was headed. My fingers had tightened around my cell phone.

Jump had snorted. "Yeah, this is perfect. Her and Butler can cry on each other's shoulders and be fuck buddies 'til we get what we need. We just gotta pave the way."

My pulse had pounded in my head. "Pave the way? You're going to manipulate her into this somehow? Put her out there? Jesus, you're all efficiency, all the time, aren't you?"

"You wanna keep breathing, that's how you gotta be. Bring her home, man."

This whole goddamn Butler mess had been brewing for years. Having to spy on a brother was a shit thing to do, but it had to get done. Now with all this Demon Seed crap rearing its ugly ass head. . .

"*We just gotta pave the way.*"

The thought of Grace as a pawn in these fucked up plays had put me on a razor's edge.

Could she be hiding something?

I'd headed back up to our room with my gut twisted in a tight knot. I'd been looking forward to the ride home with her. Now I despised the very idea. I was going to have to deliver the most beautiful thing that had ever happened to me on a silver platter to the club. Now that I'd finally had her—her whispers in my ear, her breath in my lungs, her tongue on my skin, her heart beating against my chest—I was going to have to let all that go, abandon my secret miracle. Yes, abandon her and stand back, watch and pretend I didn't care. Abandon her like all the other men in her life. That's how she would see it, and that burned.

The blood had drained from my head. I'd have to be the one to push her in front of the hurtling train and effectively reconnect her to her old life. Jump didn't know about me and Grace, and I didn't want him to. It was going to be up to me to make a move and quickly. Christ, we were just starting to climb out of that ditch of the past together, and now I was going to have to let her drop right back in it and land in Butler's fucking bed. Grace would figure it out eventually and despise me for it, wouldn't she? I wouldn't blame her one bit.

I despised myself already.

My head had sunk against the door of our hotel room, my hand had tightened over the knob.

She'd noticed the change in me from the moment I'd walked back into the room. The light in her eyes had dimmed, but she'd gone with it. I'd avoided her eyes and gotten us on my bike. After we'd finished a tense lunch where she'd needled me about my family history, and I'd somehow ended up telling her more than I had ever shared with anyone else, I'd finally got us back on the road.

The less we talked the better.

The less I looked into those beautiful eyes of hers that constantly shifted in color from greenish-brown, to greenish-gray depending on her mood, the better.

I'd pushed the bike into high gear, and the Harley had surged forward. I'd held my breath for a split second.

There it is.

Her body had slammed into mine, and her arms had pressed tighter around me, but I'd stopped myself from putting my hand over hers. And I'd felt the loss of that contact deep in my gut.

Like tonight.

Tonight.

I got up from my bare mattress, stripped off my clothes, and got in the shower. I shoved the handle all the way to cold. My mouth hung open as icy needles of punishment rained down on me.

Tonight, Butler had been all over her from the minute he'd gotten to the club, but I'd felt her eyes on me. I knew I was going to have to provide the incentive for her to be with him, although my every instinct was screaming the very opposite.

I would have to stomp on what was priceless to me.

Iris and her new friend had climbed all over me, and I'd let them. As the night wore on I had seen that sting all across Grace's face, and it had ripped a hole in my chest. But later, when I had heard her uninhibited laugh and had seen her draped all over Butler, it had screwed with my head.

Butler was no Dig; maybe one day he had been, but no more. He didn't deserve a woman like Grace. She didn't belong in his arms, she belonged in mine. I had sent over the cup of ice with the lemon. Yeah, she'd gotten the message. When she'd suddenly taken off inside the clubhouse, I'd tracked her like I was going in for a kill. I'd pinned her to the wall. Her gorgeous smell and the feel of her warm soft skin under my hands had done me in.

Would this be the last time?

What I'd really wanted to do was get her on my bike and put thousands of miles between us and the club. Instead, I'd lost control, and nasty, vile shit had spewed out of my mouth. I hadn't regretted making her come on my fingers and moan my name. It had been phenomenal and sheer, ugly torture all at the same time. But it was mine.

I was glad she'd slapped me; I deserved it and more.

Under the shower I scrubbed this entire freakish night along with Iris off my skin. I wiped the mirror and stared at my murky reflection.

Feeling any better now?

I would never feel better.

I knew that the moment I'd seen Grace reappear in the courtyard twenty minutes after I'd assaulted her. She'd taken on the look of a hard, glamorous woman with a purpose. She'd gotten drunk. She had been the life of the goddamn party. Butler had her in his arms, the two of them singing, laughing, whispering together like some sort of couple. I'd choked back the bile in my throat. Then they'd left together, and I knew.

I knew.

Mission accomplished. *Well done, soldier.* Yeah, I'm a damn good soldier, always have been.

I'd grabbed Iris, headed for my room and pushed her face down onto the bed.

"You going to blow your load inside one of those skanks now?"

Grace's voice had ricocheted in my soul daring me, mocking me.

I'd stood there at the edge of the bed, my clothes on, my cock out, and lasted all of two minutes inside of Iris. Grace's urgent moans and her sweet smell had clung to me. I'd detested myself all over again for lying to her, for driving her away, hurting her, stealing from her, disappointing her.

I'd hated myself for once again wanting what I couldn't have.

My father's bitter voice hurled through time.

That musty, mouse-ridden cellar in my grandmother's house...his stumbling steps...his slurred words filling my ears: *"You are nothing, a mistake. You'll never be nothing but nothing, boy. Just like me. And that's just what you deserve."*

I scrubbed my hands over my face, kicking the wet towel out of my way, slamming my dresser drawer shut. I shoved my legs into clean jeans, stretched a fresh shirt over my head.

Didn't make a difference.

Still feel dirty.

I couldn't get air in my lungs. Everything was covered in a haze.

Got to get out of here.

Socks. Boots.

My hands shook as I reached for my colors.

Jacket. Keys.

I threw open my door.

Bike.

Road.

"Want you with me, sweetheart. You say the word. I'll come down and get you," Butler told Grace.

I adjusted my sunglasses at the sight of Butler on his bike, his one hand at Grace's waist.

It was the Grace and Butler show, the big goodbye.

I had ridden back into the club by twelve noon. Butler's crew had finished packing up and gotten on their bikes. The girls collected their empty coffee cups.

Bear jerked his chin at me. "Where you been, bro?"

"Out," I muttered.

His eyes narrowed. "You okay?"

"Yeah." My teeth dragged across my lower lip.

"I can't make plans now," Grace said. "I need to be here for Ruby. I'll give you a call, though, and if I can, I'll get in my car and come right up."

"I'll come get you," Butler said. "I'd drop everything for you. You know that."

"Even the coke?" she asked. "I don't want to ride with you high."

Butler's face tightened. "I only ride sober, babe. I ain't a fool."

Bear smirked at me and shook his head.

"I'm just worried about you." Grace squeezed his shoulder. "I want you to stay alive."

Yeah, yeah, blah blah blah.

"Oh really?" Butler grinned at her. "So I can give it to you regular?"

Shut the fuck up.

He pulled her body in closer to his and whispered some shit in her ear. She laughed, and I gritted my teeth. Bear handed me a cup of coffee, and I took a swallow. Tasted like liquid ash.

Butler kissed her. His hand slid down and gave her ass a squeeze, and then he finally let go of her sweet body. "Call me the minute you're free to fly."

He strapped on his helmet and aimed his gaze at her, a grin splitting his face as he throttled the engine and toed the kickstand. The roar blasted in the crisp autumn air, and the rest of his boys started up their bikes. Butler finally led his men and their women off the One-Eyed Jacks property and onto the asphalt.

Good riddance, motherfucker.

Grace stood there until they were no longer in sight. Jump came up next to me, a faint smile creeping across his lips.

Grace strode past us without a word, without a look.

My heart thudded in my chest. My insides were torn, bloody, gutted, the urge to puke overwhelming.

What the hell had we done?

Motherfudgemycake.

SEVENTEEN

GRACE

DAWES TAPPED OUT A BEAT on the steering wheel of Alicia's Grand Cherokee, Bear fiddled with the radio stations, and I sank into the backseat and sighed. Visiting with Ruby had been difficult today. She was paler, weaker, frailer, distracted.

Every muscle and fiber in my body was as worn out as an old rubber band. I wasn't getting much sleep at the club. My brain stayed awake at night deliberating, dealing the cards of possibility, chance, and risk over and over again in an endless game of poker night after night. The sound of my nephew's breathing at my side only made it worse.

Bear shut the radio off. My eyelids fell. A nap would be glorious before we got back to the club and I had to plaster a smile on my face for Jake. Alicia slid in the back seat next to me slamming the door shut. I flinched.

"Before we go home I want to stop at Lenore's Lace, hon."

Dawes's eyes lit up in the rearview mirror. "No problem." He shifted the Cherokee into gear and turned out of the hospital parking lot.

Alicia gave me a wink. "I want to take you shopping. Since we're out, why let the opportunity go wasted?"

"Shopping?" I asked. "I thought I was on lockdown?"

"It's a boutique in Meager, two minutes from the club, and we're riding with back-up. We worked hard putting together the bone marrow drive, and it did well. We deserve a treat, and *you* deserve a few tasty bits to make your next time with Butler extra special." Alicia clapped her hands together. "Oh, I can't tell you how thrilled I am that you two hooked up. Long time coming. I'm really excited for you, Sister."

She put her hand on my leg and leaned in closer to me. "He's got a hole he just can't fill. Frankly, I think you're the only one who can do that for him. From what you've told me, you've been on your own a long time, too. I think it would be great if you could get away for a few days and head up to North Dakota."

I raised my eyebrows at her. "You lost me at tasty bits."

"Me too," said Bear. Dawes glanced at him, and they both shook with laughter.

A grin curled Alicia's lips. "Sister, when was the last time you spent money on yourself in the lingerie department, hmm?"

Actually, I had always enjoyed splurging on nice underthings for myself and had a number of choice pieces. But something told me not to let on, and not in front of Dawes and Bear for God's sake.

I only shrugged my shoulders at her.

"That's what I thought." Alicia frowned at me. "We're going to get you something fine, something steamy, something high-class. I don't think Butler's had any high-class tail since Caitlyn. He's never going to let you go once I'm through with you."

I was certainly impressed that Alicia considered me "high-class tail," however I wasn't sure I liked the idea of her having her way with me. I was older now, set in my ways, and I really wasn't in the let's-go-shopping-with-my-BFF sort of mood at the moment, especially after my visit with Ruby earlier.

"Don't give me that face, babe," Alicia said. "You deserve some fun. Let me treat you."

"Alicia, you don't have to—"

"Stop." She flipped up a hand at me. "I want to."

I sat up and stared out the window. Alicia was wrong. Only Butler could fill that hole inside himself; nobody and nothing else could do it. Living with my mother and Ruby had taught me that.

"Who's Lenore?" I asked.

Dawes grinned at me in the rear view mirror. Bear chuckled.

"Lenore's got the hottest boutique in the area," said Alicia. "Forget that mall shit. Lenore's stuff is top of the line. She designs a lot of it herself, and a lot of it is handmade. You and Butler both deserve it, and I'm going to make sure you get it." Alicia let out a throaty laugh. "You're going to get laid but good when you get up there!"

I slid my sunglasses back down over my eyes. Little did she know my experience with Butler had hardly been the stuff dreams were made of.

"Every man likes a show of appreciation." Alicia leaned forward and tapped Dawes's upper arm. "Am I not right, honey? You're a man. Bear? Come on, you two—am I not right?"

"You're a goddess!" Dawes exclaimed throwing me an amused glance in the rear view mirror.

"She knows what she's talking about, Sister." Bear slowly nodded his head.

Alicia grinned. "Damn straight."

"Speaking of which—" Bear turned in his seat inclining his head towards Alicia. "Last night Suzi finally let me—" He caught my frown and let out a deep, rumbling laugh. "Well, anyway, it finally fucking happened. Thanks to Alicia."

"Really?" Alicia asked. "Excellent!" Bear rubbed his chest like a self-satisfied gorilla.

"And did Suzi enjoy it?" I asked. "Whatever *it* was?"

"Fuck yeah." Bear made a face as if I had asked an obvious, ridiculous question.

"Sister, you don't argue with the goddess," Dawes said.

I raised an eyebrow and went back to staring out the window as we entered Meager.

Alicia made Dawes and Bear stay in the car in front of the store much to their disappointment. I recognized the black hanging sign from when Lock and I had had coffee at Erica's.

Entering Lenore's Lace was like entering a gothic version of the inside of Jeannie's bottle in *I Dream of Jeannie*. Violet, fuchsia and mandarin orange swags of gossamer fabric flowed down from the walls. Large pieces of stained glass in the front window filled the interior with other worldly colored light. Moody synth music and wind chime elements floated through the boutique. A cinnamon and sage scent wafted through the air from an incense stick that glowed on a small table in the center of the shop.

Lenore was a striking older woman with dyed blue-black hair, cat-lined brown eyes and colorful tattoos all over her chest and down her arms. Her gaze carefully scanned me up and down like a laser beam, and she smiled slowly. Alicia immediately made herself comfortable on a small lemon yellow sofa and explained to Lenore what I needed. Or what Alicia *thought* I needed. Thus, the quest began.

Lenore pulled a number of delectable pieces for me to try on as Alicia sipped on green tea and either nodded her approval or made faces. Lenore outfitted me with a matching bra and panty set that was truly beautiful. Delicate sheer black fabric with lilac swirls embroidered on the front of the panty and on each demi-bra cup. Lilac trim and elegant thin satiny straps finished off the pieces. The demi-bra made my girls look irresistible, and the matching and very revealing sheer panty was cut high on my rear. I was impressed.

"Try this." Lenore handed me a short slip nightie in a luscious plum color trimmed in black satin. I squeezed into the form-fitting fabric and modeled it for the women. Thank God for all my years of yoga and Pilates.

"That does wonders for your skin color," Lenore murmured. The otherwise sheer slip had only a skimpy halter of satin covering my breasts. Lenore had paired it with a crotchless panty.

Alicia nodded. "Fantastic."

"You're going to love that panty, Grace," Lenore said. "He definitely will." She grinned at my reflection in the mirror. I only averted my gaze.

Lenore had kinky ensembles, of course, but I refused to try them on. Alicia laughed at me. "Next time, you're getting that black topless corset with all the straps."

I rolled my eyes at her.

Lenore's workmanship was very fine, and her prices equally extraordinary. She wrapped each piece I had decided to take in lilac tissue paper and rang up the bill on her cash register. Alicia poked through a selection of vibrators and sex toys that lined a long shelf.

I nudged her with my elbow. "You can forget about it."

She smirked. "I'm looking for me, honey. I love this shit." She held up a package of anal beads. "Have you ever tried these?"

I shook my head at her.

"You don't know what you're missing. Now I know what I'm getting you for Christmas. You're going to thank me big time." She wiggled her eyebrows at me, and we both burst out laughing.

"By the way, what was it you convinced Suzi into doing with Bear?"

"Anal sex. Poor thing was so nervous about it. I get it. Bear is pretty big, from what I hear. But I explained what it was like, talked her through it. Oh, and I got her these really nice oils and a—"

I squeezed Alicia's arm cutting her off. "You're such a good den mother."

Alicia grinned as she dug in her designer handbag. She absently handed Lenore a wad of cash. Lenore tapped on her register and handed her the change with the receipt.

"Thanks, Alicia. This was fun. It's really sweet of you."

"I want you to be happy, Sister. You just got to be open to new opportunities."

Would Alicia ever learn that copious amounts of sex would not cure all of life's ills? Although, it does ease the pain temporarily. Lenore handed me the purple, rectangular shopping bag with her name scripted in black over it, and I took the thick ropy handles in my fingers. Alicia snapped her hand bag shut and shot a cool, tight smile at me.

A chill spiked through my insides.

I remembered that brittle smile. It was the one she always flashed while dishing out her primal old lady authority at the sluts who'd hang out at the club. It was that I'm-gonna-crush-you-if-you-don't-behave smile, that I-don't-trust-you-but-I'm-putting-up-with-you-smile. But never to me, never before. Alicia and I had started out together. We'd reigned together.

I knew what this was.

This shopping trip was right off the club expense account for Operation Butler; a pretty lie cast like a fishing net over what they knew were my chaotic, conflicted emotions. This was Jump and Alicia's attempt to prettify my having to lie to Butler. Yes, this was Act Two of the coercion: a vanity splurge in the name of sisterhood and a second chance romance fantasy for lonely me and lonely Butler.

No way in hell was I going to wear this lingerie. Ever.

I flashed Alicia a smile right back, turned on my heel, and headed outside. Dawes and Bear glanced up at me. I flung open the door of the Cherokee and tossed the shopping bag in the back seat.

My cell phone buzzed in my handbag. I found it and tapped it open.

"Hey, Alex."

"Grace—"

His voice dragged on my name and then abandoned it in the air. My blood froze.

"Alex, what is it?"

He made a noise in the back of his throat. My chest constricted at the struggle in his voice.

"You need to come back to the hospital, Grace."

"What? Why? What's going on?"

Alex let out a slight moan.

My eyes squeezed shut. "Oh no. No."

"Grace, please."

I pleaded with God. I pleaded with the universe.

Alex cleared his throat. "Bring Jake to the hospital. Bring him now. He needs to see his mother. He needs. . ."

"Alex?"

"Come now."

I touched the end call button on the screen and gripped the hard electronic rectangle tighter. I stared at it. It was no longer a mobile phone, just a loathsome object. A brutal black shiny object of torture straight from hell.

"Sister, you okay? What is it?" Dawes swatted Bear on the arm and leaned over him. "Sister?"

My heavy eyes cut to his. "Got to pick up Jake and go back to the hospital."

Is that my voice?

Bear snapped out of the Cherokee. "Get in, babe. Come on." He guided me into the backseat, put my phone in my handbag, and then darted towards Alicia who was chatting with Lenore in the doorway of the shop.

Dawes got out his phone and tapped on the screen. "Mary Lynn? Listen. Get Jake ready, we got to bring him to the hospital to see his ma. Be there in five."

EIGHTEEN

"THE CANCER HAS TAKEN A VERY AGGRESSIVE TURN. It's metastasized through her lymph system and spread to the membrane around her heart. At this point her one lung is in danger of collapsing."

Dr. Braden's lips moved. His clear voice floated over me, everything separated into pieces.

"It's a very aggressive disease."

The pieces broke.

"Mrs. Quillen? Do you understand?"

My mouth was ridiculously dry. I took in air through my nose. "And there's nothing else we can do?"

"I'm sorry. We're making her comfortable with painkillers. There's a room available at our hospice, just a couple blocks away. She'll be taken there within the hour, I believe."

Hospice.

"Do we know how . . ."

"You should be with your sister now."

Dig's remains and Ruby's rather aggressive turn. Remains and aggressive turns. The ingredients of my existence.

"Thank you, Doctor." I stood rooted in the hospital hallway and stared after Dr. Braden in his crisp white coat and expensive sneakers as he receded from my line of sight.

"Grace, go in and see her," Alicia whispered. "We'll be right here with Jake." My gaze darted down to my nephew who held Wes's hand. He pressed his head against Wes's long arm, his round hazel eyes full of water, his lips sealed in a squiggly line.

"I've got to call Ray." I fished in my bag for my phone. I found it, but Dawes plucked it from my fingers.

"Who's Ray?"

"Her father," said Alicia.

He jerked his chin at me. "I'll talk to Ray."

Bear squeezed my arm. "Want me to get Boner over here? He and Lock went to Deadwood today. Should be on their way home by now."

I blinked up at Bear and nodded. My teeth jabbed at my lower lip.

This wasn't real. This was someone else's life playing out in mine. Ruby couldn't be leaving us this fast.

I opened the door to her room and forced my heavy feet to move across the speckled beige floor. Alex looked up at me, raking a hand through his hair. His face was drawn, his strained eyes were dark against his pale skin. "Talk to her. She's in and out."

I nodded at him and sucked in air. The door clicked behind me.

"Hey, Sleeping Beauty," I whispered. Her one eyebrow jumped, and so did my heart. My hand smoothed over her forehead. "I love you, Ruby. Love you no matter what, so just suck it up." The edges of Ruby's lips curled up then fell.

Her eyes fluttered open slowly. "Grace." Her dry lips formed the word.

I willed the tears to stay put behind my eyes. "I'm here."

Her cold fingers wrapped around mine. "You gotta promise me."

"Anything."

"My baby." Her chest rose. "Have to help Alex."

"Yes, yes, of course, Rube." My knuckles swept over her cheek.

"Promise." She struggled for air. "He needs you, you gotta make sure—"

"Shh. I promise, Ruby. I'm going to stay and help Alex raise him. I'll never leave Jakey. Never."

"Be his mommy."

"You're his mommy." My voice broke. I pressed my wobbly lips together. Her eyes widened for a moment, and she struggled to suck in air. I leaned over her to hear her better.

"You love him good and big and deep. You love him the way we never had, the way we always swore we would."

I crushed her hand in mine. "I will. I will."

"Don't let him be—" Her breath caught, her eyes closed for a moment, "—too crazy wild like me."

"Come on, Rube, just a little bit. Can't fight DNA."

A faint grin swept her lips then faded. "He's my little bit of gold, Grace. Yours too."

My chest caved in. "Yes, he is." Her hand reached up and curled into my shirt. I squeezed her wrist. "What is it, honey?"

Her eyes widened again. "Try." She tugged me down close to her once more and wheezed. "No more ghosts, new dreams. Get on with joy."

"Simple as that?" I breathed. She only nodded at me. Her eyelids closed and her raspy breathing somewhat evened out. My eyes darted up at the monitors. They continued their sonorous beeping and blipping.

"You're my grandpa?"

Ray nodded at his grandson. "Look at that, you have my eyes. Just like your momma and your aunt."

Tilting his head, Jake wiped his tiny fingers across Ray's brow. "Are you here to see Mommy?"

"Yes, I am, Jake." Ray's palms were splayed on his jeans. "Can I give you a hug first?" Jake nodded. Ray scooped him up and squeezed him in his arms, and Jake nestled his head in his grandfather's neck. Jake's eyes widened up at me, and I smiled at him. Boner's arms tightened around my middle.

"I'm glad you came, Grandpa. Mommy needs us."

"Yes, she does," Ray said. "She certainly does." He patted Jake on the back and set him down on the floor.

"Jakey, you want to stay with Lock and Boner while Grandpa and I go in to see Mommy?" I asked. "Daddy's inside with her now, he'll be out in a bit." Jake nodded absently.

Lock held out his hand to Jake. Jake swung his head up at him and put his tiny hand in Lock's large one.

"Time for chocolate, what do you say?" asked Lock, his voice low.

Boner released me and touched Jake's shoulder. "I think we need to try out those video games in the lounge, huh?" Jake's eyes lit up at the two tall leather-clad bikers covered in dust and dirt smiling down at him. Anyone else might have run for the hills.

"Okay." The corners of Jake's mouth tugged down.

Lock's heavy gaze held mine for a moment. He leaned down and swept Jake up in his arms popping him on his back, his hands wrapping around his legs. Jake flung his arms around Lock's neck.

Boner clapped his hand on Jake's back. "That's some big horse you got there, little dude," he murmured. Jake smiled at me, and I blew him a kiss. Lock and Jake ambled down the carpeted hallway of the hospice with Boner in tow.

I pulled on my father's arm. "Dad."

His watery gaze jumped to mine, his brows pulled in tight. "Say it, girl."

"You got to make this right." My voice faltered and I took in a breath. Breathing. Something so simple, so natural. Something Ruby could no longer do. "You got to make it right between the two of you before she goes. Please."

His hands rubbed at the sides of his face. "You think I don't know that? You think this hasn't been weighing on me for years?"

"Oh, it has? Shocker."

"Grace."

I clamped my jaw shut and swallowed hard. "There's no more time to be nice and step carefully on the millions of eggshells we're standing on."

"I know." He nodded and let out a gust of air "Want you in there, too." I pushed open the door to Ruby's room, and my heart broke. Alex was slumped on the bed asleep with his arms draped over Ruby's middle.

"Alex, honey," I whispered over my brother-in-law's haggard face.

His eyes bulged open one after the other. "W-What?"

"You fell asleep."

"Oh shit." His body jerked, and he grabbed his wife's hand. "Ruby?" She blinked at him. Alex planted a kiss on her forehead, and he sat up glancing at us. "Oh, Ray. Just get in?" Ray only nodded, keeping his hands in the pockets of his plush hunting jacket.

"Lock and Boner took Jake for a snack and video games in the lounge," I said.

Alex rubbed his eyes. "Okay. Think I'll go find some coffee." He took Ruby's hand in his and kissed her finger tips. "Be right back, baby." He squeezed my arm as he shuffled out of the room.

Ruby smirked and let out a wheeze of air. "Father and daughter."

"Hey, Rube," I said.

Ray approached her bed. "I need to tell you, Ruby. I need to say it." Ruby trained her tired eyes on him. "I know. I was a crap dad to both of you girls. I know that. At the time I couldn't do any different. Wasn't in me. It was selfish, and I'm sorry you two suffered for it.

Ruby nudged at her oxygen mask. "And Ma."

"And your mother, yes. Oh yes. Wasn't right of us to take our problems out on you two. Just wasn't right. You both paid the price for it." Ray glanced at me. I sank down on the edge of Ruby's bed, putting my hand on the thick cotton comforter over her shin.

"It's way too late for excuses and explanations, I know that," he continued. "After Jason died, nothing fit right for me no more. Not even you two smiling at me, tugging on my hand, not even your ma trying so hard to be a good wife. Nothing. I was all wrong. I was suffocating in that house, choking."

"Montana has. . .fresher air?" Ruby wheezed.

Ray shook his head tightly. "Couldn't go too far away." His breath snagged. "I want you to know that I always loved you. I'm sorry I couldn't show you. I thought it'd be better for everyone if I left, stayed away. That was very shortsighted of me. Then it was too hard to come back."

Ruby turned her head, her lips parted slightly.

"I'm sorry I couldn't be the dad you two needed me to be. I regret that." He leaned over Ruby, his fingers brushing across her cheek. "Forgive me, Ruby girl. Forgive a stupid old man. I want you to know it was all me that was wrong, not you. You were. . .you were wonderful." The air swirled from the room. Ray sniffed in air. "Your Jake's a beautiful boy. You did good, Ruby."

Ruby forced in air. "Got one thing right."

"Oh, no." Ray shook his head. "Whole lot of things, girl. You took care of your momma and your little sister all on your own. You did good. Yes, you did."

Ruby's eyes blinked slowly. "Can't be a part. . .of my boy's life if you're going to be a. . .shit grandpa." I grinned and bit my bottom lip.

"Straight shooter, as ever. I'll be here for that boy, Ruby. I'll be right here."

"And be good . . ." She fought for air, her gaze darted to me. "Be good to Grace."

Always looking out for me, my big sister, no matter what. Even on her dying breath.

"I'll be here for your sister." Ray's voice broke. Ruby's eyes drifted. Ray turned away from the bed and staggered towards the window where his hands reached out and gripped the frame. His body sagged, his shoulders shook.

Two days after she entered the hospice, at a few minutes after four o'clock in the morning, Ruby passed away.

Alex and Ray were stretched out on pull-out armchairs. Jake and I were curled up together on the sofa. A slight cough followed by a choking sound woke me. I opened my eyes and jerked upright. Alex's face was buried in Ruby's pillow, his muffled cries filling the room. Ray stared blindly out the window as he sat on the edge of Ruby's bed, his silent tears streaking his face. I glanced down at Jake, his face swollen with sleep, and I folded him in my arms, burying my face in his hair to stop the world from spinning.

Ray and I left the hospice and went to the funeral home in Meager to make the arrangements. You couldn't tell it was morning as the vast sky was thick with those gray popcorn clouds. On the way back to the club where I had my car, I told Ray to stop at our old house.

"What's the point, Grace?" His thumbs flicked up from the steering wheel. "What for?"

I clicked my seatbelt into place, my gaze trained on the road. "Just go."

He swatted at his blinker. Within five minutes we pulled up alongside the driveway of the scene of so many crimes. Ray inhaled a deep gust of air.

"Is it hard for you, Ray? Being here?"

He shoved the gear stick into park. His gaze remained straight ahead.

"Well, isn't that too damn bad," I muttered snapping the seatbelt off. I jumped out of his SUV, slammed the door, and strode over the thick emerald lawn. The cracked driveway that in another era had once been filled with loud pickup trucks and great gleaming Harleys had been re-paved. A brand new silver Mazda minivan stood still over its black smoothness.

A banner decorated with colored leaves and acorns flapped in the gentle breeze from a pole by the cobalt blue front door. The windows had been reframed with matching blue shutters and replaced with brand new storm windows. My eyes fell on the window of my old room. It was the one Ruby used to climb in and out of in the wee hours because my room was further away from our parents' bedroom. She'd tell me all about her adventures of the night, and I'd soak in every crazy detail, then we'd both drift off to sleep on my bed.

Wheat colored curtains were now drawn in the living room window. In that living room, Dig and I often found refuge from the club for a spell of quiet time alone together before we bought our own small house. We would cook together, then eat in front of the television or listen to music and talk stretched out on the sofa. Those nights were rare, though, weren't they? If I wasn't at work, there was always somewhere he had to be, something he had to take care of.

I pushed my hair back from my face and peered at the side yard. The rusty swing set that Jason used to love and that none of us had the bravery to get rid of after he'd died, was gone, replaced by a solid wooden fort. I stood transfixed on that lush, green lawn, my pulse thudding in my neck.

I had to see if the house was still here. Still standing. Like I was. Like Ray was. Standing, breathing. But the house had moved on. It had survived us and had been transformed. What did I expect? That it stood here untouched as a monument to my experiences? No, it most certainly hadn't.

Our old house now contained new lives and new hopes, dreams, and memories that belonged to another family, another generation. The Hastings clan had been wiped clean, exorcised. Today I'd wanted to see that. And I saw it.

Today.

A new day.

A rotten, bitter day.

"Grace? Grace, is that you?"

My head snapped to the side. "Karen?"

Karen still lived next door, and she still had that strawberry-blonde hair, wide smile, and those dimples. She and her husband Bill had been newlyweds when they had moved in next door to us just before Jason died.

"Hey, honey! Haven't seen you in so long. Oh my gosh!" She swept me up in a robust hug. "Ruby used to stop by for a cup of coffee here and there. She's got herself a beautiful boy. Did you ever get married again, Grace? You got kids now?"

"House looks good." I gestured at my former home.

"Doesn't it? A nice young family bought it a couple of years ago. Two kids and a third on the way, would you believe? They really do a good job keeping it up, just painted it last month. They're out here gardening all the time."

I nodded, my gaze drifting over the property once again.

Her eyes narrowed over me, and she frowned. "Have you moved back now, Grace, or just here on a visit?"

"How's Bill?"

"Bill's good. Now we're home alone. The twins are both married and living in California."

"That's nice."

"We want to take a road trip to see them. Bill's got his birthday in a few months. Thought I'd surprise him with a new car to get us to California. Something with pizzazz that's also dependable on the road, but I'm not sure what exactly. He's at that age now, when he wants a little sizzle in his life." She rolled her eyes.

I glanced at Karen's driveway. A green Ford Explorer was parked there. "Does he still have the Nova?"

Karen let out a laugh. "Are you kidding? Of course he does. Wouldn't part with that car for love or money."

My mother had slammed into Bill's prized Nova one night trying to park in front of our house after a drunken spree at Pete's. She had overshot our driveway, jammed on the gas instead of the brakes, and rammed right into back of the Nova. Bill had been furious. Ruby had been hysterical with laughter for days.

"Honey, you okay?" Karen asked.

"Does Bill ever take the Nova to Wreck's Repair?"

"At the club?" Karen tilted her head slightly. "Yeah, he goes there for his tune-ups."

"He must know Lock who runs the shop. Lock does custom paint jobs, original designs. He could give the Nova some of that sizzle."

Karen grinned. "Oh yeah?"

"I'll give you his number." I took out my cell phone. "He does good work. Usually works on bikes. Insist on an appointment, Karen."

"Okay. I'll insist." Karen touched my arm. "Honey, what is it? You don't look so good."

"Come say hello to Dad."

Her eyebrows shot up. "Is that Ray in that SUV?" I nodded. "I'll be damned!" Karen charged over to the Enclave. My father opened the door and hopped down. She let out a laugh and clapped her hands together. "Ray Hastings, is that you?" Dad grinned briefly as his hand reached out to shake Karen's.

I stayed rooted on my formerly scabby lawn, which was now velvety green and bordered with white and gold chrysanthemums. Ruby and I had never done any gardening. Never even thought about it.

I raised my head at the sky and admired the billows of puffy popcorn clouds in gray blue and ashy white. I couldn't get enough of them.

"Good to finally meet her sister. Ruby used to talk about you a lot, you know. I'm so sorry."

I nodded at another one of Ruby's friends. My hand was finally released.

Ray covered the costs of Ruby's burial in Meager in the same plot with our mother, as well as the coffin and a huge spray of white roses. Ray had taken care of her birth and death, but not a hell of a lot in between. Funny how that worked out.

He stood with me and Alex as friends of Ruby's expressed their condolences. Many I remembered from high school, others were from her work at the addiction counseling center. Their names were familiar, but their faces were foreign to me. Erica was there with her husband. So were Karen and Bill. Lock, Jump and Alicia, Kicker and Mary Lynn, Suzi and Bear and Boner had come along with Dawes, Peck, Dready, and Clip. Jump had made it an official event for the chapter.

"You will always be a part of this club."

Even though there were just a small number of people here, it was a huge relief to finally not have to shake hands, not have to smile, or listen to small talk any longer.

It was over.

"Oh, Grace!" Karen pulled me into a deep hug. Lock stared at me over her shoulder, his eyes smoky, his jaw tight. "I'm so glad you're staying. That boy, that poor boy!" she said through sniffs.

"Let the woman be, darlin'," Bill's hands tugged on Karen's shoulders. He shook my hand, then Ray's.

My eyes stayed on Lock's. He drank me in.

Grace. Baby . . .

My gaze drifted.

Mary Lynn and Suzi put their arms through mine. Dee stood in front of me, her mouth moving. I couldn't hear what she said. Her mascara was badly smudged, her face red. My arm moved. Jake pulled on my hand, swinging it up and down.

Ray gave Jake a hug, and they shared a few words. He shook Alex's hand, nodded at Lock and turned back to me. Suddenly, he embraced me, sighed heavily, then released me and strode away.

Alex swept his son up in his arms and planted a kiss on my cheek. Jake waved at me. *My beautiful boy.* Father and son disappeared down the green hill towards the big iron gate.

Lock stood with Dawes and Kicker smoking a cigarette. His mirrored aviators now cloaked his eyes, the angles of his face tight as he watched me.

My gaze slid to the open grave. The cemetery workers hovered over Ruby's coffin and fiddled with their system of pulleys and belts. She didn't belong to me anymore. To any of us. The earth was claiming her. The coffin jerked slightly and down it went into the cold hard ground of Meager. A rolling, manicured green expanse of lawn had this one hole in it today. A gaping gash yawned wide to receive my sister's cancer ravaged flesh now locked in a beautiful wooden casket lined in white satin and sealed forever.

Ruby hated satin, didn't she?

Alicia's throaty voice called my name. And again. A hand pressed on my arm. I wiped it away. The sharp wind pricked my skin.

Remains.

What remains of me though?

The roar of pipes made me turn. A huge chopper came right down the long path halfway towards the gravesite and stopped. Ruby would have loved that. My eyes lifted to the rider.

Butler.

Lock moved towards me. Boner's voice boomed behind me.

Butler lifted his black sunglasses, and his icy blue eyes pierced mine. The insolent rumble of his engine arrogantly ripped through the eerie calm, proclaiming, protesting, objecting.

I sprinted forward.

I flipped my bag's long strap across my chest, jerked my stretchy black skirt up my thighs, grabbed onto Butler's shoulder, and swung my leg over his bike.

We tore out of the cemetery in a dizzying blur.

NINETEEN

"MORE TEQUILA FOR MY WOMAN!" Butler slammed his fist on the table. We both roared with laughter.

The small party at Butler's clubhouse was in full swing, and I was tightly wound on booze, nerves, and plenty of denial. Sally, a plump woman in her mid-fifties, ran over with the bottle and filled my glass.

Sally was a former VP's widow who still hung around the club and kept things somewhat organized and clean. However, there was only so much one woman could do. The North Dakota chapter's clubhouse was a freaking pit. The windows were streaked with grime, and the odor of stale beer and mildew permeated the air. Black smudges from drinks and stomped-on food bits marked the worn, patchy linoleum.

"Thanks, Sally."

She grinned at me. "Sure, Sister."

Butler plucked the glass from my hand and knocked back the tequila. "Hey!" I slapped his large bicep. He grabbed my face with both hands and bent to kiss me. I parted my lips, and the liquor from his mouth flowed into mine. I arched up against him and swallowed the warm stinging nectar in one go. I straddled his lap and gave him a fat kiss in return. His laughter tickled down my throat.

This was the Butler I remembered.

The hot Dionysus, the god of the unquenchable good time, and the endless party. I was not on his periphery anymore. He was no longer stealthily flashing that killer smile and those arctic blue eyes at me, after which a spray of ephemeral gold dust would scatter over me. Now I was the center of his fucked up magic kingdom.

Lucky me.

As one of Dig's new recruits for the One-Eyed Jacks right around the time I had hooked up with Dig, Butler had shown his exemplary flare for the dramatic. That summer the club had had rough dealings with another club in Colorado. Negotiations over transport had not been going well, and one of the other club's prospects had been needling Butler, calling him "pretty boy" over and over again.

The guy had made repeated demands on Butler to bring over beers, food, check on their bikes, a whole variety of the usual little chores and tasks. Butler had kept his cool until the idiot told him to get on his knees and shine his boots. That's when our blond god had finally lost it. He'd broke a beer bottle and jammed it into the jerk's throat, shouting, "What do I look like—your fucking butler?"

"Hang on, beautiful." Butler planted a kiss on my forehead and pushed up from the sofa where we had been lounging and necking for the past hour. He jerked his chin at Tail, his VP who shoved his woman of the hour to the side. It was Iris, Lock's black-haired concubine. She glared at me for the hundredth time that night as she leaned against the bar.

Hi-ya! Slut power, girlfriend!

Tail approached Butler and listened to what he had to tell him. He nodded and went back to Iris, a hand landing on her ass. Butler gestured to one of the prospects behind the bar. The guy leaned over the bar.

I blinked. Familiar. Familiar. Who was he? I bit the inside of my cheek. Wasn't he one of the Demon Seeds who had held onto me in that warehouse in Montana? He handed Butler a small envelope and the two of them tapped fists. Dammit, I couldn't be sure. I rubbed at my eyes, fatigue and booze had caught up with me. I sat up on the sofa and straightened my back as I sucked back some beer from Butler's bottle.

"What you looking at?" It was Creeper, one of Butler's brothers who definitely fulfilled his name. In his early forties, Creeper sported long stringy brown hair, permanently dirty fingernails, raggedy jeans, and a perpetual leer on his face. He'd sported the same look twenty years ago.

I gestured at Butler's back. "I was appreciating my fine piece of ass until you got in my face."

"Yeah," he said on a long sigh nodding at me. His eyes were pinned and they seemed to pulse.

"You got a problem, Creeper?"

"Me? Fuck no. I just hope my prez don't, that's all."

"What's the matter, couldn't get a little girl to climb into your lap tonight?"

Creeper threw his head back and laughed.

"What's going on?" Butler's voice sliced between us.

"Just yakking," Creeper said.

Butler scowled at him. "Get lost." Creeper made a face, took a drag on his cigarette butt, and slunk off. Butler tugged me off the sofa and led me down a short hallway to a room. Once inside I immediately kicked my boots off and rid myself of my black tights. He peeled me out of my blouse and skirt. I slid his colors off him, and he tugged off his T-shirt revealing his bare chest.

His fingers ran down my sides. "Baby, you're a sight to see." Butler sank down on his knees in front of me, his hands gripping my ass, and licked at my inner thighs. His pierced tongue prodded at my clit through the sheer fabric of my panty, and I let out a tiny gasp as my fingers dragged through his spiky hair.

The door to the bathroom creaked open, and I flinched back. Two giggling nearly naked blondes appeared in the lit doorway draped over one another. Their nipples and belly buttons were pierced with small gold hoops, and they wore only teeny-weeny thongs.

"Aw, it's my kitties," Butler drawled. "Get your asses over here." He tottered up and pushed me back on the bed. I fell against the edge of the mattress.

"Butler?" My head swam. I propped myself up on my elbows.

He planted a wet kiss on each girl's mouth and fondled their breasts "What a nice surprise." They giggled.

He released them and threw himself into the armchair opposite the bed. He took out the envelope from his pocket, leaned over the table next to him, and poured cocaine onto a small mirror. He arranged it and snorted two lines through a small, rolled-up paper. He slumped back against the cushioned chair and inhaled deeply, rubbing the sides of his nose and wiping at it with the back of his hand. The blondes got down on the floor between us and started kissing, making moaning noises as they flicked their tongues over each other's nipple rings. Butler's gaze was riveted on them, his mouth hanging open.

"Good kitties." Butler barked out a laugh and leaned over and snorted more coke.

"Baby?" I asked from my tequila haze, barely able to sit up. Could he even hear me? The room began to wobble.

Butler grunted and pulled his cock out of his jeans. "Do it."

The girls crawled over to me. Their hands reached out and caressed my thighs. "What the hell?"

"My kitties'll take care of you, beautiful. Relax."

The girls were obviously twins, practically identical. Very young, blonde, blue-eyed with perfect, small breasts. They looked eerily familiar. My clouded brain strained. *Dammit, who? Who was it . . .?*

My body froze. They looked just like Caitlyn, Butler's dead wife.

Caitlyn was the one who had a thing for piercings. She had them everywhere and had gotten Butler to join her in the fascination. She had been determined to get me a belly ring once, but I had chickened out at the last minute. Getting a tattoo didn't bother me, but a piercing was a whole other kettle of soup in my opinion. Caitlyn had laughed at me when I had decided instead on an extra hole in my right ear lobe for a tiny diamond stud.

The air in the room suddenly got hotter and pressed in on me.

Kitty One tugged my panty down my legs, then nudged my knees open. Kitty Two climbed up on the mattress and took one of my breasts in her mouth. My eyes widened at the sensation of a small metal ball rolling over my skin. "Stop it!"

Butler jerked his cock faster.

Holy shit.

I had never been with a woman before, and I didn't intend to start now. I kicked her away and twisted on the mattress. "Butler?" Two hands clamped down on my wrists and others dug painfully into my thighs.

"This is all for you, baby. Gonna feel so good," Butler said through ragged breaths.

That choking sensation in my lungs tightened. I twisted against them, but I had no strength left. My joints had turned to jelly, and those four hands and two mouths had a firm grip on me. I could barely breathe, barely think. Butler spit out a slew of curses from his armchair, and the girls emitted breathy moaning sounds as if on cue.

"I'm gonna get you a hood ring, sweetheart." Butler laughed. "I'm gonna make your pussy sing." Yeah, a piercing down there was what I was missing. Frankly I didn't think Butler could put forth the effort to make anyone or anything sing right at this moment.

He stumbled over to us and stood over the bed, his wet erection in his hand, his eyes burning. The Kitty on the bed scuttled over to the edge of the mattress and sat up on her knees. Butler shoved his cock in her mouth and grunted.

I pushed at the other Kitty twin with my foot, and she fell back on the floor giggling. Butler fisted his fingers in the other one's hair and ground into her face. He screwed his eyes shut, lost in his own world.

Just fucking lost.

I crawled up the bed, leaned back against the headboard and watched. Butler muttered a round of expletives and pumped harder, his breathing growing even more labored. The other Kitty got up from the floor, pushed her sister out of the way, and took Butler in her mouth working him furiously. Shit, this could go on all night long.

Butler's strained eyes found mine. His face reddened, his body stiffened, and he let out a yell, finally shooting whatever wad he had into her mouth. She groaned and licked him dry. Her sister let out a soft giggle and flopped back on the bed. Butler dropped onto the mattress and crumpled over the girls. All three of them snickered and groaned.

I crawled out of the mess of a bed, found my panties and bra and tugged them back on. My legs shook as I stood over them. The Kitties glanced up at me and surprise flickered over their dazed features.

"Get out," I said. They only laughed and sighed.

I disengaged their limbs from Butler's body and rolled them off the bed. The two of them slithered over to the cocaine table and rubbed some coke along their gums.

"Get the fuck out!"

They frowned at me, stumbled to the door, and banged it shut behind them.

Butler snored from the bed. I pulled his jeans off of him, and he curled into a ball on the twisted sheets. He went back to snoring, and I dropped the jeans on the chair, glanced at him once more, then nabbed the envelope from the table. I went into the bathroom and turned on the light. Words were scribbled on the inside of the envelope:

Canada is on.
Will text details.

I returned the envelope to the table.

"Baby?" Butler mumbled. "Come here." I laid down next to him and wrapped my arms around him like I would a child. My hand stroked his back.

"I'm here," I whispered. He sighed and settled into me. A smear of blood smudged the edge of his nose and the top of his lip.

"That was fun, huh? Gonna have lots of fun together, baby. Wanna make you happy." I planted a kiss on his forehead. If only that gentleness could help ease his lonely, crazy wild. Of course it wouldn't.

I forced my muscles to relax into the mattress and tried not to think about the questionable sheets underneath me. My dazed thoughts tripped over themselves and eventually landed on Lock. As they usually did.

Lock. Lock. Lock.

Tall Lock. Lanky Lock. Silent Lock. Lonely Lock. Lock's cock.

I wonder where Lock's cock is tonight?

My gut swirled. My brain spilled over.

Alicia will really be disappointed, won't she? Tonight was not the romantic reunion she had in mind.

I closed my eyes, but I knew it was useless. Sleep wouldn't come.

I was now officially flapping in the wind.

Dig had once promised me that he and the club wouldn't leave me 'flapping in the wind'.

So this is what it felt like.

Flappin' flippin' flappin' flap flap flap.

Oh no, wait. Lock was out there somewhere, close by, keeping tabs on me. Maybe he couldn't sleep either.

Yes, we're on a job here, aren't we?

And Daddy was back in Montana, back to not being inconvenienced or held back by his family. Oh wait, I was all that was left of that family.

No, there's Jake.

Yes. Concentrate on Jake. This is all for Jake.

I rubbed a hand over my sore eyes. What was that song that Phil, a neighbor of mine at my apartment in Seattle, used to blast with hellish regularity during his drawn out divorce drama? I had learned the words against my will over the course of those months. It was some British synth duo. . .ah, Hurts, that's it.

Perfect.

The bittersweet words came to me. My hoarse, creaky voice ruptured the darkness in Butler's room.

Yes, the lyrics to "Blind" made complete sense to me now.

TWENTY

MILLER

I WAITED ON MY BIKE in the parking lot of the Mandan Harley store just outside of Bismarck, North Dakota.

I had my leather jacket on over my colors. I was on my second hour and onto my tenth cigarette. It was Saturday afternoon and the place was busy.

But no sign of Grace and Butler. Yet.

Grace had called Alicia early this morning. In the course of their superficial conversation Grace had said the previously agreed upon magic phrase that let us know something was up, and she needed a meet to share important information. I had been up here since yesterday anyhow. Whenever she came up to Butler's, I came up and hovered nearby. Boner had wanted to do it, but I had insisted on the job. I couldn't leave Grace on her own with that shithead and his merry band of assholes. And I couldn't not punish myself for putting her here. I needed to be here, to see it. Until my eyes burned.

A twisted, bleeding, pathetic guardian angel.

A group of four North Dakota One-Eyed Jacks roared into the lot up front by the entrance to the store. Finally.

I flicked my cigarette to the ground.

Butler pulled his bike to a stop, and Grace hopped off. Her hands reached out and smoothed down the bandana he wore on his head, and the asshole grinned up at her. Butler got off his bike, hooked his arm over her shoulders, and they strode into the store. His three brothers trailed behind them.

Game on.

This was the second time she had spent a few days with Butler. The first was when she had taken off with him at the cemetery a week ago, which had shocked the shit out of me. She hadn't shed one tear at the service. Her face had been an unreadable mask. On Grace it was bizarre.

That beautiful face was usually so expressive, a combination of girlish innocence and thoughtful seriousness that I found damned irresistible. But at the funeral it was blank, as if she had bled out. It only got worse at the cemetery. She had been in her own world. She had ignored Alicia. I had moved towards her, but she'd jumped away from me as if I was some kind of freak she had to escape. Boner had called out to her, but she didn't even turn around. Nothing. She bolted and got on the back of Butler's bike. That gouged me deep. She was hurting, and I couldn't help her.

I checked my watch. Over twenty minutes had passed since Butler and Grace had entered the store. Time to move.

Families and couples browsed through the ridiculous variety of pricey clothing and accessories, plenty of folks inquired about bikes and parts at the other end of the building. Lots of movement, some noise. Perfect. The brothers were on their own in the repair and parts shop.

I stood in a thick forest of leather jackets against a back wall on the other end of the store and waited for her. My hands smoothed over the thick, fresh leather, and I inhaled that epic scent. The display racks were high at this end and full of bulky merchandise that provided good cover. I took a few steps back into the leather jungle and waited for her.

Three teenage girls rifled through a rack of tank tops and T-shirts in the women's section, and there was Grace going through the rack of kid's T-shirts on the other side. She plucked one hanger off the rack, checked the tag, looked over the design on the front, then the back, then the front again, and put it back on the rack. Her back was stiff, her movements sharp. She did that same exact thing three times over until she held onto two T-shirts in her hand. She weaved her way towards the leather jackets.

Towards me.

She stopped just a couple of yards away. I pushed my sunglasses up on my head. My pulse raced. "Hey."

Her face was pale, dark circles shadowed her eyes. Her lips seemed taut, thinner. Her opaque eyes, more gray-brown than green, darted around us.

"I don't have much time. He's clingy."

My jaw clenched. "Yeah, I noticed."

She tilted her head at me. "You noticed?" Her voice was brittle.

"Every time you come up here, I'm here too." My lips sealed into a firm line.

"Right." Her face darkened. "Hope it's been entertaining for you."

It's been total shit, baby.

Grace adjusted the sunglasses on her head with a quick flick of her fingers. "I recognized someone at their clubhouse last week, from our trip to Montana." Her fingers absently stroked the textured sleeve of a brown leather jacket that hung in front of her.

"A Demon Seed?"

"Yeah." She blinked up at me then returned her attention to the jacket. "He was one of the guys who brought me into the warehouse in Montana where Vig was waiting for me. He looked like a Demon Seed recruit at the time, but the other night he wasn't wearing colors. Thought that was strange. I would have said something sooner, but I wasn't sure it was him the first time I saw him. He's in and out of their clubhouse pretty regularly. I've been trying hard not to pay him any attention, just be in a Butler tizzy all the time." She rolled her eyes. "But I know it's him."

Oh God, her voice was flat, the richness gone. I swallowed hard. "Got a name?"

She didn't look at me. Her eyes darted everywhere: on her boots, the jackets, price tags. Everywhere except at me.

"Crank."

"Anything else?" I took a few more steps back closer to another line of jackets against the wall, and she followed me casually, a finger pushing back a lock of stray hair.

Baby, look at me. Please, give me that much, just once.

"I get the impression most of the crew doesn't really fall in behind Butler, especially Creeper," Grace whispered, her eyes finally on me. "I can't say I blame them, he's high almost all the time. Too much coke and plenty of weed. Then he throws in the booze at night and it becomes a three-ring circus." Her face tensed momentarily, and my eyes narrowed over her. "He can't be making many good decisions like this." She let out a huff. "Creeper seems to be the one watching over the henhouse."

"Grace . . ."

"Crank brings him the coke in an envelope. I checked it out when he was asleep. I found a message that Canada was on and to expect a text. I've been checking his phone regularly whenever he's asleep. He finally got the text yesterday from Vig. Butler and his boys are bringing in a truck from Canada on Thursday, switching it out here, then bringing the goods to Montana for him on Friday."

"This Thursday?"

"Yeah. Must be a big payoff. Butler, Creeper, and Tail were all smiles and happy feet last night after the text came in. I wrote down the coordinates for the location of the switch out for you." Her voice was low.

She stepped forward, inches from me, took a tiny crumpled ball of paper from her front jeans pocket, reached out, and stuffed it in the front pocket of my jeans, tucking it in, her eyes glued to mine. Her fingertips barely brushed my body, but it was electric. The sweet minty green scent of her shampoo drifted over me, and our nights together came crashing in on my memory, my cock stirring in my jeans, my pulse racing. The breath caught in my chest and pinched there.

A frown shadowed her face, and she took a step back. "Butler's going to hang on to it for one night, then make the delivery into Montana the next day." Her gaze slid back to the jackets hanging high over us against the wall.

I wanted to pull her in my arms, stroke her back until she relaxed into me. But that was a fucking fantasy right here in the middle of the store with Butler and his boys under the same roof. Anyway, that was done with. She wouldn't want that from me anymore, would she?

Not after you sold her out and let her fall into the snake pit.

Maybe she and Butler had rekindled their long lost fucking fire? I could barely think about that without my skin crawling and a red rage whipping through me. But, no, I didn't think so. No way. She didn't look too happy. In fact, she didn't look happy at all.

"Grace, how are you holding up?"

"It is what it is," came her reply in an unrecognizable, flat voice.

I wasn't sure I wanted to know what that meant. The thought of Grace in the middle of a club brewing its own poison led by a dick off his rocker who thought he had her in the bag was making me come unhinged with every passing minute.

"When are you coming home?" I said through my clamped jaw.

236

My eyes scanned the clothing section for any movement through my lookout gap. Those teenage girls were onto another rack comparing handbags and gabbing on their cell phones. A saleswoman opened the sunglass case and took out several for a waiting customer. Two older heavy set bikers and their old ladies checked out the stand with the rain gear. Grace blinked up at me, her hands twisting the T-shirts on their tiny hangers.

"Tomorrow. I called Boner to come pick me up."

"I'm here. I can come."

"No, not you." She averted her gaze once again. She might as well have ripped a knife through my gut. Grace always seemed to drink in my eyes as if she was absorbing some sort of secret from them that only she understood. Our gazes had always lingered, but now she avoided my eyes as if she didn't need to look at me, as if it was a chore to be with me. Like she'd done at the cemetery.

Look at me, Grace.

I tried to swallow past the cement blocks in my throat. The tension in the air between us was suddenly as thick as tar. "Those for Jake?" I pointed at the T-shirts crumpled in her hands.

Grace nodded. "Got to go."

Shit, she barely spoke in full sentences. She turned away, and my stomach twisted. She was leaving again. Leaving me. Getting back on that motherfucker's bike. What the hell could I offer her now? What could I say? I had no fucking idea, I only knew I couldn't let her go like this.

My hand flew out and grabbed hers. "Grace . . ."

She spun back to me, her eyes blazing down at our hands, her face tight. She jerked against my grasp. "You don't get to do this. Not now," she said on a hiss. "Now we're all about what's good for the club. You made sure of that, right? So did I."

And there it was.

"Let me go," she said under her breath.

I winced. *Can't let you go.*

I released her hand, and she snapped hers back at the same time. Her handbag went flying off her arm, its contents spilling onto the floor.

"Shit!" Grace scowled and got on her knees. She tossed tubes of lip balm, a pack of tissues, keys, pens, her cell phone, a wallet, and a whole lot of other girl crap back into her bag.

My eyes zeroed in on a brown prescription bottle. I crouched down and snapped it up. It was half-full of pills. My eyes widened over the label. A recent prescription of anti-depressant meds filled at a pharmacy in Rapid City.

"You taking these?"

Her steely eyes cut to mine, her body visibly stiffening. She plucked a hairbrush and a small round mirror off the floor shoving them into her black suede handbag. "That's none of your business."

"I've been to war, Grace. I know all about post-traumatic stress and anxiety. You need the relief?" She ignored me.

We had put her in harm's way, hadn't we? Now all her old buttons were being pushed once more, and maybe new ones were being created. How was she really holding up under the strain? She was vulnerable, way too vulnerable, but my Grace was strong. Always had been. And she had to be now. She had Jake. She had me—

Fuck.

She snatched the prescription bottle from my hand and shoved it in her bag. "If you must know, for the past sixteen years, off and on when needed."

"You're not mixing them with blow or anything else are you?"

She zipped her bag closed.

"Grace?"

Her eyes came up to mine. Hard, cold. They weren't filled with any sort of emotion, unlike that deep wash of luminous gray-green they transformed into when I moved inside her, her pink mouth gasping for air, her small hands clutching my back.

"What's it to you?"

Fucking everything.

"We done here?" That sharp coldness in her voice, a voice stripped of any emotion, pricked at my skin.

I sank back on my haunches, gritting my teeth. Grace leaned into me. "This has been such fun." The snide tone in her voice left a trail of acid in my ears which drained right down into the twisted muscle that thudded against my ribs.

She took off, her stride long, her back stiff. My palms dug into to my forehead, and I squeezed my eyes shut against the burn.

Yeah, that's what locked down looked like.

"Is that it for today, ma'am?" the cashier's voice rang out.

"That's all," came Grace's taut, rigid voice.
And that's what locked down sounded like.

TWENTY-ONE

GRACE
PAST

DIG'S EYES WERE READY TO BURST. "What the fuck?" he growled, his body still.

"What the hell did I do, brother?" Butler shouted.

Wreck shook his head. "You are such a goddamn idiot."

"Cause I looked at his woman?" Butler asked. "Shit, man! She's around, we talk, I look. So does everybody else. What do you want from me?"

"You don't just look. You *watch* her all the time," Dig said. "Think I didn't notice when we camped out last weekend? You think I'm some kinda moron with my head up my ass?"

I froze. He knew. Oh my God.

"But today you touched her. Nobody touches what's mine. Nobody touches my old lady."

I opened my mouth to explain, but I clamped it shut again. This was between the brothers. And it was a long time coming.

Half an hour before I had been organizing the shed, perched on a tall metal ladder to place three rusty Double Eagle Motor Oil cans on the highest shelf on the wall. Wreck had found the vintage cans in Wyoming and had brought them home the night before. I hadn't opened the ladder wide enough though, and it had seesawed under me. Butler had held onto the ladder as I clambered down, but then he'd slid one arm around my back and one under my knees, lifted me in his arms and pulled me close.

Too close.

"Butler, let me down. Come on." He'd only laughed and swung me around.

"Please put me down."

Jump and Dig had walked in just then, and all hell had broken loose.

"Aw, man, Come on! Wasn't anything!" Butler shrugged his shoulders and flashed a stiff grin. "Shit, brother, you used to share all the time."

I scowled. Boner shook his head and let out a groan. "Wrong thing to say, asswipe."

"True colors," Wreck said. "You show 'em time and time again, boy. Just can't help your fucking self, can you?"

Dig's burning grip on my wrist tightened. "You watch her like an alligator waiting to pounce on his next meal. You keep your fucking dick in your pants or I'm gonna have to do it for you. She's my old lady. She's mine, goddammit!" Dig smacked my ass where my new tattoo of his wildflower with our initials entwined in the leaves had just been inked the day before. I jerked and hissed in air. The skin was still sensitive. "She's got my mark on her," he seethed. "I'm the one in her day and night. Not you, not ever."

"I wouldn't fuck your old lady, man. You're my brother. That shit just isn't done."

"But you still wanna get as close as you can, don't you?" said Wreck. "You just keep pushing at her, keep pushing." He leaned into Butler and pointed at me. "And that girl's too nice to tell you to fuck off."

My gaze darted over the men. Jump glared at me, his sneer full of bitter contempt. I looked away.

"I don't think he got the message, Dig," said Boner, his eyes that unusual cold green color. "He thinks he can get away with this shit time and time again."

"Got to agree," Wreck pulled me out of Dig's grasp and tucked me behind his body. I finally let out the breath I'd been holding onto.

Dig hovered over Butler. "You hear that, motherfucker?"

A muscle in Butler's jaw tensed. His mouth fell open, and he shook his head at his brothers. "Look, I'm sorry, all right?"

Dig's eyes flashed. "Sorry?"

Wreck unstuck my hands from his arms and pushed me back, motioning me with a jerk of his chin to get in the clubhouse. I retreated into the doorway, but I watched. I couldn't not watch. My stomach scrunched.

"I'm not buying your shit, brother."

"C'mon, Dig!" Butler's hand tugged through his straggly blond hair, pulling it away from the drawn lines of his face. He swung his hands up. "C'mon man, no harm done. I swear, won't happen again."

Dig pulled out his knife from his left boot.

"Bro!"

An hour later Butler sucked on a bottle of bourbon in the clubhouse with ice packs on his face. His body was spread out on the bar top like a rag doll while Wreck, who had been a medic in the army, bent over him and sewed up deep gashes over his chest, middle and thighs. His groans reached Dig's room where I sat on the floor against our bed with my knees curled up to my chest. Dig had taken off on his bike. He'd be back soon though.

I waited.

The door banged open and slammed shut. My body shuddered. There were streaks and splatters of blood across his shirt and down his jeans, red smudges on his neck and hands. He ripped off his colors, dumping them on the floor. His face was full of thunder.

"Baby?" I whispered from my patch of humility on the floor.

"Clothes off."

"Dig. . ."

"Now!"

Under his iron glare I teetered up on my feet and pulled my shirt up off my head, peeled out of my cutoff shorts, unclasped my bra, and tugged down my panties. Dig charged towards me and wrapped his hands around my neck, kissing me hard. His one hand slid down to my tattooed ass cheek, and he smacked it. I bit down on my lip. His fingers dug into my stinging flesh.

"Ow!"

His hand clasped my jaw in a tight grip close to his face. I grit my teeth. "Never let anyone, not anyone, take advantage of you. Ever. You call it like it is. You don't have to be nice to everybody." I held his fierce gaze. "You like Butler? You want him? Huh? You want to fuck him?"

"I only want you."

His eyes glittered. "You liked having his eyes on you, didn't you? Did it turn you on?" My eyes filled with water, and he shook me. "What is it? You curious? You've only been with me, you bored already?"

"No. You know me better than that."

His head tilted slightly, his fingers gripping my jaw even tighter. "Do you like him?"

Dig would know if I bent the truth. It so wasn't worth bending, ever. We both expected nothing less than honesty from each other.

Even if it stung.

"He's. . .I'm attracted to him." Dig's gold-flecked eyes tightened over my face as he took in air through his nose. "But I don't want his hands on me, his mouth on me. I don't want him inside me." I reached behind me and put my hand over his on my tattoo. "Your mark means everything to me. You're everything to me, Dig. I wouldn't throw away what we have for. . .I love you." His hand pushed mine aside, slid from my rear up to my breast and squeezed. I clenched my teeth against the sharp pain. Our breathing turned choppy.

"Yeah? You sure about that?"

My gaze met his hard, glassy one. "What about that bottle blonde who keeps showing up everywhere we go?" I asked. "She hangs on you at every party, every event, brings you drinks. And you keep smiling at her, talking to her, lighting her cigarettes. Last week, you let her touch you. I saw it."

His jaw clenched. "She's got a great ass," he said, his voice rough. I struggled in his hold, tried to wriggle out of his grasp, but he only clasped me tighter against his body. My fingernails dug into his skin. He winced.

"You like her? You want inside that cheap ass? You want to fuck her?" His lips pressed into a firm line. "Come on. Say it!"

"Yeah, I do."

I grunted and twisted with all my might in his grip, but he only pulled me closer to his body. His forehead slid to mine. His hand dug into my hair, and his lips moved against my mouth. "But she ain't got what you got, Grace. None of 'em do. And I need you, need you to fucking breathe. Everything comes back to you. Always you."

My heart pounded in my chest, and my eyes didn't leave his as I snapped open the buttons of his jeans. I shoved them down his hips and pulled out his cock, and he let out a hiss. He clasped my ass in his hands and hoisted my body up in his arms as I clutched his neck and hooked my legs around his waist.

He turned, my body collided with the door, and I gasped at the jarring pain. I rocked my pelvis up against him, and he rammed inside me. I grunted through each harsh thrust. It hurt, but I didn't care. All I cared about was feeding our violent hunger. Our eyes were riveted on each other, our bodies jostled against the door. My fingers dragged through his hair and pulled.

"Fuck, baby." Dig breathed hard against my lips as he filled me, thrusting inside me over and over again. "Only you. Only you."

We didn't leave our room the rest of that afternoon or that night. The next day Butler took off for the North Dakota chapter. Dig and I got married the following week.

And I found the bottle blonde and told her to go fuck herself.

NOW

"What's up, Boner?"

"Came for Little Sister."

"Over there." Creeper gestured towards the sofa were I lay half-asleep.

I raised my head and swiped the dribble from the edge of my mouth with the back of my hand. My neck was stiff and my back very unhappy. My leather jacket that I had used as a pillow lay crumpled on the floor.

"Hey." Boner stood over me and handed me my jacket. He pulled his lips into a firm line. "Any coffee around? Can't stand that shit they sell on the road."

I got up on a sigh, stretched out my arms, then snaked them around his middle. He hugged me. "Don't think what they have here is much better," I mumbled into his chest.

He planted a kiss on my forehead. "See what you can come up with."

"Okay."

His hand gripped my jaw, his green eyes darkened. "Better make one for yourself, too."

I shuffled behind the small semi-circle shaped bar. Boner remained in the middle of Butler's small clubroom, his hands on his slim hips.

An infomercial hawking frying pans blared from the television. The new club mouse was on her knees between Creeper's legs finishing up his blow job. He was slumped back on the sofa across from the one where I had been napping. I had woken up to his muffled grunts and her sucking sounds along with the enthusiastic voice of the frying pan lady on TV. Two recruits prepped a bong at a small round table in the corner, and Butler sat at the bar smoking a cigarette and nursing a beer.

"You in a rush?" Butler asked.

"Got shit to do, can't stick around," Boner said.

"I told her I'd bring her, but . . ." He raised an eyebrow and brought his cigarette to his lips once more.

Boner shook his head at him "Look at you, man. How you gonna stay on your bike?" Butler only smirked. Boner leaned in closer to him. "Look. At. You."

"Fuck off, man. I'm just hanging, enjoying time with my girl. It was a long weekend, what can I say?" Butler wiped his hands over his eyes and flicked his cigarette into a dirty coffee mug. "Right, baby?"

I poured the water into the coffeemaker, smacked the cover over the filter compartment I had filled with coffee, and snapped the power button on.

Boner exhaled. "Oh yeah?"

"Yeah, man." Butler rubbed his chest and let out a soft chuckle.

"The coffee around here must be some sort of miracle brew then," Boner said.

I rolled my eyes.

Butler lit another cigarette. "What?"

The coffeemaker dripped its black liquid into the glass pot. My gaze settled on the antiquated Mr. Coffee which shuddered on the counter. Boner flicked on his lighter and lit a cigarette.

Drip. Shake. Drip. Hiss. Drip.

"Here you go." I placed the mug filled with hot coffee on the bar by Boner's arm. "One sugar."

He took the mug and drank. "You ready to go?" he asked, his voice low.

"Bag's by the door." I filled a cup for myself. Butler winked at me and jerked his head to the side. I rounded the bar, and his arm wrapped around my middle as he pulled me between his legs. Boner watched us from behind his mug of coffee.

Butler buried his face in the side of my neck. "When am I gonna see you again, babe?"

"Got a lot to do right now. Have to find somewhere to live, find a job, set up my nephew. Real life, you know?" His mouth touched mine, and the tobacco laced my lips with a bitter tang. Butler's hand rubbed over my rear, and he smirked at me. "What is it?" I asked.

His lips brushed my ear. "Love that ass, baby. You gonna let me in next time?"

Oh, for Pete's sake.

Last night in bed Butler had tried to lick my wildflower tattoo, but I had pushed him away and turned over on my back. He didn't say a word, but he knew. Instead he pulled me over again and used my rear end as a pillow for his head for optimum viewing of the Kitty Show down below us on the floor, absently swirling his fingers between my legs.

I had dozed off, but woke up when he'd suddenly flipped me on my back. He bent my knees, slid his hands under my rear, and went down on me. I laughed. Butler's eyes blazed. He gripped my thighs and became relentless. But I couldn't stop laughing, even through the multiple orgasms. I suppose all that vodka with lemon I'd had for dinner had done me in.

Boner plonked his mug down on the bar, a scowl on his face. "Time to hit the road. Let's go."

I untangled myself from Butler's arms. He squeezed my hand and released it. "Take care, babe." I gave him a small smile and a wave of my hand. Boner nabbed my duffel bag, I grabbed my jacket off the sofa, and we headed for the door.

"Drive safe, kids," Creeper muttered. He flipped channels on the television while the new girl sat on the floor at his side, wiping her neck and chest with a paper towel.

Outside we charged towards Boner's bike. His lips smashed together as he packed away my bag. "What the fuck?"

I zipped up my leather jacket, shoved my hands into my gloves, and nabbed the helmet from him. He stared at me, his eyes wide.

"Let's go, Boner!"

We mounted his Harley. He gunned the engine muttering a string of obscenities and shoved at the kickstand.

Hallefreakinglujah.

"He's a sitting duck." Jump folded his arms and leaned back in his chair behind his desk.

"Wasted off his ass, the rest of them crawling around, doing their thing. I'm telling you, they're making it real easy for the Demon Seeds to just walk in there and take what they want, and that's all she wrote," Boner said.

"What about Crank?" I asked. "Did you find him?" I sank back in the armchair. I was tired after the long ride in the cold air coupled with the stress of yet another delightful two days with Butler. My head was still in a hangover fog. Luckily, I had chained up any stray post-Butler emotions like self-loathing and guilt, and had tossed them overboard on the highway a while back in order to deal with this "debriefing."

Lock stood in the doorway, his arms crossed. His inscrutable gaze fell on me. It was still there, that enigmatic whirlpool of taut emotions. I fidgeted in my chair. The self-loathing and guilt started nibbling at me again.

"Crank's a Demon Seed newbie, but our brothers think he's a Jacks recruit," Lock said. "He's been up in ND for almost a year now playing go-between."

"Anything else?" asked Jump.

"Creeper's got a bug up his ass all the time," I said. "He's a very suspicious son of a bitch and doesn't mind showing it. Then again, he always had a problem with Dig, so he doesn't like having me around."

Lock's brow snapped. "That's it. I don't want her up there with them again. It's too dangerous. We got some good information.

Take her off it now." My skin heated at the insistent tone in his voice. I leaned my elbows on my knees and kept my eyes on the floor.

"Let's not rush this," Jump said.

"Rush? Are you shitting me?" Lock raised his voice. "She's been up there twice already. So far she's managed to avoid Crank catching on that she recognizes him. Creeper's on her ass. Not to mention the possibility of getting herself killed or maimed or worse on the back of that coked-up asshat's bike."

"I'm with Lock. Enough." Boner plonked his empty beer can down on Jump's desk, leaned back against the wall and crossed his arms over his head. "There's a seriously whacked vibe in that joint. I don't like it, and I don't like Sister up there alone. Butler's fucking lost it. She's gonna lose it too."

Lock's fingers gripped my chin tilting my face towards him. His eyes were stony, his brow rigid. My chest constricted under his merciful scrutiny. I peeled his fingers off me, turned my face away, and sank back in the chair. Just his touch after all this time, those large dark eyes on me. My breath knotted in my chest, but there wasn't any room for that knot.

"Yeah, all right. Let's focus on Thursday." Jump fiddled with a key chain and smirked at me. "Did he show you a good time at least, Sister? You got him out of your system?"

My spine stiffened, I shot him a glare. "He's not in my system. And sorry to disappoint you but no, he can't fuck. It's difficult for him."

"Aw, man." Boner rubbed his face with his palms.

"Butler needs help," I said, my eyes trained on Jump. "Your brother needs you. You need to think about that and deal with it, prez." Jump leaned back in his chair and put his feet up on his desk.

That was it, I was done. I had nothing more to give. I needed sleep, real sleep, but I wasn't so sure I'd ever get it again.

Jump let out a throaty laugh, his fingers smoothing over his mustache. "Shit, hon. You didn't even get laid out of this deal? That does suck."

Boner tossed his beer can at Jump's head. "Such a motherfucker!"

"Fuck you, asshole!"

"Why are you talking to her like that?" Boner's eyes bulged. "Look at her! You think this shit is easy for her? I sure don't like watching it. I sure didn't like what I saw today." Boner kicked the metal trash can, and it exploded against the opposite wall. Jump hurled more curses at him.

I pushed myself up off the chair.

Lock was gone.

TWENTY-TWO

"TIME FOR LUNCH, HONEY."

Jake only shrugged as he plodded to a chest of drawers and put away the spark plugs he was holding in his tiny hands.

"Grace." Lock's fingers brushed my arm.

My eyes darted up at his, and I stuffed my hands in my back pockets.

"I want to ask you something."

"Sure."

He glanced at Jake, who shuffled the metal drawer of a cabinet back and forth. "I want to take Jake for a ride on my bike. What do you think?"

I grinned. "I think it's the best thing I've heard in days."

He raised his chin, the corners of his lips tipping up. "Give me your phone."

"My phone?"

"I want to call Alex and ask him if it's okay."

My heart squeezed. Even in the eye of our current shitstorm, his compassion, his kindness, hadn't faded. I pressed my phone into his hand.

He called Alex and they spoke. Lock handed me my phone back, his eyes soft. "Get his jacket, Grace."

"Thank you," I whispered, my thumb rubbing over the smooth surface of my phone.

"You don't have to thank me. I want to help Jake any way I can. He needs us now. Really needs us."

I held his somber gaze. We weren't touching, both barely breathing, yet a tiny surge of warmth flickered through me like a small flame wavering and struggling in a dark, windy tunnel.

"Yes, he does," I said. "I'd do anything for him. Anything."

"I know you would." He let out a heavy breath as he dragged a hand over his mouth. "I've got a kid's helmet around here somewhere," he mumbled.

Ten minutes later man, boy, and bike were out on the track.

"Don't let go, Jake. Okay?" said Lock.

"Okay."

Lock revved the engine. Jake's tense gaze jumped to me over Lock's arm. I gave him a thumbs-up and a smile, and he nodded at me, his eyes round as saucers. Lock's Fat Bob roared off down the club's mile long track. Not fast and not too slow. I grinned as I used my cell phone camera to record a video of this momentous occasion. They rounded the track a third time. Lock leaned over and said something to Jake. Jake glanced up at him, and they both smiled. Warmth slid through my chest.

My ring tone went off and Butler's name flashed at me on my screen. "Hey."

"Babe. Just got back from that trip I'd told you about."

"Oh, right, it's Thursday today. Everything go okay?"

"It's all good. Very good." He let out a chuckle. "Want to celebrate with you. Take you out. Get your sexy ass up here."

"I got my dad in town, Butler. I need to be with him and my nephew right now," my voice trailed off. The bike zoomed past me once more. Jake pressed his little body back against Lock's as they both leaned into the curve. That warmth shifted inside me again. A smile danced across my lips.

"You at the club?"

"Hmm? No, I'm in town getting some ice cream for Jake. I'll call you later when I can talk, okay?"

"All right, beautiful. Later." I ended the call and went back to taking photos of Jake and Lock as they zipped by me.

"Got a minute?" Jump stood at my side, his face tight.

"I was just going to come find you. What's up?"

"Need you to come with me and check something out." He didn't look happy. He also had blood spattered across his sleeve.

"Uh, okay."

"You're gonna like this, Sister." His eyes went to Lock and Jake rounding a tight curve on the track. "How's Jake?"

"As long as we're distracting him with some sort of electronic entertainment or fast food, then, yeah, he seems okay."

Jump sighed. "Rough."

I took another photo of them as they flew past. Jake had a smile on his face and so did Lock, expressions I hadn't seen on either of them for a long while. I stood still, a flutter in my belly, as they zoomed past us once more.

For the first time in what felt like a very long time, I didn't squash the sparks of hope stirring inside me; they only grew stronger with every pass of Lock and Jake on the Harley around the track.

"Look at him." Jump chuckled. "Reminds me of Wes at that age. Shit."

"So I just got a call from Butler. He's back from Canada with bells on his toes. Wants me to come up today to celebrate."

"And you said?"

My gaze remained on Lock and my nephew cruising along the track. "I told him my dad was in town, and I had to spend time with him and Jake."

He nodded. "Get on the phone and tell him to get his ass down *here*. I need him here and very distracted tonight."

"Glad I checked in with you first, prez."

"Are you?"

My gaze snapped to his. Jump shook his head as he watched Lock and Jake. He yanked at my elbow. "You fuck whatever and whoever you want, but it does not interfere with business. Ever. You get that?"

"You don't have to remind me of the golden rules."

"Do I need to remind Lock? Never had to worry about him before. Am I gonna have an episode of "Young and the Restless" on my hands with the three of you?"

"Young and the Restless?"

Jump's face creased into a frown. "My ma watches that shit. Years now." I laughed. "Shut up, Sister. I don't have time for this shit. I got a club to run and a bike to ride."

There it was, the credo that had shaped my adult life. For good, for bad, the ugly, the worst.

"I don't like soap operas either, Jump. On TV or in real life."

Jump narrowed his eyes at me, and I ignored him turning back to face the track. His cell phone buzzed loudly. He squinted at the screen and sniffed. "Yo, big man, what's up?"

Jump smirked at me gesturing at his phone. It had to be Butler calling.

"Yeah, I hear you, brother. She's not herself, man. I don't know what to tell you." Jump rolled his eyes at me. "Alicia and I aren't even quite sure how to talk to her these days. I know what you're saying. Listen, why don't you come down, surprise her. We're all going to the Tingle tonight. It's always a good show on Thursday nights. Of course she'll be there, I won't give her a choice. That's what I'm saying, B. . .Sounds good, man. . .It will definitely be a good time. Okay. Ride safe, brother." Jump tapped his phone and snickered.

"What did he say?"

"Romeo is concerned about his Juliet. Says he ain't buying the shit you laid on him over the phone."

"Really?"

Jump grinned at me. "You're good, baby."

"And yet you doubt me."

He let out an ominous chuckle. "Motherfucker is definitely in the mood to celebrate and wants to do it with you."

"Yahoo. What's this about a party at the Tingle?"

Jump shifted his weight. "He and his boys ain't gonna turn down a freebie at the Tingle, so we'll give them a celebration they won't forget. And since he's bringing his boys down, that means the goods from Canada he's hiding tonight for Vig will only be left with a couple of dumbass recruits. No doubt, all of them will be high. Kicker's been up there with a crew since yesterday with their eyes on that truck thanks to your info. Tonight Butler will abandon it for a night with you. Oh, the things we do for pussy."

"Give me a break. The things your old lady does to keep your dick interested."

He gave me a knowing look. "It's a good thing. Live and learn, woman."

I raised my hand up at him. "I'm happy that you're happy."

He laughed, took out his phone and tapped on the screen. "Kicker, get it together, brother. We're on for tonight. He's getting on the road now, on his way here with a few of his boys, leaving it wide open for you. Sit tight. We're gonna show him a good time at the Tingle. Yeah, yeah, exactly. . .I'll be waiting to hear from you, man."

"All set. Let's go." Jump whistled hard at Lock and gestured that he was taking me with him inside. Lock lifted his chin at us.

Jump and I entered the clubhouse, passed the large kitchen, then rounded the corner for the stairs heading down to the cellar. My mouth went dry. Dig had overseen the renovation on the cellar after we had first gotten married. It was taboo territory for the women, unless you deserved to be there, of course. I had never seen it and frankly had prayed I never would. So much for that.

Dawes stood outside a reinforced steel door. His eyes shot up at me then at Jump. His knuckles wrapped on the door. "Open up, man. It's Jump."

The door scraped open. Boner stood in the center of the dimly lit room along with Bear and Clip, blood splattered on the front of their shirts and on their arms. Boner's flinty green eyes cut to me. Jump gripped my upper arm and ushered me further inside the square cement block room.

A heaving figure was crumpled on the floor, his hands fastened behind his back with plastic cuffs. Boner hovered over him, his eyes gleaming like a satisfied hunter's over a fresh kill. He dug his hand in the man's matted hair and jerked his head back. Globs of blood dripped from his bruised face onto the cement floor.

My stomach churned, and I pushed down the acid that rose in my throat.

"This Crank?" asked Jump.

"Yes, that's him."

Crank's bloody, swollen eyes strained up at me. "Fucking cunt!"

Boner let out a sharp hiss and jabbed Crank's side with the toe of his heavy boot. "Manners, motherfucker." Crank grunted and collapsed on the floor.

"Did you get anything more out of him?" Jump asked.

"Eh, a few crumbs," Boner said. "Got plenty of time ahead of us."

"It's on, brother," Jump said, his forehead wrinkling.

A smile flickered across Boner's lips. His hand reached out to his side and wrapped around a short knife that had been impaled in a table.

"Have fun, boys." Jump led me out of the suffocating room. Dawes secured the door behind us.

I inhaled a deep breath once we reached the top of the stairs. "Alicia coming tonight?"

"Yeah, of course. All the old ladies. Why?"

"I want girly backup at the titty bar."

"You got it, babe." Jump grinned and slung an arm around my shoulders. "Aw, we used to have good times at the Tingle back in the day, huh?"

PAST

I had driven Alicia to the Tingle plenty of times in the middle of the night and held my breath as she would charge through the club like an unholy avenging angel until she found Jump. She would often find him either getting a lap dance or getting blown, and then she would explode into one angry fire breathing demon. I didn't blame her.

Tonight, Dig shook his head at me in disapproval.

"What do you want from me?" I asked. "She's been spewing threats for hours and drinking non-stop. Should I have let her drive here on her own? I not only had to take her keys away from her, but the keys to all the trucks, even our car. Then she punched me in the stomach. The shit I go through for Jump's dick!"

Dig let out a laugh, hooked his arm around my neck and pulled me into his body. He kissed me hard and my arms wrapped around his middle. I inhaled his spicy cologne and smiled against the warm skin of his neck.

"What is it?" I glanced up at him. "Did you miss me?" My eyes darted over his shoulder to the two nude women dancing up on the bar who wore nothing but bright red lipstick, high heels, and thin long chains slung low on their hips. "Or maybe these lovely ladies got you horny?"

Dig's hands fisted in my hair, and he tilted my head back. "No one's getting this dick but you, baby. Isn't that what this band of gold means?" I grinned up at him and squeezed his hard ass with my one hand.

His lips brushed my mouth. "You and me, circle of life and whatever the—"

I laughed. "It's circle of infinity, Dig. Circle of life is from *The Lion King.*"

"Whatever. It's your circle around my dick, right?"

"Just your dick?"

He clasped my hand that lay over his chest. "And this little muscle right in here, wiseass." He leaned his forehead against mine. "It's got your name burned on it, and you know it." My heart stammered at the deep, gravelly tone of his voice.

"Good thing I like that dick then, huh?"

"You better. It's the only one you're getting." He eyed me. "What's not to like anyway? You got complaints?" I laughed and buried my face in his chest. "Fucking Wildflower," he said on a growl. He kissed me gently then smiled at me and grabbing my hand yanked me towards the back of the club and up the stairs.

"Baby?" I shouted over the pulsing beat of Will Smith's "Gettin' Jiggy Wit' It." I knew where we were headed. My heart raced as we reached the VIP rooms. Luckily I was wearing a short skirt and. . .oh man. . .my husband was in for a surprise tonight. My fingers squeezed his as he pushed open door number two.

"Hey!" shouted Shannon, a brunette with serious fake lashes and a mini red halter dress with a rhinestone buckle shimmering just underneath her breasts. She led a middle-aged man to the same doorway.

"Wait your turn, Shannon," said Dig.

She rolled her eyes at us. "You two take the cake!"

"Sorry, Shan," I said. Dig yanked me into the room and slammed the door behind us.

"You were a bad girl, Mrs. Quillen," he whispered in my ear.

I raised my eyebrows. "Was I?"

"Tonight was supposed to be boys' night out." Dig eased back on the small circular red vinyl sofa in the small dimly lit room. I stood in front of him. He stretched out his arms across the top of the sofa. "You weren't supposed to be here."

"My mistake, Mr. Quillen. I was just looking out for a sister. Please, don't punish me."

He only smirked, and I pulled my blouse off my shoulders and tossed it at him. Dig caught it, crumpled it to his face, inhaled, then dropped it to the floor. His heavy gaze returned to me and his eyes widened.

He leaned forward, one arm planted on his thigh, his mouth hanging open. "What the hell are you wearing, baby?"

My eyes darted down my body clad in my new, very expensive, black lace bustier. I enjoyed indulging on occasion using my own money once in a while. Today was that kind of special occasion.

After we got together, Dig had proudly paid my tuition and rented us an apartment in Rapid City until I finished my remaining credits at college. He and Boner, Wreck, Willy, Jump, and Alicia had all cheered loudly at my graduation. Unfortunately, Ruby was still in prison at the time. I had put my business degree to good use by managing Pete's Tavern full-time as Pete began his slide into retirement. I also took care of Wreck's accounting at the club's repair shop. We'd been together one year and married for just over four, and things were good. In fact, we felt ready to take the next step. Finally.

"Today was my day off from work, so me and the girls went out and did a little shopping at the new mall this afternoon, remember? I bought this." My face heated. "We got back to the club after going out for dinner, and I was trying it on again when Alicia got on her tear about Jump being here with that new dancer, Whatshername. I had to drop everything and deal with the situation, and I didn't get a chance to take if off."

Dig only stared at me.

"You like it?"

He let out a laugh and shook his head. I put my hands on my hips and sauntered over to him on my high-heeled boots. I leaned over him, my hands resting on his thighs.

"It was supposed to be a surprise for you, to celebrate," I whispered.

"Celebrate?" His eyes were glued to my breasts which spilled out of the tight corset.

"I threw away the birth control pills this morning, like we'd talked about. We're starting this for real."

Dig's eyes shot to mine. A grin lit up his face. He leaned forward to kiss me, but I pushed off his legs and took two steps back. He tilted his head at me, a hint of amusement in his eyes as he licked his bottom lip.

"Can I be of any service to you this evening, Mr. Quillen, or are you otherwise engaged?" I shimmied out of my skirt and let it fall to the floor revealing the matching thong.

Dig's eyes darkened, a slow smile building on his lips. "Otherwise—what?"

"You know, busy?" Suddenly, I was short of breath.

He crooked a finger at me, and I sashayed back over to him. He took my hand and kissed it, then pulled me in swiftly until I straddled him. Both his hands ran up and down the taut lace of the corset and tugged on the hanging garter belts. Dig nuzzled my exposed breasts, and I arched my body up into his, my fingers tangling in his silky hair. The electrifying thrill of being with him had not dulled or diminished over the years. I loved that about us; it made me feel truly alive.

His thumb nudged past the delicate fabric of the tiny thong between my legs, and I gasped. "Music to my ears," Dig murmured, an eyebrow raised. I giggled.

His thumb continued teasing me as he slid two fingers of his other hand into my mouth. His breathing grew heavier as he watched me suck on them. "Yeah, that's it, baby." He popped them out of my mouth and quickly slid them inside my wet center. I let out a soft cry, my eyes fluttering closed. "Look at me." My eyes focussed on his golden brown gaze. "Is this my pussy?" he breathed.

"Uh-huh."

That twist of pleasure unraveled inside me. I squirmed in his arms and circled my hips. His other hand left me and stroked the soft leather of my tall black boots at his side. "Shit, I don't have time to do everything I want to do to you right now."

"And what do you want to do to me?" I asked breathlessly.

His one eyebrow quirked up. "You want me to tell you?"

"Hell yes, tell me."

He chuckled and nipped at my throat. His fingers inside me and his thumb over me moved in more determined strokes. His other hand slid down my ass.

"You still sore?"

I arched my back and let out a moan. "No. Dig, tell me."

"What would I do to my Wildflower?" Dig went down his wish list in remarkably filthy detail.

My entire body shuddered and groaned. "I need you."

"I'm not fucking you here."

"What?" My fingers dug into his neck. "Why not?"

"I don't want our kid conceived at the fucking Tingle."

I laughed. "Baby, it's going to take the pills at least a couple of weeks to wear off." I reached for his belt buckle.

"Shit, really?"

I unbuckled the clasp. "Yes, really. Come on."

His hand tightened over mine. "We'll start this officially then at the Hippie Hole."

My eyes shot to his. "We're not going to have sex until then?"

"No, I didn't mean that!" He laughed. "But I want to go to our spot." He buried his face in my throat.

Explosions and screams detonated below us in the club. We froze. Were they gunshots? More screams rolled through the building. The music screeched to a halt.

"What the fuck?" Dig released me and lifted me off his lap. He slid his gun out from the back of his jeans.

I grabbed my top and skirt and wriggled back into them. I nabbed my purse and curled my fingers in the back of Dig's shirt as he unlocked the door. We crouched down, he slowly opened the door.

"Get off me, man!" A voice boomed from downstairs.

A Demon Seed stood in the middle of the club with his gun raised high. Boner and Jump held him in an arm lock.

"Stay down, baby. Don't move." He squeezed my leg.

"Dig." He glanced at me. "Love you," I whispered.

His beautiful eyes softened for a split second. "Love you, too, babe." His lips brushed mine. "You keep that thing on for when I get home later, yeah?"

He rose to his feet, and I held my breath as he strode to the top of the staircase.

"What's the problem, man?" Dig strode down the stairs to face the Demon Seed I had never seen before. He squirmed in the mens' steely grip. A hush came over the room. "Why are you shitting in my club?"

Dig leaned into the guy, nostrils flaring. The guy mumbled something in his ear, and Dig's shoulders stiffened.

"Clean this mess up," he ordered the staff. The girls hustled to right chairs, the bouncers set up an overturned table. Broken glass was swept away by the two bus boys.

"Office, now," Dig said. Boner and Jump led the Demon Seed to the back of the club. Then my old man turned back to the crowd. "Round of drinks for everyone!" A few cheers went up, and the music blared again. Dig and the men were gone.

A shadow fell over me, and I blinked up. It was Shannon again. I stood and pushed the door open for her. "Take the room, sweetie. Sorry about before."

"If you got it going on, hon, you got it going on. Good for you. But some of us got to make a living here, you know?"

"I know, believe me." I shuffled out of the doorway.

Shannon leaned into me, her hand touching my arm. "Sister, don't be sorry. You two are great together. It's good to see."

I smiled at her.

She turned to her new customer, her hands on her hips. "Come on in, honey." Her voice was sultry and welcoming. A young, short guy wearing a fancy western shirt, his fists stuffed in the pockets of his crisp jeans, shifted his eyes down the hallway then darted into the room. She winked at me and closed the door behind them.

The wild hum of the crowd battled with the music once again. Three nearly naked statuesque women danced onstage. The Tingle had returned to normal.

I sprinted down the stairs and found Alicia sitting at the bar.

"This sucks," she said, her eyes dull. I swept wisps of heavily hair-sprayed blond hair from her damp face and put an arm around her shoulders.

"Let's go home," I said.

"Yeah, this just sucks." Alicia slapped her hand down on the bar.

"Sure does." I fished my car keys out of my bag.

Clip came up behind me and plucked the keys from my fingers. "I'll take you two home, okay?"

I sighed. "That would be great, Clip. Thanks."

We each grabbed one of Alicia's arms and got her out to the parking lot.

Yeah, good times.

NOW

"To Ruby!" Jump declared. "She was a good woman who sure as shit lived her life wild and free, and she did good things for the One-Eyed Jacks. This one's for her!"

He knocked back his tequila as did the rest of us at the table. Alicia's lips twisted. She hated Jump reminiscing about his former flames, even if they were married to someone else. Or dead.

The fiery shot slid down my throat.

Yes, my sister was one in a million. She paid big time for her missteps over and over again, but it didn't seem to faze her. Her tough exterior never faltered.

Neither should mine. Just a little bit more. This should all be over tonight.

I slammed my empty shot glass down in front of me. Lock's eyes cut to mine from across the table.

There he was—just another biker brother in my club family.

He's not just another anything.

I sank back in my chair, and Butler's arm dropped around my shoulders and drew me close to his chest. My head rested back against him as I trained my gaze at our reflection in the mirrored ceiling up above. What a happy-go-lucky bunch we were.

There had certainly been major improvements at the Tingle since my day. The light fixtures hanging over us were sexy vintage style chandeliers dripping with crystals, not those eighties style bulbous lamp fixtures of old. My gaze followed the shiny chrome embellishments and moody light effects that decorated the black walls and dotted the staircase that led to the VIP rooms.

The center stage seemed bigger and sleeker, and a ribbon of tiny lights bordered the edge of the stage along the bar. There were even two small mini-stages with their own stripper poles on either side for more dancers to do their thing. Maximum exposure equals maximum returns, right? The club had spent money on necessary upkeep when needed, not to mention an improved 'wow' factor.

"Different, huh?" Alicia leaned over Dawes who sat in between us at our huge table. She let out a chuckle.

"It's amazing," I said. "It's no sleazy, small town party barn anymore."

Gone was the stifling odor of cheap sweet perfume, sweat, and carpet mildew from too many drink stains. In its place was a citrusy freshness churned in from commercial air deodorizers along the walls boosted by an improved central air system that hit me the moment we'd walked into the Tingle.

"Things in our part of the world have heated up," Alicia said. "Girls are leaving the East Coast and Midwest to head out this way what with the mining and the oil boom further north. We've been riding the wave. Those men have nothing else to spend their money on, at least the ones who aren't sending most of their pay home to their wives and kids. Some girls stay on, others keep moving, but they're all real good. And things just keep getting busier with a better crowd, not just the same old cowboys and farmers."

"Are those more private rooms over there?" I asked, pointing to two doors against the far wall.

"Yeah, they're bigger than the VIP rooms upstairs. They're for groups, like bachelor parties, who want their private show." Alicia grinned. "That was my idea. I was the house mom about ten years ago."

"Really?"

"Someone had to keep these girls in line, look after them, keep them organized. What the hell do our men know about running a strip joint other than getting free pussy and booze?"

I laughed.

"It was good, Sister. I liked it. Then I found a manager with a lot of experience at a club in Milwaukee, and I got her to come out here. Things really took off. It's been awesome."

"Good for you."

Butler's hand stroked my thigh. "You okay, babe?" His blue eyes searched mine. He really cared about me; that was the rub in all this. And I cared about him, too.

"I'm good." I sat up settling my hand over his. "Ruby would have a real laugh if she could see us all here like this."

"Yeah, I bet she would." He smiled at me and his lips touched mine. The lights flashed for an instant, and I settled back against Butler to watch the show.

"Ladies and Gentlemen, let's hear it for one of your very, very favorite Tingle ladies. . .Honeeeeeysuckle!" The announcer's velvety voice rippled through the room. Gavin DeGraw's "Sweeter" blared over the speakers. A spotlight flashed on a tall redhead.

Heather slid down the pole on the main stage.

Shit. There goes one of my favorite songs.

Heather looked amazing. She must have gotten hair extensions because her red mane was incredibly full, and it wasn't from teasing. It was sleek and shiny and flowed around her with every sensuous move she willed her body to make. She rocked a silver sequin drape halter top tied in the back over an itsy-witsy matching thong with super high silvery heels polishing off the look.

Heatherlicious pranced up and down the short walkway that led from the stage. She shook her long legs and curvy hips in tune with the driving beat of the music. The men around the edges of the stage hooted for her and clapped as she headed back to the pole. A sexy, daring smile was plastered on her red lips. She snaked herself up and down the pole in a fantastic way that surely made every woman in the audience prickle with envy.

Someone else's sugar indeed.

I could only imagine what having sex with her would be like. The girl worked it. She worked it hard. I clenched my hands together in my lap as I imagined her and Lock fucking. Raw images tripped through my fevered brain. I tugged on the open neck of my jersey blouse as I squirmed in my seat.

Onstage, Heather pulled on the tie of her halter top, and it dropped away. She stroked her breasts with satisfaction and smiled at the men at the edge of the stage waving cash at her. She popped out a hip here and there at them, and they stuffed her thong with bills. A couple of them purposely tossed money onto the dance floor out of her reach. With a smirk on her face Heather leaned over, her round, full ass high in the air, and snatched up the bills. She then got on all fours and crawled like an alley cat towards the last bill. The men high-fived each other, hooting and cackling.

Heather split her legs out to the side sliding down to the floor. She raised her rear in the air giving us a full view of all of it and humped the stage, then smacked her own ass and rocked her pelvis as if she was desperate to be fucked and daring someone to do it.

More tequila, somebody. Please.

Honeysuckle then darted at the pole, lashing herself around it once more. She slid down the damn thing, one long leg out, her hair whipping in the air. Boner and Dawes whistled for their club girl. Who the hell wouldn't?

I grabbed Butler's glass of beer and drained it. "She's good, huh?" he whispered in my ear, his hand roaming over my upper thigh. I grit my teeth as if a lead weight was actually pressing in on my flesh instead.

Had Ruby danced like this on this very stage with Jump and Dig cheering her on?

Dancing, screwing, driving fast, and puncturing her veins with chemicals—my sister had once been so good at all that. All for fun, all for men, all for the club, all to punish the daddy she didn't have, all to make her momma blow her lid. All to put food on our table, keep a roof over our heads, feed our cars gas. Once upon a time that had been the good life for Grace and Ruby Hastings.

Butler peeled the empty beer glass from my grip. My empty hand curled into a tight fist and pressed against the edge of the table. I blinked up at the stage, but my vision was blurry. Honeysuckle Heather was still holding court. The music surged, the men howled and whistled. Acid licked at my throat and spread its sour poison through my veins. Heather swung her hair in circles and sprang back into a handstand. Very impressive on those damned shoes. The dollars cascaded in her direction once more.

I glanced across the table.

Lock watched Honeysuckle Heather, a cigarette hanging from his lips. He had to be reminiscing about fucking her as he watched her dance. Even so, I couldn't help but be transfixed by him at this very same moment. Something about his quiet bearing, the lean lines of his still body. All heat-filled, combustible, restrained power.

Dammit, where's the tequila?

Bear clapped Lock's shoulder, said something in his ear and laughed. Lock nodded, scrunching his eyes. He grinned and plucked the lit cigarette out of his mouth. Suddenly, those dark eyes cut to me, burning through the smoke he exhaled over the table. My stomach seized. Butler stroked my arm, his fingertips like sandpaper rubbing against my skin.

"Be right back, got to hit the ladies' room," I whispered in Butler's ear, grabbing my small purse, and quickly pushing off my chair. He nodded, his eyes never leaving La Honeysuckle on the stage.

Shit, does every man turn to mush when titties and g-strings romp in front of him?

I charged to the back of the club through the thick crowd. I pushed through the ladies' room door, leaned on a counter, and took in deep gulps of air. Goddamn, even the restrooms were quite clean and super snazzy. Gone were the tiny grubby sinks and squeaky faucets. Why the hell did that make me sad? My head snapped up to the mirror.

Dark circles that even makeup couldn't hide smudged the pale skin under my watery eyes. I rubbed my fingers over my pinched cheeks. I switched on the faucet and held out my wrists under the cold water. Much better. Sort of. I couldn't tell anymore.

Two young women next to me traded lipsticks and giggled at the mirror, just like Ruby and I used to do once upon a time. I pushed my hair back and dabbed at my face with a wet paper towel. I quickly reapplied my lip gloss then took out my cell phone and typed a text.

On your way? Ready & waiting.

I hit the send button and tucked my phone back in my pocket. I had to stay sane just a few more hours. Then it would all be over. I hoped. With a final glance in the mirror, I exited the ladies' room.

The electric beat of Britney Spear's hateful "Work Bitch" pulsated through the club. Shucks, I missed Honeysuckle's grand finale. Shadowy figures filled the hallway. The club was even more crowded than before. *Cha-ching for the One-Eyed Jacks.* Wouldn't Dig have been proud? Time to get back to my cozy table from Hell.

An arm hooked around my middle, and pulled me backwards. That familiar heady scent surrounded me as he pressed my body against his dense weight.

Lock hissed in air. "Grace."

TWENTY-THREE

AROUSAL FLARED IN MY GUT upon hearing his deep voice wrap around my name, his heat pulsing through my flesh.

He pulled me into a semi-private alcove where the payphones used to be in the old days, but now was lined with a stylishly curvy purple banquette filled with people drinking cocktails from fancy glasses. An eerie purplish light glowed over them as they smoked, necked, and gabbed.

"What are you doing?"

He turned me in his arms to face him. "You okay?"

"Wish everyone would stop asking me that." I pushed at his chest, and he pushed me against the wall by the upholstered bench. I bumped into the couple next to me, but they didn't even notice.

"Baby—" His warm liquor-scented breath on my skin made my insides clench.

"Let go, Lock. Come on." His fingers dug into my arms, and I gasped for air unable to bear his touch that licked at me like a flame. I twisted away from him.

He pulled me into his chest, his hands cuffing my wrists. "I don't want Heather. I don't even like her."

"Oh, shut up—get off me!"

He pulled me closer, his dark eyes boring into mine. "Grace . . ."

"I don't want Butler either," I bit out.

"I didn't think so."

I raised an eyebrow. "Yet here we are."

"Doesn't fucking matter."

"Tell that to Jump."

He shook his head, inhaling deeply. "I know this is shit tonight. I know."

"You don't know anything." I struggled against his hold.

He yanked me in close to his chest again, his eyes huge, his jaw tight, his earthy scent maddening. "I need you to know that I'm on your side, Grace. Whatever's going on."

I stopped my movements and swam in his gaze. He was suspicious of me, too, but he was giving me room. He believed in me.

"This has to be so hard for you. You're grieving for your sister, and you feel like you're betraying a friend and your own self all at the same time."

For God's sake, stop reading my soul.

My eyes drifted back to the hallway. He shook me. "Look at me! Dammit, you can't even look me in the eye anymore."

My throat burned. All this time Lock and I had managed to be civil to one another. No drama. All efficiency. The both of us had that down pat, didn't we? But look him in the eyes? No, I couldn't do that. That would cut me wide open, and there would be blood. Lots of blood. I'd crumble into a heap on the floor then beg him to collect the pieces.

"It's okay, baby," he said, his voice low.

"No, it's not." My voice was on the edge of breaking.

"Yes it is, because you got me. You deserve better than all this, but I got your back. Always have."

Lock's warm lips brushed my ear, and a shiver shimmied through me. His woodsy tea aroma rose from his neck. My gaze skimmed the edge of the eagle's wing which poked up out of the collar of his black shirt. Luckily, my hands were crushed to my chest. If I were able to wrap my arms around him, I would have done it and been lost down a cartoon-like spiral tunnel. I had to keep it together. I planted my forehead in his upper chest.

"No matter what, I've got your back," he said into my hair.

My lips brushed over the arrow charm and bead on the leather cord he wore around his neck.

The arrow. . .protection, defense, power, force, movement.

My vision clouded. I would need all those virtues tonight. Because tonight I was determined it would all end. I had to end it. But couldn't I savor this rare, potent sensation of sanctuary and promise just for a moment? I sank into his solid embrace, and his arms tightened around me.

"Everything unlocks with you, Grace. Anything good suddenly fits. You're my key. I found you, and I'm not letting you go. Not ever. I've waited too long for you."

A weight shifted inside me. In that instant there was no thumping music, no uproarious commotion, no clamor of drunken voices. There was only him.

Only us.

Don't let me go.

But I couldn't say that to him. Not yet.

"Let me be your key," he breathed.

I didn't know what to do with those beautiful words, that precious confession. My soul soared. I yanked it back to earth.

"Lock . . ."

"I only want to hear my real name out of that mouth when we're together." His head dipped closer to mine, and his thumb stroked the sensitive skin of my throat. "Say it."

I knew in my soul there would be no turning back for me once I said it. Except for my nephew, this man was the only good part of me, and I didn't want to fight it anymore.

I couldn't.

"Miller."

A small smile formed on his generous mouth. I couldn't resist brushing my fingers over his warm lips. They parted slightly under my touch.

"I once let myself think that we were possible," I whispered. "But look where we are now. How are we ever . . .?"

He squeezed my arms. "Do you forgive me?"

We both knew what he was referring to. It didn't have to be spelled out. The disappointment, the regret, the hurt smoldered still. But we both understood what the terms loyalty, club business, and between a rock and a hard place meant, didn't we? I despised that we had to tangle with these thorns before we even had a chance to come up for air. Then again, maybe some of us have to get really dirty before we can become truly clean.

"I forgive you," I whispered. My fingers traced the line of his rigid jaw.

He leaned into my touch taking in a deep breath. "This shit will be done tonight." His hand covered mine. "You just got to believe in us. Nothing else matters. Not a goddamn thing."

The edges of my lips tipped up.

"What is it?" he asked.

"Are we always going to have these heavy-duty conversations in loud, public places?"

Miller chuckled. His mouth descended over mine, and his tongue swept over the seam of my lips. I opened up to him, and his fantastic taste bloomed in my mouth. Oh, I didn't think I'd have that again. My fingers pressed into his chest.

New dreams.

But our reality was cold and hard and waiting for us in the next room. Not to mention, my other harsh reality that was on its way to the Tingle right at this very moment.

My hands pushed against Lock's chest. "I better get back. Don't come out for a bit."

He released his hold on my body, but those brooding eyes of his shimmering with yearning and hunger remained on me. I drank in those sensations for a moment longer, my heart swelling in my chest, then I turned and strode towards the main room.

At the table Jump, Butler, and Alicia laughed over something Boner had said. Two dancers swung around the poles on the two mini-stages. The other dancers made their way around the room in new outfits and dazzling smiles to score their lucrative lap dances or to chat up the men and get them to buy them overpriced, watered-down drinks. Everyone knew the score in the playground, and everyone liked to play the game. I settled in my chair once more.

Butler pulled me back into his arms against his chest. "You good?"

"Yeah, sure. Got a little air outside."

Heatherlicious strutted over to our table. She now sported a skin-tight black lycra mini dress that had gaping horizontal slashes all down the front revealing most of her ripe, bare breasts, a diamond-studded belly piercing, and her silver sequined thong. Her big green eyes devoured our table.

Sorry, Lock's not here right now.

"Heather, you were fabulous tonight," Alicia said. Heather leaned over and gave Alicia a quick kiss on the cheek.

"Thanks! It's a new piece I've been working on for a couple of weeks."

"You were sensational." Alicia beamed The Smile at her. "Always are, babe." The two of them nattered on.

Yeah. From "two-bit twat" to "fabulous" and "sensational." Alicia was quite the club den mother.

She squeezed Heather's arm. "Go, do your thing, hon."

Heather tilted her head at Dawes. She dragged her fingers through his mess of curly blond hair. "Hey baby, how did you like the show?"

"You were amazing," Dawes said, his jaw slack.

Honeysuckle grinned and slid into his lap. "Oh, that's what I like to hear!" She giggled, her arms stealing around his shoulders.

My phone vibrated in my pocket. I took it out.

"Two hours out. Back parking lot."

I texted back:

"See u then."

"Who's calling this late?" Butler asked through a haze of smoke.

"It's Alex checking in," I said without looking up from my phone as I deleted the message thread. "He doesn't sleep much anymore."

That was true, but it wasn't Alex texting me. I tucked my phone back in my pocket.

On the other side of me, Dawes rattled on about Heather's sexier-than-sin dance moves and hotter-than-hot bod when her gaze drifted over his head and landed on me. Her scarlet lips tightened. I stared back at her, my face blank. This was a strip club, after all. You come here to stare at living porn, and sometimes it stared back at you. You certainly paid a high price for that privilege. I didn't move a muscle, didn't even shoot her a smirk. Her eyes darted to Butler then narrowed over me.

"Moved on, Vanilla?" she asked.

Hell no.

My lips curled into a tight smile. "You get paid to tease cock with a full wallet, Honeysuckle, not be chatty with me." Heather's face froze. "You better get to wiggling that ass. I can hear the clock ticking on those tips you want tonight." Her face blanched under her spray tan.

"Is there a problem?" Butler's voice drummed over my shoulder.

Heather shook her head. "No, sorry." She swallowed hard and returned her attention to Dawes. "You interested in a private show, honey? I'll make it special just for you." Heather leaned into him and whispered in his ear. Dawes's grinned. She took his hand in hers and rose off his lap.

Yay, VIP room for Dawes and Heather.

Three fresh packs of cigarettes smacked down on the center of the table. My gaze shot up. Miller flicked open his Zippo and lit a fresh cigarette hanging from his lips. Those beautiful austere angles of his face were illuminated by the glow of the orange-yellow flame. He settled back into his seat, and Heather slid back into Dawes's lap.

But of course. Change of plans. No VIP room for Dawes.

"Sweet," Boner muttered. He grabbed a pack of smokes and picked it open.

My gaze slid to Heather who stared at Miller while biting her bottom lip. Dawes tucked a number of bills in the strap of her thong, snapping it back against her skin. The boy wanted his time. Heather's face bent down to his. She looked lost for a moment, then her fingertips rubbed over the wad of money against her skin, and she slapped a show-stopping smile on her face. She stood up and began grinding over him.

Was this lap dance for Dawes or for Miller?

"What the hell was that about?" Butler's fingers dug into my jaw and wrenched my head back towards him. Pain flared in my neck and the air choked in my throat. "You want to tell me why that bitch sliced you, you tore her a new one, then she eye-fucked Lock just like you've been doing all night?" his voice hissed in my ear.

"Let go, dammit! You're hurting me."

Something flashed in front of us.

Miller pounded his fist on the table inches away from Butler's face, leaning all the way over the table to do it with Boner lunging next to him. "Get your fucking hands off her or I'm going to break them!"

"What the fuck are you doing?" Boner's eyes were on fire, his voice seething.

Butler released his fierce grip, and I pushed back against the table and rubbed my neck.

"Sorry, baby," he muttered.

Alicia's eyes had gone round, her hand squeezed her husband's arm. Jump shook his head, his lips mouthing the words "Young and the Restless" at me. I shot him the finger.

Bear pulled Lock back off the table and clamped a hand on Boner's shoulder. All three parked themselves down in their chairs once more, but continued to glare at Butler. Boner drained his glass as if his life depended on it.

"Sorry." Butler lit a cigarette, his hands shaking slightly.

"You want to know about Heather?" I asked, my voice sharp.

"That's Heather?" He exhaled a long, thick stream of smoke as he watched her dance over my shoulder. I glanced over at Boner, Miller, and Bear, all of them still extremely unhappy. Butler's attention remained on Honeysuckle jiggling over Dawes next to me.

"Jesus. Butler?"

His eyes slid back to me, his fingers stroking the edge of his mouth. "Tail tapped her ass last time we were in town. I got to hear all about it. Now I get it. So, what's up with the two of you?"

"She got her panties in a twist when I first came back to the club. There was a party, and she got pissy that my sudden return stole her thunder with the boys. One of those girl-competition things."

Butler grinned. "Were you dancing on the table, putting your titties out there for everybody to take a lick like the other bitches, and the boys liked yours better? That kind of competition? Shit, I missed it?"

I smirked and shook my head. He offered me a cigarette, but I waved it away. "She was all over Lock that night," I said. "Lock being Wreck's little brother, we had a lot of catching up to do, and Heather was annoyed with me for taking up his time."

"That so?" His eyes strayed back to Heather's body swirling and surging over Dawes.

"She's young, she'll learn," I said.

"She's a brat. Better snap out of that bullshit or else."

"I guess she was under the impression it was a pissing contest. Still is."

"Sister, you need a dick for a pissing contest."

"True. Pissing contests are definitely a man-hobby."

"Glad you don't have a dick, baby." Butler entwined our hands. He fingered the silver skull ring on my index finger. His body stilled against mine. "This Dig's?"

I nodded. "Feels good to wear it, especially on occasions like this. He and Ruby worked here, and it's strange being here without them in the world. Then again, this place looks totally different now. Looks good, though. Like a real gentlemen's club."

"Yeah, right. Big City, South Dakota style." He chuckled.

"Why not?" I sipped on my glass of water. Butler didn't answer. He only settled my hand in his and rubbed over Dig's ring with his thumb.

"Another round, people!" Jump gestured to the new serving tray lined with tequila shots that had just been set on the table.

"Perfect." I slipped my hand out of Butler's grasp, reached over the table, and grabbed a shot glass, raising it in the air. "To good times, the old fashioned way!"

Everyone cheered and hollered. Mary Lynn giggled loudly.

"Mary Lynn, I think you've reached your limit, hon." Bear took the shot glass from her hand and swallowed down its fiery contents. Mary Lynn's eyes focused on the suddenly empty shot glass he put back in her hand, and she let out a stream of laughter. Alicia got up from her chair and went over to her. Suzi climbed into Bear's lap and pushed her empty chair at Alicia.

"Where's Kicker anyway?" Butler asked.

"Don't you worry, my man is on his way!" Mary Lynn slurred, dancing in her chair to the beat of yet another Rihanna song.

"He's on the road. He'll be here," Jump said, popping a handful of peanuts into his mouth. He eased back in his chair and enjoyed his view of Honeysuckle's undulating hips at work over Dawes.

Dawes had melted into his chair. Heather's tongue fluttered over the huge bulge in his jeans as her almost bare ass circled in the air.

"Aw, man!" Dawes groaned, his eyes huge. We laughed.

Heather swooped up his body, brushing her breasts over his torso as she went. Her mouth hovered over his. "Later, big man," she said, snapping up off of him.

She turned away and strutted towards the group of men sitting at the bar along the stage who had thrown so many bills at her when she had danced earlier. They clapped and hooted.

"Here she comes!" one shouted.

"Hey, y'all!" Heather crowed, hands in the air.

"Why don't you go find Butler?" Jump leaned over me.

Over an hour had gone by since Butler had left the table allegedly heading for the little boys' room, and I'd heaved a sigh of relief. After Heather had taken off, he had felt me up under the table, his lips at my neck. He'd whispered crude remarks about various dancers, the half of which weren't even that funny. He had lost me, and he knew it.

But I had never been his to lose.

A very tense Miller remained across the table from us. Once Butler had left the table, Boner had come over and sat with me, and Jump had kept his eye on me. I'd played happy-tipsy, and it had kept everyone off my back. The girls and I had laughed and made silly toasts, and I'd finally relaxed and enjoyed myself.

Dee and I settled into a more serious conversation over fresh beers.

"Why is the timing always off?"

I sipped on my drink. "What do you mean?"

"Sex, what else? Last year I was like Peg Bundy, I couldn't get enough, wanted him all the time, and he was bitching, would you believe? I swear, I felt like a wild eighteen year old boy, but with a forty-five year old woman's psycho moods to match."

I snorted and clinked my glass against hers. We laughed.

"It's true! Get ready for it, Sister. Judge couldn't keep up with me. This year, he wants it all the time, and I'm totally off my game. I mean, what the hell are we supposed to do with that? Not to mention I suddenly have to watch what I eat all the freaking time or it goes straight to my hips. I hate this."

"Are we talking about early menopause?" Alicia slid into a chair next to me. Not surprisingly, Alicia had a solution to that predicament. She rattled off a list of vitamin supplements Dee should take and books she needed to read.

"Sister?" Jump squeezed my shoulder.

I hadn't noticed that Butler hadn't returned to our table until Jump just now pointed it out. I assumed he was busy rewarding himself with a mighty fine dose of blow in some dark corner.

However, it was my job to keep him busy tonight. I checked my watch. I had a rendezvous with fate in exactly thirty minutes.

I smiled at Jump. "Why don't you look for him, honey?"

"Why don't we go together, sweetheart?"

I got up from the table, putting the long strap of my purse across my shoulders. "Later, girlfriends." Dee and Alicia smiled at us and continued gabbing. With my arm through his, Jump and I went for a stroll through the Tingle in search of Butler.

"Kicker called. He highjacked the truck and secured it in our safe house. He's ten minutes out."

"Good news."

"Now where's that douchebag?" We walked through the hallway towards the restrooms and stopped at the purple alcove lounge. Two lipstick lesbians were there alone kissing frantically on the couch.

Jump let out a growl. "Fuck me, that's what I'm talking about."

I pushed him towards the men's room while I hit the ladies', but there was no sign of Butler.

"Bet he's getting himself a private dance in a VIP room," I said.

"Ya think?"

We pushed through the lingering crowd on the stairs. A few couples danced together on the second level, and several lap dances were going on in big armchairs tucked in dark corners. Every VIP room door was closed.

"Who you looking for, boss?" asked a tall African American woman in a tight long black dress flecked with gold and wearing gold lipstick to match. She raised one elegantly groomed eyebrow at us.

"Sandra, this is Sister. Sandra's our manager."

"Hello," I said.

She smiled at me. "Hello there." Her voice was smooth as silk.

"Looking for my boy, Butler. You seen him?" Jump asked.

Sandra nodded. "Number two with Heather." She moved forward swiftly and unlocked the door with a key. Jump pushed it open.

Heather was on Butler's lap facing away from him pumping up and down over him, her hands clasping his thighs. Butler's jeans were partly pulled down his legs.

Giddy-up, cowgirl.

A scowling Butler leaned back on the sofa admiring her quivering ass as he held his dick in position and jacked his pelvis up into her grunting loudly. A grimace was pasted on Heather's face, her lips parted.

"Fucking perfect," Jump muttered grinning. He clapped his large hands together. "Yo, party's over!"

Heather's head flipped up, her mass of red hair went flying, and her eyes were wide. Very wide. She sniffled.

Someone had been in the snowy powder.

"Get lost, Heather," Jump said.

Butler's jaw slackened. "What the fuck?"

Heather pushed up off of Butler's lap and stumbled forward. She yanked her dress down her body, and skittered towards the doorway. She righted herself quickly, adjusting her silver thong. She made it to the door where I stood and leaned over to adjust the strap on one of her platform sandals.

Her eyes flared at me, her breathing choppy. "Did you enjoy that?"

Wow. The girl had an agenda.

I smiled at her. "I did. Very much. I can't thank you enough, Heather."

She jerked her head back at me.

"I needed to scrape Butler off in a big way," I said.

Heather's arm shot out and gripped the door frame. She shuffled back a step.

"Worked out great for me. Hell, you did all the dirty work."

"What the—"

"You better go," I cut her off. "The grownups have to talk now."

Heather hustled out the door, and I closed it.

"Baby?" Butler said tucking his dick in his pants.

"Save it." I leaned back against the door. Jump laughed. "I get it, Butler. Your boys tried Heather, said she was a hot piece of ass, and you had to stick your dick in her too, right?"

His forehead rose and he blinked. "She came on to me, beautiful. Offered me a flippin' dance thingy. Oh come on! This is the Tingle for Chrissake!" He wiped at his nose with the back of his hand and sniffed loudly. His fingers fumbled with his zipper.

"I'm done."

"Nah, wait! Baby, wait!"

"I'm done with you, and I'm so done with your addictions, *baby*. I've had enough." I frowned and turned to Jump. "I'm out of here."

Jump's heavily ringed hand reached out and cupped my face, his lips twitching. "Have Lock take you home."

"Lock?" Butler yelled. "What the fuck? What the fuck?"

I smirked at Jump, turned, and opened the door.

Butler let out a howl. "Hang on, wait!"

"Shut the hell up and sit your sorry ass back down," Jump spit out.

I shut the door behind me and checked my watch. I charged down the stairs, darting in between people. Miller stood at the bottom of the staircase. His heavy gaze stopped me in my tracks, and I held my breath.

Boner perched in front of me. "Sister?"

"Room Two. Jump's got him. He's a mess."

"You good?" he asked. I nodded. His hand slid down my arm, squeezing it, then he charged up the stairs behind me.

I landed on the bottom stair in front of Miller. My eyes soaked in his.

"Fuck, I've got it bad for you," he said.

You have no idea.

MILLER

Grace reached out and touched the side of my face. My hand covered hers, and I tilted my mouth and pressed a kiss into the edge of her palm. Her breath hitched, her lips parting like an innocent schoolgirl's.

I took her hand in mine. "Shit's done with. We're out of here."

She pulled out of my grip. "Wait—"

"What?"

"Not now. I can't now."

My scalp prickled. "What are you talking about?"

"I can't. Not right now. . ."

An uproar rose up behind me. I swung around. Vig bulldozed through the club along with five other Demon Seeds and Creeper at his side. My arm shot around Grace, hooking her behind my back.

Vig jerked his chin at me. "Where's Jump? I want my goddamn truck!"

"And Crank? He better be in one piece, man," said Creeper.

Vig's vicious eyes slid to Grace. "I'm on my way to you, and I hear my truck's gone missing. This all a set up from the start with you as the main event?"

Grace's body stilled, and a prickle shot down my spine.

Creeper scowled at her. "Where's Butler? He came down to see you, bitch. What are you doing with Tonto?"

I shook my head as Grace moved to my side. "He had to go fill his nose, and I just found him fucking some stripper. I'm over it."

Vig threw his head back and laughed. "Oh yeah? You keeping him entertained while you were getting me down here and my property was being jacked?"

The door to a VIP room blew open. Bear and Boner barreled down the stairs dragging a bloodied Butler between them. Jump strode behind them. Dancers and customers screeched and yelled, darting out of the way.

Vig muttered under his breath grabbing Grace by the arm and pulling her close. She didn't protest, and she didn't look scared either. In fact, she only looked annoyed.

"We agreed to do this outside," she said to Vig through gritted teeth. "We'd be done by now."

"What the fuck—" I moved towards them my pulse speeding, but Creeper got in my face, one of his hands shooting out against my chest. I slapped it away.

He sneered at me. "Nuh-uh, Red."

"All bets are off now, Mrs. Quillen." Vig's voice was full of venom. "You fuck with me, I fuck with you."

I'd heard enough.

I grabbed Creeper's wrist and jerked it, twisting it hard. He grunted and fell against me, and my knee shot up pummeling his chest. Grace let out a yelp. Scuffling and urgent yells zig zagged through us. A gunshot detonated. Butler crumpled and staggered in Boner and Bear's grip.

"Aw, hell no!" Boner cocked his gun.

I reached for mine, but a ripping burn gashed at my arm. I flinched, but didn't let go of Creeper's wrist. The metal of a long blade flashed in front of me and plunged into my arm once more, the pain tearing through me. Creeper dropped to the floor, and I clutched my bloody limb close. Women shrieked. Punches, cracks and curses exploded over me.

"No!" Grace shouted. "Vig—don't hurt him!"

I twisted back towards her voice. There was the pop and crack of another shot, and in the next instant, Dawes appeared out of nowhere, collapsing at my feet, shuddering and choking out a groan. Blood gushed from his side smattering across the last steps.

A heavy weight rammed into me from behind, and I swiveled, slamming my leg into the head of the Demon Seed who hovered over me with the knife. Peg sneered at me. My leg shot out bashing him in the chest, sending him flying back with a wail, his bloody knife dropping at my feet.

"Dawes! Goddammit—" Jump hollered as he pulled me back.

"Aw shit, we gotta call 911!" Boner said.

Bear's hands wrapped around the bleeding gash on my arm and pressed in. "You okay?"

My heart was beating overtime. All I could think of was Grace. Something was wrong, very wrong. My insides rattled and scraped against my skin.

"Grace—?" I clawed at Bear's jacket. "Where is she?" I pushed away from him and staggered forward. "Grace!" My jagged voice boomed through the now empty club, my arm throbbing, burning.

She was gone.

Vig and Creeper were gone too.

TWENTY-FOUR

GRACE

"ONLY ONE WAY THIS BITCH is gonna give you what you want," Creeper said. "I've had enough of this fucking bullshit!"

Creeper knocked me off his bike and kicked me to the ground. This hallowed ground.

There was no marker, no sign that a thousand hopes and dreams had been destroyed at this bend on a small country road in the middle of nowhere. It was the same dirt-edged asphalt, littered with rocks over the dry, cold earth and tiny green shrubs breaking their way through to the surface. My personal ground zero. It was time for all the ghosts to rest and all the living to live. I had insisted we stop here to make that happen. Right here. Right now.

I lifted myself up on my hands. Tiny sharp stones jabbed at my palms and knees. "Vig!" I shouted. "Call him off. This is between you and me."

Creeper's boot landed on my back and shoved me down. "Shut it, cunt!" My stomach rolled at the clang of his belt buckle and the slide of his zipper.

"Creeper, that ain't the way right now," Vig said. "That's for later, if you're a good boy. Now I need her. Afterwards, do want you want."

"Fuck that!" Creeper said. He yanked my hips up. My limbs locked, my stomach hardened. "Dig's old lady deserves what she gets. Thought his shit didn't stink."

"Vig!" A cracked voice boomed.

It was my voice.

A wail ripped through the night air. Creeper went flying, blood splattered on my hands. Vig stood over us holding back a bloodied palm.

Creeper writhed on the ground. "What the fuck? My nose! You broke my fucking nose!"

"You don't listen, asshole," Vig said. "Now do as you're fucking told."

My eyes went to a shiny object on the road, which gleamed just beyond Creeper's right foot. It must have fallen out of his jeans when he went flying.

God gives you an opportunity, you take it.

I shot forward. My fingers wrapped around the Glock, I pulled the slide back, crunched up and, bracing, took aim at Creeper's thigh and squeezed. Creeper howled grabbing his leg. Blood seeped over his hands. I twisted up and turned the gun on Vig. He already had his gun aimed at me.

I tilted my head at Vig. "Insurance."

"My thoughts exactly." His eyes tightened. "How's this gonna end now, Pretty?"

"Let's finish it, Vig. I'm done."

"That's not up to you."

"I want out. Ruby's dead, and I'm staying in South Dakota now to take care of her son. It's over. For the past sixteen years I've done just what you wanted. Haven't I?"

"You did."

I gulped in air. My incessant adrenaline rush kept my arms taut and raised high enough for my gun to remain trained on Vig's chest. A cold sweat beaded along my brow. "We need to make a deal."

"Honey, this ain't no deal-making meet." Vig chuckled and shook his head. "That's over with. The minute the Jacks took my truck, all the rules changed. I'm holding you hostage, pretty. Who the hell do you think you are?"

"Just an old lady trying to make things right."

"Oh yeah?"

"They wanted to get your attention by taking the truck tonight."

"Well, they got it. And now I've got you."

"You and Jump should get your shit organized. You used to be on the same side, remember that?"

Vig groaned. "Sounds sweet. You gonna serve tea and cookies at that meet?"

Creeper howled behind us. "My leg! My fucking leg! Shoot her ass. Now!"

Vig and I kept our eyes locked on each other, our guns still raised. Vig's cell phone rang.

"It's Jump. Should I answer it? Or send him one of your fingers instead?"

"I have all the keys on me right now, Vig. Every single one from each and every bank. All for you."

He said nothing, only stared at me. His phone stopped ringing.

"I never told, not to anyone," I said. "I've kept your secret safe."

PAST

"You're joking. Please tell me you're joking."

I held Dig's small black nylon travel case open in my hands. I was looking for his extra pair of sunglasses. Instead, I'd found a baggie filled with raw gold granules and two small diamonds.

Dig's eyes were hard, he didn't say a word.

"How could you agree to work with Vig?" I asked.

"He needed somebody outside his immediate circle to trust. He knew I was that man."

I sputtered. "I can't even begin to comprehend. . ."

"Vig's been going underground working with the Russian mob doing odd jobs for them out west. Making big contacts for the Demon Seeds. But he took a few more diamonds than he was supposed to have for his cut, and now they're out looking for them. He managed to pin it on somebody else, of course, but they might see through that one day. Those two there in your hand are a very tiny sample."

"Oh my God."

"He needs to keep his diamonds out of circulation for a long while, leave no possible trace to himself. I agreed to stash them until he needs them. For a healthy cut."

"A healthy cut? And how much are all these diamonds worth anyhow?"

"The whole load is easily worth over half a million."

The blood drained from my head. "Do your brothers know about this?"

His jaw tightened. "What do you think, Sister?"

"Holy shit."

"Calm down."

"The Russian mob could be after you?"

"No, there is no way in hell," Dig said, shaking his head. "Everyone thinks, no, everyone knows me and Vig can barely stand to be in the same room with each other ever since our disagreement over Ruby taking the heat and butting heads over you, and a hundred other things we've disagreed on. It's been that way for years and probably always will be. But I can have respect for my enemy. We can both find a way to strike a bargain when it comes to a once in a lifetime opportunity."

"A bargain with the devil," I breathed.

"Oh come off it, Grace."

"You're not going to tell your brothers?"

"Not right now, no. Later, when it's done. I always share though, they know that. They won't question me once they see what I can bring to the table. I'm going to have to tell you where I stashed them, just in case."

"Just in case of what?"

"Now that you know some of this, you should know the rest. You'll be the only one."

"That explains the diamonds, but what about this gold?"

Dig made a face. "Last week this freak tried to outmaneuver me when buying a bag. It got ugly. Afterwards, I found it on him. Bonus. I figure I can work on flipping it in a few months, a year. No one knows about that either. It's safer this way, considering.

"You killed him?"

"Grace . . ."

My voice shook. "Bonus? Oh my God."

"Relax, baby. It's all good. Things have been real quiet, haven't they?"

"It is not *good*, Dig! How can any of this possibly be good?"

"I know what I'm doing."

I shook my head. "All I did was forget my sunglasses at home."

"This is why I don't tell you this shit."

"It's never enough is it?" I yanked on my ponytail. "Whatever variety of shit the club has going on, whatever money comes in, it's still never enough."

Dig's eyes flared. "Sister, I saw a play, I made it," he bit out, his voice harsh. "You always have to be ready for a new play. You know that."

"Always have to think one step ahead?"

"That's right." His eyes flared. "I don't sit back on my ass and wait to get served. That's not me. How can you not want better for the club? For us?"

"We have better for us, don't we?" My hand passed over my middle.

Dig's eyes shifted to the movement. He exhaled and licked his bottom lip. It had taken us months to finally get pregnant. Now I was three months along, my bump barely starting to show.

"Baby, you know what I mean." He held out his hand, and I handed him the nylon travel case that held a sample of his blood-laced investment in the future. A veritable Pandora's box. But Dig didn't see it that way. He tucked it inside his jacket.

"Hop on, we're out of here." He swung a long leg over his bike, settled in the saddle and revved the engine.

I didn't move.

His eyes cut to me. "Babe." The muscle along his jaw pulsed.

My back stiffened. "Coming," I said through gritted teeth, my tone harsh.

"What did you say? Didn't hear you," he spit out, his face tight.

Any irritation or worry I expressed was sometimes translated by Dig as a personal challenge, especially when he was already ticked off or tense. My stomach seemed to drop ten feet like a boulder over a cliff. I detested that particular tone in his voice, that chilling authority.

I swallowed the quiver in the back of my throat and shuffled over to the bike. His arms were rigid, his knuckles white around the handlebars. I placed my hand on his stiff shoulder to steady myself, but he grabbed onto my wrist and pulled me in to him.

"Grace." He pressed his lips together. My fingers pushed his golden hair back. The sun was setting, and the orange pink glow in the sky broke over his handsome face. "Get on, baby," he said softly, planting a kiss on my temple. His lips lingered on my skin just a moment longer, and I let out a sigh. I got on the back of his bike and leaned into him, wrapping my arms around his middle.

"Your doctor said no more riding for you after this, right? So let's enjoy it," he said over his shoulder. The bike thundered to life under us, and we took off.

Less than half an hour later, the colors of the sky seeping into dark night, gunshots exploded over us. Blood, flesh and bone rained over me. The bike skidded out of control. My breath choked and I went flying through the air, landing on the green earth at the side of the road. Stunning pain radiated through me. My blurry eyes struggled to focus on the once glorious vintage Harley that now lay on it side crushing Dig, his one leg horribly twisted back.

I dragged myself up on my knees despite the jabbing pain that streaked through my abdomen. "Dig?" I hobbled up and scrambled over to the groaning Harley. The bike's wheels spun slowly, eerily, their burning scent scalding my nose.

"Dig!"

"Baby," Dig's bloodied lips quivered. "Grace?"

"I'm right here." I dropped down next to him. My hand stroked his blood and dirt-streaked face. I pressed my hands over his chest. Charred bullet holes. I counted. One. Two.

One. Two. One. Two.

No. So cold. So cold. No. No. So much blood.

My hands were red, wet, swirling in sticky blood. His strained eyes flitted to mine.

"Diamonds . . ."

"Where? Where are they?" I leaned over him. He told me what I needed to know. I swept the matted hair from his face.

"Get gone," he breathed. "Want you. . .safe." His eyebrows jerked up. "Get gone. Now, sweetheart." Dig's breath choked.

One. Two.

"I love you, Dig. I love you. Dammit, you stay with me! Please! I can't. . .Please, Dig, please!" His head jerked back in a soft, strange way, his Adam's apple kicked back. Blood gurgled in his mouth. His beautiful golden brown eyes were dull, unmoving.

One. Two.

"Dig?"

A sharp pain tore through my abdomen again. I clutched my stomach and heaved for air. "No! Don't you leave me. Don't leave me!"

I pleaded with Dig.

I pleaded with our baby.

Slow crunching steps approached me in the shadowy darkness. The hair on the back of my neck stood on end. My heart banged wildly; it would surely explode.

"You do what you have to do. Always be ready for it. Never hesitate." Dig's voice from years ago pumped adrenaline into my veins. *"Don't be a girl about it."*

"I am a girl!" I'd retorted.

"You're my old lady!" Dig had snapped at me.

"You know what to do, Sister." Wreck's voice assured me and pushed air into my lungs. *"You know."*

That motherfucker was coming for me now.

He destroyed my old man. He destroyed his bike. Now he would destroy me and my...

My eyes darted down over Dig's mangled, lifeless body. My shaking, bloody fingers reached out and snapped open the small hatch at the side. It was there, the extra gun. Dig's favorite. The .357 Python revolver. My fingers wrapped around the grip, and I tugged it out. The crunching had stopped. I cocked the safety, held the gun low at my side and pushed up off the hot metal of the fallen bike. I bit hard on my lip, ignored the intense cramping in my belly, and sucking in air, raised myself up.

A single shot lashed through me. My thigh spasmed, enflamed, and I crumpled. A wail broke from my throat, and I choked on my breath. *"Don't look down!"* I hissed at myself. *"You're shot, but you're still alive."* I stayed down holding my breath. The dark figure popped out from the shadows and moved towards me once more. Closer.

"You do what you have to do."

I raised the Python again and took aim. My entire being squeezed and squeezed and squeezed that trigger.

My vision blurred.

My body shook, my ears rang, my arm throbbed.

I flexed my hand, the gun dropped onto the asphalt.

I fell on Dig.

My fingers sunk inside his jacket and tugged on the travel bag. My eyes rose over the small rock tunnel that we didn't have the chance to go through. Clenching my jaw, I pushed through the searing pain in my leg and clambered over to the tunnel clutching the small nylon case to my tummy. I clawed at the dirt with my hands and buried it on the side of the tunnel. I repacked the soil and padded the top with a pile of small rocks, then I retched over the rocky earth.

I took in deep breaths and crawled back to Dig sinking my fingers in his damp hair. Was it sweat? Blood? It was dark now. I couldn't see Dig's eyes or his face anymore. I wouldn't see them ever again, would I?

Never again.

My fingers stumbled over the mobile phone in my jacket pocket. Somehow I managed to locate Boner's name through my dazed vision. I tapped the center button. The ring droned on and on. I twisted to the side, and my stomach churned out its contents onto the road once more.

"Sister? Sister? You there?" Boner's voice cut through the pressing velvet darkness.

An intense cramp sliced at my insides and took my breath with it. A warm sticky river of wet seeped down the inside of my legs, another oozed over one thigh. My pulse thudded. I was draining.

Life was strangled, shredded, and drowning inside me. My fingers scurried up the side of Dig's throat.

No pulse.

No life.

No life.

Yes. Let's die together, baby. All three of us, together.

My phone clattered onto the warm pavement. Another slash tore through me, and I gasped loudly. I slumped to my side against the smoldering bike. My eyelids sank.

And that was all there was.

Vaporized.

NOW

Vig fingered the flakes and granules of gold. "Price of gold is five times now what it was back then."

"If I hadn't hidden it that night along with a couple of your diamonds that Dig had in that case, the Feds would have found it and been all over me," I said. "They were watching us day and night as it was, remember that? They would have been all over the club, and they eventually would have been all over you. How would that have gone down for everybody, I wonder? Where would you be now? I'm not sure orange is your color. I know it's not mine."

His jaw tightened, his teeth dragged across his thick lower lip.

"Here are all the keys." I placed the small padded envelope into his hand. "And the gold."

When I'd finally regained consciousness in the hospital, the first thing I did was beg Ruby to go to the tunnel and retrieve Dig's travel case that I'd buried there under the tower of rocks. I'd made her promise not to open it and just head straight to the bank and open a safety deposit box with both our names on it and stash it there. Yesterday I went to the bank in Rapid and retrieved the case.

For the past sixteen years I'd been stashing all of his Russian diamonds in safety deposit boxes in both our names in every city I had ever lived.

"You keep the gold, Sister."

"No. I can't even bear looking at it, Vig. A stupid drug deal gone bad with your nephew led to Dig finding that stolen gold on him and taking it. Then it got him killed when your other nephew came searching for it on a revenge mission. All of that totally unrelated to your diamonds and your crime lords. How perfect was that? How perfectly fucked up was that?"

Vig slid the small bottle back in the envelope. "Those punks were my sister's kids. Good for nothing meth addicts that wanted to patch in. No way in hell was I gonna let that happen. Fucking morons." Vig shook his head. "Everyone assumed I had Dig killed as revenge for my nephew. Like I gave a shit. Dig did me a favor without knowing it. And so did you when you killed the other one. Who'd ever suspect that Dig and I would ever work together after that? That I would trust him with those diamonds? Nah, it only continued the legend of hate between us. Ah, Sister, the last thing I wanted was your old man dead. It was fucking perfect, though. A fucking perfect stroke of fate."

"Perfect for you."

"Yeah." He studied me for a moment, gnawing on his lower lip. "Shit's over between us when I get my truck back fully stocked."

This shit would never be done. We all knew that, didn't we? This was the way of things in Outlaw Land. There were no smoothly tied up Hollywood feel-good endings to be had here. But it wasn't my burden any longer. At least those keys, the diamonds, those grains of gold weren't anymore.

"Vig, all I want is to be free of this."

"No cut?"

"I only want my family free."

He nodded inhaling deeply. "I'll give it to you."

"My nephew. He's off your radar. Forever. Say it."

A different ring tone went off on Vig's phone.

"Talk." His lips tipped up at the edges as he listened to his caller. "All right. Later." He glanced up at me. "Got my truck back. It's all good."

"Vig. My nephew."

He frowned. "Kid's safe." Vig packed away his goodies. I swiped my face with a shaky hand. My shoulders shook. I had to get out of here. The fire-spewing silver dragon painted on Creeper's gas tank glittered in the moonlight, goading me, beckoning me.

Spoils of war.

I tucked the gun in my waistband and mounted his Harley.

Vig's eyebrows shot up. "You sure you can handle Creeper's hog?"

I turned the ignition and gunned the engine. My eyes cut to Vig. "Are you done talking?"

"My bike! Get that bitch off my bike!" Creeper wailed in the darkness.

"Your bike rides like shit," I said. I turned to Vig. "Jerk doesn't take care of his own bike?"

"Fucking disgrace. Son of a bitch, gotta deal with his ass now." Vig took out his cell phone once more.

I gripped the handlebars, hit the kickstand, made a tight U-turn, then tore off through that tunnel.

"Sister!"

Boner roared up alongside me just as I had turned off the hillside road which led back to the club. I shot him a glance. His long hair flew behind him. I could see the whites of his wild eyes in the inky darkness lit by our headlights.

I knew that look. Last time I'd seen it was when I had regained consciousness at the scene and watched Boner fight with the responding police officer, Trey Owens, and the paramedics to get to me, but I'd lost consciousness moments later and had never found out who'd won that battle.

That look clawed at my heart now. It was that same mixture of pain, anger, and sorrow that Boner wore when I insisted he bring me whatever pills he could get his hands on so I could end it in the hospital. He did it for me, but it didn't work. Caitlyn had figured it out. She had screamed for the nurse, and they had pumped my stomach. I'd woken up to face my hell all over again.

That's when Vig had paid me a late night visit in my hospital room. He had sat at the edge of my bed, taken my hand in his, and peered into my eyes. "You know why I'm here?"

I'd nodded.

"He told you?"

"Only because I found a couple by mistake. Then he told me. Just in case, he said."

"Smart man. I'm sorry he was taken from you. I'm sorry about your baby. But I need you now, Sister. You're my only option."

I'd tried to pull away from him, but I hadn't had the strength. His thick fingers had pressed in on my hand.

"Shh. I heard about what you tried to do to yourself last night. Don't throw your life away, pretty girl. You be strong. Hardest thing you ever gotta do after everything you lost. But you got it in you, I know you do."

"I don't," I'd whispered through dry lips.

"You do. And I'm gonna make you a deal to inspire you. You stay alive, your sister stays alive."

"What?"

"You stay alive, get better, and get the fuck out of South Dakota, away from your club. You go wherever the hell you want. But you keep moving every so often, spreading my diamonds as you go. You do what Dig was doing for me, but in a new way, a better way. I need this done. My shit's on the line until things settle down. Your old man gave me his word. Now it falls on you."

"Vig, please."

"I'll have eyes on you, but you won't see me again. We'll be in touch through email and unregistered cell phones. I'll set you up." He'd planted a kiss on my lips. "You open that sexy mouth of yours or anything goes missing, your sister pays the price. And I'll come for you. You know how all this works. I don't have to explain it. Do I?"

I'd only shaken my head.

"You do this right, keep it between us, she stays safe. So do you. Just stay alive and stay away. No contact with your club ever, or I let them think that Dig betrayed them. I'm very creative that way."

"No . . .Vig . . ."

"You in, Pretty?"

He was keeping me alive and killing me all at the same time. That was sheer fucking poetry.

"I'm in."

Vig had kissed my lips again. "Yeah," he'd murmured. He picked up the styrofoam cup filled with stale ice water from the table by my bed and held it before me. A slight smile had tugged at the edges of his mouth as I'd taken the straw between my lips and drank.

I had kept my word.

I didn't want to stay in Meager anyway, and Ruby had insisted I leave and start fresh somewhere new. She had wanted to come with me, but I'd known that wouldn't work. So I'd sent her back home after my first month in Boulder to sell off my and Dig's small house and everything else we owned. She'd sold our parents' house too and moved to Rapid.

In every city and town I'd landed in I had immediately opened a safety deposit box in my name and one of Vig's aliases, and had put in five diamonds. I would send him the bank card to different post office boxes each time. He would sign the card and mail it back to me for the bank. I'd kept the keys, so there was no physical proof at his end. But of course, if he ever wanted access to his goods, he would arrange for me to send him a key. I had become Vig's bandit concierge for his ill-gotten mafia gains.

And now it was finally finished, thanks to cancer, thanks to Butler spinning out of control, and thanks to me wanting more out of my life with Jakey and Miller in it. I just wasn't sure what living without that particular hell hanging over me anymore would be like, did I?

"Pull over!" Boner's booming voice snapped me out of my fog. My eyes flicked to my mirror. Clip was behind me.

I sped up, cut off Boner, and made a reckless left at the fork in the road.

Away from the club.

TWENTY-FIVE

MILLER

BONER'S NAME FLASHED on my cell phone. I wasn't sure whether to be relieved or go out of my mind. I silently made twisted bargains with the devil for positive news.

"Talk to me," I practically barked into the phone.

"Didn't you do that custom paint job for Creeper? That silver dragon with the red eyes?"

"What the fuck are you talking about?"

"Sister's on her own driving Creeper's bike, bro! I just saw her. Get me now?" Boner screeched.

"Where's she headed?"

"Looked like she was on her way back to the club, but she saw me and took off."

"And?"

"Blank, man. Her face was fucking blank, but hard as steel. Reminded me of when she—"

"Of what?"

"Shit. I've gotta find her."

My every nerve skidded along the edge of a knife. "Boner, what the fuck?"

"Years ago in the hospital, right after. She was a fuckin' mess. She tried to … Fuck!"

I squeezed my eyes shut, my lungs slamming against my ribs. "Are you on her?"

"Clip's on her trail. Soon as I get off the phone with you, I'm on my way. How's Dawes?"

"Still in surgery. You tell Clip to stand off. I know where she's heading. Neither of you talk to her or approach her. You got me? Stay on her, but back off. I'm on my way."

"What the hell are you talking about? No way, I'm not taking any chances."

"I'm there in five, stand off 'til I get there. You hear?" I yelled into the phone.

"Hurry up! This is fucking with my head. I'm not letting her do this again."

I shut down my phone and grabbed my jacket. My taped up arm screamed in pain as I shoved it through the sleeve. Blood had seeped through my bandage. Fuck it. I had taken a few ibuprofen while Willy sewed me up and we'd waited for Boner to call.

"You good to ride?" Jump was in my face. "You bleeding again?"

"Move!" I shoved him out of my way.

Jump charged out to the lot behind me. "Vig just called me. She's fine. He let her go. He said she shot Creeper and took off on his bike. She's got his gun."

My heart skidded against my ribs, every muscle in my body seething. I stopped in my tracks glaring at him. "This shit's on you, motherfucker. On both of us!"

I jumped on my bike and roared out of the club hitting the one lane road that circled Meager and would eventually lead me straight to the town cemetery. Creeper's bike stood in front of the tall iron gate. My red-eyed silver dragon on his gas tank glowed in the lone overhead street lamp. I leaped over the low stone wall that circled the old cemetery. Boner and Tricky flashed their headlights at me, and I signaled them with two of my fingers.

I ignored the jagged throb up my arm and charged around the headstones that shone in the moonlight. A brittle, thin laughter rang in the air, and a chill stole down my spine.

"Congratulations to me!" Grace's voice cried out. I stopped. She stood maybe four yards from me drinking from a bottle. She turned it over and poured its contents over a headstone. I quickly closed the distance between us. "End of Story, Dig," she said. "Thank God Ruby doesn't have to look over her shoulder anymore. But that's 'cause she's dead now. Like you. So let's celebrate." She raised the bottle in the air and smashed it over the gravestone.

I stole behind her, wrapped my arm around her waist and swiftly pulled her into me. "Grace!"

She howled and kicked. I clutched at her hands to keep her from punching up at me. "No!" she spit out. "You can't make this better. Hell, no!"

"I got you, Grace." The side of my face pressed against hers. Faded traces of her perfume wafted up to me from her neck. "Not letting you go."

She squirmed and pushed against me. "No!"

"Stop it!" I raised my voice. "Grace!" I shook her. Her head fell back against my shoulder, and she fought for air. "It's over," I murmured. "Whatever it is, it's all over now."

She stared at her husband's gravestone, her legs wobbling. "Wreck's death shook him up. Made him harder. Made him take some strange risks."

"I know how that is."

She twisted in my embrace and faced me, gripping my arms, her eyes wide. "I want to tell you everything. I need to. I want us to be nothing but honest with each other. Always. Is that too much to ask of you?"

"No." I held her steady gaze, clenching my jaw against the pain shooting up my arm. "Tell me." I held her close and she told me everything in a long whisper as we stood there together over Dig Quillen's grave.

Jesus Christ.

She wrapped her arms around my middle, took in a deep breath, and the tears came. I pushed back her hair, my lips brushing her forehead, and I held her close while she cried and shook in my arms.

"You protected your old man, Grace. From the cops, from a killer, even his reputation with his club. You stayed away and kept your sister safe all these years, and now you did the same for Jake." My hand rubbed down her back. She settled in my arms, and I pressed her in closer to me.

"All these years, along with the grief, you've been feeling angry and resentful, haven't you?" I said against her hair.

"We had it all—at least I thought so."

"Dig took risks. That's who he was."

She pushed against me, but I tightened my grip on her. "And I—I should have protected my baby. I should have stayed put, pretended I was dead. Something, for God's sake!" She groaned up at the night sky, her head slumping against me. "Instead I was thinking about the fallout with the police and the FBI, and Vig and his almighty stash."

"And you will never know how that might have turned out, Grace. The killer might've shot you at point-blank range to make sure you were dead." I tucked my face in her neck, my lips moved against her ear. "You'll never know. You made a bold, ballsy choice out of love. You didn't hesitate. And you survived. Then you kept your head up under Vig's gun all these years. Cling to that."

A bitter chuckle bubbled out of her. "Bold and ballsy just about bled me dry."

"It didn't though, Grace. You're here, baby. Alive. Breathing. With me."

Her body trembled slightly. "I came here to share the good news with my husband. Lucky for me, Creeper had a bottle of bourbon in his pack." Her trembling transformed into shakes. Christ, she was laughing. Laughing hard.

"Grace?"

Her head fell back. "Dig hated bourbon!" Her fingers curled into my shirt underneath my jacket. I tilted her face up to mine in the moonlight. Her lips parted, her wet eyes blinked up at me.

My beautiful Grace. My lost girl. My determined survivor. My vivid bright in all my cloudy gray.

I swallowed her whimper with my mouth. Her fingers pressed into my skin. I took her tongue over mine and drove through every corner of her silky mouth. The taste of her salty tears drove me on. I wanted to sandblast that sadness out of her for good. She wrapped her arms around my waist clinging to me. My head reeled. I didn't give a damn that we were standing over her husband's grave. Grace was mine, and I was hers.

I dug my fingers into her thick hair. "All this shit's done with. All of it. You made that happen. Be proud of that. I'm proud of you. You're done with the agonizing and the fucking guilt. You did good, Grace. You took on huge burdens for everyone, and now it's over. Let it go. Let the rest of them scramble over their scraps now. You live your life. You hear me?" I wiped away the streaks of wet that stained her cold face, then loosened my hold on her hair, letting my hands sweep down her shoulders.

She studied me. "Are you going to scramble for scraps too?"

I shook my head. "There's only one thing I want."

"What's that?"

My breath stalled. "You, baby." Her round eyes searched mine. "You going to cut out now that everything's over? Now that Ruby's gone?"

She shook her head. "I've got Jake."

"You got me, too."

"Yes, I do," she whispered. Her thumb reached out and brushed over my cut lip. "You're bleeding."

"It's nothing."

She took my mouth and sucked on my cut lip. The sting darted over my face. "Tastes good." My insides pitched at the husky tone in her voice.

"You're going to taste my everything when you get in my bed tonight," I said. Her lips parted, and she made a little breathy noise I felt all the way in my cock.

My hand slipped down her lower back and swiped the gun from her jeans. Her eyes flared at me. I held the gun up. "After we clean it, we'll consider giving it back to Creeper in the name of good faith. Or maybe you want to hang onto it as a souvenir?"

Grace's eyebrows lifted.

I grinned at her. "That's what I thought."

Grace got on the back of my bike at the cemetery, and we shot straight to the club with Boner following us. Clip called Dready and Tricky and got Creeper's bike back to the Club. Butler was recovering under Willy's watchful eye.

Boner charged towards us once we got inside the clubhouse.

My eyes flared at him. "Tomorrow, not fucking now!"

"Okay, okay," Boner muttered, hands in the air.

I locked us in my room. We fell on the bed together. Grace's fingers dug into my shoulders. Her cheeks were streaked with blood from my gashed lip, and my tongue licked over the smudges as she trembled in my arms. I inhaled her warm scent as if it was life-restoring. To me it absolutely was.

"Miller . . ."

There was need scorched in her voice. Need that matched my own.

We tore off each other's clothes.

"Yes, yes," she murmured over and over again as I pressed her against the bed and sucked on her tits, gorging myself on her soft flesh as if it were for the very first time. I was lost in her, enflamed beyond reason. Oh, reason had nothing to do with it. This was real desire, genuine hunger, a torturous ache ages-old that only Grace could cure.

No, I didn't want to be cured.

My hands slid down over her fantastic ass, and I pulled her down hard over my cock. Our eyes melded.

"Grace. . . oh, yeah."

Her mouth devoured mine. I would never tire of that mouth, my personal fountain of life. I tugged her hair back and tasted her throat. She let out a cry and moved faster over me, desperate to consume me, as desperate as I was to consume her. Her wet heat gripped me, pulled me in deeper, her body sliding and throbbing around me. My fingers swirled over her clit as her legs tensed and her back arched. I slammed into her, and her whole body tightened around mine, holding me in, harboring me.

"Fucking give it to me, Grace."

She exploded with me.

And so did everything I thought I knew.

That huge part of me that had never before let go, did just that.

"I missed you so much, baby. Every minute of every fucking day," my voice shook against her skin. Her arms tightened around me, her lips brushed over my flesh, soothing me, inciting me, comforting me. "I'll never get enough of you, Grace, never." I buried my cock deeper inside her, dragging moans and whimpers from her mouth.

Her warm body melted into mine. The two of us floated, nestled. Neither of us spoke, only touched, our fingers skimming, grazing over hot skin as we breathed. She touched the bandage on my arm. "You need more meds?"

"In a little bit, I'm good now," I mumbled.

"Are you sure?"

"I'm not moving." I planted a kiss on her cheek. "So tell me, hot-shot Harley Lady, you haven't been just selling T-shirts and boots all these years have you?"

"I sold bikes and then managed several stores." She brushed her soft lips over my chest. "There are a hell of a lot of women riding these days, you know."

"I know." My fingers traced lines up and down her damp back.

"You have your brother to blame," she said. "He got me on a bike first. He even yelled at Dig for not teaching me sooner."

"Good man."

"Dig was nervous about it. He said I'd be a lamb out among sharks on the road. So he taught me how to use a gun."

I filled my hand with one of her beautiful breasts, my fingers rubbing over a nipple. "Thank fuck for that."

"They taught me how to keep my cool in dire situations." She laid kisses across my abdomen.

"Again, thank—"

"Miller?"

"Hmm?"

"I missed you too," she whispered. "I tried really hard to ignore it. I've always been good at ignoring it and coasting on numb. It didn't work this time though. This time it just kept hurting."

I held her gaze. "No more numb, no more coasting, missing or hurting. We're done. We're going to live this together. Every goddamn day."

I pulled her up over my body and drank from her sweet mouth, my hands digging into her silky hair. Her thumb traced dizzying circles around my nipple and a tight shiver wound through me. My cock got harder than hell, and I rolled her over tucking her underneath me.

"Second time."

"Wh-what?" Her warm hands slid up my back, her pelvis squirmed underneath me searching for friction. I pulled up her knees so they were bent at my sides, then I sank inside her heat with one long, slow stroke.

Oh shit, there it is. . . .that little gasp from heaven escaped her lips.

"Miller, oh God."

"Second time you got taken, and my life flashed before my eyes." I withdrew and thrust into her again. Her walls pulsed and throbbed around me as she took me in deeper. Her eyes were glued to mine. Every cell in my body was set to bursting. Only Grace did this to me. No pretenses, no holding back.

Only my beautiful Grace.

"I can't lose you." I barely recognized my tense voice. I drove into her again, and she cocked her legs higher, taking me in even deeper.

The bolts inside me loosened, the bars unhinged, the latches fell.

"I need you, baby. Can't lose you."

"You won't."

"I love you, Grace. God, how I love you."

"Miller . . ."

My heart soared out of my chest. "I love you. Love you so goddamn much."

Words I had never spoken before to a woman, were suddenly the most natural and instinctive in my soul's vocabulary.

Her hands dug into the flesh of my back, her hips rolled up towards mine. "I want to feel more of you. Give me more, baby."

My blood surged, and I pounded into her. Heat rushed through every inch of me, and I drilled it back into her. She moaned loudly, her head tossing into the pillow, her wet eyes staying on me. We clung to each other, her body squeezing around mine.

This is genuine, total, absolute.

And I'm taking it and holding on.

I let out a hiss and poured myself into my woman's luscious body and stayed rooted deep inside her.

"Goddammit, I love you."

GRACE

My head rested on Miller's practically hairless chest. His steady heartbeat filled my ear, and I listened to it as it revealed its secrets to me. I took in a slow, easy breath and enjoyed the looseness in my every limb and the lazy caresses of Miller's fingertips down my back.

I raised my head up and kissed a nipple, my tongue swirling around it. His breath hitched and heat flared inside me at the sound. I licked and nuzzled the wing of the tattooed eagle on his upper chest all the way up to the hollow at the base of his long throat. He cupped my ass, pulled me up his body, and settled me in his warm embrace. I inhaled the musky scent on his sleek, damp skin. It smelled like. . .*us.*

That carefully constructed hollow, empty glass box I had lived in for so long had been rendered useless, unnecessary, pitiful even. In fact, it could no longer hold me in. I liked this new fresh, sweet air in my lungs. I breathed out and the glass walls disappeared around me. I stood on the edge unfettered and looked over without a trace of fear or hesitation.

Truth is a painful sword. It cuts deep and stings, but the pain evaporates, the blood dries, and in the place of such savagery is a gleaming absolution and an absolute purity.

It's blinding. It hurts.

And it is utterly beautiful.

"I love you, Miller Flies As Eagles."

A slow growl vibrated in his chest. He twisted my body back onto the mattress. His fierce eyes glittered over me. "You're all mine now, Grace." He laid a trail of kisses over my face. "These eyes, these lips and tongue." His hands and lips roamed over my body, savoring, biting, sucking, claiming. "These tits, this stomach, these legs."

I held my breath. He was baptizing my flesh with his mouth.

His fingers sank into my rear. "This ass is mine." He nudged his nose into my wet heat, and his tongue lashed through my slit. "This pussy. . .all mine."

"Baby—"

Miller's mouth sank between my legs, and he sucked hard on what was his.

My fists uncurled in the sheets.

TWENTY-SIX

"GET OUT HERE, YOU WHORE!" Fists pounded on the door.

Oh no.

"The fuck you say!" hissed Miller. He knifed up from the bed, pulled his boxer briefs up his legs, grabbed his Colt 1911, turned the lock on the door, and threw it open.

Butler exploded in the doorway. "Been listening to you two fuck all night and all fucking morning!"

Miller aimed the Colt at Butler's face, his long arms taut, his entire body rigid. "Glad to hear it, asshole."

In a flash, Miller tossed the gun to his left hand as his right fist snapped back and landed in Butler's face. The crack zipped through the air, and my heart rammed up my throat. Butler staggered against the wall and crumpled to the floor. His red eyes hung on mine.

"I've been wanting to do that for weeks!" Miller pulled him up by the throat.

I scrambled over the bed to the doorway, the sheet wrapped around me. "Miller—He's injured enough as it is."

"Did you hear what this fucking worm just said about you?" Miller spit out.

"I heard, but I owe him an explanation."

"You don't owe him anything!"

"Please." I wrapped my hand around his elbow just under his bandages. Miller released Butler with a jerk of his hand.

Butler stumbled once more, struggling to stand up. "Fuck this shit," he muttered.

"You got that right." Miller put his gun back on the dresser and jerked his chin at me. "Get some clothes on."

I scooped up my twisted jeans and bra from the floor and went behind the door and tugged them on, then grabbed a heavy sweatshirt of Miller's that was thrown over a chair and pulled it over my head. I stepped away from the door and went to Butler.

"Let's get a cup of coffee, all right?" I touched his arm. He shoved my hand away grimacing.

"Butler?"

"Yeah, yeah." He ambled down the hall.

My gaze flew to Miller who stood in the center of his room, his hands on his hips, a dark scowl on his face. "You've got ten minutes with him and that's it."

I closed the distance between us, yet the tension in his face didn't fade. I raised myself on my toes and planted a kiss on his mouth. He cupped the back of my head and gave me a deep tongue devouring kiss in return.

"That's the way I wanted to start our day." His thumb tugged on my now swollen lips.

"How about I meet you in the shower in ten minutes and we start our day then?"

"I'm thinking that would be a very good idea." Miller released me and headed for the bathroom.

I pulled on my boots and headed for the clubroom.

Butler hunched over the bar and lit a cigarette. His eyes scorched mine as I crossed the room. I poured the fresh brew from the coffee machine on the end of the bar into two mugs and hopped up on the stool next to him and passed him a mug.

"Thank God that bullet just scraped your skin," I said, swiping my hair behind my ears.

"Yeah, big fucking lucky, that would be me. Just plain lucky. Over and over again." He took a long drag on his smoke.

"Would you rather be lying on a tray at the morgue?"

He looked me in the eye. "Honestly?" He sighed heavily. "I don't know anymore."

"You might need to consider getting out for a bit and getting clean."

"It always comes down to that, doesn't it?"

"Yeah, it does. Haven't you hit rock bottom yet? Don't you want to see things clearly? Trust yourself again? Run your club right? Don't you want men around you who trust you, and you see that trust in their eyes? Do you even remember what that's like?" He clenched his jaw and took a gulp of hot coffee. "Vig was going to take it all away from you, and who knows. . .give it all to Creeper? Where would that have left you? Where would that have left the club you put your heart and soul into all these years? Maybe you can still make things right with Jump."

His brow snapped together. "I wanted to make things right with you and me."

"I can't get on that particular carousel with you. I've been there with my mom and with Ruby. There's no room for anybody else in the house when it's you and your addictions keeping company."

He snorted at me, his blue eyes stiffening into icy rocks. "But you can get between Lock's legs right? How long you been fucking him anyway?"

"We actually met by chance before I hit town, before you and me started up. There was a lot of on and off."

"I hit you on an off night then? See—lucky." His gaze shifted around the room. I slid an ashtray close to him.

"I wanted you that night at the party, Butler. That wasn't a lie. But yes, I had feelings for Lock that I was avoiding."

That was the truth, but there was no way I could tell him the whole truth. *Hey, honey, actually after our first time together, the club took advantage of us and had me spy on you and your chapter. No hard feelings, okay?*

"Guess you're working them out now, huh?"

"Yes, we are."

He rubbed his hands over his face. "That's my problem, Sister. I know what that's like, working on it, making it good." His voice was low, thick. "Half these assholes don't know, don't care, and that's just pathetic 'cause they have no idea what they're missing. But you know, same as me. You know." I only nodded, my fingers squeezing my coffee mug.

He sniffed as he ground his stub into the ashtray. "It's that treasure you keep shiny and safe at all costs. That thing that drives you to be a better you, that pushes out the garbage you got stuffed inside. Once it's in, it keeps out the cold and fills you with real heat. I thought I had a shot at that again with you."

My chest tightened. "I have that shot with Lock. I tried to ignore it, because it scared me, it was overwhelming, but I just can't ignore it anymore. It's as if I got bitten and the sting won't stop."

"Yeah." Butler's hand closed over mine on the bar and squeezed. His forehead sank into his other hand, his eyes slid closed for a moment.

"I never wanted to hurt you or mislead you," I whispered. "Please forgive me."

Butler made a noise in the back of his throat and averted his gaze. I planted a kiss on his stubbled cheek. "I'm so thankful you're alive. Stay that way."

"Maybe," he said, drawing out another cigarette from his pack. "Maybe."

"Grace! Thank God you're okay!" Mary Lynn's arms flew around me. The intensive care waiting room at the hospital teemed with club members.

"I'm fine. Any news about Dawes? Has he woken up yet?"

"We're still waiting," Alicia said. "The surgeon said the bullet nicked a couple arteries, but they were able to patch them up. He's lost a lot of blood though."

"He has to be okay." Mary Lynn bit her lip. "Dawes even babysits for us, Grace. The kids love him." Alicia took her hand.

An arm encircled my waist. "How you doing, Sister?" asked Jump.

"I'm okay. Better."

Jump glanced over at Miller who was leaning against the wall speaking with Kicker and Clip. "You good?"

"Better than good."

He let go of my waist. "Look, I want you to know that I appreciate you putting yourself out there for the club."

"Is that a thank you?"

"Yeah."

"How are things with Vig?"

He quirked an eyebrow. We'll see how it goes. You all squared with him?"

I nodded. "Blowback from his nephews and Dig. It's over now."

For my best interests, I, too, could cooly take advantage of the renown legend of animosity that Vig and my husband had carefully maintained, couldn't I? Some secrets you just can't share.

"I'm not gonna ask."

"Don't. There is one thing I want to ask you, though."

"It's never one thing with you women." He stuck his thumbs in his waistband and tugged on his jeans. "I'm listening."

"Help Butler get clean. And if he does, give him another chance. What he did to the club was stupid, and I know he's going to have to pay for that somehow, but don't throw him away. Ruby turned things around for herself. Give him a chance. We're all he's got."

He exhaled, his gaze holding mine. "Thicker than blood, right?"

It had proven true for so many of us.

His brown eyes searched mine. "You still hate me?"

"Yes, but it might wear off one day."

"Here's hoping."

Miller took my hand and gestured down the hallway. Boner was slumped on the floor by the doorway to the intensive care unit.

My heart squeezed. "Boner?" His strained eyes lifted to mine. "He'll be okay, honey. He'll pull through."

"He was my recruit. I was with him. Right next to him. And it wasn't a Demon Seed that got him. It was fucking Creeper. I'm gonna—"

"Just concentrate on Dawes now."

Boner inhaled. I sat down on the floor next to him and put my arm through his.

"You scared the shit out of me last night, Little Sister."

"I know. I'm sorry."

Boner sank his head in my neck. "Don't ever do that to me again," he whispered.

I hugged him close. "I won't. Not ever."

Two hours later after Dawes finally woke up and recognized us, the doctor declared his prognosis for a full recovery was good. I took Miller's hand and we left the hospital.

He held out his lid to me in the parking lot. "I'm taking you to my house."

My house.

Outside in the chilly air, the soft rays of the afternoon sun beating down on us, those two simple words said in his deep voice filled me with swirls of honeyed warmth and promise.

I took his helmet.

Miller's Harley roared out of Rapid City. I leaned my chin against his broad back, and his one hand pressed into mine at his waist.

"Have you been fixing this up yourself?"

"Yeah. You remember the way it used to be?" Miller asked. "Been taking my time with it. It's shaping up slowly. Don't have much in the way of furniture or a kitchen, but the bedroom and bathroom are set up."

Miller swung open the front door of Wreck's cabin in the hills outside of Meager and led me inside. The interior had been converted into one great room, whereas originally it had been separated into a strip of a kitchen, a living area and dining corner. Now the space was open and airy. I entered and the sunlight filled the room from the new large picture window. My hand went to my throat. Luckily, I noticed the construction supplies and tools before I tripped over them.

Miller grabbed onto my arm. "Careful."

"You cleaned the place out."

"Yeah, I did."

"Oh my gosh."

"Wreck was a hell of a pack rat."

"Yeah, it was kind of bad."

Miller let out a laugh. "You're being real generous, Grace."

I placed my handbag on the mottled black granite of the kitchen island. My hand slid over the cool, silky surface. The rest of the kitchen had remained the same from Wreck's day. A faded green fridge from the seventies, a portable electric stovetop, and rustic wood cabinets with scratched black metal knobs.

"The kitchen's up next."

I smiled at him. "I've cooked in this kitchen, you know. It was in bad shape back then."

"That was brave, baby."

"Yeah, it was." We both laughed.

"You want to take a shower? Got brand new towels you can try out."

"God, yes." I shrugged off my heavy leather jacket, and he took it from me.

Miller led me down the hall and switched on a light in the bathroom. My eyes popped open at the sight of fresh white tile on the walls and floor, the brand new shower stall, toilet and sink with sleek nickel fixtures, the well-lit mirror.

My eyes widened. "You don't mess around."

"No, I don't."

He disappeared for a few moments then returned with a long-sleeved thermal shirt in black and a pair of cut-off black sweat pants. "I don't think you'll need any underwear. Although, if you want, I do have a black panty I found in a motel room a while back." A smirk was plastered on his face.

My eyes shot up to his. He had my lost black panty from our first time together at the motel.

"You didn't."

"Oh I did, baby. Finders keepers."

"Well, tomorrow I'll need it."

A grin stole over his lips. "Not so sure about that."

My fingertips dug into the soft fabric of the folded clothing in my arms. The faint fresh fragrance of his laundry detergent wafted up, and I breathed it in, my eyes sinking closed.

"Grace?"

I blinked up at him. Miller lifted my chin and planted a kiss on my lips. "I'm going to light a fire."

"Okay." My arms wrapped around his waist, and I nestled into his chest.

He chuckled. "Babe, you going to let me go so I can get to the fireplace?"

"Not yet." I squeezed him tighter.

The heat from the fire instantly warmed me when I entered the great room. A Lakota star-patterned quilt was thrown on the large sectional sofa. I stood still and let the heat of the fire seep through my bones.

"Get in," Miller said, his hand at the small of my back. I crawled onto the sofa and nestled under the quilt. Miller, wearing only loose fitting pajama bottoms, got in after me and tucked the thick quilt around us.

"Better?"

"More than better." My gaze was riveted by the flames leaping in the hearth.

"I made hot tea, and I've got these." He held up a package of oatmeal raisin cookies.

I squealed. "Perfect!" He grinned and dropped the package in my hands. My fingers tore open the plastic and tugged out a cookie. I leaned my head back on his upper arm and munched. "Can we sleep here tonight?"

"You sure? I've got a big bed inside."

"The fire is too perfect. The sofa is roomy enough for both of us, isn't it? I'm much too cozy to move." He slid his arm around me and tucked me into his bare chest. The warm smell of his skin eased the tension in my joints a little bit more.

We stayed that way for a long time, sipping tea, watching the licking flames of the fire, breathing side by side, me slumped in his embrace, and Miller's steady heartbeat under my ear. I was secure, on solid ground, and for the first time I loosened that iron grip I'd had on myself for so very long.

I offered him the last bite of cookie. His full lips grazed the tips of my fingers, and heat spread through my body like a balm of warm oil.

I pressed closer into him. "After I got out of the hospital, I only wanted to crawl into a hole, but Ruby wouldn't let me. She kept reminding me that even though I had lost a lot, I was still young, still had my whole life ahead of me. I had a second chance. I didn't really want to start over, but I did in a colorless, drab way.

Never laid roots anywhere, never accumulated many things. I just kept moving on. Of course I had to keep moving because of Vig, but it was just as well."

"Drab?"

"Yeah, just dead in the water."

"You weren't dead in the water, Grace." Miller glanced down at me, his eyes reflecting the light of the fire. "You were just floating. You've been floating a good long time."

"Floating," I said to the fire.

"Yeah," he sighed. "You've got to swim to shore."

I took his warm hand in mine under the thick quilt. "Miller . . ."

"Shh." He wiped wet strands of hair from my face. "My grandmother used to say that there are times when we should hush and listen to the wisdom of the fire."

My lips curled into a slight smile against his smooth chest, our fingers entwined under the quilt. The burning logs crackled and fizzled as the orange flames lashed over them and reached higher. Miller's fingers caressed my skin, and I exhaled as I drifted off to sleep.

"Hold on, Sister, hold on!"

"I am holding on, Wreck!" I shout. My grip tightens around his waist. We fly down a black road on his Indian Chief motorcycle. I choke back a scream as the vintage bike roars under me. We zoom ahead even faster, piercing the black velvet night.

But there's something different. Something unusual.

No headlight.

"Wreck, your light! Can you see?"

Wreck laughs and the Indian surges forward even harder, taking my heart with it. "I can see, Sister. You hold on!"

In the infinite darkness another deeper blast of pipes screams behind us. My throat tightens. I desperately want to look over my shoulder, but I can't move. I struggle to turn my head to the side.

"Somebody's coming."

Wreck doesn't answer, he only increases the speed of the Chief. The muscles in my legs ache as I hold onto the bike with everything I have. The powerful engine vibrates right through my jaw, my eyes, my skull.

"Baby, baby, where you going, baby?" a voice behind me teases.

Butler's Harley comes up to the side of Wreck's bike. Butler's eyes are glowing an eerie dark violet color. Caitlyn sits behind him, her long wavy blonde hair glaring like neon in the black night sweeping behind her. A punk Lady Godiva whose violet eyes flicker at me.

"Baby, where you off to? I need you, baby!" Butler laughs. Caitlyn licks his neck and groans loudly as if she's having an orgasm. She shoots me a smile and licks her lips with an incredibly long red tongue, like some kind of freaky supernatural being. My stomach lurches. I try to shout, but my voice chokes in my throat.

I hold on tighter to Wreck. My legs squeeze around the hot, screaming metal. Butler's bike comes closer to the Indian Chief. I try to hide behind Wreck's massive frame, my fists tightening and thumping against his back to get his attention, but he doesn't react. Butler and Caitlyn continue to laugh and suddenly recede into the darkness. Wreck disappears, evaporating from my hold, and only the roar of the Indian remains as the night swallows me whole.

"Grace—Grace!"

My skin prickled with cold sweat. My lungs strained for air.

"You're having a bad dream. You're okay, I'm with you. It's okay, baby," Miller held me in his arms. He swept my tangled hair from my face. I struggled to open my eyes and flinched in his arms. "You with me?" He planted a kiss on my forehead and stroked my cheek. "It was just a dream," he whispered. "Just a dream."

"So real."

"It's over. It's okay."

"Freaking crazy."

"It's over now."

I turned in his arms and we spooned, his broad chest pressed into my back. His one hand went around my middle, and I reached for it and brought it under my shirt to my bare breast. I needed to feel him on my skin.

"I was with Wreck on the back of his Indian Chief. We were riding in the dark with no lights on, then suddenly Butler was behind us on his Harley looking like a freaky ghost, and he had a zombified Caitlyn with him. They were following us, teasing us.

Wreck just kept going faster and faster in the dark, just looking straight ahead."

"What was that about the bike?"

"What?"

"You said the Indian Chief?"

"Yes, it was the one he fixed for you. I haven't seen that bike in a million years. Just ... bizarre."

Miller's arms tightened around me. "I have it here in the garage." He swept my hair to the side and planted a kiss on the side of my neck. "Tell me about the dream."

"Wreck was happy. We were riding so fast in the dark. He kept telling me to hold on. He didn't care about the darkness, his speed, or Butler. He just kept going faster and yelling, "Hold on, Sister!" Miller chuckled softly. "But Butler and Caitlyn, they were damn scary."

"That's done, babe."

I rubbed over the hand that cupped my breast. "I like it when you hold me," I whispered.

He turned me back onto the sofa. His brow had knit together, and his mind was churning behind those troubled eyes.

"What is it?" I asked.

"You still living it, Grace?"

My eyes widened. "What?"

"The past. A lot just went down, and I know Butler was a part of your past."

"Do you think I haven't let go?"

"I don't fault you for it. Being back here, it's only natural."

I shook my head. "Those old buried feelings came up, but they were like. . .powder. Being with Butler was suffocating. I couldn't breathe. He's so lost, just stuck. Butler's been trying to fill the holes inside him with a bunch of crazy shit. Of course, I took a different route. I never let anybody too close, so I wouldn't let those empty holes get filled by anyone or anything else. I think I wanted to hold on to that empty somehow, not fill it, like he did."

"You can't hold on to empty." Miller's fingers dwelled at my throat.

"I tried, though. I tried very hard and trudged on. I made it an art form." My fingers swept over his broad cheekbones. "I was so scared to come back. Scared because my sister needed *me*, not an empty version of me. Now Jakey needs me, and all that empty is just useless, isn't it? Every time I'm with him, I feel that pull, that demand."

"It's a good kind of demand, isn't it?"

"It's humbling. I want to give that boy everything," my voice shook in the darkness.

My heart beat quickened under his exploring hand. I reached up and touched the side of his face. "I feel that with you, Miller Flies As Eagles." His hand stilled at the base of my throat. "It's almost—" His lips crushed mine. "Yeah, that," I breathed into his mouth. "That—just everything."

My hands slid up his sleek skin over the rippled muscles underneath. His breath snagged when my fingers lingered on his chest and brushed over the leather cord around his neck from which hung his beads and the arrow. My legs rubbed against the long muscular length of his.

There, I had confessed my darkness to him as I had done with no one else. I did not combust or go poof in a cloud of smoke. I survived, and it felt good.

A flaming ember popped out on the edge of the hearth, and the mountain of thin logs tumbled in on itself, snapping and fizzling. Miller went to the hearth and rearranged the logs. He wiped his hands and came back to me, taking me in his arms and rearranging the quilt around us. My body settled into his. We stared into the fire again in silence for a long while, my fingers dragging through his short hair.

"A brave cuts his hair off when in mourning for a loved one, doesn't he?" I asked.

"It's the sign that he's lost a part of himself."

"You've kept your hair short since Wreck died, since you were discharged, haven't you? You're still holding onto that loss?" He didn't reply. "Miller?" I whispered. My fingers brushed his stiff jaw. "You've cut off your spirit all this time?"

His head jerked down at me, his eyes tight. "I don't need a white girl telling me . . ."

I gripped his bicep. "You're the same as me. I've been floating for years, but you shouldn't be locked down either. Not locked down in your soul and not locked into the club if that's not what you want anymore." My fingernails dug into his skin. "You should be flying with eagles." His chest expanded under my hand, and my

316

fingers slid across the wings branded on his skin. "I want to see you fly, Miller. I want to fly with you."

His eyelids sank, his hands curved over my rear and pressed my body into his. His warm lips touched mine and the kiss was sweet and urgent, his liquid eyes melting into mine. His teeth nipped at my lips, my jaw, then down the sensitive skin of my throat. A shiver skittered over my flesh. His teeth sank into my shoulder.

"Baby—" The tips of my fingers scored his back.

"Touch me, Grace. For God's sake, touch me."

My fingers grazed the waistband of his pajama pants and tucked inside them, and my hand immediately wrapped around his velvety smooth cock. A deep groan escaped his lips. Heat coursed through me at that beautiful sound. His pelvis arched up into my hand, and his erection grew and hardened under my strokes.

The need to envelop him with affection overwhelmed me. I shoved the quilt out of my way, sat back, and took him in my mouth. A hiss escaped his chest, and his fingers dug in my hair. My body ached for him more intensely with every heavy breath and grunt that I wrought from him.

Stroking his balls, I took his cock in deeper, lavishing its hard length with my tongue then sucked hard, my other hand skimming over his hipbone. He groaned and mumbled words I couldn't decipher. I wanted to be his refuge, the same way he'd made me feel safe and cared for. I wanted him to know that I cared about him, that he was worthy of living full and real. Full and real with me. Most of all, I needed him to know that he mattered, that every little thing about him mattered to me.

Ruby's words blasted right through my heart. *Let go of that sadness and get on with the joy.*

I slid his wet cock from my mouth brushing my lips across the velvet tip. "I want to feel you inside me. I want you to take what you need from me."

The logs crumpled in the fire and hissed at us. The orange glow flickered over the taut angles of Miller's face. He pushed me back against the pillows and shoved his pajamas pants all the way down his legs as I swiped off mine. My gaze darted down the length of our bodies. I wanted to see us joined, watch his fantastic, sleek body work over mine. I wanted it all.

His tip nudged at my pulsing entrance, and my swollen flesh hummed. I spread my legs wider underneath him hooking a leg over his hip, my hands smoothing down the bunched muscles in his taut lower back. I wanted all of him, as much as I could possibly get. His body rocked against mine, and his thick cock slid inside me slowly.

The blood drained from my system and rushed through my veins all at once. This was bliss. This was...

"Miller—" I clung to his body.

"Grace," he rasped. He pulled out slowly, paused for a gasp-filled millisecond, then thrust himself inside me, burying himself deep. My body throbbed and spasmed all around him, stretching and pulsing at his demanding invasion. I raised my hips up to meet his thrusts, and he stopped, his fingers gripping my face. "Maybe all those other guys you fucked over the years let you take care of yourself, but not me. I'm giving this to you. When you come, baby, know it's mine."

My heart skipped a beat as he pinned my hands over my head and raised himself over me, his eyes boring into mine, almost savage in their determination. "Me in you," he breathed and thrust deep once again.

My desperate breaths quickened, shivers stealing over my skin. I lifted my legs higher against his sides to take all of him.

"Yes." I moaned with every rough and devastating jolt of his powerful body. "All yours." He thrust harder, faster, hitting my clit with every deep stroke, sending me into an overwhelming spiral of emotion and pleasure.

"You feel so good, baby. Oh God. Grace—" his voice pleaded with me, as if he was at my mercy. I knew I was at his. I tightened my insides around him, and his mouth fell open, his grip tightening over my wrists. "Aw, fuck . . ."

My heart pounded through my chest and into his. I broke apart and flew. A savage grunt escaped his lips, his body stiffening, plowing into mine one final time. I whimpered, licking at his neck, desperate for the musky, salty taste of his hot skin His large hands released my wrists and cradled my face as he struggled for breath. I took his earring in my mouth and sucked gently on his earlobe, my shaky legs rubbing his.

He released his grip on my wrists, and my hand slipped between us. He groaned softly as my fingers swirled through the fantastic mess we had made, settling over the root of his cock still embedded inside me.

That's truth for you. That's as real as it gets.

"I'm not floating anymore," I whispered against his ear.

TWENTY-SEVEN

I STRETCHED MY LIMBS under the soft cotton quilt and turned my eyes from the glare of the morning sun pouring through the large front window. Miller definitely needed curtains. He'd woken up earlier and whispered something in my ear about getting coffee from the store and with a tender kiss took off on his bike.

I sat up and smiled to myself. I leaned over onto the floor and nabbed the henley when a thick white sketch pad caught my eye. It was open to a charcoal sketch. *Of me.* Under this very quilt.

I tugged the henley over my head, smoothing it down over my body and studied the drawing. My hair was swept across my one arm. A faint, secret smile was etched on my lips in my sleep. The long lines of my throat, the curve of my shoulders, arms, bare breasts stretched out across the rough paper. I bit down on my lower lip, my breath catching in my throat.

The thought of Miller studying me and sketching me early this morning, his fingertips rubbing over the paper to create the lines of my body as I slept sent stabs of heat through me. My fingertips skimmed over the textured surface of the paper. My vision blurred.

I flipped the page over and there was another sketch of me. This one showed my bare legs twisted in the quilt, the curve of my naked rear leading to my bare back, and one arm stretched out under my head. Simple, sensual. I turned the page. There were no more. It was a new sketch pad and had only those two drawings. I had to find more.

I shot up off the sofa, hungry for a peek into Miller's concealed artistic self. Oh, this quiet man had a secret beauty all his own hidden deep inside, and I wanted to uncover it. I wanted to know it.

On the opposite side of the room from the construction supplies were piles of worn sketchbooks in a rickety pine bookshelf. I grabbed one, and my fingers flipped through the thick pages. A variety of motorcycles, skulls with plenty of accessories, phantom skeletons flying on wings, stars in a naked woman's long hair that floated through a dark night sky, eagles, eagles, always eagles. The pages flapped to an intricately patterned butterfly in dark midnight-hued colors. My breath tripped. I turned over the page. An ominous landscape of hills with a grouping of three trees, the land saturated in blood red. That one over and over again. A souvenir of war?

I flipped over page after page of this treasure in my hands. My heart stuttered at a portrait of an older Native American woman, the severe lines of her face softened by her large dark eyes. Miller's eyes. Her long smooth hair had been worked in a variety of rich jewel colors giving her a magical, otherworldly quality. Colored butterflies took shape from her strands of hair and flew into the sky. She shimmered with intense color, with vibrant life.

"Grace?"

I gasped and swung around. Miller, wearing a knit cap and his worn leather jacket, held a grocery bag in one hand and his keys in the other. He stared at me. "What are you doing?"

"I found these." I held up the drawing pad in my hands. "They're wonderful. I really like them." I cleared my throat and raised the last drawing to show him. His eyes darted to the portrait in my hands and stiffened.

"Is this your grandmother Kim?" He only nodded. "It's stunning."

"Stunning?" He dropped his keys and the shopping bag on the granite countertop, peeled off his jacket carefully, and leaned his hip against the island. "Come on, Grace."

I grinned. "It is. It's also fantastic and magical all in one. That's what this is." My eyes returned to the portrait of his grandmother. "Fantastical. Oh, and I liked mine too." I gestured at the sketches of me I had left on the sofa.

A shy yet mischievous smile crept over his face. "Get over here." Thick bubbles popped inside my chest. I loved that rough tone in his voice, the one that held a secret just for me. I scooted over to him, threw my arms around his neck and gave him my mouth. He pulled me in tightly against his chest, lifted me up, and deposited me on the kitchen island.

"Good morning." His dark gaze lingered on my lips.

I plucked the slouchy knit cap from his head and mussed his short hair with my fingers. "Make the coffee, baby."

"Hmm. . .bossy." He leaned down, and his tongue swiped over my smiling lips.

I opened the shopping bag, pulled out the package of ground coffee and smiled. Miller spent money on good, high-end coffee. "Brazilian?"

"Always. You like it?"

"I do. Very smooth and rich."

I held out the bag to him. Miller took it with a kick quick kiss on my cheek and busied himself preparing his equally high-end coffee maker. He sauntered back over to me stretching out his arms on the counter at my sides, studying my face. My stomach dipped and that hum took over my body. "We've got a few minutes before the coffee's ready."

"Hmm?"

"I've got an idea," he whispered. He leaned in and gently kissed one corner of my mouth and then the other.

I sighed, my thumb rubbing over his lower lip. Those sensuous lips of his were what a few of my fantasies were made of.

"I like you in my shirt and nothing else," he murmured. His cool hands slid up my bare thighs, and my breath caught. He rubbed his nose against mine. "Come here."

I nestled closer in his arms. He swept me up, chuckling as I let out a squeal. I hooked my legs around his waist. He snatched the sketchbook and a pencil from a drawer in the island and carried me to the living room to the oversized leather armchair.

My body sank into its thick softness. There was room for two on this chair. I could imagine the two of us curled up on it under a blanket before the fire, TV on, necking, reading, eating popcorn, napping. Very domestic daydream.

He pulled my legs apart and kneeled down before me. My breathing accelerated. "I want to see you, Grace. Haven't really had a chance yet." His eyes were somber, wide. "Lose the shirt."

I wriggled out of his shirt, and he took it from my hands and let it drop to the floor. I licked my suddenly dry lips. His heavy gaze swept down my body and I shivered, my nipples hardening immediately. He groaned softly as he cupped my breasts kneading them together and then suckled each one gently. I let out a cry, desperate to kiss him, touch him, feel him against me, my back arching off the leather chair. The pads of his fingers glided over my ribs, the curve of my waist, down my hips. His touch was feather-light, full of reverence, yet there was possession in it. A tremor betrayed me.

"Are you cold?"

I shook my head, unable to speak, mesmerized by his soft, heavy gaze. My fingernails dug into the thick leather.

Miller's hands pushed my knees further apart. Sparks flew through me as his fingers lazily stroked my inner thighs. His thumbs lightly caressed over the center of my own cataclysmic tornado. "Oh, Grace," his husky voice pulled at my name. "So beautiful, baby." My eyes fluttered closed, my face burned. His lips nuzzled their way up my left thigh, the anticipation of his luscious mouth on me unbearable.

"Yes," I breathed.

He took my one leg and slung it over the wide arm of the chair, my other remaining on the floor, then he draped my upper body at an angle against the other arm. He sat back on his haunches, a thick eyebrow raised.

"Touch yourself, Grace."

I blinked up at him. "What?"

Miller sat on his knees on the floor in front of me and picked up the pencil and sketchbook. His pencil began moving quickly over the paper. He was sketching. Sketching me. "Touch yourself, baby. But keep your other hand up over your head."

Heat flared over my skin. I watched his eyes dart between me and the paper as his pencil outlined and filled. My fingers went between my legs as my other hand clutched the soft leather of the chair arm under my head.

"Take yourself there slowly, but don't come. I'm going to make you come."

My insides seized and melted at his words, the commanding tone of his voice. I relaxed my head and my fingers moved, my gaze riveted on him studying me, drawing. My breathing deepened, my one heel raised up off the floor. I surrendered to my own rhythm and to his focused gaze.

He suddenly dropped the pad and pencil. His hand pushed my fingers away and his tongue snaked over my throbbing center, his eyes scoring through mine.

My hips jerked. "Oh God, yes!"

Sharp shards of pleasure tore right through me as his tongue pulsed over my clit then swirled in lazy strokes up and down my sex pulling me under. He sat up suddenly, his tongue swiping over his lower lip, and went back to sketching.

I let out a moan. "Miller?"

His pencil dashed over the paper. "Don't move, baby. I just tasted everything we did last night," he murmured, his eyes not leaving the sketch. "Tasted real good."

My head sank back into the leather and I squirmed, my blood still simmering. He sketched with quick and long, drawn-out strokes. I could practically feel the pencil on my skin.

"You need to feed me," I said. "Now."

His eyes remained glued to the sketch pad. "What?"

"I want to have enough energy to keep up with you."

He flashed me a grin. A boyish abandon swept over his features, and I melted all over again. He dropped the pad and pencil on the floor and grabbed the T-shirt. I pushed up, and he smoothed the soft cotton down over me. My fingers tugged at the hem over my legs.

"And after I feed you?" His dark eyes teased me.

My thighs pressed together. "And after you feed me. . .what?"

His fingers went to my chin raising my face to his. "My bed. For the rest of the day."

"I hope so, because you need to finish what you just started."

"Screw the dishes, Grace. We'll deal with it later."

I stared at the tumble of greasy frying pans, sticky plates, mugs, glasses, and an empty orange juice container in the small kitchen sink. Ordinarily my hair would have stood on end at such a sight, but I only giggled. We had devoured the bacon, egg, cheese, and English muffin extravaganza I had concocted and now lazed on the stools at the kitchen island.

"Later on this afternoon we'll go get your stuff." Miller swept over the granite with a wad of damp paper towels.

I slid the salt and pepper shakers to the end of the island. "What do you mean?"

"I mean your moving in here. Today."

"What?"

He looked up at me and stopped wiping. "What do you mean—what?"

"Today?"

"Yeah."

"Um, I can't do that. I have to work myself into Jake and Alex's schedule. They're over in Rapid, so I need to find a place there. Then I need to find a job there." I swept my hair away from my face.

He stared at me.

"And I need to go through Ruby's stuff. God knows what I'm going to find. Then I really, really, need to find a yoga class and some kind of cardio so I can sane and still consume all this hearty food I'm suddenly surrounded by. And—"

His lips smashed together. "You're not making a lick of sense."

"Are you kidding me?"

"No." He shook his head. "You're kidding yourself."

"I am not. I need. . .time."

"Time?"

"Yes. I need time, to get into the flow of. . .this."

"What flow, Grace? Flow of what?"

"You know . . ."

"No, I don't know." He tossed the paper towel on the granite and crossed his arms.

"I need time to get organized, get focused. I can't just . . ."

"Can't just what? Get a life?"

"Miller!"

"Sixteen years worth of rolling and drifting, and you've got nothing and no one to call your own." He planted his hands on the granite and leaned towards me. "What the hell is there to organize?"

My shoulders stiffened. "Excuse me, I do have a few possessions, a quality vehicle, and, I'll have you know, plenty of money saved in the bank!"

His dark eyebrows snapped together. "Congratulations. And how's that working for you?"

I flexed my feet against the footrest of the barstool. My eyes swept over the clean, shiny granite.

"And where do I fit in to this "flow" of yours, Grace? Do I even fit in? Or maybe you don't know yet? You need time to see if I fit in to your flow?"

"That's not what I meant." I cleared my throat. "Miller, look. I'm going to be settling down for the first time in a long time, and that's going to be a huge change for me. I need to get used to that, get comfortable first. It's freaking me out a little, which I realize may be strange. But then I can think about..."

"Think? About what? About me? Us?"

"Well..."

"Grace, I have money saved in the bank too, a job I like, and my brothers who always have my back. I've got my own house that I'm fixing, and a slew of amazing bikes. The one thing I don't have, the most important thing, is you. And I'm not waiting for you to get organized, get in a fucking flow or find a yoga class or whatever the hell you're babbling on about to have a life with you."

"I'm not babbling!"

"You're panicking. We need to be together, Grace. Now. Yesterday."

"Okay, but —"

"'Okay' doesn't factor into this at all. And neither does the word 'but.' Jesus, nothing about us is 'okay.' We are good, amazing, dream come true. What have we been talking about and fucking about for the past two days and nights? Us, together, that's what. We need to start making our home, Grace. I want a place that's ours, where we can rest together. Don't you get that? I need that. I need it now, and so do you. I can't wait. I won't."

I took in a deep breath and exhaled. His hand clutched mine. "Are you scared?" he asked in a throaty whisper.

My eyes fell to our hands on the granite.

"I'm not your dad, Grace. I won't just pick up and leave you. And I'm not an alcoholic like your mom or my dad. We're not them."

We held each other's gaze in thick silence. "I know," I whispered.

His hand squeezed mine. "We're human. We're going to make mistakes, right?"

I nodded, my eyes prickling.

"Grace, I've never done this before, well, not really. Can't say I know how it works."

"That doesn't matter."

"No?"

"As long as we're both in it, all the way."

"I'm in it. Way the fuck in it."

I leveled my gaze at him. "Amazing, huh?"

"Yeah."

"Dream come true?"

"Definitely."

My blurry gaze drifted around the kitchen, the hall to the bathroom and bedroom, the huge front window where light poured through and illuminated the sectional sofa with our crumpled quilt, the massive leather easy chair where he had me pose for him, the crap shelf where years of his beautiful artwork was piled, his neatly organized stash of tools in the corner.

"No more ghosts, new dreams. Get on with joy," Ruby whispered in my heart. I rubbed my eyes and blinked.

"We'll fix this house any way you want." Miller circled the living room. "Do up the kitchen with whatever appliances you like. We'll build an extension with a bedroom and bathroom for Jake."

My body stilled. "You'd do that for Jakey?"

"Of course. We can have an extra room for a play room or a project room for sewing or . . ."

I laughed. "I don't sew."

"Whatever." His hand ruffled through his short hair. "I'll extend the garage for your quality vehicle."

"I've got lots of books. And you have lots of sketch pads."

"Adding built-in shelves to the list. Anything else?"

"A porch out front would be really nice."

His lips curled up. "Good idea. Done."

His smile filled my insides with warmth. He was right, of course. My instinct to step back had kicked in, having been skittish and careful for so very long. Yet it no longer applied, did it?

I hopped off the kitchen stool and strolled towards the hallway. My fingers traced the blank, freshly painted wall. "Miller?"

"Yeah?"

I ripped off my shirt and dropped it to the floor. I glanced back at him over my bare shoulder.

"Babe?" A slow smile formed on his lips.

"You haven't shown me your bedroom yet, and I might want to make a few changes in there." I continued down the hallway. "You coming?"

"Ah, sweet fuck."

We were wrapped around each other, our muscles wobbly, our breathing unsteady. "Moving inside you bare goes right to the core, Grace," he whispered against my throat.

The dark golden light of the late afternoon sun glowed over his huge glossy wood platform bed. "I have to say, I like your bed. A lot." My fingers traced over the sleek live edge slab of wood that was the headboard. "It can stay."

A chuckle rose in his throat. "Glad to hear it."

My body still hummed with him. My mouth had taken its sweet time indulging in the taste and feel of every inch of his smooth bronze skin. My hands had memorized the firm lines and dips of his entire body, his flesh shivering under my touch. I leaned over him and kissed him gently. His molten eyes caressed me. The silver threads in his eyes intrigued me all over again, just as they had the first time I had noticed them that night in Dead Ringer's. His fingers traced a trail down my forehead, then my nose and rested on my lips.

"Marry me, Grace." He let my name out on a sigh, his heart pounding under my palm.

I shook with laughter.

"What the hell is so funny, woman?"

"You're a brave man. You just had to convince me to move in with you. And now, hours later, you're asking me to marry you?"

"That's right."

"You're confident, aren't you?"

"I figured I had the advantage after all those orgasms I just gave you."

I bit his fingers, and he laughed out loud. "Babe, do you need to try me before you buy me?"

I shook my head, my lips sucking on his fingers.

He stared at my mouth, his eyes heavy. "So, was that a yes to my proposal?"

I nodded, my lips releasing his wet fingers with a pop.

"Say it." His wet fingers teased my nipple.

I gasped and let out a laugh. "Yes."

He grinned, his lips brushing my forehead. "Get up, baby. I want to show you the bike."

I blinked up at him.

"The Indian Chief, Grace." Miller gave my bare ass a pinch.

"Ow!" I let out a huff, and he shot me a wicked grin as he pushed off the bed and sauntered from the room.

I hugged his king-sized pillow and enjoyed the show: long powerful legs, lean hips, a small sculpted rear, a broad back, and even broader shoulders all in a fierce, yet graceful package.

My man. All mine.

I hugged the pillow tighter. I thanked God, the Spirit of the Great Eagle, all of nature, and the universe for him.

For us.

Miller's rich laughter rose from the bathroom. "Babe, get your sweet ass out of that bed already!"

I rolled onto my back and smiled at the ceiling.

The garage door shook and rattled as Miller dragged it up and jerked it open. The dark garage yawned before us. Rusted steel and chrome glimmered in the afternoon light. Mustiness and the smell of gasoline and metal assaulted us. We stepped inside, and I took his hand in mine.

"It's over there." His chin jerked towards a hulking mass in the corner covered in a dirty tarp.

Years before he had taken in Miller, Wreck had found a rare Indian Chief frame from the early fifties and had stored it in his garage. When he had brought Miller home from Pine Ridge, he had decided rebuilding the Indian would be their project to work on together, and they had done it. He had taught Miller everything he knew about a motorcycle and more.

Wreck had once shown me the bike and also a photo of a grinning, skinny, long-haired, teenage Miller straddling the Indian Chief with Wreck at his side, an arm hooked over the boy's shoulder.

Miller pulled off the tarp.

I froze.

His lips pressed together. "Is it the bike in your dream?"

I nodded. "How can that be? I've only seen it once, and that was so long ago. Wreck never rode it when you were away."

"Dreams are the language of the mind, Grace. Over time your mind catalogues random items and experiences in your life and uses them as symbols to work things out when it needs to."

"More Grandma Kim wisdom?"

"No, but she did have a deep respect for dreams." Miller rubbed the back of his neck with his palm and grinned at me. "A buddy of mine in the army was a psych major in college and was really into dream interpretation. We used to talk about this shit for hours on patrol."

"Oh." My gaze returned to the bike.

"The key is to understand what the symbols in your dreams mean to you. Then you can unweave the meaning of the thing. And maybe you'll learn something from its message about what you're dealing with or where you need to go."

Okay then. My brain flipped through the imagery of my dream.

Wreck on the Indian. His passion for bikes, for freedom. Passion for the One-Eyed Jacks.

What does that mean to me?

I was on the back of that bike holding on to Wreck.

Wreck, my substitute older brother, quasi-father figure. Wreck on the vintage bike he restored for his long-lost brother, the brother he hunted for and found, cared for and loved. Something I admired enormously and would want for myself: security, love of family, refuge. It meant safety, masculine protection—Father. Brother. Lover.

Miller.

Driving in the dark faster and faster without lights.

Wreck was the most experienced rider I had ever known and had taught me how to ride. Riding with him in the dream was scary, but I trusted him. It was exhilarating. Maybe I've got to trust my new feelings for Miller. Maybe I've got to move forward in general in my life, because yes, it is like flying over a dark highway in high gear.

And I'd been roving blind and bound for too long.

My fingers brushed over the rusted, mangled handlebars of the damaged bike.

The Indian, the treasured Indian. Rare. Found and restored over the years by the hands of a man who loved and gave and safeguarded. The Indian company. The first American motorcycle company that later struggled to reinvent itself over the years and blast back into a very competitive market after several resurrections.

My life. I grinned.

"What is it?"

"I'm thinking over the dream," I murmured.

Butler and Caitlyn. The past and all its losses and the residual guilt. That was done. Life pushes on.

Miller's fingers rubbed over the scratched logo on the engine tank. "When I went into the army, we stored it in here. Then when I got out and joined the club, I rode it, but I rode it down into the ground. I was on a huge tear. One night I had been drinking too much, and I was on my way here from the clubhouse. It was raining hard. Didn't give a shit. I was going too fast, didn't pay much mind to the ditch at the head of the main road here, and she went flying. Not much happened to me, I had my gear on, but the goddamn bike took it hard. I hauled it back here, and here she's been sitting ever since. Stupid."

He exhaled, his chin hung low for a moment, and then our eyes met. His face was blank, yet for a second I saw the pained expression of a boy on those features.

This special bike, this treasure, now all banged up and bruised, somewhat maimed and pretty rusted, had lain under a dirty tarp in a dark cave of a garage for so many years. Yet this vintage bike was still a thing of unusual beauty, even if, right now, it looked more like a gaping wound.

"You never tried fixing it?" I asked.

His fingers tugged on his hoodie around his neck as he shook his head.

"You've got to fix it, Miller. It tells a story. Yours and Wreck's. There's a lot of love and honor in this buckled metal. You've been fixing up the house. Baby, you've got to fix this bike."

Miller's gaze remained on the Indian. "Willy's been after me to do it. He's good for leads on the parts, which are pretty scarce these days. He knows a lot of the old timers still around. I'd definitely need his help."

"Do it."

His gaze met mine. "By the way, who the hell is Karen, and why is she insisting I trick out her husband's Nova?"

My eyes widened, and I threw my head back and laughed.

TWENTY-EIGHT

"THAT'S MY NOVA?"

Bill's eyes creased, his gaze darted at Karen then back to the shiny hot muscle car tearing around the club track with Miller at the wheel. Karen smiled broadly and shot me a look as if she would burst any minute like a loaded piñata.

Miller had not only tricked out, but amped up Bill's Chevy Nova. Going over Karen's budget, but figuring it was well worth the potential word of mouth marketing, Miller had put in some extras out of his own pocket. He and Tricky and Clip cleaned up the car inside and out, repaired any minor damages and updated key details in the interior, making everything glossy and sharp. Tricky had installed a new transmission and cleaned up the engine that was still in pretty good condition. Miller had updated the exterior of the Nova with a sleek midnight blue paint job and detailed it with silver and black scallops and pin stripes down the hood and across the sides reminiscent of 70's muscle car glory, Bill's favorite decade.

"Karen? What the hell is going on?" Bill asked, his face red.

"Happy birthday, honey!" Karen threw her arms around her husband's neck. "Isn't she beautiful?"

Miller roared past us once more. Jake hopped up and down whooping and clapping. He raised his hand at Clip and the two of them high-fived each other. Tricky laughed.

"What do you think, Bill?" I asked.

"I. . .I. . .Holy shit!" Bill hands tugged through his silvery brown hair. Miller slowed the car down and brought it to a smooth stop in front of us. Bill swallowed hard. "I can't believe this." He slid his arm around Karen and laid a fat kiss on her.

"Does that mean he likes it?" asked Jake.

Tricky draped an arm around his shoulder. "I think so, my man."

Miller got out of the car, glanced at me, and put the keys in Bill's hand. "Happy birthday, Bill."

Bill grinned at Miller and shook his head. "Shit, son!" He clapped Miller on the shoulder and pumped his hand in a firm shake.

"Woohoo! He likes it! He likes it!" shouted Jake sprinting towards Miller. Miller grinned and swept him up in his arms.

As I watched Bill take his fab and very sexy Nova for a rip around the track, Miller came up behind me, wrapped his arms around my middle and pulled me back into his chest.

"Thank you, babe," he murmured in my ear, his voice thick. I turned in his arms and kissed him thoroughly.

Karen got herself that extended road trip to visit her sons in Cali. Little did I know, but Bill belonged to a muscle car club, and he and Karen traveled frequently to club events across three states. They showed off Miller's creation everywhere they went and left his new business card behind. Upon Bill's return he had the boys replace the engine for a meaner, higher powered driving experience. The calls started coming in.

Miller and Willy got to work on the Indian Chief soon after the Nova Experience, as we called it. Willy contacted all the old timers he knew who might still have Indian parts, and he rode off with plenty of cash one morning and came back a week later with a smile stamped on his whiskered face. He and Miller man-hugged for the longest time mumbling into each other's ears as Tricky unloaded the truck.

Jake, their official junior intern, helped organize and clean all the bits and pieces, and then the re-build began. It took months, especially once new custom paint job customers started rolling in and things got busy. When it finally did get done, it was magnificent.

We frequently took the Indian Chief for rides through the Black Hills or the Badlands beyond. Especially sunset rides. We'd pack a blanket and pick up goodies from Erica's cafe and head out to soak in the purply-pink orange sky over the endless expanse of rolling land, both dry and verdant, austere and lush.

Miller was right. That bike was a thing of beauty.

EPILOGUE

"YOU LIKE IT?"

My breath caught in my throat.

"Grace?"

I stared at the delicate white gold diamond eternity band studded with small emerald cut diamonds around my finger.

I lunged at Miller. "I love it!" I whispered in his ear.

His soft laughter filled my chest. "I was going to give it to you tonight over dinner, but, screw it, I couldn't wait."

"Oh, I liked it over breakfast."

"Yeah, you are a morning person, aren't you?"

"I do like it in the morning, baby."

"Hmm. I've noticed that." He nipped at my lips, and we kissed through our laughter. "I figured you'd like to have a few rings like that to stack. We'll get another one for your wedding band, another for our first anniversary. Yeah, a new one every year, baby. I'm gonna fill your fingers with them." He swept the hair from my face. "Happy engagement, Grace."

"Happy engagement, Miller." My hands tugged through his hair, and I pulled him closer for a deeper kiss.

He groaned in my mouth. "Baby, I'm getting hard again. You don't let go of me, you're going to have to do something about it at lightning speed, and you know how I'm not into lightning speed with you these days."

"Get over it," I murmured.

I pulled down his zipper, released his grateful cock from his boxer briefs, and slid down his legs to the floor.

"Oh, Jesus." He let out a hiss.

His jet black eyes shone, his lips parted. I licked at his hard shaft then immediately took him deep in my mouth and showed my fiancé my enthusiastic appreciation for my glittery engagement ring. He came in lightning speed, his hands digging in my hair, his hips thrusting, my hands squeezing his gorgeous, tight ass. I took a final lick at his tip in farewell then smoothed his black boxer briefs up over him, tugged up his jeans, zipped them and stroked my hands over his taut abs. I held his somewhat astonished stare and grinned. "Ready for work now?"

He fisted a hand in my hair and pulled me close. "Mr. and Mrs. Flies As Eagles. Cannot fucking wait."

Miller and I got married just before Christmas, a few months after we had moved my things into his house.

Initially, we'd wanted to go to Vegas and make it a week long escapade, but then we decided our friends and family could really use the boost, and, frankly, so could we.

We put together a wedding ceremony at the local church where Mary Lynn's brother-in-law was the pastor. I hadn't wanted to get married at the club. Dig and I had done that. This time around I wanted a more traditional sanction from the Powers Above.

Wreck had walked me down the aisle the first time around. This time Ray gave me away, and Willy was Miller's best man. Jake, of course, was our handsome ring bearer, with Kicker and Mary Lynn's girls leading the procession down the aisle tossing rose petals everywhere.

Since winter was upon us, we had the reception at Dead Ringer's Roadhouse; the place where it had all begun or, actually, where it had all ended. Luckily there was no snow that weekend to make traveling difficult, but it was pretty damn cold. Ray insisted on springing for the party. There was good food, plenty of booze, balloons, flowers, the works. Erica was thrilled to bake us a three-tiered dark chocolate cake layered with whiskey-flavored caramel. The cake was covered in a cream fondant with a simple beaded trim and flourished with dark pink peonies on each tier. It was perfect. Simple, yet elegant.

We hired one of the bands that played at the Roadhouse, and the party went all night long. All the One-Eyed Jacks brothers and their families were in attendance. Everyone except for Creeper, of course, and Butler.

Butler had given up the presidency and checked himself into a rehab. I hoped he'd stick it out. There was plenty to celebrate though. Jump and Vig had worked out a truce that satisfied everyone. At least for the time being.

I wore a strapless cream-colored floor length gown with narrow pleats and a thin lilac silk ribbon at the waist. Underneath I wore an amazing cream-colored corset that Lenore had made for me, and later that evening Miller showed me his keen appreciation for it. At the church I wore a faux fur wheat-colored bolero jacket over the dress, which I took off at the party.

Unfortunately, I had on extremely high heels for the ceremony which I did not feel comfortable in, but which Alicia, Lenore, and Dee had insisted I wear. Ray caught on to my ineptitude with heels right away. He held my one hand and put his other arm around me. "Relax and hold on tight, girl," he whispered in my ear as we waited for our cue. I squeezed his arm, and we made it down the aisle just fine under Miller's strong gaze.

My groom's dark eyes were glassy and full as he took my hand in his. "You take my breath away," he whispered, his voice catching. He brought my hand to his lips and kissed it gently.

"I love you," I whispered, my eyes filling with water.

After a few prayers, our simple vows, and a blessing, Miller slipped another diamond eternity band on my finger, and I slid a white gold band on his.

As soon as we got to Dead Ringer's, I tossed the stilettos off at Dee. She handed me my pair of brand new and very amazing light brown leather cowboy boots embroidered with different colored flowers I had splurged on at Pepper's to suit the occasion. Of course, I made sure the band played plenty of country music.

"You don't know how much your sister wanted this for you," Alex whispered in my ear as we danced.

"I know she did."

"She's smiling down on you, Grace."

I hugged my brother-in-law and planted a kiss on his cheek. "I can feel it."

"You sure you're okay with the arrangement?"

"We're thrilled that Jake will be living with us. Never doubt that. The new addition to the house was all Miller's idea. I'm sure both of them will probably turn the new playroom into a man cave."

Miller had hired a contractor right away. The kitchen was turning out great with new hardwood cabinets, dark wood flooring and granite countertops to match the one on the island he had already installed on his own. The stainless steel appliances had just arrived and were huge, gleaming and begging to be used.

Willy had built a mantel for the fireplace out of layers of stone. I had found two incredible frames made of driftwood from a local gift shop and had Miller's small painting of a dark butterfly along with his portrait of Grandma Kim encased in them and hung over the mantle. They were the perfect blaze of color in an otherwise calm, earth-toned room.

I'd found the photo of Miller and Wreck with the Indian on an old bulletin board at the repair shop. I had it enlarged and mounted in a black frame and hung it along the wall in the hallway along with other prints of a teenage Miller in his high school football uniform and one of him in his army uniform hugging Wreck good-bye before shipping out for the last time.

There was another photo of a young Miller with Wreck, Dig, and Boner working on bikes in the shed. I had never seen that one before. I also put up a photo of me and Ruby at her high school graduation, me squeezing the life out of her, and another of Ruby, Alex, and Jake when he had taken his first steps.

I had framed three of the nude sketches Miller had drawn of me and hung them in our bedroom. All the others, and there were plenty more he drew later—most of which were not for public viewing—I stored in a large leather file box with special tissue paper in between each one to preserve them. What few belongings I had were now installed in our house. For good.

"I'm very grateful to the both of you," Alex said. "I have to take this assignment on site in North Dakota. All the work I've been doing over the past two years has been leading up to this, but when Ruby got sick they let me delay it."

"Alex, there's barely any housing up there for families, and as a single dad how are you going to take care of Jake while you're going to be so busy? It makes sense to leave him with us. It's not that far away." He only nodded and averted his gaze. "We're family, honey. You do what you have to do, we'll be right here. Miller and I want to be a big part of Jake's life." I planted a kiss on his cheek. "Thank you for letting us be."

Alex's hand on my back tightened as we moved to the music.

I cleared my throat. "By the way, it's official." My fingers smoothed down the crisp white collar of his dress shirt. "Ray is selling his house in Montana. He's decided on a smaller house he's had his eye on here in town."

Alex let out a sigh. "I've got to hand it to him, Grace. He wants to be here for you and Jake. That's good. My son gets to have a grandpa. How do you feel about it?"

"Don't tell anyone," I whispered in his ear. "But I'm glad."

After the wedding Miller and I splurged and headed to New Zealand for an amazing three week honeymoon full of sun, swimming, seafood, and incredible bike touring.

Within a couple of months after our return, Ray completed his move back to Meager. He sent me to a lawyer in Rapid who informed me that my father had set up a very generous trust fund for Jake, of which I was the trustee, and a brokerage account for me. I was to use the money any way I deemed fit.

So I did.

I invested in our new life.

Miller resigned as Road Captain of the One-Eyed Jacks and requested to minimize his role in the club. "I want to take care of my family," he told his brothers. They all agreed with him.

We bought out 70% of Wreck's Repair from the club and renamed it Eagle Wings. Naturally, Miller designed a kick-ass logo and the lettering to match. I liked Miller's logo so much, I had baseball caps and T-shirts made with it to sell at the shop. The shed got a much-needed renovation and expansion, and now included a large shop and office space with a new computer to keep track of everything. Miller outfitted the new building with a whole range of updated equipment and tools in order to better handle all his custom detailing work and paint jobs.

He officially hired Tricky to head the car repair division and an army buddy of his from North Carolina who had become a hot rod specialist over the years. I hired a web designer to set up a snazzy web site, and I placed advertising in newspapers and biker and hot rod magazines nationwide. I hired Suzi part-time to keep the office organized giving me as much free time as possible with Jake and time to oversee our home renovation.

"How much longer until that ham is ready?" Jump asked. "Too many bitches in the kitchen." He glared at the television slumping into the sofa next to Boner and Bear, who was holding his son Luke in his lap.

"Oh, shut it, Grump." I handed him another bottle of beer. Alicia rolled her eyes as she filled the large wooden salad bowl with a variety of greens, scallions, and dried cranberries. Suzi whisked my home-made syrupy glaze on the splattered stove top, and Mary Lynn scooped the freshly made mashed potatoes into a ceramic bowl.

Miller pulled me into his lap on the roomy armchair. "Ten minutes tops, I swear. The extra glaze for the ham is just thickening," I said.

"I'm not worried, Martha Stewart. Seems like you've got it all under control in there."

"Some things I do, yeah."

Miller squeezed my hip. "What is it?"

"Nothing." My gaze drifted to the baseball preview report playing on ESPN.

"Tell me."

"It's just . . ." I shook my head.

"Grace, talk to me."

I leaned into his neck. "I want to give you a family."

His body stilled, his eyes locked on mine.

"A baby," I whispered.

He ran the back of his knuckles down the side of my face. "What's this about?"

"I want to make you happy. The happiest ever."

"Babe, I'm delirious."

"But I want to give *that* to you, too."

"Grace, I was unwanted from before I was born. I never let myself dream that one day I'd even have one bit of what we have now."

My lips brushed the side of his face. "You know you need to be grateful that your dad, for all his faults, took you from your mom. Because you wouldn't have had the reservation or your Grandma for as long as you did and when you did. He wasn't a good dad, but he did that for you."

"This is true. But all that shit is eclipsed by you."

"Eclipsed?"

"Oh yeah. You like that?" I let out a laugh as I kissed the edge of his jaw.

"I know this," he said. "That you want me for me, for who I am, not for something you think I am or what you want out of me. That means everything to me. Never had that from a woman before, Grace. Never."

"I love you," I blurted out.

"I know." He let out a small laugh. "Babe, what I'm saying is I don't feel like I'm missing anything. I'm thankful for what what we have. Is that—"

"I just wish I could give you a baby. Yours and mine. I wish I could give us that," I whispered. "Am I being greedy? I love having Jake be a part of our family. He's a blessing I never expected."

"He is." His hand stroked my middle. "I would love a kid with you, Grace. Of course I would. But that decision was taken away from us." His hand went to my hip and squeezed "You want to adopt?"

My gaze followed Jake, who buzzed around the house being chased by a red-faced Melinda and a giggling Carrie. The candied, spicy scent of the glaze filled the air lacing perfectly with the savory aroma of the roast ham and Alicia's homemade biscuits, which already blanketed the house.

"Babe?"

"There's surrogacy."

His eyes widened. "Yes, there is."

"Unless you think we're too old?"

"Hell no. Do you?"

I shook my head.

"Have you looked into it?"

343

"No." I bit my lip, my fingers tracing his jaw. "I wanted to talk to you first. Of course, as our house is now full of guests for the very first time, and we're about to sit down to Easter dinner, it's probably not the best time."

He smiled at me, his fingers digging into my leg. "Look into it."

"Wes!" Jake shrieked. "Wes! Help me! They've got cooties!" Luke hopped up and down in Bear's lap, clapping his hands.

"Got you, little man." Wes scooped up Jake, tossed him in the air, and they both hooted with laughter.

It was now early summer, and from my desk in the shop where I was taking care of a few accounting details, my eyes grazed over the framed photo of me and Miller and Jake that Alicia had taken from last week's Club barbecue.

Miller had taught Jake a thing or two about football that day with Wes and the guys. Jake had just scored his first touchdown, and I had run out to hug him. Miller had been holding him, and I tackled both of them. The three of us had fallen on the ground, the football still in Jake's hands. Jake was laughing hard, his cheeks red. That sad, long look had finally faded from his face. Miller's one arm was around me pulling me in for a kiss, his other arm around Jake's tummy.

I sighed, kicked off my boots under my desk, and clicked on the calendar on my tablet. I had several doctors' appointments coming up and an interview with a potential surrogate. We were also trying to decide when the best time would be to get away for a few days to go down to Pine Ridge and visit Grandma Kim's grave and see Miller's father who had been in touch. It was awkward, but it was something.

I leaned back in my chair and gazed out the window to the yard of the shop and admired the view of my husband rolling a chopper out front for a final polish before the client came by to pick it up. It was a very warm, sunny day, and he had taken off his

T-shirt and wore only his low slung jeans over his work boots and a bandana tied over his hair.

The sweat shone on the tight wiry muscles of his back under his One-Eyed Jack's tattoo as he brought it to a stop, the bike a flash of chrome and steel in the bright sun. I smirked at the giddy, lustful thoughts zipping through my nasty little mind.

Miller leaned over the engine for a moment, his necklace dangling away from his chest. The silver skeleton key with a skull design I had given him as a wedding gift hung from a leather cord around his neck. I fingered my own small delicate key charm studded with diamond chips that hung at my throat. Miller had it made for me for Christmas out of white Black Hills gold.

He turned suddenly, grinning at me through the big picture window of the shop. I smiled and waved. He dropped the rag on the seat of the bike, wiped his hands on his jeans, and sauntered through the door of the shop, a crooked smile tipping the edges of his lips.

Oh boy, I knew that look.

"Hey, baby," I murmured, my toes curling against the floor.

"Client's coming in an hour for his bike," he said, his voice low. "I finished early." His hand jerked on the pulley rope for the thick venetian blinds, and they clattered down the window.

"I've got the paperwork all ready."

His fingers turned the lock on the door, and the bolt clicked. "Tricky had to go out on a run, everyone else is out for the afternoon."

I raised my eyebrows at him. "Right." I bit the inside of my cheek as he prowled across the room.

He turned the lock on the back door which led to the repair shed and came to the desk pulling me off my chair and into him. I planted a kiss on the small tattoo just under his eagle. "Grace" in beautiful antique lettering was inked over his heart with a vintage key hanging from the "e". He had designed a tattoo for me of an eagle flying with a key in its claws. It was inked on my lower abdomen just over the waistband of my panties.

I swirled my tongue over my inked name. His breath caught. The briny taste of his sweaty skin sent heat skittering through me.

"Suzi coming in?" he asked.

"Nope."

My tongue found one of his dark nipples. He lifted me and sat me on the desk. My fingers removed his bandana and swept through his soft black hair. It was growing out, and it looked great. It would take another couple of years, maybe more, until it grew to his shoulders. My new favorite indulgence was combing through its silky thickness with my fingers whenever we kissed or with his head on my lap while he watched television lying down on the sofa, and always right before I fell asleep every night, his head against my chest. It was such a simple pleasure, like holding his hand, and I couldn't live without it.

"Jake still going to the movies with Ray?" His fingers curled into the hem of my T-shirt.

"Yep, then spending the night with him, in fact."

"Really?"

He yanked my shirt over my head and tossed it on the desk. His fingers skimmed over the satin of my bra as his tongue scorched its way over my collarbone then up alongside my neck.

"Geez, what are you doing?"

"Licking my old lady." He sucked on my key charm for an instant then slid it out from between his full lips.

I exhaled. "Am I your afternoon energy snack?"

He chuckled. "I could make a meal of you, baby, anytime of day or night."

"Hmm." I held his face between my hands and nibbled at his lips. He fumbled with his jeans and then unfastened mine. I slid off the desk, and he tugged them down my hips. I kicked them off me and pulled his body in between my legs.

"Shit, Grace, are you wearing those . . ."

Yes, those crotch-less panties Lenore insisted I have were pretty terrific. I had gone back to the boutique and snapped up a few more.

"Fuck me," Miller breathed, staring down at me.

"That's the idea, baby. Always prepared for snacks."

A growl escaped his throat as his fingers traced over my tattoo, then down the lace of the flimsy panty, finally sinking inside my wet pussy. I leaned back against the desk as Miller clasped one of my legs, holding it high against his shoulder, his thumb stroking my clit back and forth.

"Baby. . ."

He groaned as he rocked his hips into mine, sinking his cock into me. My body stretched around his heat, taking him in, and he settled deep.

"Oh shit, yeah." His eyes squeezed shut for a moment.

"Mill . . ."

His one hand stayed wrapped around my calf against his shoulder, the other pinned my hip down. He dragged his thick cock out slowly, and my breathing stopped. Everything stopped. He thrust in again on a fierce stroke, and life made sense once more.

I let out a deep moan, my head lolling back against the desk. "What you do to me . . ."

"Love you, Grace. Love you so much."

He rolled his hips into mine over and over again, thrusting faster. My body jerked back and forth on top of the desk. My fingers clasped onto the edge of the furniture. An empty mug tumbled on its side, pens and pencils spilled over onto the floor, a pile of envelopes cascaded over the side.

My body tightened, the harsh wave built inside me. "Oh God, every time . . ."

Miller's dark gaze darted from my eyes to between our legs where his fingers teased my clit, coaxing me higher, his lips forming a tight O, his breathing now short and quick. He loved watching, and I loved the burn in his eyes when he did. He drove faster inside me, grinding his hips against mine. I cried out as that excruciating current pulled us in, and the wave shattered over us both. He let out a deep groan filling me with his sticky warmth, and my hand wrapped around the base of his perfect cock. Miller leaned over me and took my mouth in a rough, hungry kiss.

"The clouds cleared up. Full moon will be perfect tonight. After dinner, you and me have a date with the Indian."

I kissed the underside of his jaw. "Good."

He released my one leg and hooked it around his waist along with the other. He freed a breast from a bra cup taking the tip in his mouth,while his fingers swept across my chest and teased my other breast. I shivered, and my hands slid down his damp lower back.

"Love watching my cock inside you," he murmured against my skin.

"Oh, me too."

He chuckled, his mouth brushing my lips. "Gotta finish up with that bike. Come see."

We got dressed. I raised the venetian blinds as Miller unlocked the front door. It was quiet moments like these when I felt truly happy and grateful for all that I had. Yet, still, a gnawing in the pit of my soul poked at me and whispered fragments of impending doom in my ears. I knew it would take more time for those voices to finally quiet, but I was getting there.

I closed my eyes, and a smile curved my lips. My brain felt refreshed, my body felt whole and loved-up. That was my kind of cardio, not that boot camp torture Lenore was always dragging me to.

"Baby?"

I blinked up at my husband. He fingered the wide V of my T-shirt tugging it down. I grinned at him as he planted a kiss on the swell of my breast. I entwined my fingers with his, as he swung open the door.

A streak of bright sunlight gleamed off the cherry red explosion of zig-zags freshly painted over the body of the restored bike before us. My fingers curled in Miller's firm grasp, and a billow of warm air bathed us both as we stepped outside.

THE END

OTHER BOOKS BY CAT PORTER

WOLFSGATE

RANDOM & RARE (BOOK 2 OF THE "LOCK & KEY" SERIES)

ABOUT THE AUTHOR

CAT PORTER was born and raised in New York City, but also spent a few years in Texas and Europe along the way. As an introverted, only child, she had very big, but very secret dreams for herself. She graduated from Vassar College, was a struggling actress, an art gallery girl, special events planner, freelance writer, restaurant hostess, and had all sorts of other crazy jobs all hours of the day and night to help make those dreams come true. She has two children's books traditionally published under her maiden name. She now lives in Athens, Greece with her husband and three children, and freaks out regularly and still daydreams way too much. She is addicted to reading, the beach, Pearl Jam, the History Channel, her smartphone, her husband's homemade red wine, really dark chocolate, and her Nespresso coffee machine. Oh, and Jamie & Claire Fraser and those Vikings...never mind. Writing keeps her somewhat sane, extremely happy, and a productive member of society.

Come Find Me Online!

Facebook: www.facebook.com/catporterauthor

Website: www.catporter.eu

Twitter: @catporter103

TSU: www.tsu.co/CatPorterAuthor

Instagram: instagram.com/catporter.author

Pinterest: www.pinterest.com/catporter103

Email: catporter103@gmail.com

Goodreads:
https://www.goodreads.com/author/show/8286871.Cat_Porter

Lock & Key's book trailer: http://bit.ly/16OmhZ5

ACKNOWLEDGMENTS

I COULD NOT HAVE MADE THIS DREAM COME TRUE without a great many wonderful, supportive and very smart people who deserve my big hugs and my sincerest thanks:

To editors Chelsea Kuhel and Madison Seidler. And to editor Jennifer Roberts-Hall for her polishing, buffing, and clarity on this second edition, her support, and sooooo much laughter across continents and oceans. I couldn't have gotten here standing upright with this huge smile on my face without you, my Sassenach. Words cannot express...truly.

To the amazing Najla Qamber for her artistry in creating a magical cover and for collaborating with me over and over again in our very own time zone. Dream come true! To Jovana Shirley for formatting with such style and ease.

To artist and jewelry designer Billy Blue of Blue Bayer Design NYC for the use of his fantastic original design skeleton key necklace featured on the cover and in my story. Thank you for your enthusiasm.

To David Charles Spurgeon's book "Bikin' and Brotherhood: My Journey" which provided a spectacular, vivid ride through the life of real 1%'er, "the one in a hundred of us who has given up on society." His rough and tumble ride through the outlaw life, his dedication to the brotherhood and his "love of the machine and the freedom of the open road—live to ride, ride to live" through all the many, many grim realities of the life was heartfelt and eye-opening and gave me so much to chew on. To Carol and Vlad Ononov of Scenicdakotas.com for their great Dakota travelogues and for answering my many questions about the magnificent Dakotas.

To my beta readers: Adele, Alison, Angela, Danette, Deana, Natalie, and Rachel. Your eagerness, enthusiasm, and feedback always made me smile, gnash my teeth, and kept me moving forward. Thank you for putting up with my sending you new updated versions over and over again and for answering all my questions. To Andrew and Evan, my lone male beta readers and dear friends. You two paid attention to whole other rivers of detail which was absolutely priceless. Your pointed suggestions kept it real, made me re-think the spine of the piece, and helped me spin a much tighter web. Special thanks to Natalie and Rachel for round 2 and their astute insights, relentlessness, and generosity.

To Ellen S. for your country music guidance. To Carolyn for your pushing me on through the years and your pointed comments. To Annika for your precise eye and acidic mind when proofreading my wordy first draft and for answering all my grammar questions at all hours. You had me questioning everything with a fresh eye and ear and laughing at my idiocy. To Needa for her honesty and friendship.

To Chas Jenkins and Rockstar PR & Literary Consulting for their support and guidance. To Julie Brazeal of AToMR for my very first blog tour ever. To all the book bloggers, Facebook book groups and the readers who took a chance on my book and shared the love over and over again. Special hugs to the amazing Angel Dust for L&K's beautiful book trailer, MC Rocker Reader, Clare Williams, and Kitty Kats Crazy About Books who popped my Goodreads cherry. Special kisses to Ellen at The Book Bellas, Dee at Book Boyfriend Reviews (and for Miller winning Book Boyfriend of the Week!), the Dirty Girls of EDGy Reviews, and DiDi, Java Girl and the special ladies of Guilty Pleasures. A very special thank you to Jenny and Gitte of Totally Booked whose generosity, spirit, and forthrightness truly blew me away and inspired this second edition. Big smooches! The enthusiasm, support, and the amazing work all these wonderful women do mean so very much to me as an author and a reader and always will.

A very special thanks to author Lorelei James for her zesty shout out and support. I swear, I am coming to South Dakota!

To my cousin Nicholas who set up my own e-reading app when I first bought a tablet two years ago and thus opened up a brand new world of possibilities to me as an avid reader and a writer.

Suddenly I realized the dream of full-time writing could come true, it was in my hands. Thank you for the memorable and very late night shopping trip to the "Great Temple" for my laptop when I finally made the commitment to myself (and no longer wanted to share computer time with the rest of the family). And thank you for indulging me and taking me to that Harley Davidson store. Also, thank you to my cousin Domna, the family R.N., for answering my medical questions.

To Edward who a long time ago in his art gallery every Friday afternoon schooled me and the rest of the staff in the finer points of drinking top-notch single malt Scottish whiskey, an appreciation I have to this day. My respects, sir.

To my mother who always believed in me first and foremost and pleaded with me to keep writing when I had locked it away for a long while there. To my dad who always believed in me no matter what and had given me his precious copy of Roget's Thesaurus when I went off to college, changing my inner landscape forever. You two are no longer with me, but are in my heart forever. To my husband who has always supported me in making this dream come true. (And doesn't freak out *too* much that the house is in a bit more disarray than usual!)

But most of all, it has to come down to my three children who not only put up with my long, crazed hours of writing day and night and all my emotional wackiness as I live these creatures of my mind, but encourage me to do it. Their generosity and gentle reminders to feed them a real meal, bake them a treat, resolve an argument, help them with their homework, or simply to play with them gives me the temerity and resolve to keep plugging along even on the days when everything looks and feels grey. You're my everything.

To my readers, this is truly nothing without you. Thank you for letting my words whisper in your ears and in your hearts. Thank you for reaching out to me. Thank you for your reviews. You make it all worthwhile and all the sweeter.

Please connect with me on my website, Facebook, Twitter, and Instagram. Visit my Pinterest page where I have dedicated boards to "Lock & Key" that I hope you enjoy as much as I do pinning them into creation. (Can't stop, that thing is addictive.) Please do leave a review wherever you may roam for all are very much appreciated and are very important for readers and writers alike.

xx C